The Shopgirl of Ironbridge

Also by Mollie Walton

The Raven Hall Saga

A Mother's War
A Daughter's Gift
A Sister's Hope

The Ironbridge Saga

The Daughters of Ironbridge
The Secrets of Ironbridge
The Orphan of Ironbridge

MOLLIE WALTON

The Shopgirl of Ironbridge

MLP

First published in Great Britain in 2025 by Mountain Leopard Press
An imprint of Headline Publishing Group Limited

This paperback edition published in 2025

1

Cataloguing in Publication Data is available from the British Library

Hardback ISBN 978 1 8027 9826 5

Typeset in 10.32/13.76pt Sabon LT Std by Jouve (UK), Milton Keynes

Printed and bound in Great Britain by Clays Ltd, Elcograf S.p.A.

Headline's policy is to use papers that are natural, renewable and recyclable
products and made from wood grown in well-managed forests and other
controlled sources. The logging and manufacturing processes are expected
to conform to the environmental regulations of the country of origin.

Headline Publishing Group Limited
An Hachette UK Company
Carmelite House
50 Victoria Embankment
London EC4Y 0DZ

The authorised representative in the EEA is Hachette Ireland,
8 Castlecourt Centre, Dublin 15, D15 XTP3, Ireland (email: info@hbgi.ie)

www.headline.co.uk
www.hachette.co.uk

This book is dedicated to the memory of Dr Chris Sutcliffe, who tragically passed away during its writing. One of the kindest, wittiest, most erudite people I've ever known, he was my teacher mentor: when I wanted a fancy new overhead projector for my classroom, he gave me a birthday card soon after with a picture of a teddy bear next to a blackboard, inside which he wrote, 'See how Ted is happy with the old ways.' When I left full-time teaching to become a novelist, he remembered how I'd told him I adored cricket when I was a girl, and he gave me an old cricket game of dice and scorebook. He loved W. G. Grace and looked a bit like him too. In my writing career, he was my champion: he read all of my novels and wrote reviews under the pseudonym of his PhD subject, a celebrated Shakespearian actor. He was my dear, dear friend: he looked after my daughter who was at school near his house. And he gave the greatest advice. He told me the best way to beat the stress of work was to have many strings to my bow – he called it portfolio working, and I still follow that to this day. Also, he once told me the single most useful piece of advice I ever heard about how to be an excellent teacher. He said, 'You have to be the most interesting person in the room.' He was so right, about teaching, but also about writing, about persuading your reader to ignore all other distractions and to start reading and not stop. The truth was, in any room anywhere in the world, if Chris was there, he was the most interesting person in the room. No less of a wonderful person is his wife Carol, an angel in human form. All my love to you both. This story is for you.

The Ironbridge Saga

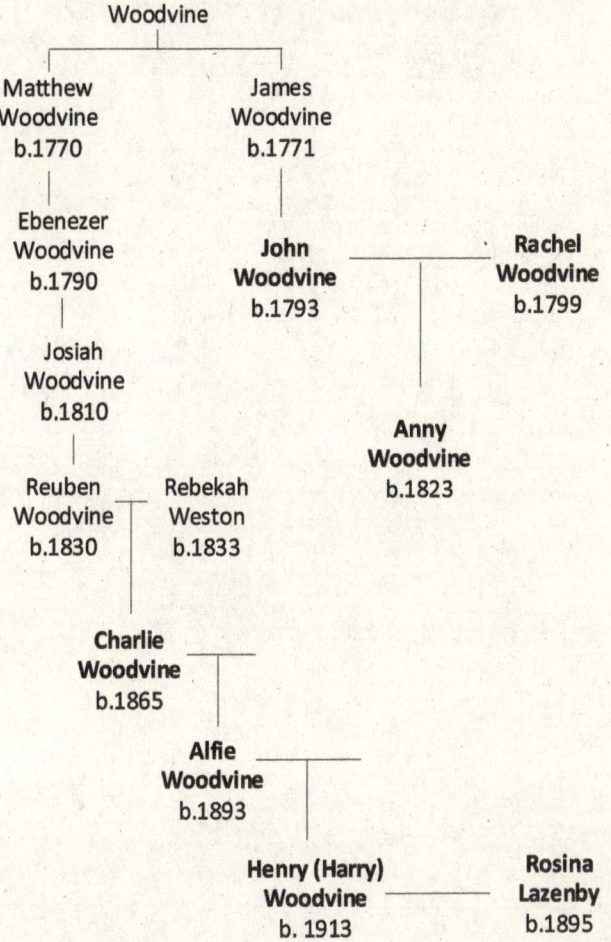

Woodvine

Matthew
Woodvine
b.1770

James
Woodvine
b.1771

Ebenezer
Woodvine
b.1790

John
Woodvine
b.1793

Rachel
Woodvine
b.1799

Josiah
Woodvine
b.1810

Anny
Woodvine
b.1823

Reuben
Woodvine
b.1830

Rebekah
Weston
b.1833

Charlie
Woodvine
b.1865

Alfie
Woodvine
b.1893

Henry (Harry)
Woodvine
b. 1913

Rosina
Lazenby
b.1895

The Raven Hall Saga

Prologue

Ironbridge

March 1882

Maria didn't want to walk into town. Her feet hurt. She sullenly dragged them along, trying to muster tears to prove how hard done by she was. She wanted to stay in their cosy little home on Paradise and be lazy that spring Sunday, to sit in a patch of sun in the woods and read a book, maybe take a nap and dream of forest fairies. But her mother and father insisted. They were all trooping down to Ironbridge to see her uncle, who was visiting for the day and would meet them at the Tontine Hotel, opposite the bridge. She'd never met her mother's brother before. All she knew was that he was a farmer and lived a few hours' ride away. After a long week at school and helping her mother with sewing work most evenings, the last thing Maria wanted was another walk after church and then to have to listen to the adults droning on about tedious matters all afternoon. Enough was enough. She stopped dead in the road and burst into faked tears, pointing at her feet.

'Ah, come now, there's a good wench,' said her father. 'It inna far.'

'My feet are aching summat terrible!' she sobbed.

'That's only because you were skipping all evening with that little chit of a girl from number seven,' snapped her mother, losing her patience. 'You're too old at seven years of age to be carried or to be whining like a babby. Don't take on so!'

But Maria wouldn't budge. She would stand there till kingdom come if necessary.

'I canna walk another step, not a single step.'

She folded her arms and stuck out her chin, until she heard a slow clip-clop approaching from a side road and glanced towards it.

'See here, my beaut,' said her father nicely, a softer touch than her mother. 'That's our friend Mr Transom, the miller. Maybe he'll give us a ride to town on the back of his cart.'

'Can we, Mam?' Maria beseeched her mother, all tears gone. It was never Dad who had the final say in the Keay household.

Her mother rolled her eyes. 'You spoil the lass, Alfred,' she sighed at her husband though she smiled a small smile too, maybe at the thought of a ride into town to save her own tired feet, maybe at her husband's kindness. Maria saw him approach the miller, who called out 'Whoa' to his horse. The nag looked old and tired itself.

Maria watched her father share cheery hellos with the miller, who laughed heartily at something else her father said. Everyone liked Alfred Keay, the maltster: all the men at the malthouse where he worked the cooler months, all the men at the Talbot Inn where he worked the warmer months, all the folk in the rented cottages beside them along Paradise. He was just one of those people who got on with anyone. His wife was shyer and more reserved, while his daughter was just like him.

'Afternoon, little'un,' said the miller and winked at Maria and she grinned back at him. 'Hop on, then.'

'Say thank'ee to Mr Transom,' said her mother. Maria called up her thanks to him and he nodded, then she stopped on her way to thank the old horse too, who stood patiently, staring at the road.

'What's her name?' asked Maria.

'She's no name as such, this'un. I've had her so long and always called her Oss. Just Oss.'

'Thank'ee, Oss,' said Maria and touched the horse's soft muzzle. The old mare nudged her warm, damp nose into Maria's hand.

'Stop with your messing about, lass,' scolded Maria's mother, as her husband took her hand to help her onto the back of the cart. He lifted her up to seat her and gave her waist a squeeze.

'A fine figure still, Charity Keay,' chuckled Maria's father, making her mother blush and push him off, smiling as she did so. He turned to Maria and called, 'Where's my devoted darter then?'

'Here I be!' she cried and trotted over, to be grasped and lifted up high in the air, giggling all the way. She was plonked down next to her mother on top of a flour bag, her father climbing up to sit beside her, the three of them in a comfy cwtch. The flour dust from the bags made her mother sneeze.

Off they went, swaying down the road to Ironbridge. It wasn't far. She'd made a big fuss about nothing, Maria knew that. But just look what rewards her tears had brought! A ride on Mr Transom's cart and a horse's-eye view of the journey, looking down her nose at roadsters as they passed.

It wasn't too long before they turned off Paradise onto Wharfage. The road was busy with pedestrians and horse-drawn vehicles, as usual, the centre of Ironbridge a hubbub of activity clustering around the iron bridge of its name arching gracefully over the mighty River Severn, which also teemed with traffic, a bringer and taker of goods and people, industry and economy. Maria understood little of the world of work, just loving the river for its sparkle on sunny days and its darksome moods on dull days. She was fascinated by its speed and its murky depths. As they plodded on along Wharfage, she wondered what monsters may live in those waters, along with the fish her father sometimes caught for supper. She was an imaginative child, often prone to flights of fancy. The river was high and fast-moving that day and she saw it rush by with dark purpose.

They were coming up to The Swan inn opposite the Severn Warehouse, that extraordinary gothic building that looked more like a church than a place to store earthly goods and always gave Maria a sense of wonder. She heard a dog barking madly nearby, disturbing her little reverie. At first, she did not see the ox passing by the inn but she heard it. An unearthly sound: an animal in distress, panicked by the stray dog that yapped and snarled at it. The great ox bolted from its owner and charged across the road. In its panic, it headed straight for the miller's cart. Maria whipped her head round to see where the strange noise was coming from. She just caught a glimpse of the brown bulk rushing at them before the poor horse reared up in terror. The cart tipped violently to the right and Maria was thrown into the air. The world spun over as she tumbled through space and landed with a thump on her side in the mud. Bags of flour seemed to explode around her, filling the air with thick white dust. She heard a great splintering of wood and the crack of metal and snap of leather as the cart smashed back down onto the road.

In her confusion and pain, she did not see the miller's horse career down Loadcroft Wharf into the river. She did not see her parents and the miller hauled into the water by the horse gone mad, dragging its load, its passengers, its cart and itself into the roaring Severn. The swift, deep river took them all, tumbling and tangled. She did not see her parents and the miller dragged into the depths of the river as the cart sank, nor the horse itself sink from great, panicked gulps of river water. She did not see the miller caught on a branch of a tree that had fallen into the Severn and gasp for air and survive. She did not see her parents lose their fight against the rushing current and drown downstream.

All she saw was a kindly face, a woman, older than her mother, looking down at her in the mud, the white flour from the upset bags swirling about them both like a thick and dusty snow. The woman asked her urgently if she could move her legs and arms.

'I can,' said Maria and scrambled to stand up, helped by the lady. She was too shocked to cry.

People were crowding around, shouting and chattering, pointing and shaking their heads. The lady helped her over the road into The Swan inn and sat her down on a wooden stool.

'Where are they, Mam and Dad?' Maria asked the lady.

'Oh, my poor child,' said the lady. 'My poor, poor little ducky egg.'

Maria looked up into the lady's pitying face. Suddenly, her arm ached like billy-o. Shock had kept the pain away and now it assaulted her with a ferocity she'd never known. She cried out and grasped at her arm, which made it worse. For the second time that day, she wept and wept, real tears this time, tears of pain and fear, confusion and questions, tears of the most terrible loss a child can fathom.

Chapter 1

Ironbridge

January 1892 – ten years later

'You're the lass who wrote me such a fine letter, then?'

'I am. I'm Maria Keay.'

The barber squinted at her. His unruly eyebrows were as thick as well-fed caterpillars and seemed to wriggle as much, as he regarded her with scrutiny.

'Said you're seventeen. You dunna look it. You look younger'n that.'

'Fresh-faced: that's what they say about me.'

In fact, she was only just seventeen as she'd had her birthday a few days before.

The barber muttered, 'Hmmm . . .' and eyed the top shelves behind the counter. 'You're little too, a ratlin of the litter. You think you can reach top shelf?'

Maria looked at the tobacconist section of the barber's premises. He cut men's hair and shaved their beards in the three raised chairs, each with a step up, in a row on the right-hand side of the shop, while the tobacco products were kept in drawers and on shelves behind a decidedly dusty and cluttered counter on the left.

'All I'll need is a milking stool to step on. I've got one at my lodgings. I'll bring it tomorrow. I can do this job, Mr Boden. I promise I can.' She held herself upright and tried to look as tall as she could.

The barber sighed and glanced at the clock on the wall behind the counter. It was five minutes until opening. His appointments were scribbled on a slate propped up on the countertop, just a barely legible list of names. Most of the barber's customers would come whenever they felt like it, Maria guessed, but some arranged it in advance to fit their busy work days. There were no times written down. There were several heaps of coins scattered across the counter too, in no particular order, mixed up with a fallen pile of blank receipt notes, screwed up knots of waste paper and all scattered liberally with flecks of dried tobacco. On the floor were strewn hair clippings mixed with dust balls and crumbs of mud and leaf litter brought in from outside. The two small windows facing the street were smeared with a deep layer of grime. He must have to squint to see his customers' necks when he scraped a blade up them.

'I'll clean this place from top to bottom, every day. I'll get you a proper ledger and write all your names and appointment times out in a neat hand, just like my letter was. And I'll keep a track of money in and money out, so your accounts will be as neat as a pin. I'll give this counter and all the drawers and shelves a good dusting. I'll arrange a proper good display in the windows and give them such a polish they'll shine and show off all your most expensive items. And I'll serve customers with a smile and persuade them to buy things they didna know they needed. You wonna be sorry you hired me, Mr Boden, I swear you wonna.'

'How d'you know all about accounting, eh? Slip of a wench like you.'

'I was taught by the village shopkeeper back in Middleton-in-Chirbury, the lady who wrote such nice words about me in the reference I put in the same envelope as my letter to you. She taught me everything I know.'

Maria could feel her cheeks blooming. Normally, she was a hopeless liar. She never had the knack for it. Exaggeration, yes. Embellishment, certainly. But she wasn't a born liar. Luckily, instead of eyeing her, Mr Boden was looking about his shop with an expression of annoyance. Her little speech seemed to rouse him, perhaps to realise she was right about what a mess the shop was, but he was also a bit put out that she'd detailed it all so precisely. It was a gamble. So was the reference she'd forged from the village shopkeeper. She'd been in that shop every chance she could get in the last ten years, but she'd never officially worked there. She was good at faking handwriting and taking on the persona of a kindly shopkeeper giving a glowing reference. She just hoped Mr Boden never wrote back to check it. Seeing what a muddle his paperwork was clearly in, Maria doubted it.

She knew it was wrong when she did it, but she knew also that finding shop work with no reference would be hopeless. After all, it was a white lie, really, as she hadn't had a job at the village shop as such, but she'd been so enamoured of it – filled with a cornucopia of goods to serve the rural folk for miles around – that she'd spent as much time as she could there, the patient shopkeeper putting up with her presence, her dawdling and her questions about how shops worked. So she knew a thing or two about shop work, enough to start her off in a small place like this, she was sure. But had she done enough to get the job? Maria waited and watched him. She'd come a long way. She was tired but driven to succeed. She just needed a little bit of luck.

'You're on then, lass. Start . . . now?'

'Now it is! Shall I clean first?'

'Do the cleaning. It needs it, you're right. I'll deal with customers this morning. When it's shipshape, then maybe you can start serving custom, we'll see.'

'Yes, sir,' she said and nodded emphatically.

Maria got to work straight away. She didn't ask questions, just used her common sense, as well as the years of experience cleaning the farmhouse, from where she'd travelled eastwards the day before. She wanted to sweep first, so went to the back room between the counter and the barbering area, finding a broom and some old rags out there. She also came across a few odds and ends of cleaning materials in crusty containers, yet with the lids off she saw they were adequate and would do the job fine. She set to sweeping the floor. Mr Boden opened up the door and the bell rang, while a rush of chilly January air assaulted them as a man came in for a shave.

The customer, a middle-aged man with mutton-chop sideburns and a stooping gait, stared at her.

'New wench?' he said to Mr Boden.

'Started today.'

'Bonny lass,' said the man and seated himself, ready for a shave, yet turned his whole self round to keep looking in her direction. 'Hair as yellow as a Viking and eyes as blue as forget-me-nots. She dunna cut gents' hair?' he added, hopefully, with a wink at her.

'Nay. She'll mind the tobacconist while I do the barbering, thank'ee. Now, stop yer jabbering or I'll slice yer throat and it wonna be an accident.'

The customer turned back around in his chair and settled himself.

Maria continued her cleaning frenzy as the barber's customers came and went, all commenting on the girl and what a peach she was. She wasn't haughty with them, but she didn't encourage them either. She'd dealt with enough farm boys to know how to keep a male at bay. She was polite with them, yet focused on her work. She tidied all of the paperwork into piles and found the wooden cash tray in the drawer beneath the counter with sections, where she arranged the different coins, each type in its own compartment. She polished the counter as well as she could and cleaned up and down its sides. Soon, the whole shop was brighter than ever and it seemed to cheer Mr Boden, whose mood improved as the morning went on. Every time she finished a job, he inspected it briefly and nodded. Maria was pleased with her work.

Now the shop was as clean as she could make it, she tackled the two window areas. The so-called displays had a few items strewn about, with some advertisement cards propped up, thick with dust. She took everything out and cleaned the whole area. She used water and soap to scrub the windows, as they were mucky as mud, the day beginning to stream through as she did so.

'Let there be light!' said one of the customers, having his hair trimmed, watching her in the mirrors placed all along the right-hand wall.

She smiled and carried on scrubbing till the glass was gleaming, then began to place items back in the display areas, neatly arranging them in patterns that were pleasing to the eye. There were all manner of pipes, including clay pipes from Broseley Pipeworks down the road and a selection of wooden pipes. One curious pipe had the bowl held by a carved wooden hand. She put that in pride of place in the centre, raised on a little box, to catch the eye of passers-by. There were several earthenware jars filled with tobacco from faraway continents, including Africa and the Americas, each with its tobacco's place of origin lettered on the front: exotic locales such as Martinique, Cairo and Tennessee, which filled her mind with wonder. How marvellous it would be to travel to such places one day. She organised the jars in arcs, as well as dusting off the advertisement cards that sang the praises of their wares in once-bright colours: *Smoke Ogden Midnight Flake! Enjoy St Julien Tobacco!* She took some cigars from their box behind the counter and arranged them in an intricate tower, to lure the smoker to lick his lips and want a puff enough to come in and buy. That was the whole point of having a window display, she knew from her time ogling the windows of the one village shop for miles around, not far from the farm she'd grown up in this last decade – the farm she was taken to the day after her parents were lost to the Severn, the farm run by her uncle with an iron fist. The farm she hated with every fibre of her being.

By lunchtime, the shop was transformed. Mr Boden was delighted. He told her she could have a half-hour off to go and eat but she said no. She'd brought bread and cheese with her and would eat it in the back room, while she cleared it up. While there, she found an old ledger that had once been used, perhaps by a previous owner. There were once neat accounts kept there in a sloping hand. Maria dusted it off and brought it through, asking her employer whose work this was.

Boden looked down at his toes and muttered something she didn't hear.

'It's my wife's,' he repeated gruffly. 'It were, I mean to say. Lost her three year ago. I'm a widower.'

'I see,' said Maria quietly. 'She did a grand job, I can tell.'

'She had a lovely hand, so she did.'

'She did indeed. Wouldna'it be nice if I carried on in the same book, keeping your accounts all nice and neat, like before?'

'It would, lass,' he said and, with a sniffle, he turned away to hide his emotion that had spilled out momentarily. Boden paid his full attention instead to his chairs, brushing them down of hair detritus before the next customers came to be seated. Maria took up the broom and cleared the floor in readiness.

She was putting the broom away behind the counter when the doorbell rang and in came a young man. Maria looked up and instantly knew the face. She was expecting to see boys and girls from her childhood, grown now like herself, around and about in Ironbridge – that was, if they were still recognisable from the last time she saw them ten years before. But this man was older than her, she was quite sure, and yet his face was sharply familiar – though the last time she'd seen it, she was sure it hadn't included his current broad brown moustache.

He had beside him a dog, a black and white Border collie. She knew collies, as her uncle had two who lived out in the barn and were called Collie younger and Collie elder, their names being both their breed and the name of their owner, oddly. They were treated rather roughly by her uncle Solomon Collie, as he treated everything close to him, and so she never made friends with either. This pretty Border collie, however, was wagging its tail like mad, its tongue lolling out good-naturedly. The dog was on no lead, yet behaved perfectly as the man pushed the door to. The handsome dog seated itself neatly next to its owner and looked up at him expectantly, lovingly. The man was looking at Maria.

''Ow bist, Mr Woodvine?' asked the barber.

'Fair to middling, Mr Boden, more middling than fair,' said the young man, still looking at Maria.

She turned away. Whose was that face? And that name – Woodvine – it was familiar to her. She scanned her memory scene by scene, trying to conjure it up, as she retrieved the papers from beneath the counter that she meant to sort that afternoon.

'And Biscuit?' added Boden, leaning down and ruffling the collie's fur. 'Fair or middling, boy?'

'Biscuit is always well above middling,' said Mr Woodvine.

'And what brings'ee here this time o'day?'

'Lunchtime, when I take Biscuit for a walk, and thought I'd just pop in on the off-chance.'

'Shave or a cut?' said the barber, addressing the owner, not the dog.

Maria was leafing through the paperwork at the counter, but she glanced up twice to keep an eye on Mr Woodvine to find he was watching her too. He must know her then.

'Tobacco, actually, Mr Boden.'

'You dunna smoke, mon.'

Maria looked up sharply then. The man coughed nervously and said, 'I do, I do. I've just recently taken it up.'

Boden squinted at him, but then was distracted by another customer coming for a shave.

'Can you serve this gent, Maria?' said the barber and she nodded vigorously. Her first customer! She was glad of it, for she wondered when she'd be allowed to actually serve rather than clean.

'Afternoon, sir,' she said and smiled.

'Good afternoon, miss,' he said, smiling back. That was when it came to her. That smile. His hair was longer now, as he'd always had it cut close to his head as a younger man. Now his light brown hair was curled and a little unruly on top, perhaps from the winter breeze that had reddened his cheeks. Now she knew exactly who he was. As a girl at school, from time to time an older pupil helped the school children with their lessons as a kind of apprentice teacher. This man was the eldest of them, around sixteen or seventeen the last time she saw him. And oh, did she have a girlish crush on him back then? *Did I ever!* she thought. It was Charlie Woodvine. Charlie, that was it. How she broke her girlish heart over Charlie, the apprentice teacher (minus moustache, in those days).

He asked Maria which tobacco she would recommend. It was obvious he knew nothing about smoking. She knew even less, but she had made herself familiar with Boden's stock that morning and so knew enough to make some suggestions.

'I would like to try some from Tennessee. I should think it'd feel quite special to relax of an evening by the fire and puff on something that crossed the Atlantic to sit in the bowl of my Broseley pipe.'

She smiled at that. Charlie had a nice turn of phrase. She went over to Mr Boden and asked him how much to weigh and how much that would cost. That would be another job needed: writing out cards with prices on them. Boden told her and she weighed it out, then wrapped the tobacco in a fold of paper for Charlie, yet the saleswoman in her was not done with this customer so soon. 'Would you like anything else to go with that, sir? Do you own a Broseley pipe?'

'I do not,' he said and cleared his throat. The ruse was up, surely. The man clearly did not smoke. So why had he hung around to buy some tobacco from her? Especially when he so obviously needed a haircut. As Charlie smiled at her again, she thought she guessed the reason why. Maria glanced at Boden, who was busy arguing with his customer about local politics. She looked back at Charlie.

'I believe I know you, sir. Or I used to.'

His eyes widened then. 'I believe if I'd ever known you, miss, I'd have never forgotten a moment of it,' he said matter-of-factly.

'You were Charlie Woodvine, the teacher's apprentice.'

'I was! Well, I was a pupil-teacher, so they called it. Were you one of my little charges?'

'I was. I was seven years old the last time you might've seen me, ten year since.'

Biscuit the collie dog was pushing his muzzle into his owner's hand.

'All right, boy,' Charlie said gently, but did not take his eyes from Maria. 'Where . . . have you been?' he asked her hesitantly.

'That's a long story,' said Maria. 'Too long for a shopgirl at work to tell.'

She was acutely aware of her boss eyeing them both as they chatted, as another customer was just coming in and was lining up behind Charlie, who registered the other man's presence by fumbling in his wallet to hand over the cash for the tobacco he'd probably never smoke.

'Thank you, miss . . . Miss . . .?'

'Keay,' she said. 'Miss Maria Keay.'

'Hurry yourself up, schoolmaster,' said the man behind Charlie. 'We havna got all day for you to learn the wench her times tables.'

The barber laughed at that and so did Charlie. So, he was the schoolmaster now. He'd kept to his younger purpose, then. It was impressive.

Charlie made his apologies and clapped the man on the back, telling him his son was doing well with his reading these days, which made the man puff with pride and thank him. Charlie took one last glance at Maria and gave her a small smile, which she noted but did not return. Charlie left, Biscuit close at his heel.

Maria had to be careful with the customers. Every man that had come in that day had given her a good look. She had to keep her wits about her with the male of the species. It was odd, she knew, for a young woman to be seen in this kind of shop and she was grateful to Mr Boden for taking her on, despite her not being a male. She never wanted him to feel she was enjoying the male attention too much, and get a name for herself. Instead, Maria wanted to work so hard that he would wonder how he ever got by without her.

Chapter 2

Maria spent the next couple of hours going through the barber's papers and recording his receipts in the ledger in the most sensible order she could find. She also turned to the back and began a trust book, where she'd record the names of those paying later on account. She wrote with a pencil, using a penknife she found in a drawer to sharpen it, as she couldn't locate a pen nor ink. Maria could tell her new boss was pleased with her hard work and her initiative. By three o'clock, the whole place looked like a new shop. He'd be there till eight or nine that night, catching the working men after their long day of industry. But he let her go early.

'Be off home with yer, wench. You've earnt it. See you back here on the morrow, lark-heeled, bright and early.'

Maria said her farewells and, bundled up in her winter boots, scarf, hat and shawl, she braved the cold afternoon outside. It was not yet fully dark, but it wouldn't be long. She pulled the shop door to and stepped down onto the pavement of Waterloo Street. Boden's barber and tobacconist occupied the ground floor opposite the stone arches of the Ironbridge Police Station, with the Fire Station just around the corner.

She'd never be short of folk to call on if there was a dire emergency, she thought.

She walked down to the High Street, watching the iron bridge all the way. It drew you to it always, the focal point of the town. Maria wanted to hurry back to her lodgings, as it was a bit of a way and she was weary from her day's work and yesterday's journey, but she couldn't resist a brisk walk over the bridge to stand in the centre and look down at the river flowing beneath it. She watched the dark waters race downstream. Then, from beneath the bridge, a singular figure emerged, seated in a tiny circular boat, armed with a paddle. Beneath his flat cap and in the dimming light, she couldn't see his face, but she knew who he was. Everybody in Ironbridge knew Tommy Rogers, the boatman and coracle builder. She gasped at the sight of him, for it was he who'd found her parents' drowned bodies, the evening of the accident. With his waterway skills, he was often asked to recover drowning victims and they say he never took payment, out of respect for the dead. She thought of the wreck of the miller's cart down there, all of its pieces no doubt rotted or carried away by the current in these last ten years. The miller had been rescued, pulled from the river by strong iron workers who found him near Bedlam Furnace. Her parents had not been so lucky.

Maria watched Tommy Rogers speed along, the river bearing his coracle away swiftly. Where was he going at this time of the darkening afternoon? Poaching, perhaps? Hunting for illegal rabbits in the fields of wealthy landowners, no doubt. Those were the rumours when she was little. She watched him until she could see him no longer, lost to the twilight. *He saw my parents' corpses*, she thought grimly. *He hauled them out of the water. Mam and Dad*. She'd never seen them dead. Never seen them again, after the moment she was launched into the sky from the miller's cart. Within a day, her uncle had been informed and taken it upon himself to assume custody of her. There was nobody else to do it. There was a sister on her father's side, but she lived in Staffordshire. Her mother's brother was the only other relative around and conveniently in Ironbridge the day of the accident, waiting at the Tontine to see his sister, who never came. He agreed to take seven-year-old Maria on and back they went the next day on the long, dreary horse-and-cart ride for the thirty-odd miles to Collie Farm in Middleton-in-Chirbury. During the journey, her uncle did not speak to her once, in all those hours, not a word, a kind word or any other type of word, to the bereaved child still in pain and shock. She soon came to know that Solomon Collie was always a man of few words, except when he was vexed and would then indulge in long, self-righteous rants. He mostly communicated via grunts and nods, coldness and violence. So ended the happy Ironbridge chapter of her childhood and began her cruel exile. Maria shivered as she peered into the gloomy depths of the Severn below.

She scolded herself. Why did she come to stand on this infernal bridge anyway? Why was she drawn to it? This, the place of her tragedy? The worst day of her life? She didn't know, but she had to do it. Something about the indifference of the river compelled her. To witness, to pay homage to all she had lost within its rushing might.

Maria dragged herself away, turned about and walked back over the bridge, past the Tontine and up Wharfage past all the shops that lined the street and faced the river, their windows aglow with welcoming light and warmth. She had to pass by The Swan and Loadcroft Wharf on her way, the very site of her tragedy. She tipped her head back instead and looked up at the gloaming in the sky. Evening was drawing in. She hurried as she went up along Paradise, thickly wooded on each side and punctuated by dwellings, the memories pouring in now.

It was unfortunate that her cousin, whose house she was walking to, lived on the very same road on which her home had once stood. That morning, walking down to the barber's shop, Maria had seen with a shock that the little house her parents had rented, nearly twenty years before, had been knocked down and replaced by better-built cottages. She didn't look at them as she passed this time. It made her too maudlin to think of every scrap of her childhood smashed up or washed away. It was as if her parents had never existed. Time had forgotten them.

She hurried on to get back to the house she was to sleep in: the home of her cousin Rhoda, the daughter of her father's sister who lived in Staffordshire. Rhoda was eight years older than Maria and had married an Ironbridge man, so came to make her home here, long after Maria had left. Desperate to escape the farm, Maria had written to Rhoda asking for a place to stay in Ironbridge, telling her she would be looking as soon as she got there for a job in a shop – any shop in the area. Her cousin's response was lukewarm, yet she agreed, for a certain amount of weekly rent, enclosing details of a job going at the tobacconist and barber's shop on Wellington Street, which had a scrawled sign in the window saying HELP WANTED, ASSISTANT ALL HOURS. Thus had Maria's chance come to finally escape Collie Farm.

On the day she left, she planned to say all manner of righteous things to Solomon Collie, his timid wife Mercy – to whom he'd shown none – and their six children. There were so very many of them, from ages one to eleven, when Maria had arrived aged seven that they seemed thrice times six when the devil took their moods and they misbehaved, which was often. When Maria had arrived, she was treated from her first day as their unpaid skivvy, carrying on this role in the farmhouse for ten long years. She wanted to inflict her rage upon them all that morning she left the farm forever, never to return. But she'd not had the heart to. He deserved it, Uncle Solomon, the man who'd slipper her and the others merely for breathing and beat any of them into a stupor with his belt for leaving a bean on the plate uneaten. Solomon was a farmer of wheat, oats and turnips and only sometimes peas and beans, so beans were prized and should never be left. He complained that beans did badly in his wretched soil and he 'dunna know why he bothered', though the soil looked rich and luscious to Maria on her frequent rambles to escape the farmhouse. But, though she hated them all for the cold and lonely life they gave her among them, the rest of the family were but pawns caught up in his vicious game. Maria was the scapegoat for them all. She'd slipped away at dawn the day before and had not said a word. They were not worth the effort, she decided.

The last stretch before her destination was quite steep and her legs were tiring. She looked back on her day to cheer herself, as she had to admit it had been a resounding success. She'd got the job and acquitted herself very well, she thought. Mr Boden seemed ever so pleased with her hard work. And then there were the comings and goings of customers, the talk she overheard as the barber chinwagged away with the men whose hair he shaved or trimmed. At one point, there were three men in the chairs and one waiting, and once they'd clocked her and given each other knowing looks, they'd more or less forgotten her. She had sat quietly doing the paperwork as they gossiped about the town and its workers and bosses and talked of strikes and unrest. It was such a change to be surrounded by people who liked to talk. She'd lived in a cold, stone farmhouse of silence for so long, only punctuated by the sound of a child whinging or crying after a blow from their father. To stand behind a counter and write in her neat hand, while all about her was chattering and commerce, after years of wanting to be a shopgirl, Maria was at last achieving her dream. And the icing on the cake was Charlie Woodvine turning up, a face from her past. And what a nice face it was.

Then, there she was, finally arriving at Rhoda's house. Her cousin's husband, Eli Nott, wouldn't be home yet, she guessed, as she'd been told that his work as an insurance agent often had him out and about at the premises of his clients long past six in the evening. Maria opened the front door and stepped inside, stamping her feet on the mat to get as much of the outside off them as possible. Rhoda was house-proud and Maria didn't want to add to her work by traipsing in muck.

At the sound of the door, Rhoda appeared in the hallway, her pregnant belly the first thing to arrive. She was a few months away from her time, a tricky pregnancy filled with all manner of physical ailments, which she had told Maria about in great detail upon her late arrival last night. Maria's eyes had been drooping from exhaustion, but Rhoda had failed to notice and kept on with her litany of woes, as well as making it quite clear that Maria's presence was tolerated but not particularly welcomed.

At the sight of Maria home from the first day of her job, one might expect Maria's cousin to ask her about her day and how she fared. But no, that was not Rhoda's way and, instead, she continued the conversation from last night as if they had left off only a moment ago, and not the twenty or so hours that had passed.

'I am aware that you are a tragic person, Maria,' announced Rhoda, as Maria took off her winter gear and then stood rubbing her tired, chilled limbs in the hallway. What was the woman going on about now? Maria could not believe at times that Rhoda had come from the Keay side of the family – as Maria's father had been such a sweet-tempered, humorous man – yet her cousin had about as much sense of humour as a doorpost. 'Having lost your dear'uns at a young age, Eli and I felt it our Christian duty to take you in, temporarily of course, while you find your feet, until you secure paid lodging elsewhere. However, we didna agree to you coming home early from work and no doubt alarming your employer and disturbing me in my slumber of an afternoon. I didna expect you home till gone eight or even nine and then assumed you'd be straight up to your room. I was to put out cold cuts for you. Not a hot meal, as Eli and I will have. And there is not enough for three. I am eating for two folk as it is.'

'Mr Boden let me go home early. And cold cuts in my room will be fine,' said Maria, forcing a smile. She had agreed with her cousin and made it easy for her. But still that was not enough.

'Everyone on our side of the family was fond of your father, Alfred. My mother said as much at least once a year, as I recall. And that's the spirit in which I take you on now, into my very home, to pay respects to your personal tragedy. We have no need of you in this house, but we do right by family, taking you in. Make sure you show my husband gratitude. He inna your kin, so dunna see it like I do, but we welcome the rent you pay and any help you can give with housework while I'm struggling with this little'un inside me making me sick as a dog. But if it is God's will that this child will live, then I will put up with hell and high water to bring it into the world to live in health and ease for as long as I am permitted by the graces of heaven. Finding you here hours before your time has quite put me out of sorts and given me a new ache in my side that wasna there but five minutes before you roughly shoved our front door open, letting in all that cold and . . .'

And so she droned on. How very, very much Maria wanted to scream at this infernal person, *Hush your noise!* But, of course, she didn't and instead listened politely to every last whining word. She took her plate of cold mutton upstairs with a lamp to her room and shut the door, collapsing on the bed with relief. It was lucky Maria was so short in stature as the bed was that of her cousin's child: a boy that had passed away at the tender age of three, not two years before. This cold fact gave Maria pause to not feel too disgruntled with Rhoda. Perhaps, if two deaths were ever to be compared, then that of a child and that of one's parents were not too far apart in drodsome misery. They could have bonded over this, but Maria felt no affinity with Rhoda in the slightest, feeling only a bother to her and her taciturn husband Eli.

Maria sat up and drank down a mug of water that had been left on the milking stool beside her bed since last night and then she wolfed down the mutton, suddenly realising how hungry and thirsty she was after the hours of work and walking. She lay back and stared up at the ceiling of the tiny room, more like a cell than a nursery. She'd been told by Rhoda that she could stay until the baby to be born was a few months old, as they'd be keeping it in their own bedroom with them until it was weaned. Rhoda had explained, 'I wonna be taking my eyes off my babby for one second once it's out of me and in the world. Not for one second.'

Maria felt her cousin's pain and anxiety about the baby to come and the loss she'd suffered, which maybe explained Eli's lack of chatter too.

The January winds whistled round the house, ruffling the curtain that hung in the one window, as the wind's icy fingers seeped through the ill-fitting window frames. As uncomfortable as living there might be, Maria worried too about how on earth she'd find cheap enough lodgings after the baby came. Well, she'd have to work on that problem another day. She was too weary now.

She climbed under the thin blanket on the bed, fully clothed, so chilly it was. As the lamp threw shifting shadows of the fluttering curtain across the wall, she thought she heard a distant call. Maria held her breath to hear it better. There it was again: not distant, just small. And close. It sounded . . . like a child's whimper in its sleep. But there was no child in this house, not any more. Was she to be haunted now too, by her cousin's lost boy, as well as her parents? A last thought flitted through her mind that evening, before tiredness overtook her and she passed into sleep: *Perhaps it wasna the best idea I've ever had to revisit the place of my soul's great sadness. Perhaps I should never've returned to Ironbridge.*

Chapter 3

April 1892

The morose mood of that first night soon passed as Maria learnt the ropes of her new job. The pay wasn't much, but it was her first real job and thus receiving her weekly pay packet from Mr Boden was a source of excitement, certainly at first. Three months went by, serving customers – all men, without exception – and fending off their interest in her. Three months of cleaning daily to keep the shop spick and span. Three months of keeping Mr Boden's accounts in apple-pie order. She'd been right about Mr Boden: he'd said to her just the other day that 'I dunna know how I managed without'ee!' She'd made herself indispensable at work, if not at home, where her cousin's moaning and groaning continued. Work was an escape, yet she was tiring of the male attention and also the stink of tobacco, which she'd never liked. Her father had not been a smoker, but her uncle was and it reminded her of the farmhouse hearth, the stuffy air choked with pipe smoke as she longed to escape. However, there was one particular pleasure of Maria's days and that was the weekly visit of Charlie Woodvine and his loveable dog Biscuit. Charlie now visited for a shave at lunchtime and bought more tobacco, though Maria was still convinced he didn't actually smoke and came in only so he'd have the opportunity to chat with her. One time, Boden couldn't resist the opportunity to tell Charlie off for not letting him cut his hair shorter.

'It looks like a sheep needin' shearing,' he said, tutting and shaking his head at the curly mop.

'The sides and back are short enough. The top does have a good height to it, I agree, but that only makes me look distinguished, I'd say. I only want half an inch off, Mr Boden. That's all and no more.'

'Maria,' sighed Boden. 'Can'ee not talk this man into neatening up?'

Both men looked at her, awaiting her response, yet she was ruffling the back of Biscuit's neck. The dog loved this and he sat, gazing up at her with new devotion, as she'd discovered his favourite thing beside sausages.

'I like curls,' is all Maria said, occasioning a broad grin from Charlie and another bout of tutting from the barber.

At that moment, the door opened and in came something quite unexpected. A woman. And not just any woman, but, quite clearly, a gentlewoman. She was dressed in the latest city fashions, or so Maria guessed, as she'd not seen clothes that smart on anyone in Ironbridge. The woman's outfit was a symphony in purple, such an unusual colour to see around town. She had a lilac plaited cotton blouse with a cascade frill down the front, an indigo skirt and matching jacket with pronounced leg-o'-mutton sleeves. Both were cinched tight at the waist, where there was tied a flouncy lilac waistband bow. She was such an uncommon sight – not only in the town, but certainly in this shop – that Maria, Boden and Charlie were all struck dumb. Even Biscuit was motionless, regarding her.

'Good afternoon, sirs, miss,' she said, her voice loud and

throaty, a comfortable smile about her lips. Maria could tell this woman had that confidence that money gave, to be assured of herself that, in any situation, she was probably the wealthiest woman in the room.

Maria spoke first, to break the awkward silence. 'Good afternoon, ma'am. How may I help you?'

Boden and Charlie had not moved and were obviously awaiting the solution to this mystery, of what such a well-dressed middle-aged lady might possibly want in the town's barber shop and tobacconist.

'Thank you, my dear. I see in your window you sell some very smart-looking cigars. I see also your little advertisement for Alton's Cigars. Please tell me you have some of these. They really are my favourites.'

Maria had learnt quite a bit in the last three months about the wares she sold, and she certainly knew that they did stock Alton's. She'd read about their qualities in the order book she'd found in the drawer one day in that first week.

'They are indeed Alton's, ma'am. All hand-rolled and made from the finest Havana leaf. Shall I wrap some for your husband or would you like to take a whole box?'

The woman chuckled. 'They are not for my husband, young lady. They are for me! Alton's are the nicest I've tried and I've tried a fair few, on my travels.'

Maria was aware of Charlie and Boden giving each other a look, then turning to mind their own business as Charlie sat down for his haircut. Maria knew this woman was the richest customer they'd had in all the time she'd worked there and, if she could, she'd sell her everything she was able to before this customer left the premises.

'My mistake, ma'am, and I apologise. I shouldna've presumed such. Please instruct me how many you need and I'll wrap them for you directly.'

'It's quite all right. I know I am most likely quite an odd sight in this province. I'm visiting a sick relative, you see, up the hill. Staying there for a couple of days. I can't be without my evening smoke. It'd quite put me out of sorts.'

'I'm sorry to hear of illness in the family,' said Maria, as she placed a box of Alton's cigars on the counter.

'You're kind. It is my great-aunt. I've lived in Shrewsbury these past twenty years since I married, but she is dear to me and used to visit me regularly. But now she is bedridden, I come to see her when I can. It is my maid's day off today and I was feeling a bit house-bound, so thought I'd come for a stroll into town. Great-Aunt Mabel was sleeping, so I won't be missed, I dare say.'

'A most thoughtful great-niece, if I may say so, ma'am. How many Alton's cigars would you like to purchase? Unless madam would like the whole box?'

'Now then. I don't want to run out. I'll take the whole box, please.'

'And did madam fancy another brand to try, while she's here? Free samples are offered on request of our full range of cigars from the world over.'

Maria had never offered a free sample before and as Boden snipped away faster and faster at Charlie's curls, Maria could sense his annoyance. But she was sure that it would pay off, considering how much cash this punter was likely to spend.

'What else do you have in stock, then?'

'We stock Upmann's and Punch.'

'Why, Upmann's is considered finer than Alton's, though I still prefer the mellow quality of the latter. You should advertise those as well in the window. I'm not so keen on Punch, but I'll have some Upmann's too. I prefer those with sherry and Alton's with wine.'

'Another full box, ma'am? Upmann's do come in a quite

charming cedar box, which I warrant would look nice upon an occasional table in madam's house.'

'Well, I was only going to try one or two but . . . all right, I will. You're right, the box is nice to look at. Both boxes then, please. Wrap them, will you?'

'Indeed, ma'am.'

She'd made an excellent sale. Maria was sure Boden would be pleased. She went to the back room to fetch some paper for wrapping and when she came back in, she glanced over to see Boden had cut Charlie's hair far too short for his liking. But Charlie was kind enough not to make a fuss while such a prestigious customer graced Boden's shop. He handed over his coins to Boden and might have smiled at Maria as he took Biscuit and left, but she was too busy attending to the lady to see. Boden went into the back to sharpen his tools just as Maria had finished wrapping the cigars.

'I'll pay you cash, since I'm not a local and do not have an account here. Can you change this?'

It was the first paper note Maria had taken in all her time as a shopgirl.

'I'm sure I can, ma'am. We've had a good number of clients today. Thank'ee.'

She smoothed it out in the cash tray and admired it momentarily. *Just imagine, having paper notes about your person, just as an everyday occurrence.* She did the quick arithmetic in her head and gave the woman her change.

'It might be an idea to set up a postal service for your cigars,' said the lady. 'Put an advertisement in the local paper. I'm sure the finer families in rural areas hereabouts would welcome quality cigars sent to their homes.'

'That is a capital idea, ma'am. Thank'ee for it.'

The lady said, 'You really are quite a wonder, my dear. I did not expect to find a saleswoman like you in a small town, and one so young. How on earth have you found yourself working in such a male environment? Is the barber your father?'

'Indeed not,' said Maria. 'I recently moved here from the countryside, where I lived with my farmer uncle. I didna wanna stay there a moment longer. I've known for a long time I wanna be in shops and so I left crops for cigars.'

The lady laughed. 'Quite right too! You know, the larger towns and cities of England are now places where shopgirls can excel. It's quite a new thing, this idea of shopping for pleasure. You'll see it more and more in larger locations. They do it wonderfully in France and now here too, taking after the French model. Hordes of women customers at last being able to meet a friend in a shop without the need for a chaperone. And shops designed to be spectacles, full of elaborate displays and places to promenade, to see and be seen, and even restaurants and waiting rooms for ladies in some places. They truly have become a woman's realm. If you really want to ascend the career ladder, then a draper's shop might be your best bet. Most department stores developed from draper's, you know.'

The thought of where this woman had travelled and what she had seen filled Maria with wonder. She'd heard the term 'department store' but had never really wondered what it actually meant. She knew about draper's shops, of course, as every woman knew where to buy materials for dresses and other clothes. In recent years, though, most of her clothes came from the second-hand markets. She didn't know anything of this other world this cultured woman was describing.

'I think I would die happy if I were ever to work in a place like that, ma'am.'

'Have you considered what your next step might be?'

'I hadna, ma'am. I was just grateful enough to get this job.'

'Then I suggest you approach the draper's I was in before I

came upon your premises here. It's the large one on the Wharf-age. There was a sign in the window requesting an assistant.'

'Was there?' Maria said loudly, then immediately retreated into herself as Boden returned from the back room with sharper tools.

'There was. You know, it wasn't that long ago that all shops were run and staffed by men. But what women wanted was *women* to serve them, who knew about dresses and scents and jewellery and ribbons and so forth, who understood which colour hat would best suit her hair and complexion. Or what it truly felt like to wear a bodice that fitted just so. How could a shopman divine these things, never having worn a bodice?!'

The woman laughed and so did Maria, yet Boden looked deeply uncomfortable as he brushed off his chairs.

'Well, I shall let you get on, my dear. I've taken up far too much of your time already.'

'Not at all, ma'am. It's our pleasure. Thank'ee for coming to Boden's today.'

'You're welcome. And the pleasure was all mine. Just so you know, my name is Mrs Ethel Jameson. And you are?'

'Maria Keay, ma'am. Thank'ee, ma'am.'

'And you must be the eponymous Mr Boden, I take it?' said Mrs Jameson, turning a dazzling smile on the barber, who stood up straight, stiff as a board.

'I be Boden. Pleasure, ma'am. Thank'ee for the custom.'

'You're welcome, my man. And may I suggest a pay rise for this little gem here? She is quite the jewel of your business, Mr Boden. Good day to you both.'

They wished her good day and, in a swirl of purple, she was gone.

Maria looked at Boden and wondered if he might be annoyed at her, spending so much time with one customer, but he was so pleased with the sale he actually did a little jump and rubbed his hands together gleefully.

'Danker me!' he crowed. 'Two cigar boxes! Well done, wench! Well done!'

Maria laughed and thanked him. 'I knew she'd have the money to spend, so why not spend a bit more of it here!'

'That's the way of it. That's the way to make money.' Then his mouth turned down and he added, 'But I canna pay you more, wench. I canna afford it, not with rents such as they are.'

'I understand, Mr Boden,' she said, and then a more regular customer came in, an old man wanting his shave, as his hands shook too much these days to do it himself.

Maria did understand, but, as she took out the ledger and recorded the substantial purchase from the gentlewoman, her mind was filled with the draper's shop and its advertisement in the window, of which the lady had told her. Maria might find a way to leave a little early tonight, perhaps using this success to butter Boden up. For if she left before closing, she might catch the draper's before it shut its own doors and she could pop in and have a word about this job. She'd only been at the barber's since January, but she felt she was outgrowing this little business already. The visit from the extraordinary smoking lady had given her pause for thought. Mrs Jameson had opened a door onto a new world of commerce that awaited Maria. And the young woman was uncommonly eager to step through it.

But there was a flurry of customers that evening and Mr Boden did not let Maria go home early that day or for the rest of the week. Thus Maria could only pass by the draper's shop on Wharfage when it was already closed and ache to go in and ask about the advertisement. Had the barber heard her talking to Mrs Jameson about the draper's job? She hoped not, but it was odd that he was so insistent she remain until the last moment, as he usually let her go a little early. At least the advertisement was still in the window when she passed it the following Tuesday. The next day was half-day closing for many businesses in Ironbridge, as the market filled the square that day. Boden could not keep her when the shop was shut. So off she went bang on closing time, hurrying along Wharfage in the spring sunshine to reach the draper's before it too shut for the day. She got there just as a woman was locking the door from the inside. The advertisement still remained in the window, thankfully.

Maria knocked hurriedly on the window and saw the woman mouth 'CLOSED!' at her, clearly annoyed. But Maria was not to be put off. She knocked again and said loudly, to penetrate the glass between them, 'I'm here about the job.'

The woman frowned and unlocked the door. She was nicely turned out in a dark green plaid dress with puffed sleeves. Maria suddenly felt conscious of her grey woollen skirt and jacket, with clumpy boots and frayed cotton shirtwaist. Even though nobody could see the hems were frayed, as they were tucked in to her skirt, Maria knew they were. Mrs Jameson had seemed like a bird of paradise compared to a sparrow; that is, there were very few points of comparison. This woman at the draper's was closer in class to Maria and yet her clothes were so much nicer; Maria felt like an urchin at the sweet shop window in her shabby outfit. Yet Mrs Jameson had not looked down upon her because of it. Maria told herself to make the best of herself and be confident, that if she could glean even the smallest modicum of Mrs Jameson's confidence she'd do all right.

'Did you say the job?' the woman said.

'Yes, ma'am. I'm here to apply for the job advertised in your window.'

The woman looked her up and down and Maria's heart fell at the thought of how she must look. Her clothes were bad enough, but her spring cloak was even more threadbare, she recalled, and her boots were muddy from the April showers that had plagued the town for days before today's sunshine. Her clothes might look poor, but one thing she did know was that she could talk up a storm. Her uncle never valued her schooling and pulled her out of the village school aged eight and a half to work full-time at the farmhouse as the general skivvy. Every day began with emptying the family's slop buckets, then it was scrubbing steps, scouring the range and any other job her uncle could think up for her little fingers to slave away at. But Maria joined the village library and got books out as often as she could, reading them aloud to herself in the hayloft or the woods or any other secret places she could escape her cousins' racket and her uncle's cruelty. Sometimes her Aunt Mercy saw her hidden away, reading, but just winked at her conspiratorially and left her there. So, Maria knew for sure that she might look like nothing special, but she could talk posh with the best of them. She would act out all the different voices of the characters, rich and poor, young and old. She often wondered if she should be on the stage and fantasised about running away with a troupe of actors. But no actors came anywhere near Middleton-in-Chirbury. And, anyway, serving in retail was a bit like acting really. You had to put on the mask of the saleswoman and be someone else at work than you were in ordinary life. The village shop was the only hint of glamour in her existence, its shelves graced with everything a local lord or travelling tinker could want, from currant cakes to quills, brooms to battledores and wax to wafers. That was where her determination to become a shop-girl began. And it had brought her here, to this draper's doorstep on a warm April lunchtime.

'I shouldna left that sign up there,' said the woman. 'I've interviewed a few girls now.'

'But you havna employed any particular girl, as yet?'

'Well . . . nay. Not as yet. My assistant is getting married the end of this month, so the job inna open till May.'

'Then that suits me fine, Mrs . . .?'

The woman sighed. 'Mrs Nixon. It says it on the shop. So . . . do you have any experience of shop work?' she asked.

'I do, I do. I'm working currently at Mr Boden's, the barber and tobacconist on Waterloo Street.'

'A tobacconist? Unusual job for a lass,' said the woman. This was not going well. She looked decidedly sceptical.

'That is exactly why I took the job, ma'am,' said Maria, confidently. She had no idea what she was going to say next, or even why she'd said that, but she was desperate and saying the first thing that came into her head.

'How do you mean?'

'I came from a farming community to Ironbridge to seek a career in shop work. I decided the best course of action would be to seek out a proper big range of different kinds of experience, you see. I could've come to you straight on arrival, asked about work at a draper's, as being the traditional work for a shopgirl. But instead I looked for summat more unusual, summat that most lasses wouldna have in their career. I chose to seek work in a place that was mostly the . . . the . . .'

She thought hard about the word Mrs Jameson had used for the new world of women that shops had become.

'The realm! That's it, the realm of the shopman. I wanted to see how things were done by those who've been at this game far longer than I. And I've learnt heaps, Mrs Nixon, honest I have. I know how to serve men, and we even have some female customers buying cigars, such is the modern world. So I know how to serve both types. But I want more experience on the female side. And now I'm ready to move on to the realm of the shopgirl. I know how important it is for women customers to be served by women. For is there any woman in the world who wants to be told how a bodice should fit by a man?!'

She'd stolen it from Mrs Jameson, but nobody else knew that. *And*, Maria thought, *that's how things get learnt in the first place. It's not stealing when it's learning.*

Mrs Nixon smiled approvingly. 'That's quite a speech. I need a girl who can do mental arithmetic, who can keep accounts, measure and weigh. And who is a girl of good manners and character.'

'I can do all those things, ma'am. I've done bookkeeping for Mr Boden for four months now. And I write a good hand.'

'Would Mr Boden give you a good reference?'

'I dunna doubt it, Mrs Nixon.'

The draper looked Maria up and down again, focusing on her boots.

'The weather's been no great shakes of recent,' said Maria, trying to explain away how muddy they were. 'But also, Mrs Nixon, may I say that what I lack in funds for turning myself out to my best advantage, I make up for in ambition. A shopgirl's career should be one a hard-working person of meagre means can use to better herself and that is what I mean to do, by hook or by crook.'

'I see,' said Mrs Nixon, her face appearing somewhat amused. Was she laughing at Maria? Or was she impressed by her little speech on the rights of the working-class woman? Maria couldn't tell. 'What's your name then?'

'Maria Keay.'

The woman's face changed. She looked like she instantly recognised that name, Maria surmised but didn't know for sure.

'Maria, thank'ee for coming to see me. I shall keep your

name on file. I'll be finalising the interviews soon and, if I have need of you, I shall call for you then.'

'Thank'ee, Mrs Nixon. Thank'ee kindly.'

'All right, Maria. Ta-ta for now.'

'Cheerio, Mrs Nixon.'

The draper shut the door to the shop. A woman, running a shop. Now that was a turn-up. Maria was pleased it was a woman as she needed to learn from a woman's mind what women customers wanted. Having worked with men these past months, she had a feeling that – when it came to shopping – they were simpler creatures than female customers. Women customers seemed to have more complex needs, Maria felt. And she wanted to learn about all of them. Well, Mrs Nixon had not said yes to an interview, but she'd not said no either. So there was hope.

Maria turned around, looked up at the blue skies and smiled. There was a blossom tree by the side of the river and it was in full bloom, pale petals wafting down in the breeze. As the wind got up, so did the petals, which swirled about madly and filled her sight with white. At that moment, she realised she was just up from Loadcroft Wharf, the place where . . . She felt sick. The whiteness of the blossom recalled the dust of flour clouds of that day, the day when . . . Maria closed her eyes. She brought her hand to her face. Was she going to vomit? Her head was spinning. *Oh God,* her mind cried. *Why did I come back to this place? Why?*

Chapter 4

'Miss Keay!' said a male voice urgently. 'Are you quite well?'

Maria opened her eyes and saw Charlie Woodvine worriedly fiddling with the brown bowler hat he held in his hands.

'I am quite well,' she muttered, but it was not at all convincing.

'I dunna think I believe that. Have you eaten today?'

Maria breathed in deep and strong, standing upright and focusing her eyes downwards. She had to pull herself together. She had always told herself that she had to be strong. For nobody was coming to rescue her, nobody cared enough. She only had herself.

But then, while staring at her feet, a black and white snout appeared in her view, sniffing at her shoes. Biscuit peered up at her and whimpered.

'I am well, boy,' she said gently and stroked his head, feeling how silky his ears were. He wagged his tail excitedly, which thumped against Charlie's leg.

'Biscuit believes you,' said Charlie. 'Have you eaten though?'

'I have eaten. But thank'ee, for checking on me.'

'Of course,' said Charlie and shrugged his shoulders. She looked up at him. Boden really had shorn him like a sheep. He had but one large curl that flopped over his forehead now. It rather suited him. She could see his eyes more clearly and, as she looked into them, Maria felt a little jolt of connection that made her glance away. He added, 'Have you finished work for the day, at least? So you can rest?'

'I have,' she said. 'But what about you? You inna teaching soon?'

'Every Wednesday, when the town has early closing but the market is on, I have a very kind volunteer teacher, a fine lady of the town who comes in and takes my class for a couple of hours, so I can have some time to myself. I generally use it to prepare my lessons. Or catch up with some shopping in the market. Or sometimes I just go for a little walk along the river alone, to catch up with my thoughts. They generally have so little time to themselves that sometimes they escape me. I was on my way down to the river path, if you'd like to join me for a stroll?'

Maria could not even bear to look at the river and shuddered involuntarily in response.

'Nay, I'd sooner jump off a cliff than be near the river right now.'

She hadn't meant to say it. It just popped out. Charlie looked confused and then a realisation seemed to come over his face.

'Of course. Well, I need one or two things from the market, if you'd like to take a stroll along with Biscuit and me? But I quite understand if you need to get back to your lodgings.'

The thought of spending the afternoon being ordered about by Rhoda, who was about to give birth any day soon, was enough to keep Maria from the house for days. Also, the thought of a stroll with Charlie Woodvine was too much to resist. How nice he was. And how handsome, though he didn't

seem to know it, which made him all the more handsome in
Maria's eyes.

'The market it is,' said Maria and Charlie looked very pleased.

They walked slowly up Wharfage, the town busy around
them with shoppers and delivery boys and workers coming and
going. Biscuit trotted beside Charlie, panting heavily.

'It's a warm day for April,' said Maria. 'Poor Biscuit looks
like he needs a drink.'

'There's a trough for dogs at the Bartlett Drinking Fountain
in the square. Let's head that way, shall we?'

Maria nodded and they carried on together. There was so
much hubbub about them, as the crowd thickened towards the
marketplace, that they did not even try to make conversation,
as they'd have to shout. Wharfage was filled with the throng
and, if Maria had jumped up in the air, all she would see
would be a sea of hats. Yet, small as she was, she saw mostly
a forest of jackets and skirts, brown and grey and black, the
colours of the ordinary folk. No purples here. For sale all
around them were piles of spring cabbages and onions, apples
and forced rhubarb, beets and watercress, along with cured
fish and breads of all types, eggs and cheese, with quack pills
for the infirm that claimed to cure anything from worms to
nerves. Customers haggled for the best prices and salespeople
shouted their wares. It was a cacophony that bathed Maria in
relief, for the noise stopped her thinking of the rushing sound
of the river in her ears and it calmed her. She watched Biscuit
lap up water messily from the dog trough at the fountain, realising too how thirsty she was and taking a drink of the marble
fountain's cool spring water and feeling refreshed by it.

Charlie said, 'Did you know this fountain was provided by
a philanthropist, due to the unclean water for poorer folk and
the threat of cholera?'

'I didna know that. Who did it?'

'A vicar from Buildwas – or his wife did, anyway, in his memory. Some folk are truly good to others in this world,' he mused.

'And some are pure devils,' she said, thinking of her uncle, who used to say she couldn't have a sip of water until she'd finished all her chores. She remembered that parched feeling so keenly, it made her mouth feel like sand.

Maria took another swig at the drinking fountain. She looked up and wiped her mouth, Charlie watching her seriously.

'You can smile, Charlie Woodvine. I'm not ailing.'

He grinned. 'I'm glad to hear it.'

'What did you need to buy?'

'Buy what?'

'From the market.'

'Oh,' he said sheepishly. 'You've caught me out. I dunna wanna buy a thing. I just wanted an excuse to walk with you some way.'

'Good,' she said, smiling at him. He smiled too and it changed his face, his eyes even brighter than usual. 'Let's walk a bit further then. But not by the river.'

'Understood.'

She told him she lived on Paradise and they decided to walk there the long way, up Church Hill – past Charlie's school – to Lincoln Hill and cut across Dale Coppice to Paradise. They walked slowly and talked. She told him about the draper's and the job she hoped to get. He told her about being a schoolmaster and how much he loved his job, even the naughty children who were often his favourites, though he tried hard never to have favourites. She described her lodgings and her cousin and husband, their dour ways and their sadness, which she tried to be charitable about but, even so, how difficult they were to be around. Charlie asked where she'd been before she came back to Ironbridge and she told him of her uncle and his family, about the farm and the days when drought ruined the harvest and they'd all get beaten for that.

'If it pains you to talk of it, I dunna wish you to be in pain,' Charlie said, which touched her.

'It's all right. It's good to speak of it. Nobody else has ever wanted to listen to my stories. Well, not since . . . not since a long time.'

They walked in silence for a few steps, Biscuit's delight at new smells and places with which to acquaint himself filling their silence with the simple joy of watching the innocent happiness of an animal.

'My parents were killed,' she said suddenly. She hadn't meant to say it, but, as so often with Maria, it came out of its own accord.

'I know,' said Charlie. 'I remember it well. Everyone remembers it, what happened to the Keay family. I didna wanna bring it up as I didna wanna upset you.'

'Everyone knows?' She wondered if that's what Mrs Nixon was thinking of when her face changed at Maria saying her name.

'I'd say so. It was a terrible tragedy. I dunna need to tell you that. I'm sorry. Stupid thing to say.'

'Nay, it inna. I appreciate it. In some ways, it feels better that people remember it, remember our name. Coming back, it felt like my parents had been . . . rubbed out. Like they'd never been.'

'I can understand that. But be assured, your name is remembered well. And mourned. Both of my parents spoke of it before they passed.'

'Your parents are gone too?'

'They are. My father Reuben was a miner and died of lung disease aged fifty-five, seven years ago. My mother Rebekah died just three years hence, tuberculosis, same age as Father.'

'I am sorry to hear it,' said Maria. 'Sorry for your loss.'

'Thank'ee. Yet it was their time. They had a good life, both of them. I'm the only child and they wanted more, I know that, but it didna happen for them. So they doted on me, too much most likely. But I inna complaining. I loved them both. I miss them. I visit their graves, lay flowers.'

Maria said, 'My parents . . . I dunna know where their graves are. My uncle would only pay for a pauper's burial, so they're all mixed up with other folk somewhere.'

'Oh, there I go again, putting my big foot in it. I'm an idiot, Maria, I truly am. I didna mean . . .'

'Nay, it's all right. Please dunna feel you've to tiptoe around me. It's ten years hence. I'm over and past it.' She knew the last part was a lie. But she wanted to soothe his feelings. 'Truth is, I was too young to know details about them, only what I saw of them: a child's-eye view. I dunna know how old they were when they died, as I dunna know when they were born. But I think they were very young, as my uncle said they were foolish, as they married and had me before they turned twenty. "Young fools", my uncle called them. Once, he even said, "No wonder they drowned."'

'What a cold and coarse thing to say to a little lass!' Charlie cried. 'I shall never comprehend the cruelty of folk towards little'uns. It beggars belief. I am sorry that happened to you, Maria. Nobody deserves that, least of all a fine, good person like yourself.'

'Thank'ee, Charlie,' she said. 'That means much.' And it really did. She had not shared any of this with a soul. But Charlie understood. He knew about children and he knew how they should be treated.

'Nay, it's nothing.'

'Kindness inna nothing. And a listening ear. That inna nothing neither. It's what I've never had and what I needed. Thank'ee once more.'

'It goes both ways,' he said. 'Nobody wants to listen to me rattle on about school.'

'I'm sure that inna true. Everything you say is so interesting.'

Charlie looked at her. His eyes were shining. She had felt the weight of the water about her, drowning her in sorrow, just an hour or so ago. It was such a relief to share this with him and find a kind ear who would listen and be truly interested. And now Maria felt light as a feather as he looked at her. He had that knack, Charlie. Like his dog, Biscuit: that simple sweetness that takes away all cares.

'Maria, I think I know someone who'll remember those details about your parents, when they were born and suchlike. That lady I spoke of, who teaches some of my classes on Wednesdays, she's lived in Ironbridge all her life. Perhaps . . . well, you might like to come to the school and meet her, one Wednesday sometime. Her name is Anny Malone. Before she was married, she was Anny Woodvine, a distant relation of mine through her father. We are second cousins twice removed, or some such nonsense. She knows everything there is to know about Ironbridge. Would you like to meet her, and see my school?'

'I surely would! I was made for school and taken out of it before I was ready. I would love to do that, thank'ee Charlie.'

'Well, there's no time like the present. How about—' Charlie started.

But, all of a sudden, Biscuit stopped dead in his tracks and started barking. His ears were pricked and he barked and barked at something he could hear but no human could.

The sound of that barking gripped Maria so that she felt her skin grow cold. The barking went on and on, insistent, piercing the air. Why did it frighten her so?

'Are you well, Maria?' said Charlie, then turning abruptly to Biscuit, he went on, 'Stop that, Biscuit! Hush your noise!'

Biscuit stopped and whined, then came to Charlie's heel, his body still alert to trouble.

Charlie turned back to Maria. 'You're as pale as snow.'

'I'll be fine,' she said. And she did feel better, now the

barking had stopped. 'Let's carry on walking. Honest, I'm fine.' But all she could think of were the dark waters of the river closing over her head, even though she couldn't see a drop of it from where they were on Paradise.

Charlie calmed Biscuit and persuaded him to go on, but the dog looked jittery as he trotted along, stopping and starting, listening intently. They were on the last bend before her cousin's house when the sound of a ghostly, wailing voice drifted to them on the breeze. That must've been what Biscuit had heard. Or was it? Was it only Maria who could hear it? Was it the dead child haunting her again? Maria froze in horror. She turned to Charlie, who'd stopped as well.

'Can you . . . can you hear that?' she uttered, terrified he'd say nay and then she'd know she was truly going mad.

'Of course. It sounds dreadful. Like a woman in childbirth.'

'By gosh! It'll be my cousin Rhoda! She's due any day now!'

Biscuit barked furiously.

'Go, you mun go,' said Charlie.

'It's true, I mun go.'

'I'll take Biscuit away, he'll only cause havoc. I'll see you anon. Good luck!'

'Thank'ee!' Maria cried and took off running down the hill.

The cries of her cousin grew louder and wilder as she approached. The dread of this event engulfed her as she arrived at the gate to the house. There had been too much death in her life, in Rhoda's too. And they deserved no more.

'Please, please, Lord,' whispered Maria. 'Please let this babby stay in Shropshire. Thy dunna want such a little ratlin in heaven. Leave it be, Lord, I beg thee.'

She opened the gate, rushed to the door and went into the house, her cousin's cries filling the close air with fear and agony.

Chapter 5

May 1892

SETH NIXON GENERAL DRAPER is what the sign read above the shop. It occupied ground-floor rooms on Wharfage, with one main room housing the counter, shelves, cupboards and drawers full of stock, as well as the fabric-measuring table. In the smaller room to the right, there was an area curtained off for privacy and a small cubbyhole for the resident seamstress to make amendments.

There were two large window displays: one contained a face-less mannequin sporting a spring outfit for those women of Ironbridge who weren't as poor as Maria and yet nowhere near as wealthy as Mrs Jameson. It wore a plain brown linen skirt with a beige shirtwaist and puff-sleeved jacket, all topped by a smart straw boater with a brown ribbon. Times really were changing. Maria remembered as a child when she'd seen ladies wearing the bustle – that large protuberance at the back of the skirt – which she always thought would make sitting down very tricky. Maria assumed those ladies never did sit down and stayed on their feet from dusk till dawn. Now the bustle was almost gone and a sleeker silhouette was in fashion.

In the other window was a little girl mannequin dressed in a sailor suit jacket and skirt. Both window displays were flanked by a range of hats on one side, while on the other were parasols, umbrellas and something that suited both types of weather, which Mrs Nixon told her had the French name *en tout cas*, which meant *in any case*. A French umbrella . . . Maria realised it was the fanciest thing she'd ever encountered in her life. And she also knew that this was only the beginning of a new world that was opening up to her, now that she'd started working at Mrs Nixon's draper's shop.

The interview never happened or, at least, it did but Maria hadn't realised that her impromptu call – that day she went to the market afterwards with Charlie and Rhoda's baby girl Matilda Rose was born (a healthy, hearty babby that brought joy and screamed her demands at all hours to the Nott household) – that day was the day she got the job. Apparently, Maria had so impressed Mrs Nixon that she didn't bother with any of the other girls and had appointed Maria the moment she shut the door. It took a few weeks for Mrs Nixon's other assistant to get married and move on, and for Maria to work out her notice for Mr Boden. Mrs Nixon had visited Mr Boden personally and talked him into letting Maria go, with a glowing reference, to better herself. It hadn't been easy to leave Mr Boden. He had been so kind to her and given her a chance when she was nothing and nobody. He wished her well. Maria even thought she noted a tear in his eye on her last day, though he'd rather die than admit it.

Charlie complained that he'd have little excuse to come in and see her regularly now, so they agreed that they'd meet when they could on Wednesday half-closing, when Anny Malone took his classes. They'd planned for Maria to go over to the school and meet Anny and the children back in April. But there was a wave of illness that month and the school closed for a time. Charlie was also marooned at home, in case he was harbouring any vestige of the flu that had seized his charges. Two of the children died, which was truly awful. Maria knew Charlie would feel it particularly badly as he felt responsible for his pupils in every way.

The threat lasted until May and, when it passed, the school opened again and Maria would be going there on a visit with Charlie soon. Firstly though, she had her long days of work at Seth Nixon General Draper's. It turned out Mr Nixon had died five years before and his widow, Mrs Pamela Nixon, had taken over the shop, revamped it to focus more on female customers than male and made it into the best draper's in town by a long chalk, the clever woman.

On entering the shop in the early morning, an hour before opening, Maria had a long list of jobs to do. At the barber's, much of the time she had made herself busy by giving herself extra errands, but at Nixon's she was rushed off her feet from the moment she arrived. She was up at six and started in the shop at seven. Her first job was always to clean the windows and dust the whole shop. Then she'd open up any deliveries, arrange them neatly and record them in the order book. Mrs Nixon was chief window dresser, yet she allowed Maria to assist her, showing her how to design a display that showed off the outfits to their best advantage. Mrs Nixon explained, 'No woman on earth has a waist as small as a mannequin, so we mun pin the clothes in to match it. The customer mun believe that, with a corset and fitting from Nixon's, she can attain that shape that dunna exist anywhere in nature.' This seemed tantamount to lying to Maria. Why did a woman need a tiny waist, anyway? Corsets were uncomfortable, every woman knew that, but taking it to this extreme seemed unfair on all womankind. However, she could see the logic of it from a commercial point of view. Make them want for something. Wanting equalled sales. As one of only two drapers in town, the shop sold a wide range of products, including a large variety of fabrics, ladies' outfits, hosiery, underclothes, gloves, hats, artificial flowers, boots, mantles and ready-made coats.

The rest of Maria's day was taken up with supplying Mrs Nixon and the customers with everything they might need to make a purchase, arranging fabric and patterns on the counter, fetching items from storage, ensuring the pin bowls were full, wrapping packages and smoothing out paper to keep it neat, as well as being sent out on errands, such as fetching fancy knick-knacks and trimmings from the other draper's and haberdasher's in town (owned by Mrs Nixon's brother-in-law) or taking small amounts of cash to be deposited in the bank. She also watched Mrs Nixon sell and learnt about how to flatter women and empower them to make bold choices (that usually cost more money) or to make them feel that their choice was the most comfortable and fitting choice they'd ever made. Each customer seemed to leave not only satisfied but bolstered by their visit. Maria soaked this all up like a sponge and admired Mrs Nixon's skill in coddling her customers and making them feel special.

By the end of Maria's first week, her feet were swollen. She spent the whole of her first Sunday off in bed, listening to Matilda Rose fussing and yelling and all the noisy things a baby only a few weeks in this world liked to do to torment its parents (and lodgers). But seeing the glow in cousin Rhoda's cheeks when she proudly carried the little'un round on her arm, everywhere she went, at all hours of the day or night, whether the baby was awake or asleep – the broad smile on her face every time she looked down upon her baby – all the noise was worth it. 'She is my miracle babby,' Rhoda would tell Maria, beaming. Maria was delighted for her cousin, whose previous character had been altered out of all

THE SHOPGIRL OF IRONBRIDGE

recognition by the coming of her child. Her husband Eli had not improved though, and still looked up urgently at Maria every time she entered a room, as if she were a thief who'd broken in.

One day, he said, in a voice that seemed strangled by his own necktie (so unused to speaking to her, he was), 'Cousin Keay, I've instigated a rota for yourself to follow which lays down the opening times of various rooms and locations within the domicile.' He talked like he'd swallowed a dictionary, Maria thought. Maybe that's what stuck in his throat and made his voice so thin and reedy. He went on, 'Here is a list of all times when you are permitted to enter the parlour, kitchen and privy. At all other times, you mun be in your room or out of the house. No exceptions.'

She couldn't quite believe it, but he was deadly serious. Times for the privy? She wanted to say, 'My bowels dunna obey written rules, Cousin Nott.' But she didn't. She made a decision right there and then to find alternative lodgings as soon as possible and well before Rhoda would want to move the baby into her own nursery. Now Maria was earning better wages at Nixon's than at Boden's, she knew it was time for her to move out. The thought of living in rented accommodation enlivened yet also worried Maria. To have more freedom would be lovely, yet she heard landladies could be worse than Eli when it came to rules and regulations of the house. But where should she start looking? It'd need to be within a manageable walking distance of work and not too pricey that all her wage went on rent. She realised she'd got used to the small amount Rhoda had charged. Now she'd have to face market rates and she didn't know if she'd ever be able to manage that alone. Her answer came the day Mrs Nixon hired a new colleague at the shop.

'Maria, this is Rosie Green, our new seamstress. Show her

the ropes and get her started, will you? I've Mrs Lakelin coming in soon and she always soaks up all my attention.'

'Charmed, I'm sure.' Rosie grinned. She had curly brown hair, the same shade and texture as Charlie's, which she wore in a knotted bun on top of her head, with her curly fringe seemingly all natural. Maria's hair was dead straight and she envied Rosie her natural curls that Maria had to create with rags knotted up each night. Rosie had a scattering of freckles across her nose, which also added to the overwhelming impression that Rosie Green was going to be a big dose of fun.

'Same,' said Maria, peering behind her to ensure Mrs Nixon was elsewhere. 'I'm pleased there's a new seamstress,' she whispered conspiratorially to Rosie. 'And one about the same age as me, as the last one was ancient and so dour and bossy, then went off to live with her spinster sister up north.'

'Oh Lord, I'm glad the old crink shuffled off then!'

They both giggled, then hushed themselves, making sure the boss hadn't heard them.

That first day of Rosie's, Maria worked just as hard as usual, but it was extra fun to know Rosie was just in the other room, every time she wanted to secretly crack a joke about a customer's big nose or snotty child or whatever. And since the shop just happened to be right opposite the Severn, there were times at work when Maria would glance through the shop window, or look towards the river while running errands, and that breathless wave of horror would threaten to engulf her and she'd have to screw her eyes shut and steady her breathing with care, or else she'd faint away. Busy days at work – and now laughs with Rosie – kept the darkness at bay. At closing time, Maria told Rosie how much she was dreading going home, after Eli's new edicts.

'Danker me, what a gaoler!' said Rosie.

'That he is. I'm gonna have to start looking for new lodgings soon, but the devil knows where I should begin.'

'Begin with me, wench! I've a spare bed in my room. I'm looking for a new'un. You'd be sharing a room with little old me, if you dunna mind that. It's cheap. And no rules about privy use!'

And that is how Maria ended up moving her meagre bag of belongings from Paradise to Hodge Bower, the long road that sat above Ironbridge, her lodging house nestled at the end of a row of other lodging houses just along the road from the Crown Inn. That following Saturday evening after work, saying goodbye to Rhoda and Matilda Rose was not as simple as Maria thought it would be as she realised she'd grown fond of the pair of them. Rhoda too shed a tear when Maria left, saying, 'It inna right that Matilda Rose is losing her cousin to strangers, it inna proper!' But her husband did not shed a tear and that was enough of a push for Maria to march off along Paradise with no regrets.

That first night sitting cross-legged on her bed opposite Rosie on her own bed, giving her impressions of Eli Nott, was the most she'd laughed in ages.

'Just imagine them in bed together!' said Rosie. 'I say, Mrs Nott, according to my rota, tonight is our monthly opportunity to reacquaint our private parts. Open your knees, Mrs Nott, and present your cosy nook.'

'Cosy nook!' roared Maria and both of them fell about in hysterics.

They talked until the birds sang and spent the rest of Sunday sleeping off their hilarious night of insomnia, jokes and secrets shared. When Maria awoke on Sunday afternoon and looked over at her new roommate, Rosie, sleeping on her back with her mouth wide open, she realised she had never shared a room with someone her own age in her life, as an only child. And once she'd been exiled to the farm, the six children shared rooms near their parents', but she had been put alone in an extended closet near the larder, where there was just about room for her low bed and nothing more, cursed as she was to be the unpaid maid of Collie Farm. She hadn't known what she was missing. Rosie Green was a gift that had landed in her lap and she was eternally grateful to whatever higher power had brought them together. For the first time in years, Maria felt she'd made a friend.

Apart from Charlie Woodvine, that was. Was Charlie a friend though? He acted like one. Whenever they spoke, it was always an easy kind of chat with no awkwardness. He'd never tried to take her hand or kiss her. So she supposed they were friends. But she saw him looking into her eyes at times and she wondered if he'd kiss her, but he never did. She didn't know why. Was she not pretty enough? She knew deep down that couldn't be true, as the men at the barber's had always flirted with her. And rough boys in the street whistled at her, shouted things at her about her yellow hair. She didn't know many girls whose hair was as bright as hers. It was almost white in some lights, so pale and shining it was. She inherited that hair from her mother, who'd had the same. Her blue eyes came from both parents, but specifically how large hers were and the long eyelashes were from her father. Maria was not vain enough to think every man desired her. Yet she did wonder why Charlie hadn't tried to kiss her yet. But, actually, she liked him for that. She got quite fed up with the lascivious looks that some men gave her. Charlie respected her person at all times. And she was fond of him even more so because of it. She looked forward to visiting his school with him, which would more than likely take place that coming Wednesday.

Now it was Sunday teatime and the landlady called up the stairs for the girls to come. Maria nudged Rosie awake. They were the only lodgers at the little house on the end of the row. Their landlady, Mrs Cribb, was a widow who must have attained a great age, as she looked ancient to Maria (but was, in truth, just past fifty, as was the seamstress Maria thought as old as Methuselah). The girls threw on their shirtwaists and skirts over their shifts and rushed downstairs, starved after sleeping all day. They were seated in the little parlour next to the kitchen, with a wobbly table just big enough for the two of them to eat at. Mrs Cribb brought them a stew of some indeterminate meat and it had lots of potatoes in it and hunks of bread baked by Mrs Cribb herself, with an apple and a knob of cheese for after. It was good food, better than Rhoda's.

'This is a proper treat to have a hot meal, Mrs Cribb,' said Maria. 'At my cousin's, I was lucky to get a thumb lump of old bread and mutton.'

'Thank'ee,' said Mrs Cribb, nodding slowly. She did everything slowly.

Maria told Rosie, 'I think Cousin Rhoda mun've learnt to cook from someone who'd lost all sense of taste in a tragic accident. Everything tasted of wall!'

Rosie roared with laughter, at which Mrs Cribb emitted a sudden, 'Hush!' adding, 'You wenches mun curb yer hollering at night or you'll keep me up awake till the larks if yer dunna shut yer traps.'

But they had laughed their heads off all of the night before, so Mrs Cribb must be a heavy sleeper. When she'd gone back to the kitchen, Rosie whispered to Maria, 'She's an opium swigger, that one. She wouldn't wake if a cannon went off in her bloomers.'

That Sunday night they couldn't sleep, of course, and chatted on, Maria telling Rosie about her childhood. Rosie listened solemnly, then at the end of it said, 'Life inna fair.'

'That's the truth,' answered Maria and they sat quietly for a moment. 'Tell me about your growing up, then. I hope it's happier than mine.'

'Not much, except my mother's alive leastways.'

Maria listened to stories of Rosie's childhood, brought up by her mother with no father she'd ever known. Her mother went into the workhouse for a while, but was out now and living with her uncle and his family over in Jackfield, not far, and would most likely stay there for good as she couldn't work on account of bad joints in her hands and knees and needing to rest. So Rosie had been a seamstress for years before the job at Nixon's, sewing at home, in the workhouse, in another draper's in town and then this one.

'I'm heading up in the world and mean to conquer it,' said Rosie, eyes bright with ambition.

'Me too,' said Maria, delighted she'd found a girl with the same drive as her.

'Do you have a plan?' said Rosie. 'Of what to do next?'

'Nay, not as such. I'm just glad I got this job and dunna have to sniff the stink of tobacco all day.'

'Well, I do,' said Rosie breathlessly and reached under her mattress and dragged out a slip of folded paper. 'Look what I found in a Shrewsbury newspaper months ago. A lady left it behind in the marketplace one day and I nabbed it.'

'Shrewsbury?' said Maria. It was the county town of Shropshire and Maria had never been, had never imagined going, so far away it had felt from the farm and, even now, from little Ironbridge.

'Shrewsbury is where I'm going to make myself. I want to work here. Look.'

Rosie opened up the neatly folded bit of paper and handed it to Maria. It felt thin and fragile from being pored over many a time. It was an advertisement for a shop in Shrewsbury. But not just any old shop. There was a line drawing of the place, which was situated on a grand corner of two broad thoroughfares, with three full shopfronts that stretched around the corner. It was three floors high, with rows of windows and clusters of chimneys across the broad roofs. 'Harborne and Co' was emblazoned across each shopfront.

'I've never seen anything like it,' said Maria, in awe. 'What kind of shop is it? What can it possibly sell?'

'Everything!' cried Rosie. 'It sells everything! You havna heard of department stores?'

'I've heard of them but never seen one. A posh lady who came in the tobacconist's once mentioned them to me. She said most started out as drapers. Is that what a department store means then? A huge, hulking great thing, like three drapers' shops scrudged up together?'

Rosie grabbed back the paper and said, 'It's better than that. It has a draper's, but the biggest draper you could ever fathom! And a whole room just for seamstresses, who make up outfits for proper ladies. And there's women's fashion and men's fashion, and a milliner's, and gloves and silks and flowers and boots and a haberdasher's and tobacconist's and all sorts. And a restaurant and a room for ladies to rest. And even a funeral parlour, so they say, burying Shropshire's finest corpses!'

They laughed at that. Could it be true, though, that one shop could contain such multitudes?

'And *that* is my ambition,' said Rosie. '*That* is where I'm off to next. One day I'll be a seamstress there. And I'll meet a rich gentleman customer whose waistcoat I've adjusted and he'll take one look at me, fall at my feet and propose. And I'll be shot of this miserable life and be a rich man's wife. And Mother will never have to worry about her joints again. And she'll come live with us in Shrewsbury in a house with a garden and she'll potter about and grow sweet peas, while I produce bouncing baby heirs and get fat on boxes of chocolates bought for me by Mr Rosie.'

'Mr Rosie!' Maria roared with laughter.

'I'm dead serious, mind,' asserted Rosie, carefully replacing the folded paper beneath her mattress. 'I get a hold of the Shrewsbury papers whenever I can and look for any advertisements for seamstresses wanted at Harborne's. I inna seen one as yet, but it's only a matter of time. Girls get engaged all the time and move on, so there's plenty of turnover. It'll happen. I mun just be patient. What do you think then, Maria? Shall I look for shopgirl ads there as well? Wanna come and work with me at Harborne and Co?'

'Do I ever!' cried Maria.

A new future had unfurled before her. From her tiny coffin of a room at Collie Farm, she'd ached to one day sleep in a bedroom that had a window. From there to her cousin's house, to a barber and tobacconist's, to a draper's with two whole rooms, and now to a room with Rosie and good meals from Mrs Cribb: she thought she'd done rather well for an orphan with nothing or nobody to fight for her. But now a new ambition sat shining in the distance, a place that could not be called by that paltry name 'shop', for it was a house of wonders. Maria now knew that everything she'd suffered had one purpose: to one day secure employment as a shopgirl at that unfeasibly glamorous palace of commerce, Harborne and Company.

Chapter 6

June 1892

The weeks flew by as Maria learnt the ropes of her new job at Nixon's draper's. Her feet got used to the long hours standing up and rushing about. She became versed in every type of dress, skirt, shirtwaist, undergarment, stocking and boot a woman might want. And, best of all, there was no stink of tobacco on her clothes and all through her hair at the end of a day's work.

She saw Charlie twice more, for walks around the environs on sunny June Sundays, and they grew closer, sharing stories from their childhoods and Charlie telling her facts about history, geography, science and literature, which fascinated her. She was looking forward to visiting the school herself very soon. How lucky his pupils must be to have such a pleasant and knowledgeable chap as their teacher. She also loved discussing with him the books she'd hoarded from the village library as a girl. They had a shared favourite in *Treasure Island*, which Maria had read as a child and Charlie taught to his charges. The story of pirates and riches had satisfied her need for escape in the awful days of her incarceration with the

Collies. She still had a copy, which she kept on her bedside table at her lodgings and dipped into from time to time. As some might read the Bible at night, she instead relived stories of adventure and escape. However, she was so happy in her work these days, as well as her lodgings and her friendships with Rosie and Charlie, she did not really want to be anywhere else (unless news from a certain Shrewsbury department store might turn up). Thus, *Treasure Island* had gone unread for weeks. She especially valued her long talks with Charlie. He still hadn't kissed her and Rosie asked if he had 'summat wrong with his eyes or else he's cakey in the head. Can he not see how winsome you are?' But Maria liked it how it was with Charlie. She enjoyed his companionship and their ease together. Perhaps all that would be ruined if romance got in the way. Yet she did think quite a lot about kissing him, as the bow of his lips and his bright hazel eyes were something she loved to look at, and she wondered just how soft were the curls on the top of his head – overlong and unruly again, since he'd stopped bothering to visit Boden's so much now she'd left – and she sometimes had to stop herself from reaching up and running her fingers through them as he talked.

One Sunday evening, Maria climbed into bed early, after spending a tiring afternoon along Paradise bouncing baby Matilda Rose on her knee and hearing detailed descriptions of her sleeping schedule and bowel movements from cousin Rhoda. Maria picked up the sales catalogue that Mrs Nixon used at work and perused the newest styles of shirtwaists, some with the largest mutton sleeves Maria had ever seen. The fashion for puffed sleeves was really excelling itself these days and it was odd to see a fashion from so long ago come back into style. *Perhaps that's all fashion is,* Maria mused, *just the same random collection of ingredients reused year upon year in new amalgamations.* She laid her head back on the pillow she'd propped up against the wall. She loved Rosie's constant company and the laughs they had, but she had to admit to herself that she was glad Rosie had gone to visit her mother in Jackfield for the day and Maria had had a bit of peace in her bed. Maria loved conversation. Yet she also prized solitude, for her day job was peopled by society and sometimes the small talk they made was exhausting. She was putting on the mask of the willing shopgirl six days a week and it was a relief to take it off and just be herself for a short while. However, this peace was short-lived as Rosie burst into their shared bedroom and uttered with great excitement, 'Guess what I've seen!'

'I dunna know! A black swan?'

'Why ever would you say that?!' scoffed Rosie.

'Charlie said they exist in foreign places. Tell me, then. What is it?'

'Charlie said, did he? Ooh well, it mun be right then. For everything Charlie Woodvine says is bound to be one hundred per cent accurate, such a genius he is, eh?'

Rosie was teasing her. When Maria had told Rosie she was friends with Charlie, Rosie had told her she was a lucky devil, even though Maria had made it quite clear they were only friends.

'Tell me what you've seen, Rosie, for heaven's sake!'

'An advertisement for girls wanted at Harborne and Co! My uncle picked up a *Shrewsbury Chronicle* the last time he was there for work and gave it to me, bless his soul. He and Mother know how much I want a job at Harborne's. He spotted the advertisement in it.'

She threw down the little cloth bag she used to carry her knitting around and pulled out the newspaper. Tingles swept down Maria's spine. Just what she and Rosie had been waiting for.

'Show me, show me!'

Rosie laid the paper down on Maria's bed and pointed at a small advertisement on the front page.

'Read it aloud!' said Rosie.

Maria began:

'*Wanted, a young lady as SALESWOMAN. One who has been accustomed to commerce, specialising in all aspects of drapery. With experience in ladies' clothes; dress materials; trimmings; fancy goods and ladies' underclothing. Also wanted, SEAMSTRESSES who understand silks, lace, colienne and chiffon, alongside poplin, linen and wools. Both must have good character and abilities. Apply in writing, stating name and address of referee, to Harborne and Co, High Street & Pride Hill, Shrewsbury, addressed to Miss Bytheway.*'

When Maria got to that last word, she paused. 'Is it Miss By-The-Way? Or Miss Bythe-Way?'

'By-The-Way, I reckon.'

'By gosh, Rosie. This is our chance. Jobs for both of us! We must write to them!'

Rosie screwed up her face and replied, 'Listen, Maria. You know I'm no dullard.'

'Far from it!'

'But, well, I canna read nor write with any proficiency. I never really learnt it properly. Never really had any schooling. Too busy sewing all my livelong days. Whatever shall I do? I'd sooner land an otter than write a decent letter. I do best in person, talking my way into a job. But I canna afford to travel to Shrewsbury any time soon.'

'Here, set you down on my bed here, wench,' said Maria. 'Stop werriting about all that. I shall write a gem of a letter for us both, I shall. I'm proper good at writing.'

'You're a true friend, Maria Keay. The best!' She reached over and clinched Maria in a loving hug.

'Now then, Rosie, look sharp. Mrs Cribb has some writing paper, I've seen it. She writes letters to her sister. Since you're still up and dressed, go see if she'll let us buy a page of it from her.'

Rosie jumped up from the bed and rushed out. Maria looked again at the advertisement. She knew something about everything in the list for shopgirls. But she worried about the seamstress list. She knew that Rosie did well with linens and wools and similar common materials that the good folk of Ironbridge mostly wore, but she had little knowledge of silks or chiffon. And Maria herself had never heard of colienne and doubted Rosie had. What if Rosie weren't qualified, yet Maria was? It left a bad taste in her mouth. She decided that the letter would claim they were both experts, whatever the truth was. Then it'd be up to Rosie to talk her way into the job, if they were called for interview. Rosie had the gift of the gab. She'd talk the hind legs off a donkey.

The door opened and Rosie was back. 'Here, she let me have a couple of sheets for nothing! Good old Mrs Cribb. And she lent me her pen and ink, since you only have pencils about you.'

Maria got out of bed and moved to the small table with two chairs that the girls had in their room. She'd always been a good little writer, back at school in Ironbridge, back when Charlie was the pupil-teacher and she'd watch him from across the room, envious if he helped another girl. Invariably he did, for Maria needed little help, so proficient was she at her schoolwork. The village school she later attended at Middleton-in-Chirbury was simply one room, lazily supervised by an old lady from the parish who liked to have a nap mid-afternoon and let the children run riot outside in all weathers. They said at the time, the inspector tried to close it down, and maybe it had closed by now. Maria was only there around a year and a half, before her uncle insisted she was needed at home. She learnt virtually nothing. But, luckily, by the time her parents passed, she was already an excellent scribe. She'd used this skill to great effect in impressing Mr Boden. Now she'd have to use all her skills to even greater effect, to impress Miss Bytheway of Harborne and Co.

'I'll start with our experience at work first, Rosie. Tell me all about yours.'

Maria described everything Rosie told her, making the smallest of feats sound like award-winning talent. She added in her own experience, then went on to how their skills matched the job advertisements. She wrote carefully and neatly, praying for no ink blots so she wouldn't have to ask Mrs Cribb for a fresh sheet and start again. It reminded her of the copybooks she'd used as a child, how the old woman would whack you across the head with a ruler if you blotted yours. Rosie had no ruler to beat her with, but she scrutinised the page as Maria wrote, even though Rosie couldn't read a word of it. Once Maria was done, she read it out to Rosie, who listened intently to every word.

'Beggar my tripes, you're a genius, wench!'

'I try, I try,' Maria said, with mock modesty.

'But . . . I dunna know all those things. I canna sew all those fabrics.'

'And I knew nothing about trade or tobacco or much of anything about being a shopgirl when I got my first job. Sometimes you need to elaborate a bit. You'll soon get the hang of things.'

'If you say so,' said Rosie, unconvinced. 'But then again, truth is, if we were to be truthful in the letter, we wouldna even get a reply. Sometimes you've to exaggerate to get a foot in the door.'

'That's the spirit,' said Maria.

The next day, in their lunch hour, they both went to the post office, bought an envelope and paid for the letter to be sent. They ran back to work in a flurry of excitement. The next two days dragged by as custom was a bit slow due to a brief, heady heatwave – for who wants to be pinned into layers of clothes with perspiration running down your back? – but there was still plenty to do in the shop. Maria loved her job at Nixon's, yet she had to admit she hadn't realised how long the days would feel when a shopgirl starts at seven in the morning and often isn't home till gone nine at night. In that regard, being a shopgirl had few differences from her life as a slave in all but name at the farm. The crucial contrast, of course, was that here Maria had her freedom. She was the mistress of her own destiny and fiercely independent. And that was priceless.

Two weeks passed with no sign of a return letter. Maria and Rosie had begun with optimism and excitement, yet by the time a fortnight had passed their initial mood had dulled to acceptance, with a smidgeon of hope. Each evening when they returned from work, they asked Mrs Cribb if there had been anything in the post for them, but the answer was always no.

One night, while they sulked in bed, unable to sleep, Rosie said, 'If Harborne say no, which it looks like they will, what shall we do? I never thought I wouldna get an interview at Harborne, with my skills. Or, leastways, the skills you wrote them I have!'

'I dunna know, but what I do know is that I'm set on a department store as my future now. Working all my life in a tiny draper's is . . . well, it's out of the question, Rosie. I have a burning ambition in me. And that's to move up in the world. Being a shopgirl is one of the few jobs open to girls like us who wanna escape where we came from.'

'I inna sure the same can be said of a seamstress,' said Rosie, her voice uncertain.

Maria replied, 'Maybe not a common or garden seamstress working from home. But if you get a job in a department store, your class of customer will improve no end. And then you'll have the experience you need to work for the rich. And that's where you'll move up in the world, Rosie. Mark my words.'

This seemed to convince Rosie, but privately, Maria herself wasn't all that sure about the career path of a seamstress, though she knew she was right about shopgirls. She snuggled down in bed praying that a letter would come soon. She was sure they'd have many applications and were working their way through them.

'Any day now,' Maria said sleepily as they were drifting off. 'That letter will come. You'll see.'

To take her mind off things, Maria agreed to go and see Charlie at his school the following Wednesday, something they'd been meaning to do for ages, but Maria always seemed to be kept behind by Mrs Nixon to sort stock or supervise private fittings and other bits of work. She was paid for them, so didn't mind. But she was pleased at last to have an afternoon off. So she walked straight from work on early closing towards the school. She strolled through town, a summer storm threatening the sky, with a few fat drops of rain forming ever-increasing circles on the water's surface as they fell heavily into the Severn. By the time she reached the foot of Church Hill, the gunmetal-grey clouds were beginning to shift and blue skies lay ahead.

Maria walked up the hill till she reached the church itself and, situated opposite, in a snug building set back and raised from the road, was the Ironbridge Day School (mixed), as it said on the sign carved into the wall outside. There were two wooden doors set into the brick wall, one with GIRLS and one with BOYS on stone arches above. There was also a general entrance gate and she went through that. She could hear the sounds of a classroom emanating from the building, so went in through the front door and followed them. There was one classroom, opposite a cloakroom with hooks for hats, caps, shawls and coats. The classroom door had a window in it, which Maria peeked through and saw Charlie standing by the wall, as well as an older lady delivering the class, probably in her sixties or thereabouts, whose back was to Maria. She supposed that was Anny Malone. Then Charlie looked up and saw Maria peering through the window and his face broke out in a broad grin. He hurried to the door and came out, shutting it behind him.

'You came!'

'Course I did. I said I would.'

'Would you like to come in and meet the children?'

'All right. Though I dunna know what to say to them.'

'You can pretend to be an inspector, if you like. Then they'll be scared of you!'

Maria followed him into the class, whereupon every pair of eyes in the room focused intently on her. Maria supposed that, when at school, any interruption to the general run of things was an improvement and worthy of close attention.

'Children,' said Charlie, at whose voice every child sat up just that little bit straighter. 'This is Miss Keay. She is here to observe you today, so I'm sure I dunna have to remind you to be on best behaviour. Please proceed with the class, Mrs Malone.'

Mrs Malone had long white hair brushed smoothly into a neat bun at the nape of her neck. Her linen skirt and cotton shirtwaist were finely made, Maria could tell, but not in any way showy. She looked to be a woman of means, yet here she was teaching one afternoon a week some of the town's poorest children. Maria wondered what on earth her story might be.

All the boys had caps and all the girls had white aprons. There was a large chalkboard on a stand and all children had slates and slate pencils. In pride of place above the teacher's desk was a portrait of a cricketer holding his bat, with a straggly white wedge of a beard and stripey cap. Maria wondered if it were Charlie's father.

Maria followed Charlie to a spot at the back of the classroom, but before they got there, Biscuit appeared from a small room at the back, a kind of walk-in cupboard. Biscuit trotted straight up to Maria and pushed his nose into her hand. The children giggled and Mrs Malone reprimanded them. Maria was surprised to see Biscuit here during lessons but could imagine he would be a great favourite with the pupils. Some of the boys and girls risked a telling-off by turning round to sneak peeks at Maria, while others continued to stare straight ahead. But Maria was focused on Mrs Malone, for her face was strangely familiar. Just another face from her past, she guessed. She often recognised random people on the streets and in the shops of Ironbridge, that she couldn't place, having been so young when she left. But this face was ingrained in her memory somehow, though she couldn't for the life of her place it.

Biscuit obediently went back into the walk-in cupboard and flopped down on the floor in the doorway, his chin on his front paws. He looked very accustomed to being there. Maria turned her attention back to the teaching. Mrs Malone was talking to the children about cooking.

'Today, my dears, I shall be showing you all how to bake a fidget pie.'

'Ooooh!' came the response from the children, at which Charlie said loudly, 'Settle down and stop showing off.'

Then a boy, who had been persistently looking round at Maria, put his hand up in the air.

'Put your hand down, Arthur,' said Mrs Malone. 'I havna finished my introduction yet. Fidget pie, as I'm sure you all know, is a proper favourite in your county of Shropshire. Every household should know how to make one.'

The same boy shot his hand up in the air once more. 'But, miss!' he called out urgently.

'Are you suffering from a call of nature?' asked Mrs Malone.

'No, miss. I wanna know, why do us boys have to listen to all this? It's wives do cooking. We just come home from working hard all day and the women have our meals on the table.'

'What if you dunna have a wife?' said Mrs Malone.

'Course I'll have a wife. Every mon has a wife.'

'You wonna, not with them big ears,' said a little girl behind him and a ripple of laughter broke out.

'Now then,' said Mrs Malone sternly and everyone stopped. 'It inna daft to ask the question. And the answer inna simple. Most of you boys will have a wife one day, but some wonna, for whatever reason. And some men dunna wanna wife, for whatever reason. And some, God forbid, may lose that wife in childbirth or other misadventure. Or your wife may be ill. Or may be working hard, too, in a factory for long hours. So, as modern and new-fangled as it might seem, it's good to know how to feed yourself. So I'm gonna teach you all how to make the food of the gods.'

Maria watched in awe as Mrs Malone kept their attention with the sound of her voice. They were all rapt, soon forgetting about Maria's presence. Mrs Malone had brought all the ingredients for the pastry, as well as pork, apples and onions for the filling. She had a wooden board set up on the front desk where she rolled out the pastry. The children craned their necks to see, so Charlie intervened and said those on the two back rows could sit on their desks to get a better view, but only if they sat dead still, which they did. It was fascinating, watching her roll the pastry and carve out shapes of apples and leaves to place on the lid, as well as a perfect pastry pig to place at the top of the pie.

A girl at the front put her hand up rather reluctantly.

'Yes, Lottie?' said Mrs Malone.

'Miss,' she said in a voice little louder than a whisper. 'I dunna think I ever had pig to eat. We have rabbit at home mostly. When my mam brings 'em home under her skirt.'

Sniggering broke out, which Mrs Malone soon hushed.

'You can use rabbit instead of pork if you wish. It'll be a rabbit pie instead. And just as tasty.'

Another girl put her hand up and said, 'I know why Lottie's mam has rabbits under her skirt. It be poachers.'

This was quickly followed by a flurry of hands shooting up, but, with the general excitement proving too much for their patience, children started calling out their opinions on this thrilling topic.

'My dad got done for poaching,' said a boy. 'He's in gaol, the Dana in the big town. But he wasna there. He was there another night, for sure. But not that night. That Peeler lied about him in the court, the tommy rotter. It inna fair.'

A girl said, 'Mother goes down The Dip and sees Tommy Rogers' wife, gets the rabbits and strings them round her waist under her skirts! Peelers be none the wiser! She can walk all round town like that, dropping off rabbits to folk to buy 'em.'

Her friend sat beside her added, 'My mam sells things in her basket, cotton reels and so on. Hides the rabbits under her wares! She wonna be caught. Too clever for the Peelers.'

Charlie turned to Maria and said in a low voice, 'Lots of these children had parents in the iron industry, but it's not what it was. It's in decline. The Lilleshall Company's Lodge

Furnaces closed down three years ago and many of their parents were out of work. They relied exclusively on soup kitchens for some winters.'

A small girl in the back row, so little she looked quite malnourished, turned round and said, 'Miss, my dad's a roadster. He roves about the byways. Spends a night down at the workhouse. Then snoozes a night beneath a hedgerow. He brings me daisies from time to time.'

'That's nice,' Maria said and smiled at her, the girl smiling back wanly. Maria's heart broke for the little mite.

Then Mrs Malone called for attention once more and all fell quiet. 'I know there are topics of conversation that get you lot all worked up and this is one of them. But that dunna mean you lose your manners. Now show our visitor today that you can debate better than those lot in the House of Commons. Put your hand up and wait your turn. We've time for one more opinion. Whose shall it be?'

A sea of hands went up, desperate to be picked. But a boy at the back strained his hand so hard he more or less stood up.

Mrs Malone spotted him and said, 'You seem like a mon on a mission. And you rarely say a word in class, so I'm happy to see it. What's your view, Billy?'

'My view is that poaching inna stealing. What do those landowners and gamekeepers need with all them rabbits? They even got fruit on their tables when nobody's ill. That's how rich they are. And if it be stealing, it only be stealing from rich to give to us poor. Just like that Robin Hat.'

Laughter erupted from a few children across the room.

A girl called out, 'Robin *Hat*? You're half-soaked. It's Robin *Hood*!'

Everyone fell about laughing then. But Billy was not fazed. He simply replied, 'That's what I said: Robin Hood.'

Maria had to laugh at that, as did Charlie. Maria was

amazed at how relaxed the atmosphere was in this classroom. She'd never seen anything like that. She loved her early schooling at the Parochial School in Coalbrookdale, the school she went to before her parents died. But it was nothing like this. It was incredibly strict. Nobody spoke in class, ever. Not a word. Nobody's views were called for. It was clearly assumed that children had no ideas and nothing to offer. The cane was used regularly. Maria saw there was a cane hanging behind the teacher's desk in this room but could not imagine a kind soul like Charlie ever using it, though she supposed he had to from time to time. But perhaps not in such a relaxed attitude as this kind of teaching seemed to have. It was a whole other world from her experience. She couldn't wait to quiz Charlie about this new way of teaching.

Mrs Malone soon gained full control, after laughing herself at the Robin Hood debate. She finished off her fidget pie demonstration, calling two lucky children up to help her at various points. They were allowed to squish the pastry between their fingers and scatter flour carefully on the board for rolling. The pièce de résistance was when she first told them all that they had no oven at school so she'd be taking the pie home to cook for her own family and they'd have none of it. This elicited the most miserable faces. But, after a brief pause for effect, Mrs Malone reached into her bag and pulled out something pie-shaped wrapped in a cloth, at which everyone gasped. And she added, with a wink, 'And that's why I brought along one I made earlier, so you can all have a little bit.'

Everyone erupted into applause and laughter, which Charlie calmed down immediately, but he smiled as he did so. Mrs Malone told the class it'd be playtime soon and they should line up by the desk for their piece of pie, eat it and then wait by the door to play outside. As this joyous pie-eating event occurred, Charlie motioned to Maria to follow him as they went outside to be on duty in the playground before the children got there. Biscuit followed at Charlie's heel as they went out of the back door. All storm clouds had blown away and now the day shone cheerfully. From the top step of the playground, she could see out across the rooftops of Ironbridge and above the square tower of the church was the deeply wooded steep side of the gorge, painted every shade of green by the dappled sunlight.

Chapter 7

'Charlie, I mun ask,' Maria said, as they stood beside each other looking out at the view. 'What kind of teaching is this? I've never seen anything like it. It wasna like that when I were at school.'

'Well, my view is that children have summat to offer beside their obedience. We treat them with respect. We expect the same in return. We teach to the curriculum we must cover in order to satisfy the inspectors who come in every year. But we do it efficiently so that every Wednesday afternoon I arrange for Mrs Malone to come and teach them what we like to call "skills for life". These children – seven- to ten-year-olds – soon they'll be out in the world of work. We want them to go equipped. We have to do the job that parents would do, but many of them dunna have fathers around. They've left them in the lurch or they're in gaol for poaching or fighting or other troubles. Their mothers work all hours as seamstresses or taking in washing or working in the factories or the industries. There's simply no time at home to teach them all the skills they need. Mrs Malone teaches them how to do these practical tasks, as well as letter writing and how to speak in a job interview, that kind of thing. We dunna tell the inspector about our Wednesday afternoons. He wouldna approve. It inna part of the curriculum. So we keep it to ourselves. But one day, I hope all schools are like this. Yes, we teach them the three Rs. But also, we teach them how to be a person in the world. I'd say that's just as important.'

'Agreed!' said Maria. 'They do seem a bit rowdy. Do they ever get out of hand?'

'Not really. They respect me and Mrs Malone. They get a bit boisterous, but never too bad.'

'I saw the cane on the wall. I canna fathom you using it.'

'I hate to, I dunna mind saying. But I do, from time to time. I keep it brief. Short, sharp shock. Two for boys and one for girls, and only for the very worst of rule infringements. Never more. If it were up to me, canes would be banned. But the children expect them. If I didna use them, they'd say I was a soft touch and they'd lose respect for me. Sadly true.'

Maria sighed and thought of her uncle's belt. The buckle was the worst bit, if that caught your delicate skin. 'I suppose a lot of them have much worse to deal with at home, anyhow.'

'Sadly, yes. In some houses. But not all. Most parents of these children just want the best for their little'uns. It's the few rotten eggs that make folk think that working families are bad.'

'I'm just amazed how many you had packed in there. Twenty-five, was it?'

'Thirty-two.'

'How on earth do you get all their parents to pay?'

'Ah, well. This school is what they call a board school, funded by local rates. And just last year, the government finally saw fit to abolish school fees for all board schools.'

'Danker me, really?! My uncle went on and on about the pennies they had to pay for me to attend school. He claimed that was why they had to pull me out early. But it was such a small amount for the good it would've done me. And now, to think, these children will never have to pay for a minute of their schooling. The world is changing for the better, I wager.'

'We're getting there. It's taken decades for the government to really listen to those in education. These children will leave at ten years old, but there is talk that this will rise to eleven next year perhaps. If it were up to me, it'd be fourteen.'

'I canna see that'll ever happen. Folk wonna stand for it. They'll want their children in work afore that age.'

Charlie smiled and tilted his head to one side. 'We'll see.'

'You're like my dad,' Maria said, without meaning to. The thought was there in her mind and it just popped out.

'How so?'

'You're kind. And you're . . . what's it called . . . always see the bright side.'

'An optimist.'

'That's it. An optimist.'

'The only way to be, in my view.'

Maria was going to say she was the opposite, as life was dark and murky, difficult and long. She was always expecting something awful to happen. She felt like bad luck followed her around like a lonely spectre. And that any happiness she had would be short-lived. Sooner or later, the darkness would come to engulf her. But the children came outside with Mrs Malone before she had the chance to say it and, on second thoughts, she decided she shouldn't be darkening Charlie's outlook with her miserable ideas. *Let him be happy always*, she thought. *He deserves it.*

Then the noise of the children coming out to play was heard and they looked down at the school building to see them filing out into their two play areas: one for the girls and the other for the boys. The playing area behind the building was built on three levels, reflecting the hillside setting of the school. No doubt a child or two or many more tumbled down those steps in their enthusiastic games, from time to time. Mrs Malone appeared amidst them, directing the girls to their play area above as the boys stayed below.

'Charlie, can I ask you about Mrs Malone? She is simply dressed, but her clothes are finely made. She seems like a working woman in her experience and knowledge but talks and teaches with the manners of a wealthy woman. I am quite confused as to her background.'

'Well, you have it there in a nutshell. She is both. She has this experience from her past and present as she was an iron worker's daughter, her mother a washerwoman. Later in life, her adopted daughter became rich and gave Anny and her husband Peter the old brickmaster's house in Benthall Edge Woods. Anny's worked as a clerk for her daughter's charitable foundation. And now volunteers at the school.'

Maria shook her head in awe. 'I wish I had a rich adopted daughter!'

'You would not wish Anny's life, for it's had more than its fair share of tragedy. But Anny Malone is hale and hearty and will go on for many a year, I warrant. She could've rested on her new-found wealth and never lifted a finger for another human being for the rest of her natural life. But she didna do that. She turned her talents to charity. She works here at the school and there at the charity for no pay. She wonna hear of it. Indeed, she often pays for the children to have new things, to take pleasure trips and so forth. She's an extraordinarily kind person. A great teacher. And a good friend.'

'I am quite flabbergasted,' said Maria, watching Anny pat the children on their heads as she counted them to ensure everyone was outside who should be. Then she walked slowly across the play areas and climbed up to the top level to see Maria and Charlie.

'I'll be off to supervise the boys with their footballs, while Mrs Malone will watch the girls up here with you. She'd like to speak with you, I wager.'

'All right,' said Maria.

Charlie went down the steps to the boys' area, Biscuit trotting behind him, while Mrs Malone came up to see Maria. Some girls were skipping and singing rhymes, while others talked conspiratorially in clumps, fascinated with Maria.

''Ow bist, Maria?' said Mrs Malone, smiling.

'Good, thank'ee, ma'am.'

'Nay, nay, we shouldna have you calling me ma'am, my wench. Everyone calls me Anny. And, after all, you and I, we've met afore now.'

She smiled kindly at Maria and that face . . . that face. It was as if she'd seen it in a dream and the dream had come true.

'I thought as much. But I am sorry, Anny. I dunna remember when we met. Please forgive me.'

Anny reached out and took Maria's hand in her own. Her skin was dry and cool, her touch comforting. Maria felt as if she'd held Anny's hand before.

'There is nought to forgive. It was a long time hitherto. And I am loath to remind you of it, if you dunna recall. It was not an easy meeting, though I hope I gave you some aid at the time.'

Then it came to her. The kindly face, the comfort of her hands. Maria gasped in recollection.

'It was *you*.'

'That's right, my chicken. That's right. You know it now.'

'The air was filled with white flour dust. And then there was you. Your face. You were so kind to me.'

Anny squeezed Maria's hand. 'I did what any person would do.'

'You took me to The Swan. You sat me down on the stool. You sent for a doctor to check my arm. You waited with me all that time when they were looking for my uncle. I didna wanna go with him. I wanted to stay with you.'

'Ah, child. Family is best. It was good he was in town and could take you and comfort you.'

'But he didna. He was cold and cruel. I lived with his family ten year and it was a kind of hell on this earth. I escaped to come back here and make my way as a shopgirl. And I've succeeded in that. But I dunna mind telling you that there are times when I look at the river. And even hear a dog bark. And I am back on that day, in that moment. There are times I think I shouldna come back. That a person should never look back.'

Anny's face was a picture of sympathy. She reached out and cupped Maria's cheek. Anny's eyes were shining, so affected she seemed by the truth of what had happened next to the girl she had taken care of at the worst moment of her young life.

'I am sorrowful to hear that, my lass. Life can be cold and cruel. I know that as well as any. I have known tragedy in many forms and all that tragedy happened here, in Ironbridge. And there were times I felt misery and hatred of the place that had brought me such troubles. But I realised over time that the place itself was innocent, the place was not the architect of my sadness. The place itself is like Mother Nature: indifferent to our suffering in the way it does not comprehend it. We are the players upon its stage. We cannot blame the stage for the play. Can we now?'

Maria's eyes had filled with tears during this beautiful speech. Not only haunted by thoughts of the last time she saw

Anny Malone, but also the truth and wisdom of what she was saying to her now.

'You are a wise woman, Anny,' said Maria and wrapped both hands around Anny's now, and squeezed.

'Nay. I inna wise. Just old!'

They laughed at that and Maria brushed away her tears.

Just then, a little boy came running up the step towards them, holding a ball, his cap askew, his face rosy with exertion and the June warmth. He stopped short before Maria and said brightly, ''Ow do!'

''Ow do, young sir,' said Maria, recovering herself from her tears. The exuberance of youth was the perfect antidote to sadness.

'Do you like football, miss?'

'I dunna know a thing about it, truth be told.'

'Abel, you shouldna be in the girls' bit of playground,' said Anny. 'You know that.'

'My ball skittered over here, miss. You canna tell a ball where to go.'

'Well, that is true.'

During this back and forth, Charlie had come up the steps to join them there.

'Mr Woodvine likes football, miss,' said Abel, neatly swerving the conversation back to his preferred topic. 'He remembers when Aston Villa beat us nine to nil. He said he was shamed to be an Ironbridge mon that day!'

Charlie laughed and added, 'That is true. My old headmaster told me that football was "only fit for butcher boys"! I still love it though. And cricket. Did you see the portrait of W. G. Grace above my desk?'

'Ah, so that was who it was. My dad worshipped him!' said Maria, smiling at the fond memory of her father reading the cricket scores out from the newspaper and whooping at Grace's antics.

'Cricket is slower than a slug,' said Abel. 'Gimme football any day of the week and twice on Sundays.'

'Be off with you, back to the boys' bit,' said Charlie, straightening Abel's cap.

The boy dutifully trotted off, yet was immediately replaced by a girl with a curious look on her face. She approached Maria.

'Miss Keay?'

'Yes, dear?'

'We've been discussing it and we think Mr Woodvine might be your beau, but also we think you're too pretty for him and also too glamorous and you shouldna be a teacher or get married and have little'uns and rather you should be a star of musical theatre, if you can sing, that is. So those are our thoughts on the matter.'

There was a split second of awkwardness and Maria felt her cheeks redden, made prickly by the sunshine beating down on them. But Charlie jumped in to rescue the situation.

'Some thoughts are better not shared in polite company, Lois,' said Charlie, looking stern.

'But, sir, you always say we should speak our minds and this country'd be a much better place if the working people spoke their minds more often 'cause rich people just think us fools.'

Charlie replied, 'It is better to remain silent and be thought a fool than to open your mouth and remove all doubt.'

Lois screwed up her face and replied, 'Eh?'

Anny chortled. 'Enough of this stuff and nonsense, Lois. Run along now.'

'Thank heavens for that!' laughed Maria. 'I dunna think I could take more interrogation.'

'I'll take them back in soon,' said Anny to Charlie. 'Why

dunna you two get off? I'm doing bookkeeping with them next. No fun for you to watch that. I hope to see you again soon, Maria.'

'Thank'ee and I wish that too. I wanted to say—'

But Anny interrupted her. 'I know, my wench. I know. And we shall talk again. We'll meet again soon, I just know it.'

She smiled that sweet, kind smile again, with a hint of sadness and world-weariness in her gaze. She gave Maria's shoulder a quick squeeze, then called out to the children to marshal them back inside. They obeyed her instantly, falling in line, the girls going through their entrance and the boys through theirs, a few children in each line looking back at Maria as they went. Maria was sad to see them go as their company was so refreshing and banished all thoughts of anything, really, as dealing with them was so all-encompassing. Yet also, she felt relieved to see them going, as they were quite a handful and tiring after a long morning of shop work. Overall, though, she was tremendously impressed by the children and by Anny and Charlie's teaching.

'They're a credit to you, Charlie, they truly are.'

'Thank'ee,' he said, Biscuit yawning loudly as he did so. It was so infectious, Maria tried to stifle a yawn too, yet failed, Charlie noting it with a smile.

'Tired, boy? Or bored? I have a feeling Maria is tired too. Or bored?'

'Never bored with you!' said Maria. 'But an early start is beginning to tell on me, I fear.'

'Then let's not embark on a long walk that will tire you further. Yet it seems a shame to miss out on this glorious June day. So I have an idea. Would you like to see my garden? It is right here, behind the schoolmaster's house where I live. We can sit there awhile and you can rest.'

'That sounds perfect,' said Maria.

Charlie led the way, Biscuit hanging behind with Maria, who ruffled the back of his neck as they followed. A little path wound from the back of the schoolhouse to an annexe on its other side, entered through its own front door. The garden attached was small but well maintained. There were raised wooden-sided beds filled with a range of vegetables, growing in wonky lines, interspersed with flowering plants, bursts of orange and yellow colour amidst the green. Patchy grass surrounded the beds, and borders lined the fence with more flowers. There were quite a few straggly weeds here or there, which Charlie noted and pulled out by the root, laying them down on the grass to wither in the sunshine. A wooden bench was placed by the back wall with a patch of shade beside it, which Biscuit headed for and flopped down to rest. Charlie motioned to the bench for Maria to sit down.

'I'll fetch us two tall glasses of lime cordial. How does that sound?'

'Sounds lovely,' said Maria.

The bench was comfortable, with cushions to sit on. The sounds of the classroom punctuated the warm air here and there, filled otherwise with the buzzing of insects, some chatter from nearby neighbours and the distant clangs and crumps of industry wafting in from further downriver. Maria leant back against the wooden slats of the bench and closed her eyes, the sun warming her face, her hair played with by the pleasant breeze. *Is this some kind of heaven?* she heard her mind ask. It may well be. Its peace was like nothing she'd felt in years. It took her back to childhood summers in Ironbridge, finding a warm place in the woods to curl up on the ground beside a tree and read a book. Or helping her father in the garden, pulling snails and slugs off the cabbage leaves, which he then threw in a bucket of hot water to kill them off, the fishy scent making her queasy.

Maria always felt sorry for them, poor mites, just trying to feed themselves. But she wanted her cabbage soup her mother made with bacon more than she wanted to save them. Nature was harsh that way.

She thought of the time her mother had some kind of sickness – Maria was little and they didn't tell her the name of it, yet she recalled blood, a lot of blood, on her mother's bedsheets and her mother's face pale as snowdrops – but she spied on her father talking to the doctor and they thought she might die and a creeping coldness came across her. She went to her parents' bed and curled up on it like a cat beside her sleeping mother, the smell of her mother's soap lulling her to sleep. Her father came in and stroked her head. He always smelt malty, a thick kind of yeasty warm smell that was comforting. The terrible thing – which is how she referred to her parents' death in her mind – was yet to come. And looking back on her childhood, she often felt that it was a series of perfect days with no hint of darkness, until that day. But she realised now it wasn't true. There were sad moments and scary moments and moments when she thought the world was coming to an end, like that night when there was a storm and the windowpanes rattled and she thought the storm was a violent ghost that boomed at them and was going to kill them all. There was darkness there, the ordinary darkness of childhood. And she realised that Anny was right, that to blame Ironbridge, or the River Severn, or the barking of dogs for the terrors that often overcame her . . . that was wrong. For there was comfort to be had here too, in this place that had once been her world for seven years. What she needed to face up to was not that Ironbridge brought back bad memories – for not all of them were bad and many were shining and sweet – but that the bad memories themselves needed dealing with, and facing up to, and accepting. Only

MOLLIE WALTON

then could she move on from the tragedy of her past. As Anny had appeared to, from the tragedies Charlie had mentioned briefly to Maria. And here Anny remained, giving back to the poor children of the parish, content with her lot, it seemed. And at peace.

Chapter 8

Then here was Charlie, bringing two tall glasses of cordial. He sat beside her as they sipped, breathing in the warm and fragrant afternoon.

'How exactly are you and Anny related again?' she asked him.

'Not so close and not so far. I canna recall the exact relation, but I have a family tree somewhere my father had inked on a page. It's summat like my grandfather's grandfather was the brother of Anny's grandfather, I think that is it. Her father was John Woodvine. A good man, by all accounts. And a tragic one.'

'What happened to him?'

'He was killed in an explosion at the furnace. The owners' fault, they say, not maintaining it properly.'

'That's awful. Poor Anny.'

'Yet another industrial accident. So many have been lost and will continue to be, if workers' rights are not taken seriously.'

Maria turned to look at Charlie as he sipped his drink. His eyes fired up when he spoke of the working people. He felt passionately about the cause, she could see that. She saw it as well when he spoke about his charges at the school. It was tremendously attractive.

'You're a good man, Charlie Woodvine.'

He looked at her, smiled at her, then his face changed and he shifted position to face her. He wanted to ask her something, she could tell. But what would it be?

'Maria, I . . . I wanted to ask you, will you . . . tell me about your work?'

'About my work? What about it?'

'Does it . . . please you?'

'It does. I love it. The hours are long, granted. Yet they do fly by, as I am always busy and learning new things. I can look at any outfit, on a man or woman, girl or boy, and know what material it is made of, how each piece was cut to be fitted together, how the seams were sewn, how best to adjust it to fit the wearer perfectly. I know how to accessorise every outfit, which are the best gloves, what hosiery matches what underclothes and which hats are most in season.'

'Specialist knowledge and most impressive,' said Charlie. 'What are your ambitions? What do you wish to do with all this learning?'

'Well, I am ambitious. It wonna stop there. There is so much more I want to learn. Rosie too. We've talked about it, about looking beyond the confines of a small draper's shop in Ironbridge. Charlie, it's very exciting and I've been meaning to tell you. We have set our sights on Shrewsbury, on the department store Harborne and Co. We have sent a letter applying for a job. It's proper thrilling! Just imagine, working in a place ten times bigger than Nixon's! With all the latest fashions from Paris and three buildings' worth of window displays! And to live in a town the size of Shrewsbury!'

Before this last speech, Charlie had looked rapt at every word. As the last few utterances came, his face changed. His eyes fell to inspecting the cuff of his shirt, which he'd rolled up in the sunshine. He was not looking at her any more.

'Charlie? Have I offended you?'

'Oh, Maria. Nay, nay. You could never offend me. I . . . I find myself tongue-tied, when I have been speaking before groups of children for the last, what is it, seventeen years? But before you . . . that is a different matter.'

'You dunna wanna be tongue-tied with me, Charlie Woodvine. It is just me, your friend Maria.'

But were they really just friends? Surely friends didn't feel the need to kiss each other, as much as she wanted to kiss Charlie. But he hadn't tried to kiss her yet, so maybe he was not as interested as her. Or maybe he was the perfect gentleman.

Charlie looked intently into her eyes, then put down his drink on the ground beside the bench.

'Come, let me show you something,' he said suddenly.

'All right.'

She put her glass down too and followed him. Biscuit looked up lazily and seemed to consider going with them, as he was usually more interested in where his master was going than sleep, even if it were only a few steps across the garden. But he decided that his spot in the shade on that grass was too comfortable to bother. And he nestled his chin back down onto his forelegs and closed his eyes.

Charlie and Maria stopped beside one of the raised beds, full of pea plants climbing up stakes and curling their tendrils along the tied strings between the wooden sticks.

'Look at these peas. Think about the way I grow them, the way all folk round here grow peas. The way I prepare the soil. It's no accident these peas grow so well. It's a clay soil and gets waterlogged easily. I mix the chimney soot with it and it improves the soil no end. My father taught me that and his father taught him. The way to tie these stakes and string to allow the peas to climb and have plenty of room to thrive. The position, considering the sun at different times of day and the direction this garden faces. The compost I use to improve growth. The rotation of crops for each bed, each year, to improve the soil and its nutrients. All of this special knowledge, this useful knowledge, I didna read it in a book. I wasna taught it at school. It was knowledge passed down the generations, from working men and women to their sons and daughters. Do you think the average banker from the City of London knows to mix chimney soot with clay soil? Do you think they know how to sew a seam? Or make a perfect meat pie? Were they taught these things at Eton or Rugby? I say nay, most likely, they dunna know these things that are gold, these things that are essential for life. And answer me this: what is more important, to know how to cook and sew and plant marigolds with carrots to keep away the carrot fly? Or to know the precise usage of every type of spoon, fork and knife at a millionaire's banquet? To know how to address royalty or the landed gentry at each occasion? And yet which of these people are valued more highly by society?'

'The wealthiest among us.' She knew the answer but did wonder for a moment where on earth he was going with all this. Maria thought a minute ago that he might kiss her. But sometimes it seemed Charlie was more interested in lectures than kisses.

'Exactly. And the time has come for this inequality to end. This is the time of socialism. Workers are essential for this land to thrive. The Industrial Revolution would never have occurred if it hadna been for the working men and women who slogged for years and years to make the goods the masters sold. And many died for it. Men and women. Good men and women, like Anny's father John Woodvine. But men like that cannot even vote for who should represent them in parliament. And no women can vote at all. Hard-working, clever and thoughtful women, like Anny. Like you. It is as if you dunna even exist in law. But think of the cleverness of women, the natural intelligence to match any man. The value of their industry every day, at home or at work. Their skills and talents that are underpaid and undervalued by society. Canna you see, Maria? How noble it is to be a working person in a small town, creating small necessary things?'

'True, true. I agree with it all, Charlie. Did you think I wouldna?'

He paused, uncertain of how to go on. She was confused. What was he trying to prove to her? He took a pea pod and passed it to her.

'Taste them,' he said. He took a pod for himself, snapped it in half and shoved the peas into his mouth with his thumb. She eased her pod open, put it in her mouth and used her tongue to find the peas, each one popping its sweetness onto her tastebuds. He watched her intently.

'The sweetness,' he said, watching her lips. 'The pure, natural sweetness.'

She finished her peas and dropped the empty pod into the grass.

'They're the best peas I think I ever had,' she said and smiled at him. Yet his face was serious, so serious. He was looking at her mouth, then at her eyes.

Charlie reached over and kissed her. It was gentle, lingering. His moustache was far softer than she'd imagined.

Maria smiled. He kissed her again, longer this time, his hand at her waist.

She reached up slowly as he regarded her face and ran her fingers through that lock of hair that fell over his hazel eyes, as she had wanted to do for ever so long. It was as soft as she imagined it, softer. He closed his eyes as she touched him, lost in the moment.

'Kiss me again,' she whispered.

He kissed her again, more fervently. And this time he pulled her towards him, one hand at her waist and the other at her face, his fingers reaching into her yellow hair, as she leant her cheek into the palm of his hand. Their mouths opened and there came her first kiss that way, the warm wetness a little shocking, yet welcome and enough to make a person lose their senses.

'Darling,' he whispered close to her ear, his breath warm on her neck.

They kissed again, more passionately still, and Maria felt a great longing in her to become one with him, so handsome was he, so kind and so good. The best man she thought she ever knew, and she had known him all her life, it felt. And she had loved him all that time, without realising it now until he touched her, and it felt so utterly right and complete. The kiss seemed to last the longest time and when she came up for air, they caught sight of each other and smiled at their passion, laughing at the surprise of their desire.

Then Charlie's face changed from sunshine to rainclouds. It had that quality, of moods that shifted quick as a butterfly just landed, off again almost the instant it lands.

'What is it?' she asked, touching his cheek.

'Dunna go, Maria.'

'I wasna intending to. I have nowhere to be till teatime. Mrs Cribb will be cooking for us at five. She does every Wednesday. We have a while yet till then.'

'Nay,' said Charlie. 'I dunna mean that. Dunna go away. Dunna go to Shrewsbury.'

Maria was taken aback. 'Why ever shouldna I go to Shrewsbury? If I get the job at Harborne's, I mean.'

'I dunna want you to go. I want you to stay here in Iron-bridge and marry me.'

'Oh Charlie,' she said, overcome for the moment by the words she wondered he might say one day, but not so soon after their first kiss. 'Are you sure? It inna been long. What if we know each other longer and you grow to dislike my ways? Or find I inna interesting enough for you?'

'That will never happen,' said Charlie and he kissed her again. She felt her concerns melting as they kissed, but there was a hard nugget of something he said that did not melt. It niggled her. She couldn't let it go.

'But what if I do get the job I've applied for in Shrewsbury? What then?'

'Why, you would turn it down, of course.'

'Whatever for?!' she cried. She stepped away from him then, taking her hands from him and placing them firmly on her hips. 'Why ever would I turn down a job offer from the finest shop in all of Shropshire?'

'A married woman canna do shop work, unless she's a widow like Mrs Nixon. You'll have plenty to do here with me, at the school.'

'But I dunna wanna do that. I wanna go to Shrewsbury and work at Harborne's.'

After such an exquisite moment of closeness with Charlie, Maria felt panic rising in her chest at the realisation that her dream of working at the glamorous Harborne's and her hard-won independence could be taken away from her, simply by loving him.

'That is out of the question. I canna follow you to Shrewsbury. And what would be the point, if we are to be married and you'd have to give up your job anyway? My life's work is here, with these children.'

'I havna asked you to follow me, Charlie Woodvine. That is quite the presumption.'

Charlie breathed in deeply through his nose and fixed his gaze squarely on her. Then said, in a lowered tone, 'I dunna think I presume too much when we know what strength of feeling has just passed between us in this moment, on this spot right here. In all our moments together, since I saw you behind that counter. And I dunna think you can deny the power of that.'

Maria felt circumspect. He was right, she could not deny that. But a kiss, or even a few kisses, passionate and magical though they were, had nothing to do with her future. Did they?

'I dunna wanna deny any such thing,' she said.

'I love you,' he said urgently, as if she were slipping away from him.

Maria stepped towards him and took his hand.

'And I love you. Surely you know that. And I have done far longer than you have, for I had a thing for you when I was a mere girl. So I've felt most deeply for you ten year now. So you dunna need to tell me about strength of feeling. Or devotion. You've come late to this game, Charlie.'

'I know that and that makes finding you again here all the sweeter. And that brings me back to here, to Ironbridge and why you came back. You could've left your uncle's and gone anywhere in the world. But you chose to return. To your home. And here you are, happy to be back home. Maria, that is all a person needs. It is all I want. My home. And you. And these are not small things. These are qualities in life that people have fought for, have lost and mourned. But here we have it, in the palms of our hands. There for the taking. Home. And love. Would you push that aside for an uncertain future?'

Nothing he said was wrong. Nothing he said was unreasonable. She knew that many a girl would run headlong into

Charlie Woodvine's arms and never look back. Surely for most girls a job was a means to an end until they got married. But Maria knew that inside her was a different desire. For something else. Something beyond the confines of a kitchen range and a baby on her hip, like her cousin Rhoda. She was not ruling those out, but first she had other designs for her life. When she saw that line drawing of Harborne and Co on the newspaper advertisement, she saw a shining palace that birthed in her a need to escape. To leave the narrow confines of a life by the river, serving Mrs Nixon and the working folk of Ironbridge their linens and wools. Then to marry, to give it all up. She loved the school, the children Charlie taught. But that was *his* dream, not hers. In her dream, she saw silks and chiffons and fancy goods, ribbons and velvets and tea-gowns. She saw fashion. She saw glamour. And right now, at that moment, while Charlie spoke of all that as if it were nothing, Maria realised that nothing he could say would change her mind.

'I mean to go to Shrewsbury, Charlie, if they'll have me. If not at Harborne's, then somewhere else, somewhere bigger and better than what I have now. For why should I stop where I am on the ladder if I can go higher, see further? This town was my home, it was. But it is also the place of my greatest sorrow. I've tried to conquer it, I have. But every day I am here, the river flows on. It is everywhere here. It is inescapable. A constant reminder of what I have lost. Of what was taken from me. And so I have tried to make a life here. And no doubt I could keep trying. But it haunts me, like a spectre in the midst of my happiness. It follows me up and down each alleyway and byway of Ironbridge. I wish it didna feel that way. But it does. I canna escape it.'

'Give it time, my darling, please!' Charlie entreated her. 'It has only been a few months. You will get over it. You will be able to move on. I promise you.'

'You dunna know that!' she cried, filled with annoyance that he could sweep aside her fears so readily. 'I am hounded by my tragedy here! And I am sick to death of it! I mun make my life elsewhere. I loved Ironbridge with all my heart for my first seven years. And I love it still: the people, the bridge, the gorge, even the river. But it is spoilt by the corpses of my beloveds. Nothing you can say can change that.'

Biscuit woke up with a start. He was a dog finely tuned to the mood of his humans. He settled down again, but with watchful eyes.

'With my love,' Charlie said calmly, 'I could change that. I know I can. And the love you'll have for a baby in your arms, for our baby, one day. Born and bred in Ironbridge. Just like you were. You know it's true.'

'Well, I dunna know that. I know how much I feel for you. And how much I'd love our child, if we were to be blessed. But I dunna know if it's enough to banish my ghosts. And anyway, if you cared for me at all, you would see how important this is to me, to move on and find my life elsewhere. If you truly cared for me, you would come with me. We could find separate lodgings. We could have a long courtship. It's only a half-hour or so on the train, after all. You could visit here as often as you like. Or you could stay here and visit me on the train regularly. Then we'd both have what we wanted.'

'But, as I've already said, what would be the point? Once we've married, you would be bound to give up shop work.'

A new ambition had materialised in Maria's mind as she talked. The whole idea of marriage and shop work not mixing had not fully occurred to her as yet, as she had not been proposed to until a few minutes ago. But now she could see that there might be a way forward. It would take years and perhaps it would never happen. But if a girl like her could work her way up from tragedy – from orphan to shopgirl in Ironbridge to shopgirl in Shrewsbury and one day manager, or who knew what other giddy heights, maybe a girl like her could own her own shop one day. Anything was possible, if you had the ambition.

'But what if I didna have to, Charlie? What if one day, I had my own shop?'

Charlie closed his eyes and wiped the back of his hand across his forehead, as if she were a particularly testing child in his classroom. Maria did not like the way he did that.

'That will never happen,' he said.

'And why not? I am as good a person as Mrs Nixon. Why couldna I be like her, eh?'

'Because her husband died! People like us dunna have the capital to buy the lease of a shop. It just dunna happen.'

'But maybe it will!' cried Maria, undeterred. 'If I work hard enough and long enough. And if I owned my own premises, then nobody would care if I were married, not when I am the one in charge. So, that is my plan. And if you truly loved me, as I love you, you wouldna make me choose between the two things I care most about.'

His eyes were lit with indignation. 'You would ask me to leave these poor mites behind? Or make me wait an uncertain period, maybe even years? For you to sell fripperies to rich wives?'

She wasn't having that. How dare he!

'Fripperies?! For all your fine words on politics and rights and so forth, you're a snob.'

'Ha!' he cried. 'How can that possibly be? Do please explain how a man who devotes his life to the poorest and neediest among us could ever be called a snob.'

'You are! Snobs work both ways. A gent or lady might look down on us and our muddy boots. But you look down on them and say they are all worthless, because they do not earn their keep in industry or at the blackboard or coalface, or wherever hearty working people are. But there are other things in the world besides work. There is colour, and beauty, and skill, and talent, and design, and the art of selling. These can be prized too. But no, you throw them all in the same pile as heartless noblemen who turn their noses up at the paupers as they ride by in their carriages. But the world is not so contrary as you see it, not as black as coal and as white as ostrich feathers. Everything is shades of grey, dunna you see? There is room in society for the finer things, for fun and fashion and glamour. Just as there is room for education. And charity. And all the things you value too.'

Maria was pleased with her speech. He might be the schoolteacher, yet she could keep up with the best of them when she put her mind to it. As she spoke, she was standing squarely, facing him, hands firmly on her hips, utterly convinced she was right. But Charlie was still not persuaded.

'Nothing you have said has answered my question. You would have me abandon my children here for the sake of Harborne and Co, that paean of pointless and indulgent commerce? For that is all that will happen for you in Shrewsbury. Put the idea of owning a shop out of your mind, for it will never come to be.'

'You dunna know that! And your refusal to even consider moving to Shrewsbury is stubborn . . . and selfish. Yes, selfish. There are other teachers in the world! And one of them will come to Ironbridge to take your place, no doubt. And there are other poor mites in Shrewsbury. The streets there inna paved in gold. There will be poor and needy places that require you just as much there as you are needed here. Dunna you have ambition? You could become a headmaster of a big school in Shrewsbury.'

'I know that, I inna daft. I know I'm good at my job. But I inna interested in ambition for ambition's sake. I have enough money to keep me. To keep you too. And little'uns. I dunna need more than that. And why would I wanna move to a big town full of strangers, when I've built a life for myself at home? You and I were once children of parents who worked hard and earnt little. Neither of us had much growing up. And there are many more here who have even less. Like the children I teach now. Thus, I am resolved to help the children of my home town. That is my world. And it could be yours too. That is the choice you mun make, Maria.'

'But it inna mine. I dunna want that. I dunna wanna change my choice. So, it is you who has a choice to make. Not me. For I am set on my ambition. And nothing you say will change my mind. And if you canna accept my dreams, then my answer is no, I will not marry you, Charlie Woodvine.'

Maria was sick of arguing. She turned on her heel and marched off across the garden to the gate into the lane. As she fiddled with the latch on the gate, Biscuit came up to her and leant against her leg. She had to be quite stern with him to get him to move so she could open the gate. She stomped up Church Hill. Then made her way past the woods and up Paradise. She fought tears as she walked, scolding herself to not cry, to not linger on the thought of Charlie left behind in his garden, hurt by her words. She would not give in to emotion.

Since the day of her loss – since she sat on that cart with her taciturn uncle and knew in her soul that no love would come from him, that her parents were gone and so was everyone who would care for her, would speak for her, would give a damn about her life – she had known she was the only one. She had fought to carve out a space for herself in the world and now she was on the threshold of a new path towards freedom and success. And she would not let a schoolteacher stop her, however noble his socialist arguments. Or however soft his curly hair. Or however bright his hazel eyes . . . She couldn't help replaying their kisses in her memory, over and over. She felt her resolve weaken. Then suddenly she thought, *Nay! I mun be strong.* Instead of staring at Charlie's fine features in her mind, Maria pictured the line drawing she'd seen of Harborne and Co. *There is my future,* she thought. There it stood in her mind's eye, the great triple-fronted department store, like Camelot shining on the hill in the stories she once read as a lonely child hiding in the hayloft. And nothing would stop her from reaching it. Not even the kisses of Charlie Woodvine.

So much marching, after a long day, and her feet ached like mad by the time she reached her lodgings, but that did not stop her stomping up the stairs and slamming her bedroom door. Rosie wasn't home and Maria threw herself on her bed and burst into tears, sobbing for a few seconds. Mid-sob, she heard a voice call up the stairs.

'Maria?'

It was Mrs Cribb.

'Letter for you.'

A letter? Maria shot up and threw open the door, flying down the stairs to find Mrs Cribb at the foot of them, holding onto the letter, the most important letter of Maria's life. She had to restrain herself for snatching it out of Mrs Cribb's hand.

'Dunna slam the door against the wall that way, please. You'll shake the foundations and cause a crack in the wall if you're not careful.'

'Sorry, Mrs Cribb. It'll never happen again. Now, the letter?'

Mrs Cribb peered at her. 'Are you quite well? You've the look of a babby that's been bawling.'

'Not at all, Mrs Cribb, I'm fine. Please, the *letter*!'

Mrs Cribb passed it over so slowly, time seemed to stop.

Maria at last had it in her hands and pounded back up the stairs and shut the door – carefully – behind her. Then tore into the envelope and yanked out the letter inside.

Harborne and Company
Pride Hill
Shrewsbury
SALOP
30 June 1892

Dear Miss Keay,

Thank you for your letter of last month applying for the role of saleswoman for yourself and for the role of seamstress for Miss Rosemary Green. We are pleased to inform that Miss Keay has been invited to interview for the role of saleswoman on July 30th. You must present yourself at Harborne and Company at 10 a.m. sharp. We look forward to seeing you then.

Miss Green's application was not successful on this occasion.

Yours sincerely,
Miss L. Bytheway.
Head of Ladies' Drapery

Chapter 9

July 1892

The reactions to Maria's news were mixed, to say the least. Mrs Nixon was pleased for her and offered her a new outfit from the shop to borrow for her interview, for which kindness Maria was very grateful.

'I like to see girls get ahead,' said Mrs Nixon. 'But listen, Maria. It wonna be like it is here. I work you quite hard, I know, as hard as I work myself. But in those big stores in the big towns, it's quite different. Hours'll be longer and, though the pay be better, they're much more strict, so I've heard. So dunna get yourself too excited, as your life will change and not only in good ways.'

But Maria didn't want to hear such things, and what did Mrs Nixon know anyway? She'd not worked at Harborne's. And how could there be longer hours than she was already working? Mrs Nixon was being cautionary, that was all. A shopkeeper from Ironbridge couldn't know for sure how a palace like Harborne's truly worked. But Maria soon would. Perhaps Mrs Nixon was trying to make her stay. *That's probably it*, thought Maria. *She's trying to put me off.*

Mrs Cribb, her landlady, was annoyed that she might be losing Maria's rent.

'Life in the big town inna a patch on Ironbridge. Rowdy, scurrilous men everywhere. Be careful of your virtue, Maria.'

Maria rolled her eyes at this. Mrs Cribb was an old widow, born and bred in Ironbridge and never travelled further than Broseley, by all accounts. *So, what does she know? Nothing, that's what.*

But worst of all was Rosie, of course, who had been specifically snubbed in the letter. Maria was frightened to show the letter to Rosie but knew she had to as Mrs Cribb knew and might mention it. So Maria had to grasp the nettle. And Rosie's initial reaction was fury.

'How dare they snub me that way! What's wrong with me then?'

'There's nothing wrong with you. I said all the right things in the letter.'

Rosie squinted at her. 'Well, I wouldna know, would I? Seeing as I canna read nor write proper. You coulda written any old thing, coulda made out I was useless.'

Maria asked incredulously, 'Why ever would I do that, Rosie?! You're my best friend!'

Rosie threw herself down on the bed and sulked. 'I dunna know. Just seems a bit suspicious they want you and not me.'

'I'll tell them all about you at the interview, Rosie. I'll persuade them they canna do without you.'

'Will you, though?' said Rosie, looking at her doubtfully, tears of anger in her eyes.

'I will, I promise.'

Thereafter, they spent the following weeks until the interview in an uneasy truce, not mentioning the event once, as if it would never happen. Maria had to celebrate her excitement inwardly, alone. She feared telling Charlie too, and didn't at first, but then she felt she ought to get it over and done with and see what his reaction would be. She hoped he'd changed his views since they'd last discussed it. She met him on a Wednesday at lunchtime and they walked down to the town together.

'If it's what you truly want, then that's good for you,' he said.

'You inna proud of me for earning this triumph?' she asked, not in an angry way, though she felt annoyed inside. But in a supplicating way, as she wanted to get him onside and realise that there could be a future for them, but only if he saw things as she did.

'I am proud. Of your industry. And your ambition. It's impressive.'

But she could see his heart wasn't in it. Charlie was good about it, polite and quietly encouraging, yet she could see in his awkward manner that he was clearly disappointed she was actually going through with it. They didn't see each other again after that, before her interview. Things were frosty all round. Thus, those people closest to her were the least excited for her, if not downright unsupportive. And so it was with a heavy heart that she climbed into bed the night before the interview and stared at the smart outfit hanging up that Mrs Nixon had given her and she would wear the next day: a new cream-coloured shirtwaist with puffed sleeves, a blue skirt with a black chevron at the waist and black trim at the hemline, and a smart straw hat with a matching blue ribbon. It was the nicest outfit she'd ever worn, a perfect fit and very smart. She would be sad to give it back, but at least she'd have the pretension of appearing above her station and thus have more of a chance to impress her interviewer at Harborne's.

Maria had begun to realise that there was something curiously hinterland-like about being a shopgirl: you weren't as fully working-class any more, due to being seen as above domestic service or factory work, yet, of course, below those you served who could afford to buy at such shops. Shopgirls earnt little but had to appear genteel. She thought that she didn't really fit in anywhere now: too poor to identify with her customers, yet her new status too middling to fit in with her working-class brethren. And this drove a wedge between her and those she loved best: Rosie and Charlie.

Thus, the following morning, walking down to the Iron-bridge and Broseley railway station, she did so with a touch of melancholy, not the feeling she expected to have on the way to an interview for her dream job. *Why canna things just be straightforward?* she bemoaned inwardly, as she paid the toll for crossing the bridge, then arrived at the station. But then her heart lifted as she'd never taken a train journey alone before. She'd only been on ten-minute ones with her parents to nearby nice places for walking when they had a rare day off and never to Shrewsbury. She asked the guard where to go and soon enough the Shrewsbury train rolled in, puffing away, bringing with it clouds of steam and a scattering of soot on the breeze.

Once she was boarded, comfortable in her seat and the train had pulled away from the station, her cares began to fall away as she looked out of the window at the Shropshire greens and browns of the deep, wooded gorge and rolling hills, and the greys and blacks of ironworks and coal pitheads that gouged the country with industry due to its rich geology. The train chugged on through Wenlock, Buildwas, Cressage and Berrington. Next stop, Shrewsbury. Her chest tightened and she felt further away than ever from everything she knew, despite it only being just over a half-hour on the train. Yet along with her fear was a light-headed excitement. It was really happening. The most thrilling moment of her short life so far. Weighing in the balance was a chance of something incredible:

a job in the county town, far away from everything she'd known. The alternative was failure and she couldn't bear the idea of that, of coming home with her tail between her legs, having to admit defeat to all those around her who'd doubted her. She had to succeed. She had to act the part of the genteel shopgirl and impress them. All she had to do was not be herself.

When the train drew into Shrewsbury and everyone rose to disembark, Maria looked again at the invitation letter. The address of Harborne's was there and yet no explanation of how to get there from the station. High Street and Pride Hill, it read. Well, which was it? High Street? Or Pride Hill? Then, she realised, the department store was so big it stretched around a corner, as the line drawing showed, so it was located on two streets at once. She disembarked and followed the throng of travellers along the platform. There were men in boaters, homburgs and bowler hats, and women in broad-rimmed hats of every conceivable style, some with flowers, veils or other fancy trimmings. An old military man in full uniform held up the flow as he perambulated slowly with a cane. She saw a boy going to the big town with his father, the latter dressed dapperly in a three-piece grey suit, the boy wide-eyed and excitable. She felt like the boy herself, an innocent abroad.

As the platform opened out into the main concourse, she made her way through the crowds to the exit and out into the sunny, warm July day. She stopped and looked around her. Glancing back at the railway station building itself, she real-ised it was the largest building she'd ever seen, built from a lovely pale stone, more like a church or town hall than a rail-way station, with dozens of windows, pinnacles and a tall clock tower. The streams of people coming and going from its exits and entrances gave her a thrill, thinking of all the places they were visiting and returning from, all the possibilities of different lives they represented to her. But there was no time to mess around. It was nine-thirty already and with only thirty minutes left, she needed to get walking to Harborne's: she had no idea where it was.

Maria couldn't afford a taxicab, but perhaps someone would be kind and tell her directions to Harborne's Department Store. She saw two cabbies chatting cheerfully with each other and approached deferentially, asking if they could kindly tell her the way.

'Up Castle Gates yonder,' one of them said, waving his head vaguely in front of them. 'Then Pride Hill. Stop at High Street. Harborne's on the corner. Canna miss it, wench.'

The other one puffed on a pipe and tutted at her as she walked away. Perhaps they thought in her fine outfit that she should've been able to pay for a cab ride. Thus, again, she felt between two worlds. She felt like a fraud. But Maria had to banish these thoughts and start believing in herself. She had as much right as any girl here to work at Harborne's. Hadn't she been invited? Of course she had. *Chin up, lass*, she told herself in her father's voice.

She found the beginning of Castle Gates by asking a passer-by and set off along it. Packed with shops, the variety of premises amazed her. There were so many more shops than Ironbridge and of every kind, from the common or garden butchers and bakers and so forth to the more obscure and niche: watchmakers, photographers, staymakers, music shops, French glove shops, point lace shops. Every need a person could ever want satisfying seemed to be found in the streets of Shrewsbury. Over the shopfronts hung advertisements for the shop's wares, such as a white globe with WHY WEAR HEAVY HATS? hanging over a 'cork headwear' shop; and a lamp with the shop-owner's name on, in this case, someone called Ellen Stubbs. *So, a woman owning her own shop*, Maria thought. *And her name sounds quite ordinary. That's one in the eye for Charlie and his pronouncement on how it'll never happen for me.*

She walked past a huge bakery offering *Fry's Chocolate* and ices in all flavours. The window display made her mouth water, chock-full of cupcakes, buns and sweets in jars. She spotted a Freeman, Hardy and Willis shoe shop, with more shoes in one place than she'd ever seen in her life, offering grand bargains in their 'End of Century Sale', even though they were a few years away from that as yet. Even a chemist's, which usually was the most practical and dull of shops, had impressive windows with boxes and bottles of Hall's Wine, apparently a health drink, arranged in circles and towers and arcs to fill the whole window. It claimed to be a 'supreme tonic restorative', though when she'd seen folk drunk from wine before they didn't look particularly restored.

Then, on her left, Maria saw ahead an extraordinary building, huge and set back from the road, with walls of yellow contrasting with the black beams of wood that held it up. She gazed at it as she passed, imagining how rich a person must be to live there. It looked like a palace and just sat there, in the middle of town. But there was no time to dawdle, so she hurried on. Before long, she was coming along Pride Hill, flanked by rows of dozens more shops. Finally, she spied the mighty three-storied edifice of Harborne and Co. There must have been fifty windows or more! Maria stood at the corner of Pride Hill and High Street and tipped her head back, gawping at its magnificence, from its six separate window displays, full of ornate settings filled with a cornucopia of goods, right up to its top floor topped by slate roofs and the many chimneys she'd seen in Rosie's picture. In fact, the drawing did not do it justice as what was missing was the vastness of it and the splashes of colour in every window. People streamed in and out of its doors: three entrances, one for each building. She had no idea where to enter and find Miss Bytheway, who was to interview her. So, she chose the middle entrance as the most likely. A tall, handsome man with a neat black moustache smartly dressed in a long buttoned-up coat and stiff cap stood by the door, welcoming customers inside.

'Excuse me, sir,' she asked.

'Yes, miss,' said the doorman, giving her a quick scan up and down. 'How may I be of assistance?' He must have found her acceptable as he spoke politely to her, so didn't assume she had no place in a location as fancy as this. She silently thanked Mrs Nixon for providing her with the right clothes. If she'd come here in one of her cheap outfits from the market, she had no doubt this chap would've thrown her out on her backside with a thump in the middle of the High Street.

'I'm here for an interview for the position of sales assistant in drapery. With Miss . . . Miss . . . By-the-way, is it?'

'Oh,' he said, instantly losing interest as she wasn't a customer. And he wasn't going to help her with how to say Miss Bytheway's name either, as he simply barked, 'Go to the back there, see those stairs? Go up 'em. Turn right. Offices down there. First one on left.'

'Thank'ee,' she said and nodded, but his attention was already elsewhere, talking to another lady, a customer, someone much more important than her.

Stairs, turn right, first office on left. Maria said it over and over to herself as she walked across the floor. She didn't want to forget it. But all she wanted to do right then was stop and stare at the wonders that surrounded her. She couldn't be late, so she hurried forward, but her eyes darted everywhere, taking in the grandeur of the place. There were mosaic floors in the entrance, with lush carpets beyond. All around her were display cabinets with electric lighting, oak fittings and panelling, chairs for customers, huge mirrors to make the rooms look even larger and for customers to admire themselves or otherwise find fault with themselves that perhaps a purchase from the store would remedy. There were chandeliers, carved ceilings, potted plants dotted everywhere and in the centre of the room was a sweeping staircase, leading up to the second and third floors designed as galleried storeys where customers could stop and look down at the rest of the shoppers below. There were headless mannequins swathed in the latest fashions for men and women, with everything put on display to tempt customers, compared to Ironbridge shops where most goods were kept in drawers and cupboards behind the counter. Shoppers in Ironbridge mostly knew exactly what they wanted when they entered the shop. They didn't need it all displayed for them. But here, in this magnificent cathedral of commerce, the shopper was encouraged to wander and watch, look at all the goods proudly set out for their delectation and be lured into buying things they had no idea existed, let alone how much they now wanted them. *It's so clever*, Maria thought. This was how shopping should be. Not a chore but a pleasure.

She hurried past the main staircase to the doorway at the back where the smaller staircase was, heading upstairs to the offices. A sign instructed shoppers this area was *PRIVATE*, so Maria guessed she must be in the right place. She climbed up the functional stairs and noticed all the grandeur faded, away from the shop floor.

'Turn right, first on left,' she said aloud to herself and a chap coming downstairs eyed her suspiciously. And though Maria smiled at him, he ignored that and hurried on down the steps. Then there it was, she guessed. There was a corridor of offices and the first one on the left had a gilded sign fitted into

the dark wood of the door that read *HEAD OF LADIES'*
DRAPERY and below it was affixed a small plaque reading
MISS L. BYTHEWAY. It was thrilling to see a woman's
name on a door like that. So this would be her first ambition
here: to attain the status of having her name on a plaque on a
door in an office in a long, darkened corridor. Firstly, though,
she had to get through this interview.

Maria raised her hand to knock and hesitated. Should her
knock be firm and confident or quiet and polite? Enough dilly-
dallying. She knocked loudly. Self-assurance was the way to go.

'Come in,' came the voice from inside.

Maria opened the door to find a very small office with no
window, wood-panelled and dim, with an empty chair placed
before a desk piled with papers and envelopes and writing
paraphernalia. Behind all that sat the person who Maria
assumed was Miss L. Bytheway, a woman in perhaps her thirties, older than cousin Rhoda and younger than Mrs Nixon.
She had a pale face of even features, with brown hair scrupulously neat, pulled back so tightly in a bun at the nape of the
neck, it looked as if it had been ironed into place.

'You are?' she said without smiling.

'Miss Maria Keay, ma'am.'

'Ah, yes. Right on time. You say it KAY then, not KEY?'

'That's right, ma'am. To rhyme with STAY, not FREE.'

'Very nice, very quick,' she said, with a flash of a pursed-
lipped smile so brief it almost wasn't there. 'And I am Miss
BYTHE-WAY. And not BY-THE-WAY, as some idiots say.
Now, shut the door and come in and sit down or we'll be here
all day.'

Maria did so and suddenly realised how grateful she was
that Miss Bytheway had said her own name aloud. Thank
heavens she herself had a confusing name! Or she would've
been branded an idiot.

Miss Bytheway reached for a piece of paper on a pile on the far side of her crowded desk. Maria recognised it as her own letter.

'You write in a fair hand.'

'Thank'ee, ma'am.'

'Thank'ee? You need to stop with all that nonsense. We're not on the farm or in the gutter now, Miss Keay. We say *thank you* at Harborne's and we enunciate clearly. We will not be having any of your *dunnas* and *wonnas* here. We are in the county town, not a sleepy backwater. We speak the Queen's English here. Now, you are not going to say *thank'ee* any more in this building, are you?'

'Nay, ma'am.'

'Not *nay*! You are no horse! *No*, ma'am! *No*!'

'No, ma'am.'

'I should think not.'

Why didn't Maria know about this? How could she have been so stupid as to speak like a country bumpkin? But everyone in Ironbridge spoke that way. Well, everyone except the ladies and gents of the richer families. They all spoke like the books Charlie taught from at school. You never read Shropshire words in books. It was just what people said out loud. But not here. Miss Bytheway had a Shropshire accent, there was no mistaking that. But she spoke in the way that ladies did, omitting all dialect words that a schoolteacher would never teach you to write. Maria felt as if she were in a new country now and must act accordingly. She had to speak like books did.

'Please forgive me, ma'am. I was a country girl, once upon a time, but I've lived in a town these last months and spoken properly for all the customers I serve. I am well read too, ma'am. I can speak however you want me to speak, I assure you.'

Miss Bytheway considered her a moment and Maria prayed

she wouldn't be thrown out. Miss Bytheway sighed and continued.

'Well, then. I see you have experience of all the major departments of ladies' dressmaking. Your reference from a Mrs Nixon of Wharfage, Ironbridge, was glowing, I must say.'

Maria beamed. Good old Mrs Nixon.

'So why should the first and the greatest department store in the whole county hire a shopgirl like you, Maria? What special qualities do you bring to this role?'

'Ambition, ma'am.'

'Ambition? You mean you'll be off with the first gentleman bachelor who gives you the glad eye and get married, eh? I've lost too many good shopgirls that way.'

'N—' Maria was about to utter a *nay* at Miss Bytheway and for a split second pictured herself hauled out of the room by her hair and thrown down the stairs. 'Indeed, no,' she switched to and hurried on, to cover the near-error. 'In fact, I've already had a marriage proposal and turned it down so that I could come and work here.'

'Have you now? So, you have different ambitions.'

'I am ambitious in my work. I have found my calling. I knew from a young age that shop work was the life for me. Not only do I know the ins and outs of all aspects of drapery, as you see from my letter and my current employer's reference. Yet also, I believe I have the measure of commerce, of how to please customers, and yet, at the same time, persuade them into spending more money than they ever intended.'

'Well, that is always welcome. And how do you propose to do that?'

Maria was warming to her theme now, shifting forward in her seat. 'My belief is that the best shopgirls form relationships with customers. We become their friends, the ones they confide in. A woman buying underclothes wants to talk to a friend about which combination to buy, which corset, which petticoat, which corset cover. Things they would never usually want to talk to a stranger about. This is why women want women to serve them, because they understand. We are here to listen, to make suggestions, to solve their little problems. And to serve their every need, being willing and polite at all times, even five minutes before closing on a rainy Friday night when we are on our last legs.'

Miss Bytheway smiled at this. She actually smiled! *I must be saying summat right*, Maria thought.

'I do not spend as much time on the floor as I used to,' said Miss Bytheway with a sigh, eyeing her paperwork. 'But I do recall that feeling of exhaustion very well. You make a good point, Miss Keay. Carry on.'

'Well, I think the best shopgirls know how to flatter the customer, without it sounding like you're flattering. Instead, it has to seem like we're just there to help them to make the right choices and that makes them feel good about themselves. And then they start to link in the back of their minds that coming to this store feels good. And, sooner or later, you'll find that ladies come to your shop more often than they actually need to because they *want* to, because being in your shop makes them feel better about themselves . . . And that's when you've got 'em.'

'*Them*, you mean.'

Maria had been so pleased with her little speech but now was terrified she'd tripped up, saying *'em* instead of *them*.

'I'm so sorry, ma'am. Of course, I meant *them*.'

But Miss Bytheway did not go off on another tirade about sloppy grammar. Instead, her eyes fell and she looked about her desk for a few moments, thinking, making up her mind. Maria literally held her breath.

'Well, Miss Keay. I have my doubts about you. About the accuracy of your spoken language.'

'I'm such a fast learner, I swear. Ask Mrs Nixon, she'll tell you. And Mr Boden, he'll tell you too. I learnt all about tobacco and haircutting in the blink of an eye, before I turned my attention to drapery. I'll learn the right ways of talking in a jiffy, I know I will. And I promise you, Miss Bytheway, I could sell anything to anyone. Even milk to a cow!'

Then a magical thing happened. Miss Bytheway actually laughed. But was she laughing at Maria or with her? Another agonising moment passed and then Miss Bytheway sniffed decisively and put her hands flat on the desk.

She looked Maria square in the eye and said, 'Miss Keay . . . welcome to Harborne and Co.'

Chapter 10

August 1892

On the train home after her success, Maria relived every moment of the interview and its aftermath, when Miss Bytheway told her that she was to start work at Harborne's in a week's time, the following Monday. She'd be given two black dresses with white trim to wear for work, fifty per cent of the cost of which would be taken out of her first month's wages. The pay for her job as assistant would be twenty pounds a year. Twenty pounds! Much more than she was currently making. And that included board and lodging, something Maria had been worrying about as she had no idea where she'd start looking for lodging in Shrewsbury. But now she didn't need to. Miss Bytheway had explained that Maria would need to travel to Shrewsbury on the Sunday evening before, for five o'clock sharp, and she'd be given a room above Harborne's itself. What good fortune! Her own room above the shop!

Maria felt breathless with excitement still, as she sat on the train home, watching the landscape fly by. She felt like a totally different person than the one who'd seen this view in reverse, just that morning. Then something hit her with a jolt and made her heart sink: she had completely forgotten to mention Rosie to Miss Bytheway. How could she have forgotten her best friend so easily? She felt sickened with herself. It was just so all-encompassing at Harborne's, the whole experience, everything to take in and feverishly trying to say the right thing. Her mind had been overloaded and couldn't think of everything, she told herself, trying to excuse her terrible oversight. She wracked her brain, trying to think how to explain this to Rosie, and came up with nothing, every excuse sounding more like a slap in the face. She'd think about it later. She also had Charlie to think of, how she'd break it to him that she'd got the job. She still felt resentful that those closest to her would not be happy for her. She tried to imagine what her parents would say, that their little'un had got a job at fancy Harborne's in fancy Shrewsbury. *Good on yer, wench!* her dad would've cried and lifted her up and swirled her around. Her mam would've given her a quick cwtch, which meant a lot coming from her. They would've been so proud.

Back in Ironbridge, Maria gave her notice to Mrs Nixon, who congratulated her genuinely. She even said she could keep the outfit, as a leaving present. What a generous woman she was.

'I'll never forget your kindness,' said Maria, welling up. Mrs Nixon patted her arm. It was all becoming real now: she was leaving this familiar place and entering the unknown. Exciting, yes, but also rather scary.

Then Mrs Nixon said she was just popping out for a few minutes and Maria could mind the counter. Now, Maria was alone in the shop with Rosie in the next room. She had to get it over and done with. She went through to find Rosie sewing away at something like mad, the sound of the sewing machine filling the awkward air between them. It was difficult to interrupt it, but Maria knew she had to.

'Rosie,' she said, and the sewing machine continued without pause. Rosie did not look up. 'Rosie, please.'

Rosie stopped and looked up, fire in her eyes. 'So you got it, then?'

'I did.'

'Congratulations,' said Rosie, with a heavy dose of sarcasm.

'Thank you,' said Maria, without realising Miss Bytheway's advice had changed her already.

'Thank *YOU* ?' gasped Rosie. 'Oh, she's a fine lady, this'un. No more thank'ees for this'un. Thank *YOU*, says the wench, like Lady Muck. You're a kelter-jumper is what you are.'

'Whatever is a kelter-jumper?'

'You wouldna know since you're a lady now. It's a working girl who gets above their station, that's what, and turns her back on her own kind. And I dunna suppose you mentioned me at all? I dunna suppose I entered your busy little mind for a moment.'

'Course I did!' cried Maria, without meaning to. She'd half-decided to tell the truth, but the lie came so easily and, now it was done, she couldn't take it back.

Rosie narrowed her eyes at Maria and said, 'Did you though?'

'I did.' She had to go through with it now the lie was begun. 'I said all about your skills and different outfits you've made and different materials you handle and all that. But the lady who interviewed me, Miss Bytheway, she said they have more than sufficient seamstresses at present and they've had a slew of applications from girls claiming all sorts of experience. Yet at their interview they were given a test and it proved that hardly any of them actually had the skills they claimed, wasting their time. So they're taking applications only by word of mouth now, referred from other trusted staff members.'

She astonished herself at how easy it was to lie, how good she was at it. She even convinced herself, for a moment, that this had really happened.

'Danker me, you lie easily, Maria Keay,' said Rosie, with venom.

Maria was dumbstruck.

'And see, you're not even bothering to deny it. Too much detail, that was the giveaway. When people tell the truth, they dunna go into all the story of it, not like that. You've given yourself away now. It's bad enough you stole my dream from me. But then to deliberately not mention me in the interview to keep your precious job to yourself. And then to lie about it afterwards? You're wicked. You're . . . you're a prize bitch.'

Maria had nothing to say. Rosie wasn't totally right – it really had been a mistake not mentioning Rosie and she doubted Miss Bytheway would've listened anyway – but Rosie was correct about the lying and that just made Maria seem a hundred times worse. She had to take it on the chin.

'Sorry you feel that way. None of this was intended. I was just overwhelmed in the interview and I forgot, I truly did. I'm sorry. I didna want it to work out like this.'

'You did, you did!' cried Rosie. 'When I showed you that drawing of Harborne's, you decided there and then to take my dream from me out of spite.'

'I didna! I'd never do such a thing. How could you think that of me?'

'Everyone thinks that of you. Everyone in town thinks it. Getting above your station. Walking out with Charlie Wood-vine, the schoolmaster, with your nose in the air like the Queen herself.'

Is that what everybody thought of her? Maria had no idea. She didn't think she was better than other people. It was all so unfair.

'Rosie, you know me. You know I inna like that. And what's Charlie got to do with it?'

Rosie laughed, a cold, hollow laugh. 'Charlie Woodvine is in his late twenties and unmarried, the nicest-looking, sweetest and most upstanding bachelor in Ironbridge. Dunna you realise every girl in town has been trying to get Charlie sweet on them for years? But nay, he's turned his nose up at all the local girls, until you swanned in and stole his heart. You put a hex on him. Witches can have yellow hair and big blue eyes too, you know.'

'I did no such thing. This is madness! Rosie, I'm sorry for what's happened. But none of it is my fault. And I dunna think I'm better than anyone, least of all you. You really are my best friend. Please, canna we get past this? I'm sorry I made a mess of things. But when I get to Harborne's I will be trying night and day to get that interview for you, believe me, I will.'

'I dunna want it now! You've ruined it for me. The sooner you've left, the better. And more fool you, following some stupid shop job and leaving Charlie Woodvine behind when you coulda been his wife already. You're a fool, Maria Keay. I canna stand the sight of you.'

'Those are cruel words, Rosie,' said Maria, with all ideas of mending her friendship gone now. It seemed that months of resentment had been brewing in Rosie unknowingly. And others in town. To think, Maria had been the focus of the town's gossip for months and she had no idea.

'Ach, get away from me,' spat Rosie and set to her sewing machine again.

At that moment, Mrs Nixon came back into the shop and Maria hurried through to the counter to look like she was busy.

The rest of the day dragged by and then came home time when she and Rosie would normally walk back together, but Rosie rushed off first without her. And a good thing too actually, as Charlie appeared at the door as Maria was about to leave just after eight at night.

'Walk you home?' he said with a smile. It was so nice to be smiled at, after hours of Rosie's anger radiating throughout the shop.

'Yes please,' Maria said. 'But where's Biscuit?'

'He's at home. We went on an epic walk this evening and he's flat out, asleep on the rug. I didna wanna disturb him. And anyway, I quite wanna be alone with you, Maria, if that's all right?'

'That is indeed.'

They set off.

'I got the job,' she said.

Charlie smiled again. 'I knew you would. Who could turn down Maria Keay?!'

'Oh, believe me, Miss Bytheway could've easily!'

As they walked through the town, some shops still open and others pulling down their shutters, Maria told him in great detail everything about Harborne and Co. He listened and nodded and asked lots of questions.

'Well done, Maria. Truly. What you did was not easy at all, by any stretch of the imagination. For a young woman in your position, with your background and the tragedy you've come from, to walk into a job at the best store in the county is really quite something. I think you're an extraordinary person.'

'You do?' said Maria, suddenly overcome. She hadn't realised how much Charlie's approval meant to her until she got it.

'Listen, let me tell you something,' he said. 'I just read in the newspaper that a new member of parliament had been elected. An ex-collier called Keir Hardie for the Independent Labour Party: a brand new party to represent the interests of working people. It's quite something. He taught himself to read and write, just as you educated yourself after being removed from school too young. Hardie supports women having the vote as well. People like Hardie give hope to working folk everywhere. Things are moving on. Change is coming. They say when Hardie entered parliament, he wore a cloth cap and tweed suit, unlike all the rest of the toffs in their frock coats and top hats. I wish I coulda seen their faces!'

'Times really are a-changing!' said Maria. She didn't know much about politics, but she did know it was mostly the domain of the rich and to think of a working man in a cloth cap entering parliament was mind-boggling.

'They truly are! And listen, Maria. I want to tell you that I am extremely proud of you for all you've achieved and are yet to achieve, truly I am.'

'I'm so happy to hear that,' said Maria and took his arm, sliding hers around his. 'I've missed you. I've missed our talks and walks. I've missed having your good regard of me.'

'I've missed you too. And you never lost my good regard. You never could. And I'm sorry about how unsupportive I've been. It was wrong of me. You're absolutely right, that if I love you, then I must support your dreams and ambitions. And I do. I understand that will mean that we canna marry, so I wanna say that I will always be your friend. And I hope you'll allow me to write letters to you, to keep in touch. And perhaps to visit you from time to time to see how you are getting on.'

This idea, that they could never marry, was not one that Maria had fully considered. And it felt like a heavy stone in her pocket to hear Charlie speak it aloud. Perhaps his feelings for her had changed. Perhaps he'd gone off her. She withdrew her arm and felt suddenly lumpish and unwanted.

'But I'm not saying no to marriage in the future, Charlie . . . Are . . . are you?'

'I know that and, nay, I inna ruling it out and you know it's my heart's desire. But also I think it is unfair on you to be engaged when you're just about to embark on this new enter-prise. You will have the engagement hanging over you, knowing that it acts in direct counterpoint to your ambitions in your work. An employer like Harborne's would never allow one of their workers to marry and stay in the job, we both know that. So, if you would do me the honour of being friends, that is how I would like to be. I canna think of not having a place in your life, even in some small way.'

'Of course we're friends, Charlie!' Maria said, so relieved to hear his feelings hadn't changed on that account. She linked arms with him again and he responded with a squeeze of her arm that brought them closer as they walked. 'And, Charlie, I'll need your support. I'm terrified!'

'Dunna feel afeared. It's time for a change and I'm proud of your place in that new movement towards a better future for all. You'll be grand, Maria. I just know it.'

They talked on, about the day, about school, about Shrews-bury. It was so easy to talk to him. She would miss him dreadfully. Upon reaching her house, he stood apart to go, staring at the ground, hands in pockets.

'I'll see you again,' she said. 'Before Sunday, before I leave.'

'I dunna think so, Maria,' he replied, still keeping his eyes down.

'But why ever not?'

He looked up at her. His eyes told it all. He didn't want her to go, she could see that immediately. 'If I see you again before you go, I'll try to make you stay and marry me. I know I will. I dunna have the strength for it. I want you to go and not look back. Promise me that? Dunna look back. Go and live your life. And I'll write to you there in due course. And if you want to, you can write back.'

'Course I'll write back!' said Maria, her eyes filling with tears. She threw her arms round Charlie and sobbed on his shoulder as he pulled her tight towards him. The feel of his body was comfort and electricity all at once and she wondered how she'd ever pull away from him because she never wanted to, not ever. In that moment, she wanted to be in Charlie's arms always. But she wanted her new job too, more than anything.

'Dunna cry,' he said softly in her ear. 'Dunna cry, my love.'

Maria forced herself to pull away. She feared changing her mind. 'Why does it have to be this way?'

'Because you have a dream and you mun follow it. Marrying, having babbies and staying at home dunna fit in with that. Not yet, at any rate. And not on our wages. Or with employers' rules about married women. The two things you want just dunna fit, like the wrong jigsaw piece, however much you force it.'

'It inna fair,' she said, thinking of Miss Bytheway: successful yet unmarried and presumably childless in her thirties. Would that be Maria's fate? Did she want that?

Charlie seemed to read her mind, as he often did. 'Dunna fret about the future. It inna happened yet, so let's wait and see what it brings. Go and be extraordinary, Maria Keay.'

He kissed her cheek and turned abruptly. She watched him walk away. He looked so alone without Biscuit. And she wanted to say goodbye to Biscuit too, the sweet little soul. As Maria watched Charlie Woodvine go, his long legs loping off down Hodge Bower, she heard the cries and laughs of punters in the Crown Inn along the way, cheering some unknown joke, probably someone dropping a glass. She felt a thousand miles away from ordinary life, from jolly times in the pub, from friendship with Rosie, from engagement with Charlie, from home in Ironbridge. She was leaving it all behind for a new life. But was it the right life for her?

Time will tell, she thought, something her mother always used to say when Maria got impatient, as she often did.

She turned towards her lodging house and grimaced at the thought of facing the next few nights sleeping in the same room as Rosie, who now hated her. She went in slowly, her heart heavy, her mind confused, her eyes nearly closing from sleep. It had been the longest, most wearing of days. But one thing remained: her success. And Maria decided, whatever happened next, she must be proud of that. Her new life was about to begin.

* * *

Sunday came and Maria boarded the train to Shrewsbury. The last few days had flown by, packing her few things, working out her notice, telling her good news and then saying goodbye to her cousin Rhoda, Mr Boden and the rest. All wished her well. She did not see Charlie again, keeping to their agreement. She did not speak a word to Rosie all that week, only because Rosie would not speak to Maria. It was hellish and thank heavens it was over now.

The train was half-empty, being a Sunday teatime, and the weather was overcast and strangely cool for August. Not exactly auspicious. She wished the journey was longer, as she felt she needed more time to prepare herself. But actually, when they arrived at Shrewsbury and she walked out onto the street, the excitement of her situation hit her and filled her with hope. Why had she been so down in the dumps all week? She thought, *Look at this place!* The sight of the fine buildings and myriad of shops enlivened her and brushed aside all doubt. She was on this path now and she was going to make the very best of it.

Chapter 11

'Follow me, Maria,' said Miss Bytheway. They left the corridor where Miss Bytheway's office was and took another set of stairs and went up one flight, then walked along a narrow corridor on the top floor. The walls were bumpy and uneven with ominous dark patches in some of the corners, which looked a bit mouldy. Maria was wondering where her room would be as there were not any doors along here. She hoped it wasn't too miserable, like this corridor. Finally, they arrived at a sharp left turn and there was an open door that led into a room. Maria followed Miss Bytheway inside.

Maria took in her surroundings. It was a long, narrow room with low beds spaced out along one wall, with three of the beds having a mirror attached to the wall behind them. Nobody was in the room. There were windows on the other wall, all flung open wide. Small wooden crates were used as tables beside each bed, upon which were to be seen a few oil lamps and tin mugs and female paraphernalia, all neatly lined up. There were no drawers. Some of the windows were blocked by dresses hung up on the curtain rails. There were no wardrobes to keep clothes in, yet every other bed had a wooden chest at its foot. And up here, on the third floor, despite the August day being somewhat cool for the time of year, it was hot and stuffy, even with the windows open. Maria suddenly felt utterly foolish for assuming she'd have her own room alone, but that was what she'd imagined when Miss Bytheway told her she'd live above the shop. Yet here was the truth of it: a dormitory with ten or so other girls, which was dismal and rudimentary to say the least. Maria recalled the tiny coffin-like room she used to sleep in at the farm and realised even that was preferable as at least she'd had her privacy.

'Here are your lodgings. Your bed is the one at the very end, you see? I've laid out your two work dresses on there. I'm surprised there's not at least one girl here to welcome you, but they're probably all out gallivanting on their day off. When they're back, someone will explain all of the ins and outs of accommodation here to you. Be minded that there is a list of rules pasted on the back of the door behind you and that you must adhere to these at all times. Now, tomorrow morning, you start at 7 a.m. sharp. Come to my office at that time, not a minute before or after. I'll take you to your department and explain your duties.'

With that, Miss Bytheway turned and left the room, probably glad to get away from the airless third floor. So this was where Maria would live for the foreseeable future. She shuffled past the beds, noticing how neat and precisely tucked in they all were. Her bed had the two dresses. They were good quality, she could tell. Black silk, white collar, white hem and white cuffs. There was a black silk bow with long ribbons to be tied at the neck, ruffles down the bodice, and black lace layered over the narrow skirt on each dress. They would not be easy to maintain day in, day out. But they were certainly smart and fashionable and something she'd never be able to afford on her own salary.

Maria sat down on the bed. It sagged and creaked. There was one thin, rock-hard pillow and a single sheet. She certainly would need no more coverage than this, as the room was already so stifling that Maria was damp with sweat. She wanted to tear off her clothes and sit in her thin cotton combination only, the one-piece underwear comprising top and bottom over which a girl would put her corset and petticoat. Could she do that? Well, nobody was here yet, so why not?

She found a single hanger on the curtain rail opposite her bed, arranged the two silk dresses onto it and hung it up over the window. She looked more closely at the crate beside her bed to find it was empty on the back side. She spied that other girls had stored some possessions in this empty space, with the rest in the chests. The chest nearest her bed was already full of clothes, so she decided to wait until the other girls arrived to ask where to put hers. Maria was feeling even stickier now. She took off her clothes and laid them down at the end of the bed, then threw herself down and lay flat out, trying to think of icy things – like the River Severn frozen over one winter when people went out and skated on it – all in an effort to cool down. It didn't work.

Her thoughts filled with the charm of the store downstairs, the beautiful visions the customers saw as they paraded serenely around it, and then there was this upstairs. It was a far cry from the glamour of the shop. Here again was that feeling of being caught between two worlds: the silk dress would present her to the public as genteel, but up here in the dormitory she knew her real worth.

Before long, she heard the sound of feet ascending the staircase and footsteps along the corridor. She jumped up and threw on her shirtwaist and skirt: her one decent outfit that Mrs Nixon had gifted to her. Maria was quite unwilling to be caught in her underwear in front of a bunch of strangers.

She was just tucking her shirtwaist in when the first women began filing into the room. Maria stood stiffly at the end of the bed.

'New girl!' someone yelled, though Maria couldn't see who, and the others pushed and shoved and giggled to see her. Maria gulped and tried to smile. After that momentary introduction, everybody ignored Maria and went to their beds, then started undressing. The woman in the bed next to Maria had stripped down to her combination and was brushing out her hair from its previous tight bun. She was tall, with long, straight brown hair she was obviously proud of, as she brushed it lovingly and stared at herself in the mirror above her bed. She did have gloriously shiny tresses, so Maria didn't blame her.

Once she'd brushed it out, she twisted it into a loose bun and, still standing, turned her attention to Maria, thankfully, for Maria was feeling extremely awkward, standing there alone, ignored by everyone.

''Ow do,' the young woman said, politely. 'What's your name?'

'Maria Keay. And hello.'

'Hello to you. Miss Bytheway says you're to work with me on the gloves counter.'

'Am I? I didna know that.'

'It's nice on there but a bit dull. We dunna have to lug heavy goods around, but I feel like I know everything there is to know about gloves now. I've been here for a year.'

'Well, I dunna know a huge amount about gloves so I'll be very glad of your company. If you dunna mind me asking the odd question of you?'

'Course. I did the same with the old-new girl. She didna stay long though. Left to get married. To a gent she met in the shop. It happens, you know. We serve ladies, but sometimes the gents come in to buy gloves for loved ones and . . . well, some of them, they canna help themselves with shopgirls.'

'I know what that's like,' said Maria and told the young woman all about working in the tobacconist's and what the men could be like in there.

'There's summat about a shopgirl to these men,' the young woman said, sitting down on her bed and reclining, propping herself up with her one, hard pillow placed on its short end. 'I think it's because they dunna know what to make of us. Are we common or do we stick our noses up in the air? Or are we somewhere in between? Whatever it is, they like it. And they think we're all for sale, like the merchandise.'

The woman's voice was soft and soothing, as smooth as her hair. And she spoke properly, enunciating each word precisely. It was nice to listen to. She had quite beguiling eyes, like a cat's. Maria felt quite in awe of her self-assurance, as she felt very nervous herself surrounded by all these new people.

'Would you tell me your name?'

'I'm Gwen. Gwen Steele. Where've you come from then?'

Maria explained about Ironbridge and the draper's shop. She didn't talk about her parents. That wasn't something to assault someone with on first meeting, she decided. She just said she'd grown up on a farm. And that she was ambitious to make her way in the retail world.

'Ah, we're all ambitious here. We all wanna make summat of our lives. Either within the shop or without. So what do you make of the place so far?'

Maria hesitated. Would she sound like a snob to tell the truth and say what a dump this dormitory was? Would Gwen take offence?

'It's very glamorous . . . downstairs.'

'Quite right. And how do you find the accommodation?'

Gwen's face didn't give away a thing. She didn't roll her eyes or smirk to show her true feelings. Maria decided that honesty was the best policy. Start as she meant to go on.

'I think it's . . . awful.'

Gwen laughed a languid, relaxed laugh. 'You're spot on there, Maria. It's a grim little hovel.'

'It really is! I imagined . . . well, something very different from this.'

'Me too when I first got here,' said Gwen, 'and they said I'd be living in, I was all for it. Until I saw what it was like. But there's no escape from it. If you work here, you have to live in. That's the rule. And they can set any rent and any rules they like.'

'Miss Bytheway mentioned the rules on the door. I haven't seen them yet.'

'There are a hundred of them. No exaggeration.'

'A hundred?!' cried Maria. 'That sounds like the army!'

'Our great and glorious leader Mr Harborne does run this place with military precision, that's for sure.'

'What's Mr Harborne like? I havna met him yet.'

Gwen made a sharp intake of breath and raised her eyebrows. But she didn't get to answer because one of the other women called over to her.

'C'mon, Gwen. Shake a leg. We're off out in five minutes.'

'Hold your horses,' Gwen said lazily and yawned luxuriously, stretching out on her bed. So long were her legs, her feet poked right over the edge.

Maria smiled nervously. Was everybody going out? Looking around, it certainly seemed that way, as everyone was having a quick wash with a basin, jug and washcloth, before changing into evening clothes. They had the most marvellous outfits, streets above anything Maria owned. There were skirts and dresses of every hue, with fancy petticoats in contrasting colours, huge oversized leg-of-mutton sleeves on their blouses, with bows and ribbons and lace and ruffles pinned here, there and everywhere. Everybody had bracelets too and matching gloves. And the hats they pinned on were like something Maria had only seen on Easter Sunday in Ironbridge – boaters piled high with artificial flowers and little birds and all sorts, and many of the women had a parasol to complete the look. If everyone was going, which it looked like they were, would Maria be invited? She didn't want to be left here alone.

Then Gwen turned back to Maria and said, 'Fancy a stroll? We're off out for a walk. Back by ten o'clock on the dot or they lock you out. But we have a few hours yet.'

'Can I come?'

'Course.'

'But I dunna . . . Well, what I'm wearing is the nicest thing I've got.'

'Well,' said Gwen, eyeing Maria's outfit up and down, 'we canna have that. You'll have to save up for summat new with your first few pay packets . . . Till then, we've got to keep up appearances for the Harborne shopgirls out on the town, you know. I'm too tall for you to borrow from me, but I reckon Polly is about your frame.'

Gwen called over and a small, slight woman answered, about Maria's height and build. Gwen was right; they were a good match.

'New girl is coming out with us and doesn't have a stitch to wear. Lend her summat, will you?'

'If I mun lend it, I will,' said Polly, in a squeaky, piercing voice. 'But just be glad it inna raining as I wouldna let you get the hem all muddy if it were. C'mon, new girl. Try this'un on. It's a bit last season, so I dunna wear it so much any more, but it'll do for you.'

Maria hurried over eagerly and held up the dress that Polly thrust at her. Maria had never worn anything so colourful. It was a bright pastel purple, a kind of overblown lilac, with yellow frills placed at every opportunity.

'Ooh, that does suit you. What's your name?'

'I'm Maria. Are you sure you dunna mind me borrowing it? Does it really suit me?'

Polly helped her on with it, doing up the buttons that stretched across Maria's chest.

'You have a bigger bust than me!' laughed Polly. 'But it just about fits. And these colours really bring out your eyes. And your hair. You're a stunner, you are, new girl!'

Maria turned to look at herself in the mirror. She'd never looked so fancy. She didna know girls her age and class wore such deliciously gaudy things. She adored it. It felt like summer sprung to life in a dress.

'Thank'ee so much, Polly,' beamed Maria, admiring her figure in the mirror.

'Ah, you're a sweetie,' said Polly. 'It's my pleasure. You'll certainly get us some attention with your attributes, dearie.'

'Here, Maria,' said Gwen, dressed now in her own gorgeous outfit, a vibrant blue skirt and matching bodice which really complemented her shining brown hair she was pinning up. 'I've a hat with lilac flowers on it. In my chest there, at the end of my bed. Or, should I say, our chest. We'll be sharing it from now on.'

Maria came over and searched inside the chest, in a pile of layers of stunning skirts, bodices, dresses and hats in every shade. She found the boater with the lilac flowers on it, a perfect match to her outfit. Maria stood up and pinned on the hat to her hair, which was still tied in a low bun at the nape of her neck, her curled fringe nestling against the hat's brim, which looked as fetching as she'd ever seen herself. She felt like an utterly new person, reborn.

Gwen stood beside her and nodded her approval. 'Definitely worthy of being seen as a Harborne girl now.'

'Thank'ee, Gwen. I'm so grateful. I dunna know how to thank'ee properly.'

'Oh, we'll find a way, I'm sure. That's what we do here. We all look out for each other, one way or another. Come on then. Let's get going. Shrewsbury awaits.'

The rest of the girls were heading out now, all dolled up to the nines. Maria had no parasol, but she had a little evening purse she'd been given by cousin Rhoda after the baby had come, as Rhoda had said, 'My days of stepping out are over.'

Maria followed along, Gwen and Polly chatting away behind her. Everyone trooped down three flights of stairs and came out in a lobby Maria hadn't seen before. It led to a door outside, so she surmised it must be the workers' entrance. Just beyond the threshold, to the right, were the wide doors of the Harborne warehouse, where deliveries must be made, Maria guessed. They passed these by and strode out onto High Street. Maria had no idea where they were going or what they were going to do, but she was struck instantly by the effect such a brightly coloured gang of lively shopgirls had on passers-by. She saw more than one woman shake their heads and tut at them. And she saw many men ogle them all, herself included.

Maria looked back at Gwen and fell into step beside her. 'Where are we heading, Gwen?' she asked excitedly. There was little of anything to do in Ironbridge of an evening, except the pub. But here she guessed there must be a theatre and music hall and who knew what else.

'Nowhere in particular. We'll find a café at some point, no doubt.'

'So where are we walking to?' replied Maria.

'Nowhere!' laughed Polly. 'We're just out and about. On the town.'

'Perambulating,' said Gwen with a wink. 'To see and be seen by the gents of Shrewsbury. And the gents do love you, Maria Keay. Polly, have you seen the way they're salivating?'

'Dogs and hot sausages come to mind!' said Polly and

roared with laughter, then linked arms with Maria and gave her a quick cwtch. 'Come on, Beauty. Let's have some fun!'

And so the Harborne shopgirls perambulated the night away, a drink here, a snack there, laughing, walking, making eyes, telling tales and fending off any unwanted attention, while welcoming the ones they wanted. The men proliferated as night came on, seemingly everywhere, surrounding them, eager to chat with Maria and all the girls, telling saucy jokes and winking and trying to slip an arm round a waist or two, which were smartly fended off. Gwen made it quite clear to Maria that Harborne girls kept their virtue to keep their jobs. Men could look but they couldn't touch. That was the Harborne girls' way. Maria had never had a group of friends like this before. The other girls took her in as one of their own, talking about her gorgeous hair and her perfect skin and cornflower blue eyes and 'wasna she lucky with her hourglass figure!' and 'She doesna even need a corset really!' and 'She'll be netting a rich gent by the end of the week at this rate!' And Maria laughed and chatted and drank and talked all evening and had never had such fun. Ironbridge felt a thousand miles away. She was a Harborne girl now.

Chapter 12

August – September 1892

Maria was walking towards the railway station, grasping her ticket to Ironbridge. She looked up at the clock-tower, but this time, instead of a clock, there was a bell, a huge great shiny thing. And it started to swing back and forth and its bellowing peals rang out across town. She stopped and watched the bell and heard its insistent chimes when someone tapped her on the shoulder roughly and she turned around to see Gwen.

'Wake up, Maria,' she was saying. 'Wake up!'

And then Maria did wake up. She was in her hard little bed above Harborne's. And Gwen was trying to get her up. There was a bell on the wall outside the dormitory, ringing shrilly in short bursts, which then suddenly stopped, thankfully. Everyone else was up and out of bed. It must be 6 a.m., the time a Harborne girl's day started. There were jugs and basins on each chest and girls were giving themselves a quick wash all over, before pulling on their corsets and dresses. Maria followed suit. She didn't have any soap or towels as they did, though.

'Where do I find them?' she asked Gwen.

'You have to buy your own. You can borrow mine for now. Privies are on the next floor down, where the seamstress dorm is. Hurry now as there'll be a big queue. And you'll need a tinkle, as they dunna let you go all day when you're on the shop floor.'

Privies indoors? This was the first time in her life that Maria had had indoor toilets. She couldn't quite believe it and felt she really had made it now she could use a privy indoors. She rushed downstairs to sort that out and then rushed back up to wash. As she did so, she relived the previous night's shenanigans, cut short by having to hurry back at five minutes shy of ten, with one of the stern doormen from the store acting as security to ensure they'd arrived before the doors were bolted. Nobody in or out. She had put her clothes away in the chest she now shared with Gwen, as well as a couple of items she stacked in the back of the crate, such as her hairbrush and her beloved copy of *Treasure Island*. She was careful of Gwen's things, which included five books piled up, all volumes of an encyclopaedia. It was nice to know someone else round here liked reading. After that, Maria had gone out like a light, exhausted. After seven hours of sleep, she thought she'd wake refreshed, but she actually felt dead on her feet. Perhaps it was all the kerfuffle of moving, and meeting new people, and spending the evening out on the tiles. Whatever the reason, she had to shape up as it was her first day of work in her new job and she was set to impress.

At six-fifteen, another bell rang, and nobody paid it any mind, so neither did Maria. All the girls started to dress, pulling on their identical black silk frocks. As the women were dressing, it was clear that there was no alternate sizing in the dresses they were given, as for some girls the dresses ballooned around their thin frames and for others the silk stretched awkwardly across their chests. Those with fuller figures had to resort to tighter corsets to make the dresses fit. Maria worried now about her own dresses. She was quite short herself, with a little waist but a large bust, so perhaps the dress would be far too long and far too tight on top. She glanced at them hanging up and knew she had to get on with it but dreaded the humiliation of finding that her dress didn't fit right in front of everybody else. There was no choice about that, though. No privacy here whatsoever. She pulled on her dress and was relieved to find it was a fair enough fit, a little tight across the chest but not too bad. Then, at six-thirty, while she was still pinning up her hair into a neat chignon, another bell rang and everyone in the room started to move towards the door.

'What do the bells mean?' she asked Gwen, who told her each one was for a different breakfast sitting. Theirs was always six-thirty to six-forty-five. Fifteen minutes for breakfast, that was all. They trooped down the back stairs and into a large room with a row of wooden benches and tables, from which a group of shopmen were just leaving. They winked and whispered to some of the girls as they came in, with a few marking out Maria as new and worthy of attention, yet it only lasted half a minute or less as they were heading out of a separate exit as the girls came in and sat down. At the other end of the room, in a section marked off with small tables and proper chairs, sat a collection of smartly dressed men with a couple of women, all eating eggs and bacon. It made Maria's tummy rumble, so good did it look and smell. She was delighted to see they'd be well-fed here and licked her lips in anticipation. Kitchen staff brought out the plates for the shopgirls, which had bread and butter on each. A tea urn was out and the girls went up to fetch their tea, milk and sugar, then shuffled back to their bread. Maria thought she'd save her bread till the eggs and bacon came, so she could mop up the yolk and bacon fat – *mmm, delicious*. But the other girls were eating their bread already, so she felt she ought to do the same. Once they'd finished their bread and drunk their tea, a bell rang again and the girls moved towards the same exit the men had left from, another group of women coming in after them from another dormitory somewhere else in the vast building, Maria supposed. The managers stayed where they were, enjoying their meal in far more leisure than the shopgirls' fifteen minutes had afforded them.

'Where's our eggs and bacon?' Maria whispered to Gwen and Polly. Gwen just looked at her quizzically, then laughed. Nothing more needed to be said as Maria realised how things would be here. One rule for the managers and another for the minions. *Bacon for them, bread for us.*

Polly said, 'The smell of that bacon drives me stark staring mad. One day I'll marry a rich man and we'll have bacon for breakfast, lunch and dinner every day of the week.'

One day I'll earn enough to buy my own *bacon and have it for breakfast, dinner and supper every day of the week,* thought Maria, though she didn't say it out loud. It sounded like bragging, but actually, it was what she truly believed. Maria just had to work as hard as she could and impress all the right people. And that started now.

Maria knew she had to meet Miss Bytheway at her office at 7 a.m., so she decided to go up there straight from breakfast, asking Gwen the way. She found the familiar staircase and was outside the office by ten to seven. Miss Bytheway was already in there, scribbling away at something. Maria waited to be summoned. Eventually, another bell rang throughout the building at 7 a.m. and Miss Bytheway came out. She gave Maria a quick once-over glance, nodding with approval. Then she leant towards Maria's armpit and gave a quick sniff. Nobody had ever done that to Maria in her life before.

'Good. Harborne girls must be scrupulously clean and smart at all times, no exceptions. You must strive to be the neatest and most comely of all the shopgirls. That's the first step to getting ahead. Now then, follow me and I will take you on a tour of the whole store. You must get to know the layout of the whole place, including all of the departments, so that you can reliably inform customers of where they must go for any type of merchandise, in order to encourage them to visit more departments than they might have under their own volition.'

All of this was explained as they descended the staircase and then walked across the ground floor. Each department was already a hive of activity, with shopgirls and shopmen rushing around, setting up their counters with displays of goods, checking inventories, filling their tills with change and a thousand other jobs. On the ground floor was everything to do with ladies' outfitting. Miss Bytheway led Maria past dress materials, including linens, silks, velvets, lace and the infamous colienne which neither Maria or Rosie had heard of (and it seemed it was a kind of lace). They went on past gloves, morning dresses and gowns for tea, balls and fêtes alongside evening gowns, then to mantles, theatre and opera cloaks, furs and millinery. There was even a section for bicycle attire: fashionable yet practical costumes for the modern lady cyclist. Beyond this were the smaller counters for feathers, artificial flowers, trimmings, ribbons, lingerie and hosiery, shoes and boots, and jewellery, alongside umbrellas and parasols. Then they came to a wall, through which was a glass door, opened for them by a smart doorman, who winked at Maria. They went through it and found more hats and gloves, along with a large haberdashery department, and beyond this stretched rows upon rows of rails upon which were hung women's ready-to-wear outfits.

Miss Bytheway stopped then and turned to Maria, saying, 'You will have noticed, no doubt, that the goods on this side of the store are of a less – shall we say – fancy nature than those on the other side of the store. This section and the last have separate entrances, policed by our sharp-eyed doormen who are responsible for sending each customer to the part of the shop most suited to their purse. This part is for the customer who has to consider their economy first and foremost, who is quite happy to buy made-up goods which are then altered in our busy workrooms staffed by rows of seamstresses, just over there beyond that door.' Maria thought, *That is where Rosie would've worked*. But Rosie had treated Maria with such venom in those last days before she left that she decided she didn't want to put in a good word for her any more, so she kept silent on the subject.

They went up to the first floor and here was the gents' outfitters and all its separate departments, including boots, gloves and hats. Further on were hairdressing, an estate agency, services for cleaning and dyeing, funeral and undertaking, and items for hire. Lastly, they went up to the top floor, where could be found the restaurant, tea room, women's lounge and men's clubroom, alongside cloakrooms with lavatory facilities – for men only.

'You will of course note,' said Miss Bytheway in a low, urgent whisper, 'that there are no lavatory facilities for female customers, as of course, a public lavatory for women would be scandalous.'

'Of course,' said Maria. But it felt very unfair. A woman would have to go all the way home if she wanted a wee, but men could stay all day and drink as much as they liked with no fear of accidents. Rules – they always seemed to favour men.

Miss Bytheway then raised her voice and continued, 'You

will also have noticed, no doubt, that all of our goods have clear fixed, marked prices and the store has free entrance to all, unlike the bazaars of yesteryear. This is the modern way. Our floorwalkers are not here to tell people to buy or to leave and stop wasting everybody's time. Instead, our floorwalkers act as our security, sorting out interlopers, along with the doormen and store detectives. Customers are free to browse and enjoy the atmosphere. Coming to Harborne's should feel like a day out to our clientele. It is your job, however, to ensure that you use every manner of persuasion in your armoury to get them to leave with at least one purchase. That is your prime objective.'

'Yes, Miss Bytheway.'

'Good, now commit the three floorplans to memory so you can advise customers appropriately.'

The whole place was vast, and Maria feverishly tried to take it all in and remember what was where. It was, however, laid out with sense and purpose, which made it easier.

Back they went, downstairs to the gloves counter where Maria was to start her job and Gwen was already there, laying out on a counter display a selection of pure white lace gloves for summer evening wear.

Miss Bytheway continued, 'Lastly, as I'm sure you're aware by now, no assistant must at any time sit down during her working hours of 8 a.m. till 10 p.m., every day but Sunday.'

Fourteen-hour days, six days a week? Maria totted it up quickly in her head: that was nearly ninety hours of work a week. Ninety! Miss Nixon had been right. These hours were far longer than those she'd worked in Ironbridge. *Oh well,* she thought, *I'll be so busy, I'm sure they'll fly by.*

Miss Bytheway wasn't about to wait for the luxury of thinking time. She was already talking about something else, something about chairs: 'So, as I say, the many chairs you've seen dotted about the store are for customers only. You are only permitted to sit down to eat. Lunchtime is from twelve till two, staggered in four sittings, half an hour each. Teatime is six till eight, similarly. If you have no customers at any particular moment, then you keep yourself busy. It is imperative that customers see you busy at all times as that show of industry encourages them to buy more. You may busy yourself with other jobs, such as reordering the drawers and cupboards, dusting displays, watering pot plants, cleaning stock, polishing the counters and shelves, checking available stock lists and compiling reorders to send to me, if necessary. Understood?'

'Yes, Miss Bytheway.'

'The hierarchy within the store is as follows: Mr Harborne; the senior managers; the department heads – such as myself; then floorwalkers and other security staff; next, floor managers of each area; then shopmen and warehouse staff; then the lowest layer is shopgirls and delivery boys. Know your place, Miss Keay. I will be observing you at a distance, as well as having instructed specific other members of staff – as yet unknown to you – who will be observing you as well. I hope I receive good reports or I think we both know what will happen next.'

'Yes, Miss Bytheway.'

Then Miss Bytheway glanced up at the huge central clock, which hung from the ceiling and could be seen from just about anywhere on the ground floor, and she tutted.

'It has passed a quarter to eight. I must be gone. I will leave you in Miss Steele's capable hands. Do not let me down, Miss Keay.'

'I wonn—' Maria said with great confidence before stopping suddenly and correcting herself. 'I will not, Miss Bytheway.'

The woman squinted at her momentarily, then walked away swiftly.

Maria turned to Gwen and they both burst out laughing.

'I nearly said, *I wonna*!'

'You'd've been sacked on the spot if you had!'

'I know! Oh, my Lord!'

'Right, come on. Nearly opening time. Help me with this. Some new price cards to write out. We're having a little sale this week. Here's the list.'

And so Maria began her job at Harborne and Company of Shrewsbury. The first customers walked through the door just after eight, already eager to shop. None came to the gloves counter for a short while, so Gwen and Maria continued with their myriad of little jobs that needed doing. Maria glanced up to see the floorwalker for the ground floor approaching them, a stern-looking man in his later years, tall and exceedingly slim, slightly arched over like a longbow, with an impressive handlebar moustache. He walked by the gloves counter in a stately fashion, eyeing her with disdain.

'That's Mr Savage,' whispered Gwen.

'Savage? Is that your nickname for him?'

'Nay! That's his real name! He hates me. He hates everyone! Dunna smile at him. Or try to be nice. It never works. His favourite thing is finding reasons to dismiss people, especially us girls. And watch out for him if you ever see him behind the scenes. He has wandering hands.'

Maria made a mental note to avoid him as much as possible. Then their first customer of the day approached. A woman in middle age, beautifully dressed, looking for summer gloves for a garden party. Gwen took charge and Maria observed, to get the feel for how Harborne girls spoke to the customers. It was similar to how Maria had worked at Mrs Nixon's, but there was less natural friendliness and banter, which was common in the Ironbridge shops, where everybody knew everybody and often stopped to gossip. Here, in this much bigger town, there was the anonymity of strangers, and the shopgirls

147

had to breach that gap between themselves and the customer: to be polite and never over-familiar, yet also to be friendly and helpful, to put the customer at their ease.

The lady bought three pairs of gloves in the end: lace ones for the party and silk for the evening afterwards, as well as suede ones for the journey to and from the party, all artfully sold by Gwen.

Maria said, 'Well done. Three pairs! That's a proper good sale.'

'Thank'ee.'

'I think you're a very clever person. I saw your books in the dormitory. You like reading, then?'

'I like knowing things about the world. I dunna intend staying a shopgirl forever.'

'What do you want to be?'

'I dunno. What's open to girls like us anyway? We canna study, we dunna have the money to pay for it. But I do what I can to expand my mind, like reading.'

'You're a very impressive person, Gwen,' said Maria thoughtfully. She really meant it. To think, how many people came to their counter every day and would never have guessed of a shopgirl like Gwen that she read encyclopaedias in her spare time. 'And you're brilliant at sales.'

'That's kind. I suppose I am good at selling gloves. I am bored to tears of them, though. I wanna be on summat like evening gowns or furs, summat more glamorous. And where the tips from lady customers are regular and the work more interesting. I've been on gloves for a year and it's boring me to tears. And nobody ever tips for summat small as gloves. I'm sick of it.'

'You can make the time fly by teaching me then,' said Maria. 'I need it. Never sold that many gloves before. Show me the stock and the different materials and colours and qualities. I need to know everything.'

So that's what they did, in between serving customers and keeping busy. By midday, Maria suddenly realised how ready she was to eat. She was sent off at twelve, while Gwen would man the counter for a half-hour until it was her turn. Maria went to the canteen and saw Polly there, who was in millinery and as sick of that as Gwen was of gloves.

'Only good thing about it is being near the door, so you get the breeze coming in on a hot day like this.'

'It is warm back where we are at gloves.'

'It is! But constantly putting on hats to model them gets you a bit sweaty. The thing that's annoying about the front door is the gazer always coming in and bothering you.'

'What's a gazer?' asked Maria, flummoxed.

'Oh, they're hired by the shop. They're dressed up to look well-to-do and they stand on the pavement and *gaze* and *gaze* at the window displays, then talk really loudly about what a marvellous bargain it is, whatever's in the shop window, and then they make a big show of coming in the shop to buy it. So they march up to millinery as it's closest to the door and I have to pretend to talk to them and they're so annoying. I always whisper to tell them to bugger off and one time Savage caught me whispering and said he'd sack me if he ever heard the like again! I was lucky to get away with my pay docked. The damn gazer thought the whole thing hilarious till he got sacked for laughing!'

'Sacked for laughing?!'

'You can get sacked for sneezing in this place!' cried Polly in her squeaky high voice, just as they were called up to the food counter to fetch their lunch. It was white fish and potatoes. They sat down and Maria soon saw the fish was riddled with bones. It took her most of her remaining twenty minutes to extricate the meagre flesh from the poor creature's skeleton. She left the lunch table unsatisfied, to say the least.

The day wore on with more and more customers and a bit of a rush between three and five. Then it was time for tea at six, by which time Maria felt quite faint with hunger. Teatime's offering was bread and dripping. Tasty, but it didn't feel enough to sustain her until morning – none of these meals had. What she wouldn't give for a plate of her cousin's cold mutton right about now. At least it was filling. She never thought she'd miss Rhoda's cooking. They were only given fifteen minutes for tea, so she had to wolf it down and then rush back to her station, her guts rumbling with indigestion.

The one point of the day which made her wake up thoroughly was when Gwen nudged her hard with her elbow and said, 'Look, that's Mr Harborne.'

A man in a dark grey three-piece suit and pale blue cravat was walking slowly between the counters, smiling beatifically. He had the most extraordinarily large white mutton-chop sideburns, which descended to his chin and poked out on either side in fluffy triangles. His head was mostly bald, with a rim of white and grey hair around the back. He was portly and small, with a puffed-out chest. All shopmen in his path stopped, stepped aside and gave a quick bow, with a curtsey from shopgirls. He nodded at each, then stopped to speak to some customers near to the gloves counter, so Maria could hear their conversation.

There was a rich lady complimenting him on the floral displays in the gowns department, for which he thanked her graciously. She then went on to say how impressed she was with the staff, particularly the girls, who all spoke perfect English.

'Unfortunately,' said the lady, 'one does hear the odd shopgirl speak in the local dialect and it is most off-putting. I am pleasantly surprised by how well you've trained them out of this and for such of their class to be so well-behaved in general.'

'I like to hire the best of the most best suited . . . in terms of people for the best job . . . for their type of person,' said Mr Harborne, 'regardless of social status. Here we have a daughter of a man of the clergy persuasion . . . working alongside the son of a dustman, that is, a man of the dustbins. And both have been hired for their talents, regardless of class.'

'I applaud you,' replied the lady. 'A dear friend of mine is married to a retired colonel and their daughter wishes to work in a respectable industry. You've convinced me that shop work could well be ideal.'

'I certainly do agree. Every shopgirl working at my establishment can be sure, and indeed surely be certain . . . that she is now part of a protective and righteous place, or may I say, location, or environment. Females are at the very heart of my business and, dare I venture to dare to say . . . my shopgirls are the finest in Shropshire.'

'I do not doubt it!' said the lady and took her leave, Mr Harborne continuing on his leisurely way, moving further along, deeper into the shop.

'Well, well,' said Maria. 'So that's Mr Harborne. He does speak a bit odd. But seems nice.'

'Humph,' muttered Gwen. '*Seems* is the apt word. He's altogether different behind closed doors. Look out for him if he starts paying you too much attention. He's had quite a few girls in this store and he even married one of us. They say he has babbies with a few of them. He likes the pretty'uns, although he has a type – going for them with dark eyes and dark hair – so you might be all right and escape his attention.'

Maria knew of the wicked ways of men, but she was surprised to hear this. Harborne looked like a kindly grandfather, not a molester of young women, producing base-born offspring with all and sundry. *Just goes to show, you canna tell by looking,* she thought.

The rest of the evening dragged by until ten at night. Most of the customers were perfectly polite. But why on earth anyone would be buying gloves gone nine at night was beyond Maria. Gwen told her, 'You should be grateful at least you inna on the commoner's side of the shop, as the well-heeled are always more polite than the middling sort. They get some right rowdy types on the other side of the wall. I suppose parting with money is more urgent with them. You can afford to be nicer when you're wealthy.'

But Maria didn't feel she had much to be thankful about at all. After fourteen hours of standing up, with only an hour's total break out of the whole day, she felt deceased on her feet as she dragged herself upstairs to the dormitory with the rest of the girls. She wrenched off her dress, corset and stockings, hung them up and collapsed on her bed. She'd told herself she must look tonight at the one hundred rules that were affixed to the back of the door, but she was too exhausted. Her feet were aching like mad and her head was swimming. She heard the girls around her chit-chatting about the day while they undressed and brushed their hair. Maria hadn't even taken out her hairpins or put her fringe into rags for tomorrow's curls. She was face down on her cot and, within seconds, she was sleeping the sleep of the dead.

Chapter 13

The next few weeks of summer went by, each day more tiring than the one before. Maria's feet, having been forced to stand for over thirteen hours a day, suffered with an ever-increasing range of blisters and her ankles ached constantly. Every morning when she got out of bed and stood up, her ankles nearly gave way as a sharp pain radiated up her legs. She wondered if this was how it felt to be an elderly woman, but it was her young body that felt it, old before her time. It would've helped if the food they were given sustained them adequately to give them the energy to get through these Herculean days, but that did not improve. Breakfast was either watery porridge or bread and tea. Lunch was fish and boiled potatoes or fish soup, sometimes sheep or pig's trotter stew or boiled offal with turnips. Tea continued to be mostly bread and dripping, or they might get lucky and be given a small lump of cheese. In the evenings, most girls went straight to sleep as there was no time after work to go out due to the curfew. Sunday was the only day when they had the luxury of eating out as much as they liked, as no meals were provided by Harborne's that day. They had to time it carefully as many eateries in Shrewsbury were closed until 1 p.m. and again between three and six on a Sunday. Maria took to eating three large meals on a Sunday if she could, to somehow make up for the measly offerings she had the rest of the week.

But Maria's wage packet was slim, not only because she was paying off the two silk dresses she had to wear, but also because so much was taken out of it for rent and board there was little left. She spent much of it on her Sunday treats, as she liked to think of them, eating large portions of fish and chips from the fryer down the road, or currant buns from the baker's, as well as drinks and snacks from the girls' nights out on the town. She tried to put aside a little to save up for some decent clothes to wear on their nights out but still couldn't afford to buy a whole dress. Luckily, her dormitory friends did not let her down and each week Maria borrowed a different dress off a different girl and got by that way. Her waking hours had become a whirlwind of work and play, with little time to think of anything else. She hadn't heard from Charlie yet and hadn't written to him either. She'd barely thought of him, not because she didn't miss him, because she did, sometimes with a deep pang when he popped into her mind. How she longed to tell him all the stories of her new existence. But her brain was replete with the newness of her days and nights, or else lost to the oblivion of much-needed sleep.

And the sleeping time the girls managed to carve out was never enough. One shopgirl on furs had her pay docked for yawning at work, thus Maria took great care to stifle every single yawn that crept up on her, of which there were many. One Saturday in September, when the weather had been very warm and the week even busier than usual with a snap sale, Maria was standing beside Gwen, who was talking to a softly-spoken lady at the counter, the lilt of their voices lulling her into sedation. Maria felt that if she just closed her eyes, she could fall asleep like a horse, standing upright. Her conscious mind told her she must do no such thing, but her subconscious mind fought against Harborne's rules and needed her to sleep more than any other thing in the world. Her eyes drooped down. *I'll just let them close for three seconds,* she thought foolishly. *Just three seconds. That will be plenty.*

'Miss Keay!' came a roaring voice and her eyes snapped open in terror.

Mr Savage, the dreaded floorwalker, was on the other side of the counter, staring at her with fury.

'Accompany me immediately!' he barked, and the lady customer appeared shocked. Gwen looked down at the counter, not getting involved.

Savage stalked off in the direction of the back stairs and Maria struggled to keep up.

Oh my Lord, this is it. I'm gonna lose my job, she thought feverishly.

Savage went through the door and stopped in the stairwell, hidden from view of the shop floor and anyone descending the staircase. Maria began her defence immediately, saying, 'Mr Savage, I'm so, so sorry. Please dunna sack me. I'm just tired after a long, busy week. It'll never happen again. Please, Mr Savage!'

'Silence!' he snapped. 'You were very lucky the customer did not notice your disgraceful behaviour. Imagine the effect on sales if all Harborne girls fell asleep at their station! Imagine if a soldier on guard fell asleep at his post! Imagine the deaths and disaster that would follow!'

Maria thought, *But we're not soldiers, for heaven's sake.* She wanted to say, *Nobody died.* But she didn't.

'Of course, and I'm so sorry, Mr Savage. I can only humbly beg your understanding and forgiveness.'

Then Mr Savage's face changed. He took a step closer to her.

'You'd like to beg me?' he said.

His handlebar moustache twitched in anticipation. Maria stared at it, unable to meet his eye. Was this what Gwen had warned her about?

'I want to apologise and assure you it'll never happen again, Mr Savage.'

'But you said you wanted to beg me, girl.'

His voice had changed. No longer a bark, now low and wheedling.

Maria continued to stare at the moustache. 'I do beg you, sir. And hope you'll take pity on my error, as being new to this establishment.'

'I'll take pity, girl, if I can put my hand up your skirt.'

She looked at him then, full in the eyes. He actually glanced away, unnerved by her direct gaze.

'If you put your hand up my skirt, I will scream.'

'I doubt that,' he said, a nasty smile twisting his lips.

'I will scream and scream so loudly, they'll come running from every counter and I'll swear blind you already put your hand up there and assaulted my person with cruel and lascivious intent.'

'You never would,' he said, narrowing his eyes at her.

He was so close, Maria could smell his soap and sweat.

'Try it and find out,' she said firmly, not looking away for a moment, not even blinking. He paused, then took a step back. Tugging down his waistcoat and smoothing back his oiled hair, he composed himself.

'Miss Keay, for the offence of attempting to sleep on duty, your pay will be docked four shillings.'

That was over half a week's pay. But it was worth it to keep Mr Savage's hands to himself.

'And if I ever see you transgress any rules here again, however minor, you will be sacked. Now get back to work, girl.'

Maria walked away swiftly. She was shaking. There was sweat trickling down her back and thighs. She had no idea where that resolve had come from. She didn't know how she came up with that threat. But it had worked. She'd always said things without thinking, and sometimes that had got her into trouble, but this time it was the one thing that saved her from a horrible fate.

She arrived back at the gloves counter to find Gwen dealing with a customer who couldn't make up her mind about the colour of the gloves she wanted to buy: beige, ecru or tan. Maria busied herself with putting some stock away in a drawer from a previous customer, her hands still trembling. *Make up your damn mind*, she wanted to shout at the woman. *All those colours are the damned same anyway!* After what felt like aeons, the woman finally paid and left.

Gwen put her hand on Maria's shoulder, which made her jump.

'All right?' Gwen whispered urgently.

'Yes, all right. I escaped.'

'Good,' said Gwen. 'Any punishment?'

'Docked four shillings.'

'Crikey,' said Gwen. 'Better than the alternative.'

Maria nodded furiously, then another customer approached. Gwen took over and Maria was able to calm herself, crouching down to place items in a bottom drawer, her head spinning. She had to get a hold of herself. She stood up and took a deep breath. She felt a bit better. The important thing was she'd won. She'd escaped. At that moment, she felt the strongest she'd ever been, despite her still shaking hands. And a new hate burgeoned in her, a loathing for men who abused their power. She'd seen it before in small ways but had never been confronted with it like this, not in her very face, as this man had been. Defiance roared in her. She would never succumb to a man like that again, not ever. Men thought far too much of themselves, she decided. And yet, in the society she lived in, there was nothing she could do about that. All of the power resided in their hands.

That night, Maria told the girls in the dormitory what Savage had done and they spilled out similar stories. Savage was not alone, either. Girls had been groped in the warehouse, by shopmen, store detectives and other floorwalkers. It was the norm and almost unremarkable.

'You just have to keep your wits about you,' said Polly and shrugged.

'But it inna right,' said Maria. 'We should be able to come to work and do it without fear of . . . well, of assault.'

'But Harborne is the worst of them, so what chance do we have?' said Gwen. 'He sets the tone.'

Everyone agreed on that and the conversation moved on. But Maria could not leave it alone so easily and it played over and over in her mind: how the shopgirls were not only treated like merchandise but also were held to a much higher standard than any man who worked in the store. Since she'd started, Maria had by now read the one hundred rules on the back of the dormitory door and tried to commit them to memory. Along with obvious offences, such as stealing or being rude to the customers, there were dozens of petty issues, such as the ribbons on a shopgirl's collar being of equal length, to possessing at least a half-cake of soap at all times, which meant you had to buy more when you already had half left. It was well known that department managers came to the dormitories when the girls were at work and riffled through their possessions to check they were following the rules and didn't possess any contraband.

One night, Maria came back to find her precious copy of *Treasure Island* splayed open on the floor, its pages dirtied with mud from shopgirls' boots. Maria was furious and tears actually sprang to her eyes at the sight of it. It was much more than just a book to her; it had been her father's favourite and Charlie loved it too. Charlie . . . how she missed him now. She hoped he'd write her a letter soon. She didn't feel able to write first since she was the one who went away. Maria wanted to know if he still had feelings for her and so felt it best to wait for him to break their silence.

A few days later, the issue of rules came to the fore again as three staff were all disciplined on the same day: a seamstress from downstairs had half a week's pay docked for bringing flowers into the dormitory, another a week's pay for not lacing her boots in the right way and another girl was sacked for not securing a sale with a rich customer in the jewellery department. The day after, a special meeting was called by Harborne after closing that night. The entire staff were gathered on the ground floor near the front doors, where Harborne stood chatting with his managers while everyone lined up and waited in silence. Nobody knew what he was going to talk about and everyone was shifting nervously and shooting each other worried glances.

Harborne turned and stood before them.

'It has come to my attention that there have been a number of rule-breakers disciplined on the same day recently, which brings to the forefront a general malaise and malfeasance . . . or rather malfeasant character of . . . that is . . . among my staff up with which I will not put up with . . . which. Thus, it behooves me to pronounce a stern chastisement upon you all that if there is not an instant improvement in disciplinary discipline . . . well, then a wave of sackings will occur and I will even go so far as to cancel all leave on Sundays for the

MOLLIE WALTON

next month in order to retrain those of you remaining staff who remain . . . of the staff. If you do not wish to lose your freedom in this manner, then may I remind you that you will only have yourselves to blame if this is occurring as it . . . occurs. Therefore, and particularly seeing as the recent three disciplinaries have involved shopgirls, I have been keeping a particular eye on my female staff, indeed both eyes . . . on both staff, but mostly of female persuasion, that is the women staff . . . and yes, make no mistake, I am appalled to report that I find many of them wanting. Some of the girls in my shop are not making enough of an effort to appear attractive at all times. They must make more effort with their complexion, sleep and neatness of the hair and attire. I saw one girl just this morning with a row of spots upon her chin. This is disgusting and no customer should have to look at that and if that girl – and she knows who she is – does not get her face sorted out she'll be sacked within the week ending at the end . . . of this week. I have also had reports of girls coming back late from evenings out, being escorted by unknown males of dubious character and even having inappropriate relations with other relationships with . . . well, with other staff. This is a disgrace and will not be borne. The male staff here have their own issues, particularly involving drinking on the job, which will also be met with immediate dismissal. But I must say I find myself most disappointed with my staff of the female persuading . . . of the type of female . . . and yes, this kind of sloppy behaviour will not be brookened . . . I mean, we will not be brooked . . . that is, it will not be borne, indeed.'

Maria had never heard anything quite like it. He spoke as if he'd cracked open a dictionary and swallowed it but half of it had dribbled down his chin and he had no idea what most of his words actually meant. She imagined how much she and Charlie would've laughed to hear him speak and how much

160

Charlie would've enjoyed analysing all of his strange grammatical constructions. But these were passing feelings as her most pressing reaction was rage. The suggestion that women had a duty to be beautiful filled her with an anger she'd rarely known. *Why are men not told they have to be handsome? How can a girl be blamed for a breakout of spots?* And the hypocrisy of punishing women for having relationships outside or inside of work . . . what about the men involved in those relationships?! Did they have no responsibility in the matter? The whole thing left Maria's mind in a turmoil of wrath. Again, back in the dormitory, everyone else just laughed about it, though some were worried about the idea of losing their Sundays. Others said he was just sounding off and he'd never do that.

'He's all mouth and no trousers,' said Polly and laughed.

But Maria wasn't laughing.

Over the next few days, she noticed Mr Harborne was making more regular checks on each floor of the store, standing and watching the way his staff worked. One Saturday, when Gwen had been off having her lunch, Maria was busying herself with a stock take when she spied Harborne making his way towards her counter.

Oh Lord, she thought, and tried to carry on and ensure she was doing everything right to avoid his ire. Mostly, Harborne simply observed a while, then walked on. He rarely came up to speak to the staff at counters, but this time he was walking straight to Maria's counter and her mouth turned as dry as sand as she saw him stop and clearly wish to speak to her.

'Good afternoon,' Mr Harborne said with an insipid smile.

Maria curtseyed and replied, 'Good afternoon, sir. How may I be of assistance?'

'You can tell me your name, which I am in doubt of

which . . . that it shall be a pretty one, to match the prettiness of your demeanour.'

'Thank you, sir,' she said and curtseyed again. 'My name is Maria Keay.'

'And you have been employed here on gloves for some time, since you started your employment here with us?'

'Indeed, sir, that is right.'

'Hmmm,' he said and raised his hand to his chin, stroking his beard thoughtfully as he looked her up and down, down and up, appraising every inch, or so it felt. Maria stood proudly and took it, though if a man had looked at her that way at Mr Boden's tobacconist's, her old boss would've clipped him round the ear.

Thankfully, at that moment, Gwen returned from lunch, and she happened to be in the company of Miss Bytheway, who was saying, 'A concession of black mourning gloves seems to have gone astray and I'm wondering if they've been delivered to your counter in error.'

Maria knew about that, as she'd taken the delivery not ten minutes before, so she glanced at Mr Harborne and asked, 'If it pleases, may I answer Miss Bytheway? As I have information she will find useful.'

'Of course, of course,' replied Mr Harborne.

'Mr Harborne, can I assist you in any way?' said Miss Bytheway, shooting a quick glance at the gloves counter to see if anything was attracting his negative attention.

'Yes, Miss Bytheway. This girl, Maria Keay. Why on earth is she working in gloves?'

Miss Bytheway looked nonplussed. In fact, none of them quite understood the question.

'Maria is one of our newest and yet also our best assistants and she does a very good job here on gloves,' said Miss Bytheway, which Maria was gratified to hear.

'But *gloves*, Miss Bytheway. This girl is far too pretty to be stuck here on gloves. You know we put the prettiest ones, the comeliest girls, in millinery. Customers want to see their new hats – or potentially new if they were or are to purchase a hat or hats – perched on beautiful faces, not some old trout or plain-faced sourpuss. Move her to millinery on Monday, for heaven's sake.'

'Yes, Mr Harborne,' said Miss Bytheway.

'You can leave this one here,' he said, gesturing dismissively towards Gwen. 'And get another plain one over from millinery. Not the little raven-haired one. Polly Prescott, is it? Leave her there. Those two on millinery will do very well. Very well indeed, they will indeed.'

And with that, he was gone.

It was mortifying. Maria couldn't look at Gwen. Maria had been complimented and promoted, as everyone agreed that millinery was a bigger and better department than gloves. Yet all this was so clearly at the expense of Gwen, who'd been here much longer and had also just been blatantly insulted by Mr Harborne. It was horrible. Even Miss Bytheway looked momentarily uncomfortable, somewhat lost for words, which was most unlike her. She turned and pasted on a fake smile.

'Maria, you will begin on millinery on Monday.' She seemed to want to say something to Gwen, but thought better of it and sighed. 'Now, Maria, can we solve this riddle of the missing mourning gloves?'

'Yes, Miss Bytheway, they arrived here. I was about to report this to you.'

'I'll get a chap from the first floor to fetch them. Well, young ladies, enough standing around. Continue with your work.'

She left swiftly. Maria turned to Gwen and Gwen turned away.

'That was . . . rotten,' said Maria. 'I'm so sorry, Gwen.'

'What are you sorry about?' she replied and laughed, a hollow sound. 'You didna do a thing wrong. It inna your fault.'

'It inna any of our fault. That man is ... well, he inna a good man. To say the least.'

Gwen turned and looked at Maria, jutting out her chin. 'He inna wrong though. I am plain.'

'That is rubbish, Gwen!' cried Maria and then remembered her place, glancing around for evil looks from Savage or some other disciplinarian observing them, but there was nobody nearby thankfully. 'Listen, this is what people like that do. They divide us and pit us against each other. I know it, because I've seen it before. My uncle did the same thing. Raised us all to hate each other, so we wouldna turn on him. It's cruel. And it works. So let's not give him the pleasure, eh?'

Gwen smiled ruefully. 'You're no fool, Maria. I like your way of thinking. You're right, of course. Stuff him. Who cares what he thinks of the way I look?'

'That's right. Who cares? Not us.'

'You have the promotion though, not me,' Gwen added quietly.

'It's a sideways step, that's all,' said Maria, trying to convince herself as much as Gwen, though they both knew it wasn't. 'Your time will come. We'll get you into furs by the year's end, mark my words.'

Maria had no idea how this turn of events would come about, but she wanted it to be true, so she said it.

'We'll see,' said Gwen. Then, the shopman from the mourning wear section arrived to fetch the gloves delivery and the conversation moved on.

The next day was Sunday and all the girls went out together as usual, but Maria noticed a coolness from Gwen, not so ready to link arms or share confidences as she normally would. Things had changed between them.

* * *

Schoolmaster's Cottage
Ironbridge Day School
Church Hill
Ironbridge
15 October 1892

Dear Maria,

I hope you can forgive me for not having written until now. I didn't want to write straight away upon your departure as it felt too keen (yes, I am so shallow as to be concerned about appearing too much like an eager puppy in my regard for you). Also, too little had happened to tell you about and I do want to entertain you with these letters. After that delay, the beginning of term was upon us and I was overwhelmed with work, as usual, at this time of year. Now that the school days are running smoothly again, I felt it was the right time to sit down to pen you this epistle. I don't know why I'm being so formal, using words like 'epistle'. I probably need to calm down and write more as I speak, or how I would speak to you if you were here beside me.

So, news: the most important first, which is that the mother of a girl in my class – namely a shy little thing called Janey – came to see me yesterday to complain that a boy called Richard was pushing Janey into the bushes on the path to school, every single day for the past week. He would not further bother her, just a little shove and she'd trip and fall into a bush. She was not hurt by these actions but baffled and annoyed. Her mother asked me to intervene, which of course I said I would and it would stop immediately. I took aside Richard, the eldest boy in my class, who previously has been of spotless character and has a good future ahead, we hope, of becoming an apprentice to a wine merchant. He had never acted this way before. I took the lad aside and said to him, 'Richard, why on earth would you seek to ruin your spotless record of behaviour by cruelly assaulting this poor girl every day in such a way?' He then proceeded to burst into floods of tears and sobbed. 'Whatever has happened? It'll all be all right if you tell me, you know,' I said to him, patting him on the shoulder, man to man. Finally, he spoke. 'I love her,' he said. It turned out that he had taken a fancy to Janey and was so enamoured of her that he could not express his feelings adequately and thus the only thing he could think of to do was push her into a bush and run off. I commiserated with Richard and told him he was not alone among his brethren in being unable to voice his true feelings, but that shoving girls into bushes was not the answer. He agreed and promised to never do such a thing again. We resolved that offering a bunch of freshly picked flowers was by far a preferable approach and that he must apologise to Janey immediately and never bother her again. Such are the emotional trials of men. We are cursed with inarticulacy when it comes to matters of the heart, I fear.

I thought you might appreciate that important update from the world of education. Beyond that, there is little to report other than the usual momentous world-changing events of the 1890s that surround us each day in this extraordinary Victorian era. Just today, I was giving the older children a quick rundown of the major pieces of legislative reform that have occurred in the last fifty years or so, advancing our country and its treatment of those less fortunate. I realised upon recounting it that we are truly living through a golden age of social reform, where working people are finally beginning to get some of the recognition and help they deserve. The Health, Factory and Education Acts of this century have *transformed the lives of the poorest among us. From orphanages to hostels, and soup kitchens to the Salvation Army, we are living in a time where philanthropy is becoming seen as the norm. On that note, I hear on the grapevine that your Mr Harborne is a noted philanthropist, often contributing kindly to local charities. I'm glad to hear this, that you are employed in a business with a social conscience. This gladdens my heart more than you know. There is much yet to accomplish, yet it does one good to look back upon how far we've come, before facing the future with determination to do more and more to help others and ourselves to live better lives.*

Now, I have wittered on far enough and only hope I have not bored you too much. I would only ask one thing, that you write and tell me how you are faring in your thrilling new career. I hope it is everything you dreamt it would be and more. Folk around here still mention you and wonder how you're getting on. I would love to hear every detail of your successes, if you feel willing to tell me. I am so proud of you, Maria.

Very best regards,
Charlie Woodvine.

Chapter 14

October 1892

'Hats these days look like summer meadows,' said Polly, as Maria watched her. 'You can wear a whole flower garden on your head, if you wish!'

The lady customer laughed. 'All this ornamentation, though. It's a touch . . . too much.'

'If madam would prefer a simpler approach,' replied Polly, leading the customer down the counter to another display, 'then perhaps a bonnet veil might be more suitable. This one is bordered with blonde lace, with a clear net dotted with small spots.'

The customer turned her nose up at that too. She didn't like veils.

'Then I would suggest a boater, madam. This one has a small brim and a simple mauve ribbon and bow.'

'Can you replace the ribbon with a light blue? Or a yellow?'

'Of course, madam,' said Polly, beaming. 'I could provide two boaters for you: one with blue, one with yellow. Shall I ring those up for you, madam? We'll get those amended for you and a delivery boy will be with you by the end of the day on Tuesday. Is that acceptable?'

Maria jotted down the amendments to be made and the customer details, then took the two boaters and the instructions over to the seamstress room. On her way back, she smiled to herself. She couldn't help it. She loved working on millinery. She'd been there for a couple of weeks now and had learnt a lot. Mrs Nixon had sold a few styles of hats back in Ironbridge, but nothing like the selection that Harborne's stocked. Here, they had every shape imaginable, from bonnets to boaters to turbans, made from straw to felt, or velvet to chiffon. Her favourites were the ones the lady customer had turned her nose up at – the hats with elaborate decoration – which Maria felt were little works of art. A simple base hat could be transformed by the addition of complex bouquets of artificial flowers and fruit, feathers and bows, loops of pearls, belt buckles and brooches, even a whole stuffed bird or two. One hat they had with clusters of redcurrants was her particular favourite. How she longed to be able to afford a Harborne hat!

But despite her promotion to millinery, Maria's salary had not gone up and she was still paying off her dresses and her fine from Savage. When she'd be able to buy a new dress, let alone a fancy hat, was a way off as yet. She simply could not work any more hours in the day and, anyway, they never got paid for working overtime. So she could only look at the beautiful millinery and dream. Maria got on well with the customers here as she modelled each hat for them and could see them smiling, imagining it would look as well on their own heads as on Maria's. Harborne was pleased and often dropped by to observe her, and particularly Polly, to whom he gave the glad eye, though Polly had managed to evade his advances so far. Polly Prescott was small but mighty, a slip of a girl with black hair and large, soulful brown eyes, yet a sharp tongue. Despite her high squeak of a voice, she knew exactly how to stand up for herself. One of the shopmen was sweet on her and she on him, and rumour had it they met sometimes in their free time in discreet liaisons, their secrecy due to the fact that both would be sacked if they were found to be seeing each other outside of work. Maria envied Polly this romantic entanglement, as she missed that physical thrill of seeing someone you like, the feel of their hand on your waist, of their kiss. Her body – wracked as it was by overwork and lack of sleep – surprised her by yearning at night sometimes for the touch of a man.

She and Charlie were now friends and nothing more, it seemed. Despite this new status between them, the truth was that she'd had to stifle a sob when she'd read his letter, sitting on her bed, surrounded by girls getting ready for sleep. Just to 'hear' his voice again was balm to her soul, to hear from some-one who knew her well, someone who cared. She liked the girls around her, but also they didn't know her really, and Gwen was still perfectly nice to her, but there was that cold fact between them of Maria's promotion. Reading Charlie's words had given her much-needed recognition and comfort. Yet the content of his letter had troubled her too: this boy shoving this girl was no doubt innocent childhood games, or was it? Something about it bothered her that, again, poor male behaviour was excused and explained away. And then Charlie waxing lyrical about charity and even Mr Harborne? The grim truth of old Harborne's appetites for young girls sickened Maria. She sat on her bed that night and wrote a long reply to Charlie, detailing the difficulty of her days and the injustice of male behaviour. It was a glorious rant and she felt much better after writing it. Charlie knew enough about real life from working with the poverty-stricken children at his school. But there was another side to life he knew little about and that was how it felt to be a woman, working in an industry where you were expected to give yourself body and soul to its success and yet you saw little to nothing of its rewards. He might know this in theory, but Maria was living it in practice. She hoped to educate Charlie a little. He was not the only one who was able to teach truths to others.

Maria arrived back at the millinery counter and saw Polly off for her tea. It was gone six and she was tired and hungry. She knew better than to yawn, instead crouching down to sort the bottom drawer of hat trimmings so at least she could take the weight off her feet for a half-minute at least. But it was not to last that long even, as someone was calling for her attention.

She shot up, worried it was Savage, but it wasn't. It was a male customer, virtually unheard of in millinery.

'Good evening, miss,' he said. He had an accent, something she'd never heard the like of before. He was young, not much older than her, she surmised.

'Good evening, sir. How may I be of assistance? Men's millinery is on the first floor, if that's what you're looking for.'

'Thank you. But I am not. I am wanting to purchase a hat for a relative. A female relative. My sister, in fact.'

She liked his accent. It was unusual. It didn't sound like it came from nearby, not even in England maybe. It sounded like he came from a foreign country. Maria was intrigued.

'I can certainly help with that, sir. May I ask her age? It would help me make the right choice for the style she might like.'

'She is thirty. Nine years older than myself. My older sister. You say here in England, my *big* sister, I think? Or have I said a foolish thing?'

He looked worried. She smiled. Then he smiled. It changed his face. He had a bowler hat on, but she could see from his sideburns that he was blonde and he had light-blue eyes. She rarely saw men with her colouring.

'Not at all. You're quite right, sir. A hat for your big sister, aged thirty. Let's have a look, shall we?'

She showed him a selection of the latest fashions, yet somewhat less showy and ostentatious than something a girl like her would wear, considering his sister's age. Also, he seemed well-to-do, so she assumed his sister would be the same.

He looked carefully at them, listening to what she said about each one.

'I think I cannot decide. Which is your favourite?'

'Well, my favourite is something I'd like to wear. But I'm not sure it'd be the same for your sister.'

'I would still like to know it. To know which is the one you would choose, if you could buy anything in the whole of this place. Which one?'

'Well, sir, my favourite is this one. I just love the little red berries.'

'What are these type of berries meant to be?'

'Redcurrants.'

'Currents. Like electricity?'

'Ah no, sir. A different type of currant.'

'Well,' he said, holding the hat and turning it from side to side to get a good look. 'I like it too. Will you try it on for me?'

'Of course, sir.'

She took the hat, delighted that finally someone wanted her to model her absolute favourite. Maria pinned it to her hair and cocked it at a slight angle. It was a forest green shade, shaped a little like a bowler hat, yet with an upturned brim. Piled on top were two silk green bows, a dark red ribbon around the crown and the bunch of redcurrants. It was more of a Christmas hat really, but October would do. She checked herself in the mirror on the counter and it looked so well on her, she wished again she had the money to buy it. She turned to the gentleman and beamed, so happy it made her.

He looked at her, eyes wide, focused intently on her. He was not looking at the hat.

'I cannot possibly buy this for my sister,' he said.

'Ah, I am sorry, sir. Let us find something more suitable for her style then. I do apologise.'

'No, no, you misunderstand. I cannot buy it for my sister because I simply must buy it for you.'

Maria's cheeks grew hot and she immediately extricated the pin and took the hat off. 'That is very kind, but out of the question, I'm afraid, sir. Let us try something else. This sky-blue silk turban, perhaps? See it has an ostrich feather dyed blue, so fetching. If your sister's colouring is anything like yours, it will make her blue eyes shine.'

'Yes, yes. That will do for her. But I will not buy it for her unless you allow me to buy the hat of the little red berries for you.'

'As I say, I cannot accept. We are not permitted to accept gifts from customers.'

She couldn't afford to have her pay docked again. Or an offence of this nature might even mean a sacking.

He looked thoughtfully at her face and nodded, sympathetically. 'I can see fear in your eyes, which hurts my soul. I can only imagine your role here is overseen by tyrants. And I am sorry for that. And sorry that I have put you in an uncomfortable position.'

'You have nothing to apologise for, sir.' But his words had an extraordinary effect on her. This man didn't know her, but he seemed to be able to read her face like a book. It felt rather wonderful.

'Very well. I will buy it for my sister then. And the blue turban. You have exquisite taste.'

'Thank you, sir.'

She placed the hats in their boxes and asked him for his address for delivery, yet he said he'd take them with him.

'I am lodging temporarily not far from here. It will be no trouble to carry them back.'

So he was lodging in Shrewsbury. Maria wanted to ask where he really came from, but of course she didn't. That would be far too familiar. He took the ribbon handles for each box and held them by his sides. It was a good sale and Maria was pleased. And he did look rather funny standing there with a hatbox dangling from each hand. Maria couldn't help but let out a little giggle, which she managed to stifle immediately, glancing around to ensure no member of management saw her faux pas.

'Why, you are even more beautiful when you laugh,' the gentleman said, smiling broadly at her. 'How I would love to photograph that smile. But I sense that even laughter is forbidden here. So I will leave you. And not cause you to smile any longer.'

'Thank you, sir,' she said and curtseyed. He still gazed at her, shook his head slowly and smiled broadly.

'Please, will you tell me your name? I would like to commend you to the doorman, on my way out. I hope he will pass my commendation on to your manager and then perhaps you will receive some benefit of it.'

'That's too kind of you, sir, and I would not wish you to trouble yourself. But if you wish to do that, then my name is Maria Keay.'

'Maria,' he said, softly. 'Maria, Maria, Maria.'

Then he turned and left.

What a strange little encounter it was.

Polly was back from tea and it was time for Maria's. She ate it ravenously, as ever. But she wasn't thinking of the bread and butter with a lump of hard cheese. She was thinking of the foreign gentleman. And the way he said her name four times.

The next day was Saturday, and when she finished work at ten and hauled her weary body upstairs to her room, she approached her bed and saw, sitting upon it, upturned at an angle – as if someone had thrown it on there roughly – was a hatbox. And she knew exactly which hatbox it was. She took off the lid and there was her favourite hat, with the bunch of pretty redcurrants. Inside was a card. It read: *For Maria the milliner – the beauty of a painting come to life. Best regards, Oskar von Schoen.*

Chapter 15

Everyone in the dormitory wanted to know who the mystery gentleman was who'd given her the hat. Maria said it was just a satisfied customer, which provoked smirks from all and sundry. She asked everyone to make sure they didn't say anything to management about her receiving a gift from a customer and they all nodded assent. She hoped they'd stick to that. She wore the beautiful hat the next time she was out on the town with the girls and felt like a queen in it. She had so few nice things, it was such a treat. She didn't know where the man lived, so couldn't send a note of thanks, although she wasn't sure she should do anyway. But she was very grateful. She would have liked to thank him for his kindness personally, Mr Oskar von Schoen.

Gwen said, 'Sounds like a German name, so he could come from Germany or perhaps Switzerland or Austria–Hungary. They speak German in parts of those countries too.'

Maria had vaguely heard of these places, but knew nothing about them or what languages they spoke. 'You're very clever, Gwen, knowing things like that. Perhaps I oughta read encyclopaedias like you do too.'

'I'm not just a pretty face,' Gwen said enigmatically.

So the handsome, generous customer had a German name, then. How exotic. How fascinating. Maria wondered what he was doing in her country, if his sister was with him, what their lives might be like. She found herself wondering quite a lot about the intriguing Mr von Schoen.

And she didn't have to wait long to find out more, because a week later he appeared again at the hat counter, at exactly the same time of the evening when Polly had gone for her tea and Maria was alone.

'Hello again, Miss Keay,' he said.

'Why, good evening, sir!' she said and smiled. She hadn't expected him to come in again, but hoped he would.

He took off his bowler hat and smoothed back his blonde hair. He looked even nicer without his hat on.

'I am wondering if you received a package last week.'

'I did and I'm glad you came in. I'm glad I could thank you in person.'

'You were not reprimanded then?' He looked worried about that, and she appreciated his concern.

'I was not. I was lucky. All my dormitory mates said they'd keep it quiet for me.'

He looked relieved. 'I too am glad. It was my pleasure to give it to you. You were so helpful about the hat for my sister.'

'And did she like it? If not, it'd be no trouble to return it or swap for another style. Maybe she'd like to come in herself.'

'Ah no, my sister lives back in my home country. I sent it to her by post. I wanted her to see the English fashions, as she wears the most revolting hats at home in Germany.'

Maria laughed without meaning to and instantly covered her mouth, glancing around for surveillance. She knew she should not be having any sort of conversations like this with any customer, especially not a male one.

Mr von Schoen looked concerned again. 'Miss Keay, I can see that speaking to you at work is troublesome for you.'

'It is . . . very strict here,' she said, wanting to be polite but also ensure he understood it wasn't that she didn't want to speak to him, as she very much did.

'That leads me to a request that I have, which I will deliver quickly to you and then I will depart and you will be troubled at work no longer.'

'How may I be of assistance?' she asked. Another hat for his sister, perhaps. *Or,* she wondered, *perhaps his wife?* He looked young to be married and, after all, wouldn't he have bought one for a wife before his sister, the last time he was in? Maria realised she felt pleased that it was unlikely he had a wife.

'I am a photographer or, at least, an amateur one. But amateur or no, I believe I have a skill for it. I am looking for models for portrait work and I believe you would make a perfect model. Your features are ideal for what I need.'

Maria had not expected this, or anything of the sort. Become a model for a photographer? She didn't know anything about it, but it certainly didn't sound respectable.

'I . . . I . . . This is a subject I know nothing about,' she said hesitantly.

'Of course, I have come in with two big feet, as you say, and not prepared you for such a question. Please allow me to explain.'

Maria glanced over his shoulder to see if any managers were nearby. This conversation was going on longer than it should be and, though she certainly didn't want it to stop, she knew it would look odd to be talking to a male customer for this long.

'I think, perhaps, it is not possible,' she said. 'It does not seem . . . seemly.'

Mr von Schoen sighed and looked about him. 'And I think, perhaps, this place is akin to a kind of prison for its employees. And if your wages are anything like that of your German counterparts, then they are scandalously low for extremely long hours. Let me assure you that this kind of modelling work for a photographer is perfectly respectable and it is paid work. And I pay well, Miss Keay. Very well. Thus, if you find yourself interested in another paid position that would increase your monthly salary, then here, please come to my studio at this address any Sunday lunchtime and I can explain the whole process to you and we can do the work.'

He had retrieved a slim, silver case from his inside pocket, opened it and took out a business card, which he placed on the counter, pushing it towards her with one finger before putting his hat back on and taking his leave.

'Good evening, Miss Keay. I hope to see you soon. I will not bother you at work again. Our next encounter is in your hands now, if you wish it.'

He smiled, nodded at her, then turned and walked away. Maria hadn't said a word in reply, too nervous after the placement of the card in front of her. She looked about the store carefully and spotted Savage walking across the ground floor, looking for trouble, as usual. Without thinking, she snatched up the business card and thrust it into the pocket of her work dress. Lots of dresses didn't have pockets, but this one did, thankfully, as shopgirls often needed to stow little bits and bobs there as they worked. At that moment, Polly returned from her tea.

'I always feel so sleepy after a meal,' Polly said, stifling a yawn. 'I'd give my right arm for a nap about now. Anything interesting happen while I was away? I need a bit of gossip to stay awake.'

'Nothing of interest,' said Maria and took her leave, going off for her meal. On her walk to the canteen, she surreptitiously took out the business card and looked at it properly for the first time.

Mr Oskar von Schoen Esq.
Student of Chemistry – Rhein-Universität of Bonn
Photographer's Studio – top floor, 4 The Square, Shrewsbury

The words were surrounded by a border of leaves and lilies. A student of chemistry. And a photographer. He was growing more interesting by the minute.

Maria wasn't sure why she'd lied to Polly and not told her about his visit. It was something to do with the offer he'd made, she realised. It felt wrong, somehow, and yet his business card certainly looked respectable. And the work would be paid. And he had a studio. It all sounded above board. She was tempted, very tempted. The extra wage would be wonderful for her. She could finally pay off her debt and start buying more clothes, nicer soap and better food. What other kind of offer would afford her such luxuries? What other form of work could possibly fit with her current employment hours? And she liked him. He was polite and well-spoken. His English was better than that of many English people she knew. He was clearly intelligent, a student of chemistry at a German university. *Dunna look a gift horse in the mouth,* her mother used to say. Maria always thought it was such an odd saying, but the meaning held true: if you're offered a gift, don't criticise it. And this gift came with pay that could possibly change her life.

But however much Maria sold it to herself, there seemed something quite wrong about going to a man's place of work alone. He didn't mention he had any staff working for him, or maybe he did, she wasn't sure. She tried to imagine telling the girls at work, or telling her cousin, or Mrs Nixon, or Miss Bytheway. She was sure that all of them would warn her against it and Miss Bytheway would probably sack her, for doing something that only loose women would do. Actresses were frowned upon, so surely models were worse. She'd have to put it out of mind, however tempting the whole prospect was. But she kept the card anyway, stashing it secretly in her copy of *Treasure Island* when nobody was looking.

That Sunday evening, she was out with the girls as usual, frequenting as many cafés as they could find before being asked to leave each one, due to nursing the same hot drink for as long as they could manage. Maria sat in a window seat with half a cup of cold tea in front of her. Everyone was chattering about the latest fashions. She stared out of the café window into the Shrewsbury street. It was a chilly autumn, character-ised by low-lying fog that held the kind of drizzle that soaked you through and through. She was wearing her own woollen dress she used to wear in Ironbridge as the girls were getting fed up of lending her their nice things. She felt frumpy and fed up herself. Polly was sitting opposite her, flashing her eyes at fellows who passed by, her gorgeous red silk dress showing off her dark hair. How Maria wished she could afford a dress like that, but it would be weeks before she could. How did Polly afford such nice things? How did Gwen? And all of them?

At that moment, Polly jumped up and left the table. She often did that, left suddenly. Maria always assumed she was off to meet her beau, in secret. But this time, she saw Polly leave the shop and stop in the street. There was a young man there, George, terribly good-looking with a lean, tall frame, dark slicked-back hair and a prodigious moustache, who Maria recognised as a doorman from the store. In fact, the very same doorman she'd asked for directions that first day she came for her interview. He and Polly had a few words and then walked off in different directions. *That's odd*, thought Maria. She turned to Gwen sitting beside her.

'Gwen, I just saw Maria meet that doorman from work, George.'

Gwen just nodded and didn't say anything.

'He's a looker, is George. Is that her young man?'

Gwen laughed. 'One of them!'

'Oh! She has a few suitors then?'

'That's one name for them,' she said and winked.

Maria stared at Gwen. 'But . . . what does that mean?'

Gwen sighed and took Maria's hand in hers. 'Time you heard a few home truths, my little country mouse. That doorman, he . . . well, he helps some of us out. Finding . . . clients for us.'

'Clients . . . for what?'

'We go with men. For money. We're all Judies. For rich men, though. Gentlemen. Proper mashers, you know. Not common types. It's the only way we can afford to live. How do you think we got all these nice things?'

Maria was shocked, truly shocked. She had had no idea. She'd wondered and wondered where she was going wrong, as everyone else was on the same wages as her and getting their pay docked for minor rule infringements like her. Yet they all had money for clothes and accessories, and food and drink on Sundays. Some were even engaged and saving up for their trousseaux. There were two other girls in her dormitory who had little to spare, like her, and they often went off on their own on Sundays and didn't walk out with Gwen, Polly and the others that Maria went out with. Maybe they were the only ones not doing what Gwen was talking about.

'You're all . . . Judies?' asked Maria. She'd heard the term bandied about in Ironbridge, usually used as an insult for any girl who had kissed more than one young man. But it also meant a woman who'd let a man bed her for payment. She couldn't bring herself to say the other words people used for such women. Prostitutes . . . or whores.

'I dunna do it that often these days. I did at the beginning. I got sick of it, though. The men. George does a good job, finding the best class of masher. He arranges it with the gents who come in the store. He takes a cut for his services. But these days, the gents inna as . . . gentlemanly as they used to be. Times are hard, spare money is hard to come by. These mashers claim they dunna have the change to spend on us, so they try to stiff us, take more than what they've paid for. It's all getting a bit nasty. Polly gets her pick because she's such a looker. I get the dregs. Old duffers and drunks. I havna done it for months. If I wanna new-season dress though, I'll have to go back to it. But I just canna face it these days.'

Maria felt sick. She would never do it, never! She knew that for a fact. She couldn't bear the idea. Lying down with an ugly, old man and letting him do *that* to her. It was horrible.

'I dunna wanna do that, Gwen.'

'I know, lass. I know. None of us did. We didna sit around dreaming about being a Judy, did we? Needs must, though. You and I well know how little we earn in these shopgirl jobs. Unless we get promoted to some kind of manager, we'll always need another way to earn a living until we get married. That's what I'm holding out for, not marriage but promotion. That's the only other way of living as a shopgirl. It's either that or earning it on your back. Sorry to be blunt, but you needed to learn it one day.' She squeezed Maria's hand, then let it go. 'Chin up, though. You're a pretty'un.

You'll probably get married to that Charlie who wrote you a letter. Or some other fellow, soon enough. Plain ones like me need another plan.'

Gwen said she was tired and off back to the dormitory for an early night, leaving Maria alone by the window, the other girls all talking to a couple of men who'd come in out of the cold. Maria sat in silence for a while, staring at the rain, heavier now, dripping down the steamed-up windows. Her dreams of the glamorous life of a shopgirl in the big town had dissolved away. And what was left? The hard truth, that the hours were too long, the work endless, the body wracked by aches and pain from standing up for unnaturally long periods of time and, after all this effort, the pay was pitiful. Gwen was right that the only ways out were marriage or promotion. Or prostitution. But Maria was determined it would never be the latter. Promotion, then. That was the answer. She was doing all right so far on that count, but getting to something like Miss Bytheway's position would take years. In the meantime, she'd need another way of earning money or she'd drown in penury. And a certain German gentleman had just thrown her a rope. It was the only answer. A model she would be.

The following days until the next Sunday dragged on and Maria couldn't stop thinking about the modelling offer. She still hadn't mentioned it to anyone else. It was nice to have a secret. It felt like something warm inside, just for her. But also, there was a small voice within that told her nobody would understand. They all knew the German customer had given her a hat. And now he wanted her as his model? She knew they'd laugh about it and roll their eyes and claim he was only after one thing, that she'd be a Judy just like the rest of them and he'd be her masher. But they hadn't met Oskar von Schoen. They didn't know how cultured he was, how polite and respectable. They wouldn't understand. So she kept it to herself. And that Sunday she lied to Gwen and the others, saying she was going off to meet her old friend Charlie from Ironbridge and she'd see them that evening for their night out, as usual. She was teased about meeting Charlie. They all said she'd be engaged before the week was out and laughed about it. She let them laugh. The only one who didn't laugh was Gwen, who silently observed Maria get ready, but said nothing. Only Maria knew her true purpose that day.

Mr von Schoen's place was very close by, only a short walk down High Street to The Square, and his studio was housed in an Elizabethan building, located just before she reached the Old Market Hall. There was a little staircase in an alleyway with its own entrance next to the shop below the studio, so she took the stairs up and reached a door on the top floor. She looked again at his business card, just to double-check. This was the place. Was she doing the right thing? Why had she lied to everyone about it? *Well*, she reasoned, *a girl can have her secrets*. If it didn't feel right, she could say no, she could leave. It was in the centre of town, after all. She was surrounded by shops and houses and the Music Hall around the corner. There were people milling about everywhere. She'd be all right. She'd have to be. The alternative . . . was unthinkable.

Maria held her fist up. She felt her insides flutter with butterflies. She paused, then knocked firmly on the door. *Rat-a-tat-tat.*

Chapter 16

No answer. Perhaps he was out. After all, he hadn't speci-
fied what time to come. He'd only said lunchtime. It was
midday and she assumed that would be about right. Then she
heard movement behind the door. And it opened.

'Miss Keay!' he exclaimed. He was wearing a shirt, trousers
and waistcoat, his sleeves rolled up. 'You came!'

'I did,' she said. She wanted to remain as businesslike as
possible. This was for a job, after all. 'I'm interested in the role
you advertised. Well, the one you told me about, anyway.'

'Of course, of course. Please, come in.'

Mr von Schoen stood aside and gestured for her to enter.
Maria swallowed hard. This was never something she'd normally consider. But she wanted that extra money. And for
that, it was worth the risk.

She stepped into a small vestibule, in which was a rack of
hooks for coats and shelves for boots and shoes, as well as a
closed door to another room. He shut the front door and
turned to her. It would have been dark in that small space with
the door closed, except she saw that it was lit with an electric
bulb, which impressed her hugely.

'You have electric lighting here,' she said.

'Of course. A photographer needs all the light he can possibly muster.'

'We have it at the shop, but not in the dormitory. I've never seen it anywhere else but shops.'

'It is a new world to you, then, Miss Keay! May I take your cloak, or would you like to keep it about your person?'

She liked the way he spoke, excessively formal and old-fashioned. She supposed it stemmed from the way he had been taught English, perhaps from a teacher rather than from experience.

'I'll keep it on, thank'ee,' she said. It wasn't that cold, but she felt she needed it. Like armour.

'Ah, that word "thank'ee", yes, I hear this everywhere. It is the Shropshire way, yes?'

'It is. We're not allowed to say it like that at work. We have to speak proper English.'

'Well, I think it is charming. And if English people say it, then it is proper English, in my book anyway. Please do enter the studio, Miss Keay.'

'Thank'ee,' she said again, then asked, 'Can you tell me how to say your name? I've seen it written down but have no idea how to say it aloud, the last word. I think I can say *Oskar* and *von* right.'

'You can indeed! Imagine it has an English letter "r" in there. *Shern*. To rhyme with "burn". It is often spelt with an umlaut over a singular O in German, but my spelling exists there too. Try it. *Schoen*.'

'Schoen,' she said, thinking of 'burn' as she said it.

'That is perfect. Shall we?'

Maria went through to his studio proper. It was a long, broad room with small windows to the front, yet to the back there were much larger windows in the wall and a sloping ceiling which let in a flood of light. One room led off from this large one, with its door closed. The studio at the windows' end was largely empty, save a deep red-and-black Turkish rug, a couple of wicker chairs with ornate decoration and a chaise longue. A landscape painting was propped up against the wall in the corner. Maria supposed that would be the backdrop for the photographs. Facing this was a camera on a wooden tripod.

'I see you are admiring my camera. In fact, I have two cameras. This is a Dallmeyer, very good. I develop the plates here in my darkroom. I use this camera for studio portraits. For outside, I have a different kind of camera – an Eastman Kodak Daylight camera – light and portable, handheld, the latest thing. It is called a hand camera, or sometimes you'll hear people call it the "detective camera", with the idea of a detective spying on someone, without them realising they are being watched. It has a roll of special film, which means I can load the film outside of the darkroom. There are new developments all of the time in photography. One day, we will have all photographs and moving pictures in full colour, as sharp as your own eyes, capturing events for all time, glorifying humanity, mark my words. We are living through an age of incredible development. The future is already here!'

This speech amazed Maria. She knew nothing of photography. She'd watched him while he spoke, gesturing at the camera, at the light streaming in through the windows, his eyes wide and bright as if he were picturing the future in his mind's eye. The weak autumn sunshine shone down on his head, illuminating his golden hair. She loved to listen to his voice, his extraordinary accent. It was spellbinding, so much so that she was speechless for a moment.

'Ah, I have bored you already. I do that.'

'Nay, not at all,' she said.

189

'"Nay". That is another Shropshire word, I think. It is also charming. You, Miss Keay, are charming.' He smiled and then wrapped his arms about himself and peered at her. 'I know just how I want to photograph you. Are you wearing a white shirt? They call them a blouse, I think, or shirtwaist. I think you are, by the looks of your collar.'

'I am.'

'Perfection. Will you come and sit for me?'

'We're gonna do it then? The photographs?'

She'd never had a photograph taken of herself, not in her whole life. She couldn't imagine what she might look like, in black and white, on paper. Her parents probably couldn't have afforded it, while her uncle couldn't have cared less.

'That is what I am hoping, yes. That is why you have come, is it not?'

'I think so. I wanna know more, really. What it involves. How much it pays.'

'Absolutely. First, I will make you a cup of tea. Would you like that?'

'Tea would be nice.'

He asked her to sit on the chaise longue as he rushed about making up a teapot. Along the other side of the room was a little basin and tap, as well as a small gas stove, upon which he boiled the water. At the other end of the room was a large wardrobe and chest of drawers, as well as a set of shelves filled with books. She wondered if he'd read all of them. She could only imagine how clever that would make him.

While he boiled the water, Mr von Schoen explained his terms.

'I would like to photograph you today for an hour or so, maybe two, if that is acceptable. And, if agreeable, there would be other sessions, perhaps every Sunday, for a little while. The pay would be a shilling an hour.'

'One shilling . . . an hour?' she gasped. It couldn't be true. He must have got his English coins mixed up in his head. 'You mean a penny an hour. That's about what I earn now, more or less. Just over a shilling a day.'

'No, no, indeed, no. I mean one shilling an hour. I know how English money works, I assure you. And this is not shop work. You are unique, Miss Keay, and I pay you accordingly. It is one shilling per hour for working as my model. Do you accept?'

'Of course I accept!' Maria cried, then restrained herself. She wanted to burst out laughing. It was more money than she'd ever heard of to earn in only an hour!

'I can see I have pleased you!' he said, laughing.

'I canna quite believe it. But I wonna try to change your mind!'

'Good, good.'

He explained more about the role. She would need to sit in a variety of poses, upon a chair or the chaise longue, pretending to carry out various actions: perhaps reading a book, or writing at a table, or staring out of the window in contemplation. It was the easiest work she could possibly imagine. She said yes to everything.

Maria finished her tea and put down the empty cup on its saucer.

'Why did you choose me?' she asked. She'd wanted to know that from the first time he'd mentioned it. There were lots of pretty girls around he could've asked.

'Your features are exquisite and your colouring ideal. I work with a pioneering new form of photography called Photochrom, which I learnt in Zurich. It involves producing coloured photographs from a black and white negative. There are those who have painted monochrome photographs with coloured paint, but this is not the same thing. I am engaged in taking a variety of photographs in England, some of which I shall develop in my darkroom here. I will store other negatives and, on my return to the continent, I will go back to Zurich and transform these black and white negatives into colour prints using the Photochrom process. You have the most stunning blue eyes, deep and rich, almost purple-blue, a very special colour. And your hair is extraordinary, like something golden that has been left out on a sunny windowsill and has been bleached to such a refined state of blonde it is almost white, but not quite. These colours will look perfect in Photochrom. I've been looking for a girl with your colouring in England for months. So many browns, browns, mousy browns in this country. Nobody like you. And now I've found you.'

That all made sense. So it really was a proper job then. Maria was needed. She was unique. And she was about to do the easiest work she'd ever done, if one could call it work. Sitting around, making faces? For a shilling an hour? Only a fool would say no.

'Where d'you want me, then?'

He clapped his hands. 'So, you have agreed to be my model?'

She nodded and smiled.

'That smile . . .' he said and sighed. 'I want that smile. But not yet. First, I need some more contemplative poses. Here, please take a seat on this chair.'

He took one of the wicker chairs and placed it in front of the painted backdrop of rolling hills. But he turned the backdrop around, so it was just a plain black board.

'I do not want anything to interfere with your image,' he explained. 'You need no embellishment. Please, be seated. And may I take your cloak and bonnet?'

Maria took off her shawl and handed it to him, then drew out her hatpin and handed it to him too. She sat down on the wicker chair. Her hair was pinned neatly in a low bun and she was wearing a white shirtwaist and a dark woollen skirt with woollen stockings and boots. She wondered if it were too dull an outfit for such a fancy photographer. But she would've felt silly putting on an evening dress at midday.

'I'm sorry that my clothes are so plain.'

'Not at all. Your outfit is perfect,' he added. 'Monochrome for monochrome.'

She had no idea what he was talking about, but she just liked listening to him.

Mr von Schoen went over to the camera on its tripod and stopped beside it for a moment. He took up in his hand a curious-looking object: it was attached to the camera by what looked like a rubber tube and it had a rubber bulb on the end. She guessed he'd use that to take the photograph somehow, though she had no idea how. Maria looked at him and he was just standing there, gazing at her. She looked away from him, concentrating on the middle distance in front of her, letting her eyes blur. It was odd to be stared at like that. Men looked at her in the shop, in the cafés, on the street. But not like this. Not with this kind of scrutiny. And this was different. Those men seemed to want something from her, to take something from her. This kind of looking was different. She felt like Mr von Schoen's mind was at work behind the gaze. That he was looking at her, but, at the same time, he was moulding her image in his mind into something he wanted to produce, into a work of art. He almost looked through her. She did not feel used by him. Instead, she felt seen. It was the oddest feeling, an utterly new, pleasing sensation.

He said, 'Please, will you turn your face up towards the light. A little at a time, just so. Yes, that is the way. Now . . . stop. Right there. Hold your face there. Yes, yes. Beautiful.'

She heard the puff of the rubber bulb he held and the click of the shutter. He did that again, three times. Then he asked her to change her position, to look in different directions, to clasp her hands, or to place each hand on the opposing forearm. She had to lift her chin or lower it. Direct her gaze upwards or down. Cross her ankles or uncross them. This went on for a good half-hour or so. She was losing track of time. The minutes melted into each other. But Maria was not bored, not for a second. She felt utterly in the moment, caught in time, focused, alive.

'Here,' he said. 'Take this book.'

It was in German. She'd never seen foreign writing like that before.

'I want you to pretend to read it, to be engrossed in it.'

She held it comfortably on her lap and opened it to the first page.

'Try turning it to the middle. I do not want photographs that look too staged. They should appear natural.'

She tried it, but it still felt fake.

'If you wanna make it look real . . . well, I wouldna read like this,' she said.

'How so?'

'I wouldna read sat up on a stiff-backed chair like this. It inna comfy enough.'

He smiled broadly. 'You are quite right! Of course you would not. Nobody would! Where would you read, Maria?'

She thought about it. She hadn't read for so long, her days were so exhausting. How did she used to read when she had the time and the energy?

'I'd read it lying down. In bed. Or under a tree in the woods.'

'I wish we had a tree right now. For you to lie under. And lose yourself in a book,' he said, in a reverent whisper. 'How I would love to see you like that. But we will have to make do. Lie down on the chaise longue, would you? Here, let me position it correctly.' She stood up and watched him take her chair to one side and shove the chaise longue over, in front of the black backdrop. 'Sit, or lie down on it, exactly as you would in your own home.'

'I never had one of these things to lie on. Not in my home. And the dormitory at work has simple cot beds. But I'll try it.'

'Everyone should have a chaise longue for contemplation.'

'Shopgirls dunna have time for contemplation,' Maria replied, with a wry smile as she seated herself on the chaise longue.

'Again, you show me up for my ignorance. You were right about the chair and now you are right about my foolish assumption regarding the homes and seating arrangements of working folk. I apologise. My class is showing.'

'That's all right. You know a lot of things, I can tell. But you dunna know about working life, I can tell that too.'

Maria felt bold saying it. But something told her that, despite his wealth, this was a person who wanted to learn, who wasn't too proud and uppity to admit when he was wrong. She liked that about him. And felt it may well be her place to teach him a thing or two about the real world. It must be very nice being a student of chemistry and an amateur photographer, to have the money and the time to devote to such pursuits. He must have leisure that folk like her could only dream of.

'I want you to teach me,' he said. 'I want to know everything.'

He was gazing at her and she looked away again. The intensity of that look was unsettling and fascinating all at once. She tried to lie down on the chaise longue, but it felt too . . . abandoned, somehow. It embarrassed her. Instead, she tucked her feet under her and half-sat up, her back snuggled into the upright part of the furniture, her book resting in her lap. It was comfy but not too abandoned. Maria looked down at the book.

He took a few photographs of her like that, pretending to

read. She looked at the German words, some with capital letters in odd places in the sentences. How extraordinary it must be to be able to speak more than one language, as he could. And he did it so well. Maria wondered if he got the two languages mixed up in his head. She wished she'd had an education like his, to learn languages and scientific things. She remembered doing Geography at school when she was very young, learning about rocks and sand and mud and how river valleys were formed. But she knew nothing of the inner workings of nature, the small things inside all matter. Their teacher at Ironbridge once said that everything was made up of tiny things. That's all she knew of it. She felt so ignorant compared to Mr von Schoen. What worlds he must know of that she knew nothing about. What worlds he could tell her about. It made her mind feel like a door that was closed, and he could come and fling it open for her. And she wanted to walk through it with him. Maria wanted him to take her hand and lead her into a new land of knowledge. Then she wondered how it would feel if he took her hand. How his hand would feel: smooth, unworn, the hand of a gentleman, unaccustomed to hard work. How soft it would be to touch. How it would feel, if he touched her.

'Yes!' he cried suddenly, and Maria looked up, surprised. 'You truly lost yourself there, for a few moments. You were gone. It was beautiful to see. And capture in a photograph. What were you thinking about?'

She blushed deeply, cursing herself for her feelings showing on her face. 'Books,' she said bluntly. 'I was just thinking about books.' But she knew that he knew she was just covering up her embarrassment.

'It was impolite of me to ask such a question. I apologise. A gentleman should never intrude on a lady's thoughts. I hope you can forgive me.'

'Course,' Maria said, adding, 'I mean, of course. No harm done.'

'I hope not. I believe the work we are doing here today will be most fruitful. So many models look like models. What I meant to say is they know they are beautiful. They show it in their faces, in the way they hold themselves. They are proud and self-congratulatory. But not you. You have this quality about you, of stillness, of inner confidence, the opposite of pride, unaware of your true beauty. When the viewer sees these photographs, I hope they will feel as I do, that they are seeing you unawares. As if you do not know that you are being photographed. That you do not know you are being watched. That you do not know that I am looking at you.'

'As if . . . you are spying on me?' she said.

She met his gaze then and held it. He held hers too for several seconds.

'Exactly that, Miss Keay,' he said in a low voice. Mr von Schoen took in a sharp, deep breath through his nostrils and breathed out long and slow.

They observed each other for far longer than would be acceptable in polite company. And that was what was so thrilling about him. He seemed above the normal rules. Outside them. He was beyond them. Maria's life was bound by one rule after another after another, every second of every minute of every day, her waking hours were governed by Harborne and Company. Even her dreams were tainted by the stress of work, peopled by shadowy threats of having her pay docked, of losing her job. She had sold herself, body and soul, to her job. Mr Harborne owned her. But here, in this attic studio flooded with light through the windows above, every restraint of her other life fell away. Here, under the gaze of Mr Oskar von Schoen, she felt utterly free.

MOLLIE WALTON

* * *

Schoolmaster's Cottage
Ironbridge Day School
Church Hill
Ironbridge
10 November 1892

Dear Maria,

I read your letter with, at first, glee to receive it, then, after that, utter consternation at what it contained. I was appalled to read of your working conditions at the store. As for Harborne's behaviour towards his female employees, I was shocked and disgusted. I cannot think but that you should leave that job, Maria. I truly mean that. I understand that you want to continue in your career and better yourself. However, this particular employer has proven not to have your best interests at heart, not in any sense. The pay you receive and the hours you work alone could be considered almost criminal, let alone the discrimination shown against women in his employ. I understand how dedicated you are to your retail career. But I hate to think of you slaving away under such relentlessly dreadful conditions. It hurts my heart to think of it. And it angers me beyond all reason. I would quite like to punch this Harborne on the nose.

So I have been looking into this for you by talking to some local trade union associates, as well as writing to a contact in Manchester. I have arrived at some information for you, which you might find useful. Based in Manchester, there is now a union titled <u>The National Union of Shop Assistants</u>, formed last year. Any retail worker can join. However, I must warn you what my Manchester friend informed me, that some

198

shop managers, upon learning that any of their workers have joined this union, have sacked them on the spot. I admit I was half-tempted not to tell you that so that you would join, be sacked and finally be rid of that place and come home. But I know that would not be the gentlemanly thing to do and you would rightly accuse me of interfering in your life, when you are perfectly able to make your own decisions. Thus, I give you this information in the hope that it may be of some help to you. If you want my advice, mine would be to join this union and seek their advice on how to improve conditions at work. Yet, if you believe that Harborne would indeed sack you, and you do not want this to happen, I quite understand if you feel you are not able to risk joining it at this time. It is your decision, of course.

Please know that you can call on me at any time, if you need further help. I hope you know that I mean that. I am your good friend, Maria, and I will always have your best interests at the heart of anything I say or do.

If it's any help at all, I can share with you that I also often feel resentful towards the system in which I work. You know I love working with the children. It is my lifeblood. But the school system, though vastly improved from the beginning of this century, still has its problems. For example, all board schools such as mine are currently having to operate under a cruel, unfair system named Payment by Results. This means in practice that the money each school receives for its funding is predicated upon the results that all pupils achieve in the annual tests. In May each year, an inspector visits and tests the children (I'll write and tell you all about it in May, when it happens). Every year, we dread the visit. Not because we feel unprepared – quite the opposite – but only certain things are tested, and the inspectors can be quite capricious and decide to randomly test things on certain children to catch them out. As I told you before, the lessons which Anny

Malone teaches them on Wednesdays are not considered part of the curriculum, so we have to be very careful that the children are instructed not to mention these. It is a very difficult balancing act! We want to give the children the best education we can, yet at the same time we feel we are hampered by the system; a system, I warrant, that has not been constructed by teachers, but instead by career politicians or other busybodies. After the inspector's visit, all the funding we receive that year is designated according to how well the children performed under this unfair system of the testing of one man. That includes my salary. Thank heavens Anny volunteers as part of her charity and does not require a salary, as we would never manage if we had to pay another teacher. The system is wholly unfair, as surely any school that is struggling to deliver the curriculum requires more help, not less. I hate it. There are whisperings that Payment by Results may be scrapped by this Parliament. I hope these rumours prove true.

The systems both you and I work within are set up by the rich to benefit them and only them. Only by ordinary folk like ourselves fighting back against this kind of system can we forge a way forward for working-class people everywhere. I know, though, how hard it is to fight a system alone, especially one that so readily will throw you out onto the street for your defiance. But it is righteous to fight back against these systems and if nobody ever does, then nothing will ever change. I just wish I could help you more. Please – PLEASE – do let me know if there is anything else I can do to assist you, Maria. And also know that if you decide to leave and come back, your welcome will always be the warmest. You will always have a place to turn to in Ironbridge, I promise you that.

Very best regards,
Charlie Woodvine

Chapter 17

December 1892

'In order to provide the best coverage of the prospective sale clients, or customers otherwise, for all of the floors of the store, on all levels, high or low, for the duration of the Christmas Sale . . .'

Harborne seemed to forget what he'd called them all here on the ground floor to say. Such was his meandering manner of addressing them, he'd quite lost his way. Then he appeared to suddenly remember.

'Yes! That is, Saturdays. From now on, all shop-floor workers are now advised that for the remaining three weeks of December, hours on Saturday will be now increased from 10 p.m. to midnight. That does not include today . . . that is, this day . . . of Saturday. So, thus, today is not included. That is all.'

Harborne waved everyone away with a dismissive gesture of the hand.

Maria glanced at Polly in horror. Polly rolled her eyes glumly. Sixteen-hour days on Saturdays? As if they didn't work hard enough all week! They'd already cut lunchtime to fifteen minutes to deal with the crush. And now this! Of course, nobody said this aloud, but it was what they were all thinking.

The shopgirls traipsed up to their dormitories. The day had been a particularly exhausting one. Shoppers were gearing up for Christmas already, swamping the store with orders, demands, requests, advice and a general need for mollycoddling. She'd never seen so many men in women's fashion, desperately asking what on earth they should buy for their wives and sweethearts for their seasonal gift. There was not a moment in the day for rest or respite. Maria's feet, calves, knees, thighs, lower back, upper back, neck, eyes and head ached like billy-o. Perhaps only her ears, teeth and hair escaped the pandemic of pain sweeping through her body at the end of each day.

She threw herself on her bed. She thought about Charlie's letter. He was right about the rich crafting the system to suit themselves. He was right that she ought to be a member of a trade union. But was he right that she'd probably get sacked if she did?

She turned to Gwen, who was wearily undressing ready for bed. 'Gwen, what do you think of this? Charlie said there's a trade union for shop workers up in Manchester but anyone can join. But he also said we might get sacked if we do join. Is he right about that?'

Gwen shook her head. 'Harborne would throw you out on your ear if you tried that. He hates agitators. And Miss B would refuse to give you a reference. So you'd be knackered for finding more work in retail. They know what they're doing.'

'It inna fair. None of it. It inna right. Charlie says we should fight back. That if we dunna fight, then nobody ever will.'

'Charlie has a lot to say for himself. And you're seeing rather a lot of him. Every Sunday last month. I'm amazed he hasna asked you to marry him yet. Or has he? Are you two secretly engaged? When's the big day then?'

Maria closed her eyes, pretending to be sleepy, rather than face Gwen's questioning.

'Stop badgering me about it,' she muttered. 'We inna ready for all that.'

She turned over and mimicked sleep, but she was still fully dressed and knew she'd have to get up again soon to disrobe, as she didn't want to sleep in her corset. Her subterfuge was worth it, to avoid Gwen's keen eye. Maria had continued to lie about meeting Charlie every Sunday since she first went to Oskar's studio. *Yes*, she thought, *I call him Oskar now*. She smiled about that. *Oskar*. She'd never known an Oscar in her life, especially not one spelt with a 'k'. She'd stayed an hour that first time. And again the following week and the same throughout November. He'd taken hundreds of photographs, most likely. She'd never seen one of them printed out, not yet. She supposed that was the way of photographers as she was only the model, after all, and he was the master. She hoped one day she'd see one of them as she wondered what she'd look like rendered in this most modern technology of photography.

She'd saved up a significant amount of money already from the modelling, all the shillings he'd given her hidden in an old hopelessly laddered stocking she didn't wear any more and that was shoved in a corner of the trunk she shared with Gwen. She hoped Gwen never pried, though why her friend would look at an old bunched-up stocking was beyond Maria. She'd been careful to hide the fact of her riches, but she did want to earn some joy from her new wealth, so she told the others that Charlie had helped her out a bit and given her some money to buy a new outfit. It was a gorgeous creation, bought from Harborne's itself: there was a white shirtwaist decorated with red poppy flowers dotted all over it, then a red velvet skirt with white ribbon at the waist, white lace at the hem and a white velvet stripe all around the base. It came with a matching velvet bodice with white piping. She could wear it with her 'bunch of redcurrants' hat and look an absolute picture in it.

She'd only bought it that week and not worn it outside yet. Maria intended for its debut to be tomorrow, at Oskar's studio. He kept asking her when she was going to wear the hat he'd given her, but actually she had nothing to go with it, as her other clothes were so cheap, plain or faded. Now, at last, she had the perfect outfit for it. She couldn't wait to see his face when he saw her in her finery. She couldn't wait to see him, for any reason.

The truth was, she yearned to see him when she wasn't with him. The rest of her weeks dragged by until Sunday came, and she'd rush off at midday for her two hours alone with him. The photographs continued, but as well as that they'd sit and talk. Maria told him about her work, her life before Shrewsbury. She didn't mention Charlie. She hadn't told him about her parents. She talked about the farm and Ironbridge. Oskar told her about his life as a chemistry student in Bonn, how he was particularly fascinated by the properties of gases and what uses they could be put to in the future, other than gas lamps. He wanted to see a revolution in the concept of energy and the way we use it, he told her. He talked about photography and the way he developed each photograph. She'd never seen inside his darkroom, as yet, but hoped he would offer a tour one day. She felt he had a natural reserve that he seemed to want to break away from. There were moments when he looked as if he were on the verge of opening up to her, admitting something, or sharing a secret or two. And then he would retreat. Maria felt it too, hence not telling him everything about her past. It was as if they both knew that this relationship of photographer and model was a professional one, and that is how it would work best, for lots of reasons. And it would be dangerous to breach it, and yet . . . and yet . . . She wondered how it would unfold. In doing so, happily daydreaming of Oskar, Maria fell asleep, fully clothed.

Maria woke up on Sunday at dawn, around eight in the morning, birds chirping and scrabbling about on the roof above their windows. She was stiff and awkward in her corset and stockings and all the rest. Everyone else was still sleeping when she tried as quietly as possible to drag off her dress. She was wide awake by then, so decided to wash and get ready for the day. She brushed through her hair and cursed herself for not putting her fringe in rags last night. Now she had no curls with which to frame and prettify her face. Lots of the girls had hairpieces they used for their fringes, but Maria never liked them. It was hard to find the same shade as her near-white hair and she felt it looked faked. So she always tried to curl her own fringe, every night. And now she'd omitted to do so, what could she do with flat, straight hair? She tutted at her laziness and brushed it into a centre parting, then decided to plait it at the back, bringing the plait up and twisting it into a figure eight shape, pinning it in place. It looked becoming and would fit nicely with her hat. Without her customary curled fringe, her eyes looked bluer than usual, and she wondered if she ought to stop bothering to curl it at all. Maria got into her outfit. There was nothing like the feel of brand-new clothes. She pinned her hat in place and regarded herself. She could weep at how smart she looked. A memory of herself at Collie Farm assaulted her: straw in her hair, filthy apron, hands raw from washing. And now look at her: *a proper lady*, she thought.

She wasn't due at Oskar's until their customary twelve noon, but she didn't want to sit around in the dormitory till then, not in that get-up and everyone gawking at her. She sneaked out and down the stairs and onto the street. There was some December sunshine: not warm, but at least quite bright. She knew exactly where she wanted to go and made along Mardol Head, to Shoplatch, to St John's Hill, to Quarry

Place. And there it was: The Quarry, the magnificent public park that all Salopians loved. As the park's name suggested, its centrepiece, The Dingle, was once a quarry, but just over a decade ago, it had been transformed into a sunken garden for everyone to enjoy. She went along its paths, its trees in their winter garb stark against the pale blue sky, the band-stand and the statues of important men glowing in the low sun, pigeons milling about at their feet, pecking for scraps. The park was not at its best this time of year, but it was still a tonic after being cooped up in the shop all her waking hours. When clouds drew across the sun, she shivered and wished she'd brought her woollen scarf, but in her vanity, she had not liked the thought of it with her new outfit, thus had left it back at the dormitory. She was happy though, despite the cold, to be free, to be alone, save the Sunday passers-by who nodded to her, many giving admiring or envious looks. Once she'd sat awhile in the park, shivering somewhat, and walked a bit around the streets, looking in shop windows at goods, some of which she could now afford (but couldn't buy without giving it away to all and sundry that she had another source of income), it was finally time to go back to The Square and Oskar's studio. Excitement had been rising in her chest these last hours and now it was at fever pitch.

Maria reached the narrow staircase that led up to the studio and trotted up it quickly, breathless with exercise and nerves at the top. She knocked on the door and Oskar opened it immediately, as if he'd been waiting in the vestibule. He took in the sight of her new clothes and gasped appropriately. She beamed at him and curtseyed.

'See what a model's wage can do?' she said, chuckling.

'A stunning beauty!' he cried. 'Quickly, come in. Be seated. I have to photograph you right now with colour in your cheeks from the winter cold, rosy red just like your outfit. Quick, quick, before it fades!'

They hurried into the studio, both laughing and getting the chair and camera set up. She sat down and tried to look serious, tried to pose like a model should, but he scolded her, good-naturedly.

'No, no! I will not have it. None of that model nonsense. Be yourself! Smile at me. I told you I wanted that smile on camera and not once in all these weeks have we photographed a smile like that. Smile at me, show your happiness!'

He squeezed the bulb and the shutter clicked, time and time again, having her face at different angles, still smiling, making her laugh more, saying German words that sounded silly to her, like *lustfahrt*, which meant a pleasure cruise, and *womit*, which sounded like vomit but actually meant 'with what' or 'wherewith', or something, she didn't really care as the words were so funny. They went on like this until she was so tired out from laughing, her face ached. Two hours rushed by, as they took more shots of her in her glorious ensemble, looking out of the window, sometimes contemplative, sometimes curious, sometimes sad. He asked her to take off the bodice to see the shirtwaist and was fascinated by the little red poppies on it, taking some nearer shots of just her head and upper body, her chin lifted, the poppies clearer at closer view.

'May I ask, Maria, if you would take off your hat? I know it is a beauty, but I think I spy that your hair is different today and I would like to photograph it that way, if you are agreeable?'

Maria was reluctant. 'I admit . . . I didna style it my usual way, as I fell asleep too soon last night. I usually curl it. It looks . . . plain this way.'

'I am certain this is not true, its plainness. Your hair could never be plain in a thousand years. Its natural colour alone outshines all others. Please, may I see it?'

'If you insist,' she said, sighing, but inwardly smiling at his compliment. She'd always felt her hair was peculiar, growing up. Her uncle used to laugh at her, saying she looked like an old granny as her hair was almost white, and that insult stung like a nettle when he teased her about it. Maria hated him for that, yet hated herself more. Now here was someone who truly appreciated it, at long last. She removed her hat.

Oskar stared at her. She was used to the staring, as he did that every session. But it was different this time, somehow. He seemed somewhat moved.

'You are quite, quite different today, Maria. Your hair brushed from the centre, with none of these fashionable curls, is so humble, so sweet, your hair plaited so simply. You appear to me like a child of the German mountains, minding goats or sheep, or a milkmaid. Yes, a milkmaid, with creamy hair to match the creamy milk you carry. It has quite affected me, to see you natural this way.'

'Why, thank'ee, Oskar,' she said. She no longer blushed when he complimented her. She was used to him, but the power of his words still remained. Nobody spoke to her as he did, nobody ever had.

'Maria, will you . . . will you take out the pins and let your hair fall down, utterly natural, just as it looks when you brush it out at night?'

Oskar hadn't asked her to do this in any of their meetings. She'd always had it pinned up, in one of the latest styles, sometimes with a central bun and the rest swirled outwards as broad as a hat brim, or plaited or twisted into knots, and always those curls at the front, framing her face. No man had seen her with her hair down, not since she was a child.

'Is it important . . . for the photographs?' she asked,

hesitating. She wanted to please him, but it felt odd, somehow, almost like undressing.

'It is important to me to see you at your most natural. But I would never want you to feel strangely about my requests. You can and must say no at any time, if you are uncomfortable.'

'It inna that. It's just . . . quite a personal thing, a girl's hair.'

'I understand. Let us forget it. Let us move on.'

She looked at him and he gave her a polite smile.

Maria lifted her hands and began to take out the hairpins, one by one, slowly. Oskar did not speak. He simply watched. She placed the pins on the chair beside her and, when they were all out, she brushed her fingers through her hair to tidy it, smoothing it down with the palm of her hand. She went over to a mirror he had on the wall and looked at it. He moved behind her and watched her in the mirror. She could see his reflection behind her, looking. She looked at him and smiled shyly.

'Maria, if I asked you to never curl it again, to never use a hairpin again, to always wear your glorious mane of flaxen hair naturally flowing across your shoulders and back like this, what would you say to me? Would you want to do that for me, Maria?'

She watched him speak in the mirror. She wanted to turn around and she wanted him to kiss her, that's what she wanted.

'I'd wanna do that for you, Oskar,' she said softly. 'But if I did that at work, they'd boot me out of the shop so hard I'd land in the middle of The Quarry on my backside.'

That made him laugh. He took more photographs, this time with her hair down. It felt so liberating, to be free of hairpins and plaits and bunches and buns and all that palaver. She real-ised how much it made her scalp ache to be forever pulling her hair this way and that, and what a relief it was to have it flow-ing freely, how nice it felt against her neck and her ears, soft and feathery. Usually she only felt this for brief moments at night before she tied it back again for sleep or when she briefly brushed it in the morning.

'You look so much happier with your hair free!' he exclaimed as he snapped more pictures of her.

She thought, *Why do women have to wear their hair up all the time?* She knew it was fashion, but somehow it felt like another form of control decided by society and therefore by men, like corsets and stockings and petticoats. If women were in charge, they wouldn't have to wear any of those daft things.

Oskar asked her to stand up and she did so, then sat down again with a thump as her head was spinning.

'Are you ill?' he cried and rushed to her.

'I've been so silly. I was up early this morning and went walking and I havna eaten a thing.'

'Then we must eat. Come, we shall go and eat together. I have nothing here fit to feed a young lady.'

'All right, then,' she said and went to the mirror to pin up her hair and put her hat back on.

Oskar opened his wardrobe and retrieved some clothes, then went into the room off the vestibule, a room she'd never seen inside. He had been wearing his usual trousers, shirt and waistcoat, very plain, in grey. He emerged from his room quite different, in a fashionable tweed suit and brown homburg hat. He looked so dashing she had to look away, to stop herself staring.

'Shall we?' He gestured towards the door. They had never been out of the studio together. Would it be proper? What if the other shopgirls saw them? But, actually, the thought of stepping out with him, of being seen with such a handsome man as Oskar, she beside him in the very best clothes she'd owned in her life, felt too good to miss.

Chapter 18

They walked a short distance down Princess Street and stopped at The Golden Cross inn. Maria had never been inside before and even though it was rather too close for comfort to the store, at least she knew her friends hadn't eaten in there with her, so she hoped she'd be safely unseen. It seemed Oskar was well known there, as he was greeted by name by the landlord, who said he had a nice snug private room for the next hour, until they finished lunch for Sunday closing times. The room was comfortable and unpretentious, with benches covered in thick red material that perfectly suited her outfit. They had fat, juicy sausages with mashed potatoes rich with butter and lashings of gravy. There was apple pudding for afters, served with cream. They talked all the way through dinner, of foods they loved and foods they hated, and of pubs and restaurants Oskar had been to in his home country, in Switzerland, in Italy, in France and across the British Isles, the length and breadth of which he'd travelled extensively.

Maria said, 'It seems so curious to me that you've ended up here in Shrewsbury, when you could be anywhere in the world.

Why is that? What's the appeal, when you could be in Venice or Paris or London or anywhere else on earth?'

'You do not like Shrewsbury?'

'Oh, I love it!' she cried. 'It's the most beautiful place I've ever seen. But then, I havna seen many places. Only Ironbridge and some villages near the farm. I really havna travelled at all. So it is the loveliest place I've been. But not for you, I'd wager.'

'I have been to the Lakes, the Dales, the Cornish coast, the cathedral cities of York and Winchester and Lincoln. And London, of course, to see the sights. I asked a London hansom cab driver, where does nobody visit in the British Isles? The cabbie said Shropshire. He was born there and said when he told people that, they always said, "But where *is* Shropshire?" So here I am! And I find I adore the architecture. The age of the buildings here is quite remarkable, ancient and quaint. Also, I've met another photographer here who is training me to take landscape photographs, in which I need practice, as I've been mostly doing only portraits and indoor photographs, so I've decided to stay for a few months to continue my training. I also like taking photos of street life, when I can. Of ordinary people, going about their business. They do tend to stop and stare if they spot what you are doing, but the best shots are those where they are caught unawares. The same with you. If only I were invisible and could take a photograph of you when you had no idea. That would be perfect.'

Maria asked, 'You said you are a student of chemistry? So how is it that you can take so much time off from it?'

'I decided to take a year off to travel, to see the world. I love chemistry, but I felt I needed to escape. Luckily for me, my family are wealthy and they support my nomadic ways. Thus, I had finished my main studies and was going on to advanced level but wanted to travel first before coming back next summer to Bonn to study again.'

So, he was leaving next summer. That was months away, but Maria felt a pang inside at the thought of him ever leaving.

'I wonder what Germany is like,' she said.

'You should go! It is beautiful. Mountains, rivers, ancient woodland. You should travel there.'

'I couldna afford it. Or speak the language. How would I get by with not one German word?!'

'I will teach you. And French too. France is another glorious country.'

'You know, I heard that the best department-store shopgirls in London are expected to speak French and German.'

'Then I shall teach you both languages. I applaud you for your ambition, to work in the best stores in the country. But also, you should travel, Maria. It changes you forever.'

'Poor girls like me will never travel.'

'Then I must take you, to Germany at least. Germany is the height of civilisation, you know. The first motor car was made there only five or so years ago. Horse power is moving to electric power there too. That is the next great change. In Germany, we have electric ovens and irons and kettles and trams and telephones and even motor taxicabs. England is backwards in comparison! One day, Maria, you will never have to heat another flatiron on the range. Electricity will heat your iron for you, at the flick of a switch.'

'It all sounds . . . marvellous,' Maria said, but she wasn't really thinking about irons: she was thinking of how he'd said he'd take her to Germany. Did he really mean it? Or was it something men like him just said as a throwaway comment?

Then the bell rang for the end of lunchtime, and they had to go as the inn was closing. Oskar escorted her to the door and said he'd walk her back to the store. She was about to say no to that as she didn't want to be seen with him so close to work.

Then, just as they stepped out onto the street, someone called, 'Maria Keay!' and Maria whipped round, her face a picture of guilt.

It was Polly, Gwen and some of the other shopgirls, stopped on the other side of the street, all staring at her. At least it wasn't Miss Bytheway. But her hopes of avoiding scrutiny were dashed as the girls stood there agog, gawking at Oskar, smirking at her. Polly and Gwen crossed over to speak to her, while the others held back, giggling and pointing.

'Well, to goodness!' crowed Polly. 'So, this is your dear friend Charlie who writes such long letters and visits you every Sunday.'

Oh Lord, Maria thought. Now the lie was out.

'Nay, Polly. Please allow me to introduce you to Mr Oskar von Schoen.'

'I am charmed to meet you both,' said Oskar, who took off his hat, nodded sharply and replaced it, the model of decorum.

'The one who bought you the redcurrants hat?' asked Gwen, also smirking.

'I am indeed,' said Oskar, smiling. 'And who do we have here?'

'I'm Polly and this is Gwen. Charmed, I'm sure.'

'Delighted to make your acquaintance,' said Oskar, making a short bow to both. He was perfect. But the situation was excruciating.

Maria said, 'I mun go, Mr von Schoen. I shall see you for our next photography session.'

'Indeed, Miss Keay. And I shall say *auf wiedersehen*, in the German way, and thank'ee, in the Shropshire way.'

'Oh, very good!' said Polly and laughed raucously.

Oskar nodded once more and departed.

Polly thumped Maria hard on her upper arm.

'Ow!' she cried.

'How dare you keep a dashing German to yourself, wench!' said Polly.

'And to think,' said Gwen, still smirking, 'all this time we thought you were seeing a *friend* from home.'

'I'm sorry I lied,' said Maria, feeling utterly hopeless. She didn't know how to explain it.

Polly added, 'Nothing to be sorry about! I'd do the same and keep a rich foreign masher as pretty as him to myself!' She winked at Maria like a pantomime dame.

'It inna like that,' Maria protested. 'He inna my . . . my client.'

'What is it like then?' said Gwen deadpan. She looked disappointed and triumphant all at once.

'He's a photographer. And I'm his model. I go there to have my picture taken.'

'I bet you do!' said Polly. 'And the rest!'

'Nay, nay, it inna like that. It's a professional relationship. He takes pictures of me and pays me per hour. It's all above board. I dunna do anything like that with him and I never, ever would for money, not with anyone, at any price.'

Then the mood changed. Polly looked quizzically at her.

'You saying you think you're better than us? Us Judies who lie on our backs for our mashers? Because you inna no better than any of us, taking your clothes off for a rich gentleman.'

'Nay, I dunna take my clothes off. And nay, Polly, honest, I didna mean it that way. I dunna judge what people do, what you wanna do to make a better living for yourself. I found this way, that's all, and it pays well and I like his company. But there inna a thing going on. I promise.'

'All right, all right,' said Gwen, tiring of the conversation.

'We're off back to the store, come on. It's too cold out. You coming?'

Maria nodded. Polly was not so easily placated, giving Maria a vicious look before crossing over to walk back with the other girls.

'I didna mean to offend anyone,' said Maria miserably.

'You lied to us, though,' Gwen replied simply. She never seemed to lose her cool, always measured and careful with her words.

'Well, you lot lied to me about your mashers and all that.'

'We didna lie. We just dunna talk about it. If word got out, we'd all be sacked, you know that. And you better be more careful being seen around with your masher. None of us would dare be seen out during the day with one.'

Maria wanted to protest again about Oskar. But what good would it do? They were all angry with her for her subterfuge.

'I'm sorry for lying, for everything,' said Maria. 'I just didna know how to explain it, about Mr von Schoen and the photographs. I knew people would think it wasna proper. But it is, it truly is.'

Gwen took her arm and squeezed it.

'Dunna take on so. It's done now and all out in the open. Dunna lie to your friends again, though. It inna worth it. For all we truly have in this world is our girlfriends. We're the only ones we can ever rely on. Friendship is gold and you put a man before your girlfriends at your peril, remember that.'

Back they went to the dormitory. Gwen was nice to Maria, but Polly wouldn't say much to her. They all went out that night to the cafés and Polly came round, slowly. By the end of the evening, when they were rushing back to get home by curfew at ten, Polly gave Maria a hug and said, 'I'm just jealous, that's all, you lucky devil. You getting with such a beaut type from the off. That German feller is proper bostin!'

On Monday morning, Maria went down to work as usual but was waylaid by Miss Bytheway, who did not look pleased. She told Maria to follow her to her office immediately. Was this it? Was she to be sacked? But what for?

'You were seen in Shrewsbury entering a public house with a gentleman. It was a reliable witness, one of our floorwalkers. This is totally unacceptable behaviour for a Harborne girl. A week's pay will be docked. If you are ever seen frequenting a public house again with a man, you will be sacked.'

At first, Maria was simply amazed she hadn't been sacked on the spot. But her second emotion was anger, a new kind of anger that had been building in her for months, since she had started at Harborne's starry-eyed, which had soon turned to disbelief and now rage. But if she let that rage flow out of her at this moment it wouldn't serve any good purpose. She had to be more clever about it than that.

'Miss Bytheway, please let me assure you that the gentleman is an acquaintance and that nothing untoward was occurring.'

'That matters not. It is the appearance of propriety that is most important.'

'I understand. And I want to thank you for not sacking me, as I know that shopgirls have been sacked for less.'

'Indeed. You are very fortunate, Miss Keay.'

'Could you . . . tell me why I have not been sacked?'

'I *beg* your pardon?'

'Is there a reason why you have decided not to sack me for this offence? It would help me greatly to know, for future reference.'

Miss Bytheway looked caught off guard. It was a risky strategy Maria was employing, but there was method behind it.

'What a strange query. But a brave one. So, I will meet it with honesty. If you must know, I believe you could go far in retail. And I do not want one of my best shopgirls dismissed. But with this line of questioning, you are coming dangerously close.'

'I understand that and again I thank you for being forbearing. And for your belief in me, which means more to me than you could possibly know. I have come far for this job, from humble beginnings, and I want to better myself.'

'That is admirable.'

'But, Miss Bytheway, there are parts of this job that make it very difficult for us girls. I'm sure you know what I mean. I'm guessing you worked your way up from being a shopgirl once.'

She looked taken aback, but composed herself and replied, 'I did. And I believe I know what you're referring to. But we all have to go through it. Stiff upper lip is the thing. It is a testing environment, I grant you.'

'But these conditions we're working under. They're more than difficult. Or testing. I myself am wracked with aches and pains all over my body. I've suffered blisters like someone who'd walked a hundred miles. There are girls in my dorms with swollen knees, ankles and feet. Some girls have fainting fits and headaches that never leave them. Others have palpitations, Miss Bytheway, their hearts too weak to go on steady. I wouldna be surprised if you'd find one of us dead as a doornail on the shop floor one day, I wouldna!'

'Girl, you forget yourself. We speak proper English here.'

'I am sorry. But I have to tell you how run ragged we are. And we're hard workers, we are, every one. Not shirkers. But these rules, of no sitting down, of such long hours, and such short breaks, and virtually no time to eat and terrible food that never fills our bellies. And no half-day off, like other jobs. And the hundred rules we have to follow or get our pay docked. And now these sixteen-hour days at Christmas. And for such low pay. And half the pay of the shopmen, doing the same job! It is wrong. All wrong. Is there nothing that can be done to change this situation? We would all be better workers for it, happier in our work, more get-up-and-go to do our job right and sell more. As it is, we're like ghosts half the time.'

Miss Bytheway said nothing. Maria wondered, and not for the first time, if this was it. She'd gone too far. She'd be told to leave. And what would she do? She'd never see Oskar again. She'd have to go back to Ironbridge a failure. Charlie would welcome her, of course. But where would she live? Or work? It would be an unbearable backwards step. Why had she let her mouth run like that? What good would it do? Oh, she was a foolish girl and no mistake.

'You are right, Miss Keay.'

'What? I mean, sorry?'

'You heard me. You are right. I do not disagree with a word you have spoken. Conditions for shopgirls are a national scandal. I read about it in the newspaper regularly.'

'Do you?'

'I do. Just a few weeks ago, I read of a shopgirl in Birmingham who took her employer to court. In another, there was a call for consumers to boycott certain stores until they changed their working conditions for shopgirls. The paper called it slavery.'

'What do you think of these things you've read?'

'I agree with them all.'

Maria was astounded. Until this moment, she had seen Miss Bytheway as yet another cruel cog in the Harborne system, complicit with the worst males in management and serving the same rotten purpose. But now, all that had changed. Had she found an ally?

'But . . . what can we do about it?'

'Nothing.'

'But—'

'Nothing, Miss Keay. Nothing on the surface, at least. If any one of us women working here showed the least inclination to agitate for better conditions, we'd be out on our ears.'

'I've heard that said.'

'It is true. Even at my position, it would not be brooked. The only thing we women can do is work within the system and exploit it for all we can.'

Miss Bytheway looked absolutely determined, her fist clenched.

'But how can we do this when we're so exhausted?'

'Women have fought too long to be let into this profession, so, now we are here, we must stay in it and fight quietly with stealth and cunning. We must support each other and give other women a leg-up, whenever we can. And *that*, Miss Keay, in a very roundabout way, is the answer to your question. That is why I have not sacked you today. But hear me, if anything of the sort happens again – gentleman friend or no – then you will lose your job, be sure of that. In the meantime, assuming you behave yourself, I want to tell you that there will be a promotion up for grabs soon. We are advertising for an assistant to Miss Lafitte, the floor manager for the dress material department, as her current assistant is leaving to get married. It is the same hours but better pay. And it should lead to more upward mobility afterwards. In fact, I was most disappointed that the girl who had it before chose a husband over her career. Most disappointed. But if you can assure me, Miss Keay, that you want this promotion and you will work hard to get it, then I will put in a good word for you. But only if you strive to do me proud.'

'I will, I will! Oh thank'ee!' Maria gasped. 'I mean, thank YOU!'

Miss Bytheway gave a small smile. Maria rarely saw her smile.

'In the run-up to the promotion, the floorwalkers, myself and other staff have been instructed to watch all of you shop-girls closer than ever in order to ascertain who might be the best candidates. So, watch yourself. And work harder than you've ever worked before. You will be scrutinised. Keep your ear to the ground about this promotion. And work extra hard to prove you are a worthy contender. Many other girls will want this position, you know. Your first duty is to give as much energy as you can to the Christmas sale, as Harborne is aiming to break the store's records for money taken around Christmastime and you must play your part. If you do, I will argue your case when it comes to interviews. Now then, run along, as you are late for millinery and I am late for my duties.'

'I'm so grateful. Thank you again.'

'All right, all right, enough of that. And behave!'

Maria nodded, curtseyed and rushed down to the ground floor. On her way to millinery, she passed gloves and saw Gwen there, looking harried, dealing with two customers who were both impatient and laden with Christmas shopping. But that did not deter Maria. She remembered keenly what Gwen had said to her the day before about girls supporting girls. And she didn't want to make the same mistake with Gwen that she'd made with Rosie back in Ironbridge. So she went over to the counter and said, rather pompously, 'You are needed briefly at millinery.'

Gwen looked confused and the customers then turned their attention to the other girl on gloves. So Gwen came out from behind the counter and walked over to Maria.

'What's all this?'

'Just a ruse, to get you away for a minute. Listen, Gwen. There's a promotion coming. Miss Lafitte's assistant.'

'Well, you know why that is, don't you?' replied Gwen ominously.

'No?'

'She was . . . taken advantage of by the boss. Several times. Then she snapped and pushed him off one day. So he hit her. And she gave in her notice.'

'Oh, that's terrible. It's so unfair! Bytheway said she was getting married.'

Maria thought how easily that could've happened to her, or still could.

'They all lie for the boss. And, yes, it's unfair, but her loss is our gain.'

Maria frowned at Gwen. It seemed a cold way to look at it. 'I suppose so,' she replied, thinking that actually Gwen was right. There was nothing they could do for the girl now. And it could benefit them immensely.

Gwen went on, eagerly, 'What's the pay? What else did Bytheway say?'

'It's same hours but better pay. We have to keep an eye out as they'll be advertising it soon. But before then, they've got spies everywhere, watching us to find out who's best. So we have to be on our best behaviour. You should put an application in, Gwen. I'm going to as well. We should tell all the girls. See if we can get one of us into a better position at least.'

'Dunna tell the other girls,' snapped Gwen.

'But why ever not? I thought you said, you know, girlfriends together and all that.'

'But not when it comes to work and money. Then it's every woman for herself. Let's just keep it between me and you. Less competition, you see. Works out best for both of us.'

'If you're sure?'

'I am. Thank'ee for letting me know. Much appreciated. See you later.'

'Ta-ta for now,' said Maria and went over to millinery, a little surprised at Gwen's reaction. But it made sense, she supposed. Not everybody could get the job and the fewer who knew, the fewer could compete and make a good impression before the call for applications was advertised.

She arrived at millinery and Polly said, 'Where've you been? I've been rushed off my poor feet here.'

'I got hauled in by Miss B. Told off for going out with a feller yesterday. Some shopwalker saw me.'

'Danker me! And you didna get fired?'

'Nay! Mun be my lucky day!'

'It mun be! Glad you're still here, wench. I'd miss you!'

Maria thought about telling Polly about the promotion, just Polly. But then, Polly wasn't interested in promotion. She'd made it quite clear to everyone that she was making a good living from her second job, and she'd be off with one of her rich mashers like a shot the minute any one of them finally offered to make her an honest woman. She had no desire to rise in the ranks of the shop. So, Maria kept it to herself.

Something had changed in Maria, having spoken to Miss Bytheway. She could see that Charlie's ideas of trade unions were correct, on the surface of things. But Miss B was also right: women had to be more subtle about these things than men, in order to get their way. If they were too obvious, they'd simply be thrown out. There were more ways than one to get ahead. Maria couldn't change the system itself, but she could use it to her own advantage and that's exactly what she meant to do. But also, she had no intention of giving up her afternoons at a certain German photographer's. Whatever the risks, the gains were more than worth it. She'd keep both roles going, like a juggler at the fair. She'd outsmart those spying floorwalkers, Mr Harborne and the whole damn system of men trying to keep women down.

Maria put her application letter in the very next day. She had worked her socks off to get here and now she had a powerful ally on her side. She'd win in the end, she was sure of it.

Chapter 19

'Who is Charlie?'

Maria turned to Oskar, breaking the position she was supposed to be holding for the photograph.

'Turn back, please. Your face catches the light just right there. But you can speak.'

How did Oskar know about Charlie? Then she remembered that Polly had said it when they'd all met. Today was the next Sunday after they'd been spotted in town and she'd wondered if the meeting with the shopgirls would come up as a topic of conversation. She turned her face back to the light.

'He's a friend from Ironbridge. An old friend.'

'And you told your shopgirls you were seeing him, not coming here.'

Maria swallowed, her mouth suddenly dry. 'I did. I'm sorry for it.'

'You have nothing to apologise for. It is none of their business where you go, what you do. You are a grown woman.'

'Thank'ee, but it was wrong. They are my friends. I should've been honest with them. But I didna want them to know. About this. About the job. The modelling . . . About you.'

225

'Why is that?' he said. 'Why did you keep it a secret?' He spoke softly, slowly. It did not sound like an examination, the way he spoke with no hurry. But she knew he was not going to let it go and, actually, it was a relief to talk about it as there was nobody else she could discuss it with.

'I dunno, I just wanted to keep it to myself. The money I was earning. And I knew, if they knew you were the photographer and you'd bought me that hat, they'd . . . you know. Well, they'd jump to conclusions.'

'What conclusions?'

She sighed then, a little tired of his seeming lack of understanding. 'I think you know very well what conclusions.'

Oskar smiled then and looked into the camera and, as he did so, he said, 'So you told them you were seeing this Charlie.'

'That's right.'

'Tell me about him,' said Oskar, taking another snap and peering into the camera again, not looking directly at her.

'There inna much to tell. We went to the same school when we were little'uns. Then we met again when I went back to Ironbridge.'

'So you are friends, that is all?' he asked, still not looking at her.

'Just friends.'

'Nothing more?'

Maria knew she was lying. She hated lying. But somehow she felt unable to tell Oskar the truth about Charlie. It was as if Charlie and Oskar did not exist in the same world. There was Ironbridge and the life she had there. And there was Shrewsbury and the life she had here. Only Charlie's letters broached the gap between these two worlds. And she felt unable to let Oskar into that world. It just felt wrong.

'Why do you ask?' she said, deflecting his questioning.

'I am curious about you, that is all. Always curious.'

Maria had nothing to say to that.

Then Oskar said, 'Does he know this?'

'Know what?' she replied.

'That you are just friends. And nothing more.'

'He does. It was agreed.'

'What was agreed?' Oskar said swiftly. He was looking intently at her now. She'd let that slip unintentionally.

'That we would be friends when I came to work here. It's the best way.'

'So before that you were more than friends?'

Maria didn't want to talk about that. She didn't even know herself how she felt about it. She had powerful feelings for both of them in utterly different ways. She couldn't explain how to herself, let alone anyone else, and least of all Oskar.

'I'd rather not talk about it, if that's acceptable.'

Oskar sighed and she turned to look at him. 'I am a terribly curious person, you must forgive me. Always putting my nose in, as you say.'

'You're nosy,' said Maria and smiled.

Oskar smiled back. 'Ah, you have forgiven me. I am glad.'

'There inna anything to forgive.'

'May I speak frankly with you, Maria?'

'You may.'

She never knew what he was going to say next. It was always a thrill talking to him.

'I believe all women should be free. And men too. To love whoever they choose, whenever they choose.'

'That sounds . . . nice. But what about marriage? And children? Who'd look after the babbies if they're all off loving whoever takes their fancy?'

Maria felt she was ever the pragmatist, living in the real

world, while Oskar lived in a world of imagination and philosophy, which only the rich could afford to do.

'Oh, I believe in marriage too.'

'How does that work, then?'

He came away from the camera then and drew up a chair to sit opposite her.

'Once children are in the picture, as you say, then men should settle down and protect the mother of their child. That is natural. But before that happy day, men and women should be equal, I am sure we agree on that. They should meet and talk and love, if that's what they both want. But they should be free to choose, to try out other meetings, and conversations, and loves. How will they know who they want to marry and have children with if society only allows them to meet one and only one? These days, a man so much as looks at a woman and they are engaged. They might kiss, hold each other, fully clothed. But that is all. Then they have to wait until they are married to see each other naked. To take to a bed together. What if they find out it is no good? They are no good? What happens then?'

She'd never spoken of such things with anyone, let alone a man. 'I canna talk about this with you,' Maria said, blushing wildly.

'Why not?' pressed Oskar. 'These are important considerations that every young man and woman must think about.'

'I've never been a big Bible reader, but what you're suggesting sounds like Sodom and Gomorrah!'

'No, no,' he said, shaking his head. 'You misunderstand. What we have now is worse than that. Now, many men get engaged early to one woman. Marry her. In between times, they are having relations with other women for money. Prostitutes. Those women are ruining themselves for money and the men are lying to their fiancées. And the fiancées . . . well, they are waiting around to get married to a man and they've never even seen him with his shirt off. She has probably never seen any fully grown man with his shirt off. It's madness, all of it! Men should never have to pay women for sex.'

So many revolutionary ideas were being thrown at her, Maria felt as if she'd dropped all the balls and not caught a single one. There were so many questions to ask, and yet, at the same time, she felt overwhelmed with the topic of conversation, knowing that an unmarried man and a woman should never be discussing such things. But she had to admit to herself that the way Oskar talked excited her immensely. And, as much as she felt light-headed at this moment, she did not want him to stop. Maria decided to address the last thing he'd said, as it was the only one she'd retained.

'But why? If men want sex from women, and they are not their sweethearts, shouldn't they pay for that? Girls have to make a living too, you know.'

'Well, yes. Shopgirls like Polly, you mean. But not you.'

What? How was he throwing Polly's name about like that, having only just met her?

'You canna talk about Polly like that. And what do you know anyway?'

Oskar saw he had offended her. 'I am sorry, I did not mean to say that in such a careless manner. But you must know what Polly does. Every man in town knows what Polly does. I have seen her around in many places with different men. She is the prettiest one in town, for that purpose.'

Maria felt deeply uncomfortable. She looked away from him and shifted in her seat.

'I think I should be going now.'

'Oh no, Maria, please. Do not go. I have been a heavy-footed idiot again. Please do not go.'

But she couldn't sit still, so close to him like that. She stood up. 'It inna right, what you say about Polly. She's a good person.'

'I am sure she is, if you say so. But let us be honest. We know what Polly does. And she can be proud of that. She earns her way in life. I am just saying that, in a better society, men should never have to pay women for sex as we should all be free to have relations with anyone we want at any time. Women too. All of us. You mention the Bible as a way to live. But I *loathe* the Bible and everything in it!'

Oskar stood up at this point, gesturing wildly. He stepped closer to her.

'There is no God, don't you see? Religion is a lie. We should all be free. These times we live in will pass and one day a woman will be able to approach a man she wants and take him to her bed and none will care, none will judge, all will be free and sex will be celebrated. For what it is. An entirely natural and beautiful part of nature. As natural and as beautiful as blue skies and fluffy clouds. And flaxen hair and creamy-white skin.'

He was standing very close to her now. She felt the air between them condense with the warmth of their breath.

But Oskar took a step back. He began to unbutton his waistcoat. She knew she should leave. This was all madness. But she didn't. She stayed. She watched. He dropped his waistcoat to the floor. He began to unbutton his shirt. She stayed. She watched. He dropped his shirt to the floor. He stood there, in his trousers and boots, naked from the waist up. He was right, as she had never seen a man with his shirt off. And now she had, she could not help but gaze at him. His chest was curved, his stomach flat, his skin creamy and mostly hairless, apart from a line of blonde across the top part of his chest and lying golden down each forearm.

'There, you see. Now, you have seen a man with his shirt off.'

Maria said nothing. She felt rooted to the spot. She'd never felt so utterly still and utterly alive in the same moment.

He added, 'Is it so shocking? Is it so bad? For a woman to see a man? For you to see me as I really am?'

'Nay,' she tried to speak, but her voice broke. 'Nay,' she said again, more clearly.

'Then take my picture, Maria. I will be the model. You, the photographer.'

'I canna do that!'

'Yes, you can. You've seen me do it often enough. You know where to look into the camera. You know how to squeeze the bulb until the shutter clicks. It is your turn to look now. And for me to be looked at. Go ahead.'

Oskar turned and shifted the chair she'd been sitting on, then went to the chaise longue, pulling it into position. He sat down upon it, thought for a moment, then arranged himself. He lay on his side, facing her. His left hand rested on his belly, his right arm fell loosely, his right knuckles trailing the floorboards, his long legs stretched out, his head half on and half off the chaise longue, his hair falling across his forehead and the cushion beneath him.

'*The Death of Chatterton,*' he said and smiled. 'I enact it for you.' He closed his eyes.

Maria had no idea who Chatterton was or why he'd died. Or what it all meant. But she still had not moved, because the sight of Oskar lying there, shirtless, his head tipped back, his eyes closed, was the most beautiful thing she'd ever seen. She freed herself from her frozen stance and walked over to the camera. She took up the rubber bulb, held it lightly in her hand and looked back at him. She squeezed it and heard the shutter click. He did not move. She squeezed it again and again. He still did not move. He lay as if he were the dead Chatterton, pale and peaceful in the afternoon light. When she stopped, he opened his eyes. She stepped towards him. She looked down at herself. No fancy outfit today. Just her plain woollen blue bodice and skirt, with a cotton shirtwaist beneath. She slowly began to undo the buttons of her bodice. He observed her lying down, then slowly sat up. Maria dropped her bodice to the floor. He watched her every movement, very seriously. She unbuttoned her shirtwaist and dropped it to the floor also. He stood up and took three slow steps to reach her. He looked down at her bare arms, the corset cover tucked into her skirt, the corset beneath it, the cotton combination beneath that.

She said, 'And now you have seen me without my shirt on. Now we are equal.'

He said, 'Maria.' He took a step closer and touched her lips with his fingertips. 'Maria, Maria, Maria.'

They kissed. It was slow and tender, so soft, warm and wet. And then they opened their mouths to each other and she felt her whole world tip, her eyes closed, her body on fire.

Chapter 20

Schoolmaster's Cottage
Ironbridge Day School
Church Hill
Ironbridge
1 January 1893

Dear Maria,

Just a short epistle this time, written on this first day of the new year. The new century beckons! I wonder what wonders it will contain? Anyway, before I float off further into my reverie on the marvels of the future, I'm just letting you know that I'm going to be in Shrewsbury on your birthday – the third Sunday in January. I would very much like it if we were able to meet up while I'm in town. If you can't make it, not to worry, as I like Shrewsbury very much anyway and will take a stroll around before getting the train home. However, if you do want to meet up, shall we say to meet under the clock tower at the railway station at two in the afternoon? If

*that's acceptable. As I say, if you already have plans, I quite
understand.*

Very best regards,
Charlie Woodvine

* * *

Maria arranged with the girls that she'd see them back at the
dormitory at six, for an evening out on the town to celebrate
her birthday. This time, she told them the truth – that she was
actually going to see Charlie Woodvine in the flesh – and there
was no subterfuge involved. Polly said, 'Well done for having
two fellers on the go at once, wench!' which Maria waved
away with a dismissive gesture.

'I told you afore, it's all friendship with Charlie.'

Gwen said, 'You've enough on your hands with the German
chap, I'd warrant.'

Maria said nothing, but looked down at her feet and smiled
a small, secret smile. When she looked up, she saw Gwen had
noticed it, raised her eyebrows and smiled too, then Maria
turned away. She knew that Gwen knew that something had
happened with Oskar that last time as she'd come home starry-
eyed and tongue-tied.

'Just take care,' Gwen had said, not elaborating.

That evening, when she'd come back from Oskar's place
after their kiss, she'd been over the moon. Kissing him, with
his shirt off, touching his naked back with her fingers, feeling
his bare chest against her corset: it was like a dream one has
in a fever. And after that one delicious kiss, they'd laughed at
each other's shirtlessness, then dressed each other, Oskar doing
up her buttons slowly and deliciously and she doing the same

for him. Nothing was said or decided, it was just left as it was. Then, before she went, he told her he'd be away for the next month and back at the end of January, as he was returning to Germany to see his family for Christmas. She'd felt empty going back to the dormitory, wanting more and being denied it as he was going away. There was a part of Maria that wanted him not to go at all, and to just be there every Sunday at her beck and call whenever she required such kisses, but she knew that was silly. She'd said she was glad for him that he was seeing his family and that she'd see him next on the last Sunday in January. She didn't tell him he'd miss her birthday. She didn't want to seem like she expected anything from him. There was something about his liberty that made Maria want to appear as freewheeling as he was, not caring about such meaningless trifles as birthdays. Thus, she was actually pleased that Charlie had honoured her special day, turning eighteen, as well as a night out beckoning with the girls, which was always full of larks.

She came out onto the street opposite the station and spotted Charlie straight away, standing under the clock tower as promised. The moment she saw him, her eyes filled with tears. She almost stopped walking, overcome with it, but shook her head, scolding herself for being overwrought. Maria shocked herself with her reaction. But knew deep down that seeing Charlie again reminded her of everything that was safe, the past that had already passed and thus was contained and manageable. It was the present and future that were scary, yet also stimulating. She hurried across the road to him and when he spotted her, he grinned from ear to ear. Without thinking, she put her arms out and they hugged spontaneously, a proper cwtch, both holding on for a considerable time.

'Oh, Charlie!' she said, as they let go. 'What a tonic it is to see you.'

She saw that he was as moved as she was, though he laughed away the shine in his eyes.

'And you, Maria.'

'But there's no Biscuit here. He didna wanna come?'

'I wanted to have you to myself and not worry about that old feller. He'll be all right for a few hours.'

'Fair enough, though I do miss him almost as much as I've missed you!'

'I'll bring him next time. In the meantime, happy birthday!' he said and took out from his jacket's inside pocket a small book-shaped package wrapped in brown paper.

'May I open it now?' Maria asked excitedly. Nobody else had bought her a gift. The girls didn't have the money, though they'd collectively pay for her drinks tonight, as that's what they all did on each other's birthdays.

'Of course. It is your birthday, after all.'

She slid open the carefully folded paper and took out a book. It was titled simply *POEMS – Emily Dickinson*. Its front cover was plain, with an outline of pale purplish bluebells. She'd never owned a book of poetry and never heard the name of this one's author, but was gratified to see it was by a woman. So many of the books she'd read as a child had been by men.

'It's beautiful, Charlie. I need something new to read, not that I ever really have the time!'

'That's why I got you poetry, as I know you don't have enough leisure hours to devote to a whole novel.'

She looked up at him. 'That's so kind and thoughtful.'

'Ah, I try, I try,' he said, tipping his head and smiling. 'Look inside. It's a very new edition, only published in 1890. The poetess Dickinson had died a few years before and her poems published posthumously, that is, after her death.'

'How very sad that she never got to see her success.'

'She was a hermit, by all accounts, so I inna sure she'd even approve of her works being out in the world. But anyway, it is our gain that they are. I read them all before wrapping it for you. They're quite . . . extraordinary. I've never read anything quite like them. Deeply strange and mysterious and, somehow, quintessentially female. A friend from my teacher training days emigrated to America some years back and he sends me interesting books from time to time. This was his latest offering. I immediately knew I wanted to give it to you.'

She opened it up to see there were many short poems contained within, separated into four sections: LIFE; LOVE; NATURE; TIME AND ETERNITY. The book then fell open at a page marked with a small embroidered bookmark.

'I put that at a poem I'd like you to read. It made me think of you and our walks and talks we used to have. Please dunna read it now. Save it for later.'

'This is very deep stuff, Charlie Woodvine. Are you trying to broaden my mind?'

'I just think you'll appreciate what she's trying to get at. She's reaching for something beyond herself, beyond all of us. Time and eternity, as she says. You have something of that about you, Maria. Reaching for the stars.'

Maria looked at him. It was so good to see his friendly face, his kind brown eyes, his soft, expressive moustache. Once, she'd kissed those lips of his, run her fingers through his curls. She wasn't thinking of that now. She thought only of the rare pleasure of spending time with someone who knew her better than anyone. The shorthand of that, the comfort of it.

'Let's walk,' she said.

They went up and down the streets of Shrewsbury, Charlie pointing out his favourite ancient buildings and Maria pointing out her favourite cafés that did the tastiest sweet things to eat. They bought Shrewsbury cakes from Crump's, the best baker in town. There was nothing else quite like the buttery biscuits flavoured with lemon and studded with currants. Eventually, they made their way down to The Quarry and wandered through it. The day was chilly but not unpleasant, no breeze or rain, and as they were both wrapped up, their walking kept them warm enough, as did their friendship. They talked about their work: Charlie's little scallywags and teara-ways keeping him on his toes; Maria's glee that Christmas was finally over and its interminable sale, with a cast of thousands coming in and out of the store at all hours. Charlie told her about politics and the latest about Keir Hardie's progress in government and the Independent Labour Party. Maria told him about her conversation with Miss B about changing the system from the inside, and the prospect of promotion in the air, which had her working harder than ever these past weeks.

'I am so incredibly proud of you,' he said, as they walked back up into town from the park, the light fading as it approached three-thirty, the daylight leaching from the sky, ushering in the turn of the moon.

'I inna sure why, Charlie. I'm working myself to death, and for what? Sometimes it all seems a bit pointless.'

'Nay, dunna undermine your progress that way. The system is unfair, we know that to be true. But within it, you are carv-ing out your path with utter determination. You've already secured one promotion and now you are on the cusp of another, with a powerful ally in Miss Bytheway. So many shopgirls go nowhere with their hard work, more's the pity. But you are already tipped for greatness. You should be proud.'

'Thank'ee, Charlie. Nobody else understands how much I want this. There was a time when . . . well, I wondered if you resented it. Because of, you know, what I had to sacrifice . . . between us.' Maria looked round at him as they strolled on and he was smiling. She was relieved to see it. She hated there to be any shadow between them.

'I never did, Maria. I could see how much it meant to you. All I have ever wanted for you is what *you* want. That in itself means so much to me. I am just so happy we have remained friends and remained close. And on the subject of closeness . . .'

Charlie faltered and she swallowed nervously. Was he about to bring up their relationship again? In that brief pause, she realised she didn't know how she'd feel if he did. Would it be welcome or unwelcome? Just walking and talking with him again that day had highlighted how close they were, how much had passed between them. And her feelings for Oskar were so new, so untried and untested. But they were strong: they were almost overpowering, in truth. But what Charlie Woodvine actually had to say took her completely by surprise.

'I wanted you to know something that's happening in my life, as I always want to share everything with you. I've been teaching an adult class at the school in the evenings for those who left school early and never quite learnt to read and write with the facility they need. They're very popular, the classes, so much so we're running one for men, taught by me, and one for women, taught by Anny. And the women's class has been attended faithfully by your old room-mate Rosie Green. And I wanted to tell you, Maria, that Rosie and I . . .'

Maria felt sick. It couldn't be true. He couldn't be about to say what she dreaded he'd say.

'We are courting.'

She knew she should smile and say nice things. But she still felt sick. Charlie . . . and Rosie? The nausea she felt – at the idea of Rosie Green, who had been so vicious to her, with her paws on Charlie – was tinged with spite.

'I inna surprised,' she said, trying to sound airy. 'She always carried a torch for you.'

'Did she? I didna know that.'

'Oh, she did. And so do all the girls in town, so she told me.

She thought I was mad going away to Shrewsbury when you and I were . . . walking out together. And she hated me for cheating her out of a job at Harborne's, or, at least, that's the way she saw it.'

'I'm sure that inna true. I'm sure you two would get on again. It's all water under the bridge by now.'

'Oh, I dunna think so. She'd never forgive and forget. It inna her way. Going with you is a very nice way for Rosie Green to think she's bettered me.'

It just came out. She hadn't meant to say what she was thinking. But hearing Charlie defend her sparked a rage in Maria that she couldn't contain.

Charlie was so shocked that he stopped walking and glared at her.

'That's a cold way to act,' he said. 'And a sideways insult to me. We are very well suited.'

'Well suited?' scoffed Maria. 'I suppose she loves to listen to your long political speeches on rambling walks! And I'm sure she's a mine of information on all the books she canna read!'

It was a despicable, snobbish thing to say and Maria hated herself more with each word.

'She . . . she does her best,' Charlie sputtered. 'Rosie is a lovely girl.'

Hearing her name in his mouth was the last straw. Maria was so jealous, she could barely see straight.

'I'm pleased for you both,' she said, vitriolic and unconvincing. 'Especially since I have similar news that I'm walking out with a new fellow who's only three years older than me, a German student of chemistry and a photographer: Mr Oskar von Schoen.'

Charlie's face fell. Maria saw it and knew then that Rosie hadn't cured him completely of his feelings for herself. He looked green with envy. He attempted to speak and ended up having to clear his throat, as the words seemed to stick in his gullet.

'He sounds interesting and . . . worthy of you,' he said. 'I am glad for you.'

'And I for you. Well, it's time to go. It's nearly dark and I mun be back at the dormitory. I'm out tonight with all of my many friends. We're celebrating my birthday on the town. There's so much to do in Shrewsbury, you know. Ironbridge feels like a backward place to compare.'

Maria despised whoever this person was she'd become, whoever was this spiteful woman who spoke to Charlie this way. But she couldn't help it. He'd started it, telling her about Rosie. She had to counter-attack, she simply had to.

'I see. I wish you the evening you deserve, full of laughter. Thank'ee for meeting with me. It was kind of you.'

They could hardly bear to look at each other. They said cursory farewells. There was no hug this time. Maria turned quickly and marched off towards Harborne's. The tears were streaming down her face before she got to the corner to turn away and then she let out a little sob. She stopped along the street from the side door of Harborne's where she'd go in to reach her lodgings. She didn't want the doorman to see her like this. She wanted to find her handkerchief but realised she was still clutching the book Charlie had given her. She opened it up at the bookmark. The poem was called 'Playmates':

> *God permits industrious angels*
> *Afternoons to play.*
> *I met one,—forgot my school-mates,*
> *All, for him, straightway.*
>
> *God calls home the angels promptly*
> *At the setting sun;*
> *I missed mine. How dreary marbles,*
> *After playing Crown!*

Maria sobbed harder then. She'd always struggled with poems and working out the meaning, but she liked the way they made you feel things you hadn't expected. And this poem, as brief and strange as it was, brought a flood of tears from her that frightened her. She didn't know if she was meant to be the angel in the poem, or what Charlie meant by marking it out for her attention, but somehow, in the nebulous thoughts it conjured in her mind, she knew that something awful had happened here today and she'd never quite get over it. The man in her life she'd long relied upon to be there for her, to somehow belong to her, in the selfish way she'd kept him in mind . . . all this was gone. She had Oskar, or, at least, she had the beginnings of something risky and exhilarating with him. But Charlie, her beloved Charlie . . . she knew at that moment that he was her better angel. And now, through her own carelessness, she'd lost him forever.

Chapter 21

On the Monday after Charlie's visit, Maria slogged through the interminable day to which an hour's extra work without overtime pay had been added, to meet the demands of the January sale. After the Christmas madness, there was no respite. Thus, at 11 p.m., all the girls on the ground floor made their way slowly upstairs to their dorms, subdued and mostly silent, except for the odd yawn. It had been a rotten day after the upset with Charlie and then the news about extended hours. And Oskar still away. At least she only had to wait till the Sunday coming to see him again. And Charlie's revelation made her want to see Oskar all the more keenly. Only in Oskar's arms would she feel better about Charlie stepping out with that Rosie Green, of all people. She still couldn't believe it. *She doesn't even like books*, Maria thought grumpily to herself, though she knew that was a snobby thing to say. She made herself feel better by convincing herself that she was right about Rosie, that she only chased Charlie to spite Maria. After a bad day and now with a bad headache, she had no reason to be charitable. She was scornful of the whole idea of Charlie and Rosie. Even their names sounded silly together.

Upon entering the dormitory, every girl shivered. The shop itself was heated for the customers. The dormitories were not. There was not even a fireplace. There were times this winter, on the coldest days, where frost formed on the insides of the windows. They usually got undressed very quickly in the winter months, in order to jump into bed in the shortest time. Once under the covers, they'd pull on bed-socks and wrap a shawl about themselves. One thin blanket was provided to keep each girl warm, but it didn't. Maria couldn't decide which was worse in the dormitories: the stuffy heat of summer or the bitter cold of winter.

She made for her bed, ready to fall into it, and saw Gwen at hers, picking up a letter placed on it. Then she saw there was a letter for her too and both letters were written in the same hand. Maria and Gwen scrabbled to open them up, to find the following:

Interview for the post of assistant to floor manager for dress materials.
Location: Miss Bytheway's Office, with Miss Bytheway and Miss Lafitte.
Sunday 29 January, 1893, at 10.30 a.m.

It was perfect timing. She'd get the interview done, then head off to see Oskar for the first time in a month. What a Sunday it would be!

Maria looked up at Gwen. They both raised their eyebrows and gave each other awkward smiles.

'Got an interview?' asked Gwen.

'I have. You?'

'I have.'

'Best of luck, Gwen.'

'Best of luck to you too, Maria.'

Nobody else in this dormitory had a letter. But there were other dorms, so they didn't know how many girls there would be going for it. Bedtime that night was a little tricky, with both girls acutely aware of their now rival status. Maria had been through all of this before with Rosie and was dreading a similar outcome. The other thing to contend with was the knowledge that, whoever secured the promotion, would be moved to a different dormitory, in a building in the next street. Only the lowest-paid Harborne shopgirls were housed in the worst rooms, in the crow's nest above the store, boiling hot in summer and freezing in winter. A new job, more pay, better accommodation. A lot was at stake.

The floor manager for dress materials, Miss Lafitte, was a French expert in fashion, by all accounts. Maria had seen Miss Lafitte around, eating bacon at the managers' table at breakfast, sweeping through the ground floor from time to time. She was everything that was neat, smart and graceful. She was petite, with dark curly hair tamed into the latest hairstyles. She was in her thirties, but nobody would dare call her an old maid. Miss Lafitte could have her pick of any eligible men to marry, but clearly had chosen her career instead. The thought of working with Miss Lafitte and absorbing all she could from such an expert filled Maria with delight. This was it: the culmination of all those weary hours spent on the shop floor these past months. If she were to get this job, her rise in the profession would be extraordinary.

In the days leading up to the interview, Maria skipped lunch. Instead, she spent the time in the dress materials department inspecting the stock. She wanted to memorise the range of goods so she could answer knowledgeably on all of them in the interview. She'd look at each one, feel its quality and consider how she would extol its virtues to customers. There were serge and tweed, cashmere and merino, crêpe gauze and grenadine, velveteen and plush, taffeta silk and brocade, French cambric, cotton crépons and black moire Française. There were many, many more, in a range of shades. Each night, she took a notebook and pencil to bed and wrote down all the ones she could remember. She considered what a customer might ask, for dresses for particular occasions, and which fabrics she'd suggest. She even went to the trimmings department to consider those that would suit each material. Maria felt lucky she'd done so much dress material work with Mrs Nixon in Ironbridge. She wondered how much Gwen and any other interviewees had done to prepare as she'd not seen Gwen doing the same. Maybe she went over there at different times.

Sunday came and Gwen went down at nine-thirty, her interview just before Maria's. Perhaps she and Gwen were the only two, who knew? Just before 10.30 a.m., her stomach twisting in knots, Maria went down to the shop floor and then up to Miss B's office. She waited in the corridor, expecting Gwen to come out at any moment. Then the door opened and out came Miss Lafitte. No sign of Gwen.

'We are ready for you, Miss Keay,' she said, in her French lilt. *Imagine listening to that lovely voice all day*, thought Maria.

But once she'd sat down, she soon realised that Miss Lafitte's ruthlessness in interview was anything but lovely. Maria was quizzed on seven different fabrics as to their origins, uses, prices and more. She looked only at her notebook while Maria was speaking, which was very off-putting, while Miss B stared at her with a stony face. Maria scanned her memory for all of the details she'd been learning. She answered all of the fabrics questions with confidence. Then Miss Lafitte said she was coming to her final question.

'A gentleman said to me once, "Ah, you ladies and all your silly dresses. What a colossal waste of time it all is." I will not tell you what I said to him as I'd like to hear what you would say to such a comment, if ever you had the opportunity. What would that be?'

Maria considered for a moment before answering. 'I would say, in some ways, he is right.'

Miss Lafitte raised her eyebrows, while Miss B gave away nothing.

Maria went on, 'We women are expected to care about the way we look perhaps more than any other quality of being female. We are cursed with five or more layers of clothes, compared to two or three for men. A man can disrobe his top half in two steps. For a woman, it would take far more effort. We have to work just as hard as men, with far more clothing to carry around on our frames. And in this business, women's fashions are far more complex than men's and yet we women shop workers are paid less than half that of our male counterparts. We are told we are the weaker sex and yet we have to bear our children for nine months, we have to brave the pain of pregnancy and childbirth, we have to bear the loss of babes inside or outside of us and carry on. We must keep house, cook and clean, sew and mend, all while teaching our children how to be good people – and for many of my class, we have to work all hours as well. And all of this while we wear five layers or more, constricting our very breath. Men face the world with far fewer burdens, a world that is made for them. We have to face a world that actively seeks to put us down and keep us down. And yet, weighted down with all those layers, we rise up and succeed every day, working hard, raising children, keeping house, whatever our objectives. With all this a woman has to suffer and bear as she wakes in her bed each dawn, she knows that a well-made dress, a fabric that caresses her skin, a fit that holds her curves just so, a colour that brightens her day, a hat that shows off her face to its best advantage, a skirt and shirtwaist that let her ride a bicycle or walk the miles home or stand up at her work for sixteen hours . . . those clothes are everything. And it's our job at Harborne's to make every woman remember that. Our clothes that we sell these women do so much more than clothe us: they protect us, they support us, they present us to the world. They are our armour. And there is nothing silly about that.'

They said nothing after her speech. Miss B asked her to wait outside for a moment and not to go back to the dormitory. Maria did so and let out a breath she felt she'd been holding in for the whole interview. She'd never spoken like that before. But, somehow, it summed up everything she'd been thinking and learning the last few months. How much she'd wanted to escape her cruel uncle's world of a violent man and frightened children, to make her way as far away from him as she could get. Escaping Savage's wandering hands and Harborne's glad eye. Cheered on by Charlie and Oskar. Supported by Mrs Nixon and Miss Bytheway, women who believed in her, even the lady who bought cigars. Yes, there were bad men. But then there was her father and Mr Boden and all good, kind men like them. Yes, there were jealous women. But then there was cousin Rhoda, giving Maria a place to live when she had no other, losing her babies but soldiering on and surviving. There were Gwen and Polly and the other girls of the dormitory, lending her clothes and buying her food and drink, making her welcome and subbing her until she had her own money, all in it together. She felt fortunate indeed to know all these people and to be lucky enough to have their friendship. Even if she didn't get this job, Maria knew she lived a charmed life in so many ways. When it came to the people who cared about her, she had all the wealth in the world.

Then Miss Bytheway opened the door and beckoned her over.

'Congratulations.' She said it with her customary dourness. But she also gave one of her rare smiles.

Maria wanted to yell and jump around, but she had to contain it all.

'Truly?' she said. 'I have the promotion?'

'Yes, you do.'

'I canna believe it!' she cried, then added, 'I mean, I cannot. Sorry, Miss Bytheway.'

'I'll allow it. Just for today,' Miss B replied, smiling still.

'But, can I just ask, where are all the other applicants? Did you start interviews at the crack of dawn?'

'The only shopgirls we interviewed were you and Miss Steele. You were the only two suitable candidates of the right calibre.'

Maria thought, *Danker me! The right calibre!*

Miss B went on, 'You're an excellent saleswoman, as you've proven with your sales record to date. You also prepared admirably for this interview. Your knowledge of dress materials is excellent. Yet also, something less easy to quantify . . . you have a way about you we like. You understand retail and you understand women. A winning combination. Well done, Maria.'

'Thank you so very much!' she said. She felt it was the proudest moment of her life.

'Tomorrow morning, report to Miss Lafitte at eight. Tonight will be your last night sleeping above the shop, so say your farewells and pack up your things. Tomorrow night after work, I'll take you to your new lodgings on Pride Hill. Off you go now. And make sure you enjoy your Sunday.'

Would she ever! Maria skipped down the stairs to the ground floor and raced across it to the staircase for the dorms. She needed to change her work dress into something nice as she was at last going to see Oskar soon. She couldn't wait! She wanted to tell him her news, jump into his arms and kiss him on the lips.

Then she stopped on the first step up the stairs. She'd have to face Gwen. She'd have to face everyone and tell them she was leaving to live in down the road, instead of in the attic from hell. It felt like facing Rosie again, but ten times worse, as she would have to say goodbye to all of her dormitory mates, because she'd got a better job than them. Would Gwen forgive her? Would the other girls hate her? Would they never ask her to go out with them again?

She traipsed up the stairs, feeling depressed. It was so often that way in her life, she mused, that pure unalloyed joy gave way so quickly to sadness. She reached the top and found that nobody was there. It was gone eleven and everyone had decamped for lunch out. Thank heavens! She pulled off her work dress and chose her favourite red outfit, brushed out her hair and fixed it again, this time with more tendrils hanging down to frame her face. Maria pinned on her hat and she was ready to go. She'd be early at Oskar's, but maybe he was already there. After all, they weren't photographer and model any more. They had kissed. They were something new. Perhaps he was waiting right now, right beside his door, desperate to see her. She rushed from the room and down the stairs double-quick. Could there ever be a better day than this?

Chapter 22

Maria walked swiftly along the road to his lodgings, up the stairs, then rapped loudly on the door. Oskar opened it immediately, just as she'd hoped. He pulled her inside and she squealed with delight. He was in his customary shirtsleeves and waistcoat, despite the cold. He never seemed to feel the chill! He kissed her straight away and she melted into it, laughing at the same time as he tickled her. She was certain that Charlie and Rosie never kissed like this, never! She pulled out her hatpin and flung her hat with the redcurrants down to the floor, her precious hat, but at that moment she felt reckless.

'I've missed you, I've missed you!' he said, over and over, kissing her neck and her cheeks, even her ears. 'The world is dull without the shine of your hair and the sky-blue gleam of your eyes, my sweet Maria.'

Oh, such words! Nobody had ever spoken to her such words of love. They kissed again and it all got a bit breathy and heated, and it made her a little nervous. And, anyway, she wanted to tell him about her job.

251

'Listen, listen,' Maria said as she gently pushed him away. 'I have news!'

'What is it?'

'I have a promotion at work! I am now assistant to the floor manager for dress materials.'

'Clever girl!' he cried and hugged her so hard, she couldn't breathe for a moment. 'What does it mean, assistant of materials? Is it better than hats?'

'Oh, much better. I'll be reporting to the head of a huge section on the ground floor, all of the fabrics we use for women's dresses. And my manager is a proper French lady of fashion!'

'She is French? Ah, I shall teach you French, as I promised. And soon you'll be chattering away, the two of you. And I'll teach you German, so you can impress her.'

That reminded her of his news, the month in Germany with his family.

'That's enough about me. Tell me everything about you. How was your time at home? I wager it was proper lovely, seeing everyone again.'

Oskar pouted a little and backed away, running his fingers distractedly through his hair. 'It was necessary,' he said and sighed.

'You didna enjoy it?'

'Here, come and be seated. Let me tell you about my family.' They sat down beside each other on the chaise longue, holding hands. 'You know, I do not like seeing them really, even though they always expect me to visit often.'

'Why ever not?' Maria was jealous of him, having a family who wanted to spend time with him.

'My father is quite elderly. He had me late in life and my mother was in her latter thirties. Then she died when I was an infant. I have no memory of her.'

'Oh Oskar, I didna know. I'm so sorry.'

'I am fine! It is of no consequence.'

That was an odd thing to say about losing your mother. But perhaps he was making light of it to be brave. It was time, she decided. The right time to tell him.

'My parents died in an accident when I was seven.'

'No, Maria, no. That is tragic. It is awful. You poor child.'

He took her in his arms and held her, stroked her hair. She let Oskar comfort her, but it was him she felt needed the comfort. To have no mother, to have never known one. Somehow, it seemed worse. Maria hated to think of him so alone in the world.

'Do you have any more brothers and sisters or just the one you bought the hat for?'

'Just the one sister and, as you know, she is much older than me. And she acts like a mother, spoiling me one minute and scolding me the next. At times, I must remind them that I am twenty-one years of age and not a little baby any more!'

'It sounds like they care about you though, if they're so interested in everything you do.'

'You are kind, to see it that way. They do love me, in their way, and I them. But they are so behind the times, they drive me to distraction. They are forever speaking on and on about novels and paintings and music and so forth. And I want to talk of other things, real things. Politics, ethics, philosophy, history, science. These are real. But they like art, only art. They are hiding from the world! Hiding in their art, in their fiction. They do not want to hear my ideas, my thoughts, what is truly happening out there.'

'I thought you liked art. You're a photographer.'

'No, no. That is *why* I am a photographer, because it is the only process that truly captures reality. All other art is a sham.'

'But surely, having a different feeling about what subject matter makes for a good chat, that doesna mean you canna be a good family, does it?'

He suddenly let go of her hand and stood up. 'You do not understand!' he said, hotly. 'It is more complex than that. When a person has strong beliefs, and everything they are their family do not even try to comprehend, then it is worse than banishment. It cuts you into pieces slowly, tiny piece by tiny piece.'

Oskar was right that she did not understand it. She would give anything for a family, any family, that cared enough about her to listen to her. But she supposed that if they did not like your ways, then that would be difficult.

'But what is it you disagree on? What kind of things?'

'My beliefs. No, not my beliefs, for they are scientific facts. They have artistic brains and mine is scientific, which is why we cannot connect. I know how life should be and will do all I can to bring about change in my country and elsewhere. To ensure that my country achieves the greatness it aspires to. Only through science and politics can this be achieved. They while away their time reading poetry! It is pointless and a waste of everybody's time.'

Maria thought about the book of poems that Charlie had given her. It didn't feel pointless. She didn't understand many of the poems she'd read in bed that week, but they made her feel in different ways, and made her think hard about something that was just outside of her grasp. She concluded that she was not clever enough to truly understand them, but that didn't mean she was wasting her time. But she didn't tell Oskar any of this. She didn't want them to disagree about anything, ever. She guessed it might be difficult if she disagreed with him. It was easier to keep it to herself. Charlie was solid, his reactions more conventional, easier to debate with. Oskar had a wild unpredictability about him that attracted her immensely and, if she were honest with herself, it worried her too, in equal parts.

'It mun be difficult. Let us talk of something new, if it pains you to speak of it.'

She patted the chaise longue and he sat down and took her hand again.

'I am sorry. I feel things deeply. And I am not always successful at controlling my emotions. Especially about you. Tell me all about you now. Everything. I want to know everything!'

He kissed her cheek and squeezed her hand. She loved his strong emotions. They made her feel wanted and needed, that he felt so passionately about her.

'There inna much to tell, except the usual. Longer and longer hours at work, aching all over, needy customers. The usual kind of endless week. All except my birthday.'

She'd momentarily forgotten she'd decided not to mention her birthday because she didn't want him to feel bad that he'd missed it. But she'd let it slip, by accident.

'A birthday? You have a birthday and did not tell me? When was this? Why did you not tell me?'

'Oh, it's nothing. Dunna fuss. I turned eighteen last Sunday and I had a nice day and evening out.'

'Out with the girls? Did you have fun?'

'I had the evening out with them and so much fun. As we always do.'

'And the day out? Was that with the girls? Or someone else?'

Now she remembered another reason why she hadn't wanted to mention last Sunday to Oskar, but it was too late. And she was a dreadful liar so knew she wouldn't be able to get away with lying about seeing Charlie. But Charlie was courting Rosie, so there was really nothing wrong in seeing him, and she wanted to have no secrets from Oskar. She hated secrets. Best just to tell him and explain. It'd be fine, once she'd explained it.

'Nay, with my friend Charlie.'

'You spent your birthday . . . with Charlie?'

Maria felt his countenance change: his hand loosened in hers. A warmth came up from the tightness in her chest and spread into her cheeks. She'd done nothing wrong, she reminded herself. But then she cursed herself for mentioning it at all. She felt like a fool.

'He's just an old friend and he's courting another friend of ours, a girl called Rosie I used to lodge with. They're stepping out together.'

She felt better once she'd explained it. Surely, he'd understand that this changed things, Charlie being with Rosie. Surely, he'd see that it wasn't a problem now.

'But this man, this Charlie. You and he loved each other once. Did you not?'

His tone of voice was lower, more tense.

'It wasna like that. We were just used to each other, that's all. Because we knew each other as little'uns. We didna have feelings more than that. Just old friends.'

Maria knew she was lying now. But it was necessary.

'I do not believe you,' Oskar said and threw down her hand. 'You are lying. I can tell. How humiliating for you to be caught out in a lie.'

'Charlie and Rosie are courting, Oskar! That is a fact. You say that only facts matter.'

'Not in matters of the heart! Feelings are everything! And you have made me feel envy and sickness. And anger at this other man. I hate him! How could you trifle with my affections so callously? You do not know how much I feel for you? How I would do anything for you, to have your love, to keep your love? I am in love with you, Maria. And you have been with another man while I was away fulfilling family duties and breaking my heart with missing you. You do *not* love me!'

He was glaring at her now and grabbed a hold of her hand again, crushing it.

'I do, I do!' she cried, caressing his hand and trying to wriggle hers free. 'I've done nothing but think on you, every moment of every day, since you left. I was so excited to see you today, I came early, didna you notice? I rushed over here straight after the interview because even if I had to wait, it didna matter, for you'd be there at the end of it, and that was worth any length of waiting.'

His hand released hers and he touched her face with surprising gentleness.

'You do love me . . .' he said, as if realising it for the first time.

'Course I do. Course I love you. I havna met anyone anything like you in my life. I'm mad for you. Dunna you know that?'

Oskar said softly, 'I think I do, I know I do. I love you to distraction, Maria. It was killing me to be apart from you. It hurt me in my very soul.'

'Me too, me too,' she whispered to him, as he reached in and kissed her, so passionately it took her breath away. Her body felt transported as he eased her down onto the chaise longue and kissed her over and over, his hands on her body, touching her, pulling her towards him. And her body responded as it had ached for him these past weeks. And every move she made towards him placated him and pulled them further and further away from their argument and towards peace, by way of their passion. And took her further and further away from Charlie Woodvine and whatever she had shared with him once, and whatever paltry thing he had with Rosie Green. She gave herself to her abandonment and she welcomed it when his hand reached up under her skirts and she felt his touch there and was transported beyond herself to something new she'd never experienced, that she could never even try to describe in words. That was what she had with Oskar, something beyond words that could not be explained. But when he opened his fly and looked about to push into her, Maria stopped him.

'But what about babbies?' she whispered. She didn't want to break the spell they'd woven, but she needed to say it. 'I canna be having babbies now, not now.'

'When was your last bleed?' he said in her ear.

'Last week or so. Ended a few days ago.'

'Then we are fine. I am a scientist and I know the best times to make love each month, and if it is the wrong time, I will tell you. We are fine now. Trust me.'

He was a scientist, that was true. He would know. She did trust him, of course she did. He was the cleverest person she'd ever met.

Chapter 23

They stayed on the chaise longue all day and into the evening, wrapped in each other, naked, with only a blanket and body warmth to keep away the cold. As the dark crept in from late afternoon, Oskar lit a fire and brought her a warm woollen pullover which swamped her so that she looked like a diminutive fisherman. He fed her cooked pheasant meat and red grapes – food she'd never seen, let alone eaten, so pricey it was. It was heavenly. The darkness overcame the studio and the roof windows showcased the beauty of the stars in the night sky, so the two stayed wrapped up together on the chaise longue and watched them, Oskar telling her the stories behind the constellations, which fascinated her. His whisperings lulled her into slumber again and they nestled into each other and slept.

Maria awoke gradually, unwilling to rouse herself from such sweet sleep. It was full night now and she snuggled into her lover's body, amazed at how close two people could be. She'd never understood intimacy until now, the giving of one's self to another. Oskar was right – what if you married and never experienced this until after the wedding day? And found that you were incompatible? The horror of being stuck with someone legally forever and never knowing the completeness she felt right now with this man. She glanced up at the stars, eternal in the night sky, and felt she wanted this moment to never end, to last forever, for all clocks to be stopped and responsibilities erased.

And that was when it hit her. What was the time? She jolted to sit upright, Oskar stirring sleepily. Doors closed at her dormitory at ten. Surely it couldn't be ten yet. She squinted through the dark around Oskar's studio, looking for a clock but couldn't see one, couldn't remember there ever being one. So she shook him awake.

'What is it?' he muttered, grumpily.

'The time, the time, Oskar! What's the time?'

'My watch is around somewhere.'

He rolled back over to sleep, pushing her off the edge of the chaise longue. She jumped up and started pulling her clothes on. Wherever his watch was, and whatever the late hour was, she had to get dressed either way. She called to him.

'Wake up! I mun know the time. And you mun accompany me back to my lodgings!'

'Mun,' he said, 'mun!' and giggled. 'I love your little Shropshire ways.'

'Oskar! This inna a joke. I could lose my job if I'm past curfew. Find your watch now.'

She gave him a shove with both hands, hard. He protested forcefully but eased himself upright, stretching luxuriously. Then he found his watch in his waistcoat hung over a chair and said, 'Five minutes to ten.'

'Danker me!' she cried. 'We have to run! Quick, get dressed! We have five minutes or I'll lose my job!'

He finally understood the urgency and dragged on his clothes and boots.

They ran out of the studio, down the stairs and into the street. Any woman out on the street at that time without a chaperone could easily be accused of being a prostitute and arrested on no evidence, so Maria was glad Oskar was with her, except he was so damnably slow.

'Come on!' she shouted as she pelted round the corner and up the road to the store.

Finally, she was there and the back door was closed. Usually at this time, it was held open by the doorman to see in the last few stragglers before curfew. But it was closed.

'Oh no!' she cried and her eyes filled with tears. But she wasn't going to give up that easily. She raised her fist and bashed on the door. 'I'm here! I'm here! Let me in!'

At first, there was nothing. Oskar finally caught up with her. 'Let me try,' he said, moving her aside. He banged on the door and shouted, 'I say! Open up. There is an emergency here!'

The door opened and George the doorman (and finder of paying gentlemen for shopgirls) appeared. He looked confusedly at Oskar, then spotted Maria and smirked.

'You missed curfew,' he said with a sneer. 'No exceptions.'

He went to close the door and Oskar kicked it open.

'Oi!' cried George. 'Steady on!'

'Let this woman in or I'll beat you,' said Oskar.

George sized up to him. 'Think you can take me, Johnny Foreigner?'

'I know I can. Now let her in.'

'George, please,' begged Maria. 'I'll do anything. I've just got a promotion. I canna lose my job, I just canna!'

'Shoulda thought of that before ending up on your back with this'un,' he laughed.

'I'll kill you!' shouted Oskar and Maria leapt between them, terrified that Oskar would do what he'd threatened, which would mean she'd never get in or keep her job, if murder were on the cards.

'Call your dog off!' said George to Maria. 'And ask him if he can pay.'

A glimmer of hope. Oskar said, 'Of course I can pay, you cretin. Let Maria in first and then we shall come to terms.'

'Cash first,' said George.

Oskar sighed and pulled out the money in his trouser pockets and suit pockets, dropping it into Maria's hands as he searched. She counted it.

'Sixteen shillings and thruppence,' she said to George.

It was a huge amount: nearly two weeks' wages for her, probably less for a doorman, but still substantial. To think, Oskar had all this money just lying around in his pockets. Almost inconceivable for a girl like her.

'That is all I have on me. It will have to do,' said Oskar, folding his arms and glaring at the doorman.

George raised his eyebrows and nodded. 'Hand it over,' he said, grinning now at his good fortune.

At that moment, Maria heard someone coming down the stairs. She prayed feverishly that it wouldn't be one of the managers. A face appeared behind George. It was Gwen.

'What's happening here?' she said to George.

'None of your beeswax,' George replied and stood aside to let Maria in.

'Thank'ee,' said Maria to Oskar, who shook his head.

'A small price to save you,' he said. 'I shall see you next Sunday.'

She kissed him on the cheek, at which George whooped and laughed, then fell to counting his winnings. Maria stepped past George, furious at him, but more at herself.

George leant in close and said, 'I can get you a nicer class of gent for your money, Maria. Not a filthy foreigner, like that 'un. And they'd fall over 'emselves for pretty hair like yours.'

He took hold of a lock of it and leered at her.

'Nay, thank'ee, George. I'd rather shave my head.'

She pushed past him and went up the stairs with Gwen, who said, 'I came down to look for you. You're lucky he's rich.'

'I know, I know. Dunna scold me.'

Maria went up the stairs, just desperately relieved she was inside. Everything could've been lost. She turned to Gwen as they ascended.

'Sorry I just snapped at you. I'm grateful you came to check on me. It was just a mistake. We were busy taking photographs and lost all sense of time.'

'Taking photographs, all day and night?' said Gwen with sarcasm.

'Indeed we were. It's hard work.'

'Ever seen one of these photographs? You havna shown us one.'

'He hasna shown me one, not yet. He has work to do on them.'

She wanted to see some of them and had asked Oskar, but he said he had to develop them with different chemicals for different effects and he'd show her when he was ready.

'I still dunna think it takes that many hours to go snap snap. No need to lie to me about what you were really up to. I'm no innocent.'

Maria wanted to protest her own innocence, but it stuck in her throat. She didn't like pretending to her friend when Gwen herself had long since lost her virginity, and not for love as Maria had. But she didn't know how to explain it to Gwen or anyone. It wasn't a transaction with Oskar. It had nothing to do with his wealth. They loved each other, deeply. She wanted to say it but felt her words would ring hollow.

When they got to the top of the stairs, Gwen turned to her

and said, 'I worry for you. Taking such risks. Fact is, manager came just before curfew and did a room check. I lied for you and said you were in the privy due to eating bad fish. I wonna lie for you again. I could lose my job too.'

'Oh, Gwen, I'm so grateful. Thank'ee, thank'ee!'

'I wonna do it twice.'

'I know, I know. Thank'ee again. I wonna let you down.'

And then Maria remembered that her new promotion was at Gwen's expense. It would've been easy for Gwen to say nothing and let Maria be sacked, and Gwen would've most likely been given the position. This was even more of a sacrifice.

'I know what it'd mean for you, if I'd been sacked. I wanna thank'ee for doing that for me, when it coulda made your life easier if you hadna.'

'Shopgirls dunna betray their own,' she said, turned away and walked into the dormitory.

Maria steeled herself, then when she entered the room, she got a great cheer.

Polly said, 'Living life on a cliff's edge, eh, wench!'

Maria had to laugh, the relief was so immense.

Then Polly added, 'And congratulations, for the new job! You'll be off to sleep with the posh'uns from tomorrow. Well done and best of luck with it all. You deserve it, Maria.'

Polly gave her a big hug and lots of the other girls patted her on the back and gave her a hug too. Maria was overcome with gratitude and felt tearful as she thanked everyone for their kindness. She was applauded all the way to her bed. She smiled at Gwen, who gave her a pointed look, then turned away and sat on her own bed, unwilling to talk to her. Maria knew Gwen had jeopardised her own position for her and that she wouldn't be doing it again, and Maria couldn't blame her. Sisterly support was all very well, but not when it verged on losing your own job. None of these girls had a secure situation to fall back on. It was either work or marriage or penury.

After the fuss over Maria had died down and she'd undressed and got into bed, the lights were turned down and she lay wide awake. She'd been very fortunate tonight. She'd got away with it, kept her job, her man and her friends. But before all of that drama, something momentous had happened to her in Oskar's arms. She wished she could talk to Gwen about losing her maidenhood but feared Gwen would judge her harshly. Maria felt there was nobody she could talk to about it. But she didn't regret it, what she'd done with Oskar. She'd wanted to. She played it over and over in her mind. But then she scolded herself inwardly for putting Oskar above her job and nearly losing it. All of that work would have been for nothing. But at the same time, she felt so close to him now and knew she was in love with him. And surely he must be in love with her too, to come with her that way and pay off the doorman. *So this is what love is*, she thought. It was a world away from how she felt about Charlie. It must be the sexual union that made it different. She had been reborn somehow. And on top of all that, Maria had got her longed-for promotion on the very same day, and tomorrow she'd be leaving this poky, freezing or boiling death-trap of a room and moving to new horizons. She lay, listening to the breathing of her shopgirl comrades. She ought to be ecstatic about it all: securing the promotion of her dreams, finding the love of her life. But instead she lay awake, utterly unable to sleep, feeling that she hadn't found or gained anything. Her overwhelming sensation was that something profound had been lost, never to be retrieved.

Chapter 24

January – February 1893

After only one day with Miss Lafitte, Maria felt as if she had finally found her place in the world. Her new mentor truly took her under her wing, including her in every moment of the day when there was an opportunity for learning. After the drudgery of gloves and hats, there was the joy of discussing fabrics with customers in depth, picturing their beautiful outfits and selling them that vision every time. She hadn't failed in one sale, not yet. Every single client had bought something from Maria, and Miss Lafitte was delighted with her new protégée. That evening after work, Miss Lafitte gave her two new outfits for her new position and told her to sit at breakfast with her in the morning, at 7 a.m. Maria thought delightedly, *Bacon and eggs, here I come!*

Maria had to say goodbye to her friends to move to the new lodgings. She packed, then hugged many of them and left Gwen till last, giving her a special hug and a whispered thank you.

'Dunna fret,' said Gwen, laughing it off. 'It inna like you're going to Siberia! I'll see you around on the shop floor.'

'Can I still come out of an evening with you and the girls?'

'Course,' said Gwen. 'If you can find the time!'

Maria took her bag and went down the stairs and along the street to the building beside Harborne's, where the assistants and middle managers were housed. It was a terraced house with several rooms off a single staircase, each room housing a small number of women, with some single rooms for the most senior. Maria's was again at the top of the house, more was the pity, as she knew she'd have the same problem of heat and cold throughout the seasons. But that was the only similarity. The room had four decent beds in it, with proper bedding, and also decent furniture in which to put her things away. The other three in her room were all assistants to other section heads. They were nice enough. But Maria felt an edge of snobbery to them, looking her up and down in her old shop-floor outfit before she'd had a chance to wear her new one. She imagined telling Polly about them and knew she'd say, 'They're all a bit lah-di-dah.' But despite the rather frosty reception, the room was deliciously warm, as they had their own fire alight in there. This was another world. And Maria adored it.

The next morning, she put on her new outfit: a very fashionable black skirt with black velvet roses on the hem, white shirtwaist and black velvet bodice. This time, with her earnings from her modelling work, she could pay off her new clothes straight away. On the shop floor that morning, she swanned around in her new outfit like a duchess.

The next couple of weeks were tiring as ever, yet at least she had her relaxing accommodation to go back to afterwards. And the thrill of Sundays to come, when she'd spend all day and evening with Oskar. There was no longer any pretence between them that she was there as a model. They spent their time discovering each other's bodies in ever new delectable ways or drinking wine and eating treats (peaches preserved in brandy were her favourite new thing). She also got to know more of him and his life, seeing behind most of the closed doors at his accommodation. The door off the vestibule was a bathroom, with proper indoor plumbing and a huge bath, which she luxuriated in whenever she could. She was surprised to find there was no bedroom. They made love on the rug by the fire or on the chaise longue, and that was where he normally slept at night. When he'd moved in, he explained, he'd sacrificed the bedroom to become his darkroom, and it was perfect as it had only been a small room with a single bed in it and no windows.

'Can I see your darkroom? I still haven't seen any of my photographs. And I wanna understand how it all works. It seems like magic, bringing a picture to life on a piece of paper.'

'You cannot enter the darkroom, I am sorry to say. Nobody but the photographer is permitted.'

'Why not?' she said.

'Because, my love, there are chemical processes practised within and thus it needs to be kept scrupulously clean, as sterile as a laboratory, for the photographs to develop properly. Thus, no outsiders can enter.'

She was tremendously impressed and in awe of his knowledge of scientific things, such as the complexity of chemistry that he explained was behind photography. They spent some of these long, lazy hours talking too, discussing issues of the day. His ideas about the world were so . . . well, she couldn't think of another word for it but worldly. Oskar seemed to know everything. And he was always happy to teach Maria new things, which she hugely appreciated. She particularly found anything about geography interesting, as she had done at school.

Oskar explained to her, 'Each country is a nation, and nationhood is very important: to love your country. There are other countries in the world that are inferior to those of northern Europe, which are the finest: England, France and Germany, perhaps the Netherlands, as well as Belgium and Switzerland. Here we have everything civilisation needs to prosper. And yet it is under threat. There are dark, shadowy figures from beyond our boundaries that seek to ruin these utopias we are building. Those who bury themselves in art and fiction are blind to the threat, an existential threat, to our very borders, our very shores. We are strong but can be undermined by the weak if we are not careful. Nature itself is all about the triumph of the strong over the weak. You are familiar with the ideas of your countryman Charles Darwin?'

Never heard of him, she thought. 'Remind me which one he is?' Maria said, pretending to have simply forgotten the name. She wondered if Charlie had heard of him. Probably. Charlie knew most things.

Then Oskar told her all about survival in nature and the strong and the weak and their eternal battle. And how this was mirrored in society.

She pondered this, then said, 'Men say women are weaker, but just look at what we have to put up with. I'd like to see a man deal with the monthly curse without complaining. Or childbirth! I heard my cousin have her daughter. It was agony! She fought it like a trooper. So am I the strong or the weak?'

'You are the strong, of course. Just look at yourself. Your white-yellow hair and perfect blue eyes. You are superior to all around you. You do not see this, whenever you are out in the world? Your utter dominance over all you survey?'

'I'm just a shopgirl!' she said and laughed, though she liked the idea of being superior. That was one in the eye for the sniffy girls in her new lodgings.

'That is irrelevant,' he replied. 'It is your breeding that counts.'

Maria didn't understand what he was talking about, not really. But she just loved to listen and soak it all up. Oskar's knowledge of the world was spellbinding, no doubt learnt through travelling and reading scientific books on the subject. Many of these were scattered about the room on shelves, tables and chairs, even some left splayed open beneath the chaise longue. If only she had more time to read, maybe she'd be as clever as Oskar or Charlie one day. In the meantime, all she could do was absorb whatever learning she could from Oskar, just as she used to from Charlie.

Ah, Charlie. She missed his letters. She'd not heard from him since their row on her birthday. But considering Oskar's reaction to her seeing Charlie at all, she figured it was probably the best thing to stop seeing him altogether. And while he wasn't in contact, that was no problem. But she did wonder how she'd feel if Charlie wrote to her again. Something to worry about another day. For now, she had her Oskar and he was all she needed. Maria even stopped going out with the girls. She was never asked, so she never enquired. And she'd rather be here, in Oskar's studio with him, than anywhere else in the world.

One Sunday, they were lying together wrapped up in a sheet and Oskar stated that he wanted to take a photograph of her like that, her hair tumbling down her back, her white sheet against her white skin and almost-white hair. It was risqué, but she'd only be showing her shoulders, so she agreed. It would make a lovely image. She thought, *One day when I'm old and ugly, I can look back on it and think what a dish I was.*

Maria sat on the chair, the sheet carefully positioned, like something a Roman would wear, so it didn't fall down. She didn't want any sneaky naked shots. That really would be beyond the pale. He took a few photographs and was telling her how stunning they'd be when there came abrupt and forceful knocking on the front door.

271

'Who the devil is that?' said Oskar, annoyed.

'Dunna let them in!' cried Maria, clasping her sheet to herself. To be found like that in a man's apartment would be the end of her. 'Canna we ignore it? Or might it be a client of yours?'

'I do not have clients.'

'But . . . you're a photographer.'

'Ah, yes. Only for myself. I do not need clients. I practise photography to learn the science of it. To record life. I do not need people to pay me. I am wealthy, you know.'

But the knocking continued, then a woman's voice spoke out loudly in German. Oskar glared at the front door and Maria saw something in Oskar's eyes she'd never seen before. She saw fear.

Chapter 25

'Who is it?' Maria whispered to Oskar. 'What's she saying?'

'Get dressed,' Oskar snapped at her, as he went towards the door. Maria knew it'd take her far longer to get all her layers on and buttoned up than it took for him to reach the front door. She grabbed her things and backed away, so that whoever was at the door could not see her from it. But she was terrified they'd come in at any second and there she'd be, in her disgrace. She looked behind herself and saw the nearest thing was the darkroom door. It was time to break the rules. There was nothing for it but to go in there to get dressed. She'd have to deal with the consequences afterwards. Maria couldn't bear for this German woman, whoever she was, to see her half-dressed like a common Judy. So when Maria heard the woman's steps across the vestibule, she had no choice but to open up the darkroom door and go inside, closing it quietly behind her. The German woman's voice grew louder and Oskar answered back testily in his own language, thus Maria had no idea what they were talking about, other than that it was little short of an argument. Oskar certainly did not sound pleased to see her, whoever she was.

Here Maria was, at long last, in the mysterious darkroom. There was already an electric light on in a curious red shade, which created an eerie atmosphere. At least she could see. She'd imagined it to be totally black in here and she wondered how well she'd do getting herself ready in the pitch darkness. She heard them continue to talk, him sounding subdued and her talking firmly to him. Oskar sounded like a completely different person: not only quicker and more fluent in his own language, but, strangely, smaller somehow, less feisty and sure of himself, his voice higher too, almost like a child who was being told off.

Maria stopped focusing on that and scolded herself for wasting time. She started to pull on her clothes and fix her hair, plaiting it as neatly as she could, as she'd left her hairpins in the next room. As she did so, she couldn't help but look around at the equipment and set-up in the darkroom, hoping against hope that she wasn't contaminating anything scientific with her presence. There were trays and dishes and bottles of chemicals in disarray all around. It didn't look very scientific, instead appearing decidedly haphazard, if not a total mess. And strewn all over the floor were many pieces of photographic paper, turned over so she couldn't see the front. At last, Maria could spy some of her photographs that he'd never shown her. She finished her hair, then crouched down and turned over a few. There she was, but she could hardly see herself, as the photographs were either far too dark or too light, some with what looked like chemical spills across them. She turned over more and more and found the vast majority of them were ruined, poorly lit and badly developed. Then she saw there were also piles of torn-up photographs under the tables, shredded into tiny pieces. What had Oskar been doing all this time with the photographs he took of her? Why did they look so poor? Why were so many destroyed? Leafing through the disastrous pile, she did find one that wasn't completely ruined. She folded it up and slipped it into her pocket. She'd like to have one, just one, however badly done it was. She looked ethereal in it, like a ghost.

Then, she could hear the voices of Oskar and the German woman raised in volume. And as she stood there, in the ruins of his darkroom, listening to him argue with what she could only guess was a German lover, she felt sick with jealousy. Maria knew it was probably best to stay hidden. But she didn't want to. She wanted to know what the hell was going on. So she put her hand gingerly on the door handle, still unsure. But, damn it, the only way to find out was to be brave and go.

She saw the woman first, older than herself and Oskar, quite a bit older, with Oskar's colouring, yet her hair was a deeper gold that shone against her skin beneath her hat. She was extremely well-dressed in an emerald green dress with a dark fur about her shoulders and a fur-lined hat and boots. Now, that was the way to dress for an English winter.

The woman stared at Maria with her mouth open in a little O, clearly as shocked to see Maria as Maria was shocked by the woman's age and relatively plain face. She did not see how Oskar could be in love with a woman so much older and also less beautiful than she herself was, though she knew it was vain to think so. The only thing to do was to introduce herself. And then see what was what.

'Good afternoon, madam,' Maria said, holding out her hand like a man, as she wasn't sure what else to do. The woman took it and nodded at her, smiling yet still surprised.

'And who is this ravishing beauty?' said the woman in perfect English, with a heavy German accent. 'My dear, please tell me your name and how you come to be secreted in Oskar's apartment!'

Maria looked at Oskar, who had raised his eyes to the heavens, raked shaking fingers through his hair and looked just about done with the whole business. So she introduced herself.

'I'm Maria Keay. I'm a photographic model. I was just in the darkroom when you arrived, working as Oskar's assistant. It's a pleasure to meet you.'

'And I am charmed to meet you,' she said. 'Allow me to introduce myself. I am Lina von Schoen. Yes, I have the same surname as my brother as I am what the English refer to as an "old maid". Society may see me as disadvantaged, yet I call it freedom.'

Oskar's sister! And what an opening! Maria liked her already. Oskar, however, looked livid.

'Come, my dear,' said Lina, beckoning Maria to join her. 'Let us set ourselves down on the chaise longue, seeing as it is the only civilised item of furniture in the place.'

Oskar then shot a German phrase at his sister that, despite knowing not a word of the language, Maria could instantly tell was suggesting in no uncertain terms that she leave.

She answered back, 'But I wish to get to know your charming companion.'

Lina sat down sedately, adjusting her furs. Her hair was styled in a perfect wave across her forehead, beneath a neat green hat with a shallow veil. She dressed exquisitely.

'Miss von Schoen,' said Maria. 'Can I just say how well you dress? When I'm not here as a photographic assistant, I also work at a local department store – Harborne's – the largest one in the county. I've worked in gloves, hats and now women's dress materials, and I know fine work when I see it. Everything you wear is beautifully made, it really is.'

Lina took Maria's hand and patted it. 'You are too sweet for words! I like you very much, Maria.'

'Why are you here?' said Oskar from the other side of the room. Maria knew that voice. It was the deep, hollow voice he used when an argument was brewing. She never liked it. She glanced at Lina, whose face showed she knew that voice too, but, unlike Maria, she showed no fear of it whatsoever.

'I have already told you, dear brother. I am here to check on you and see how you're currently wasting the family money. And I find you have found a new hobby and an expensive one, in photography. Are you any good at it though? I wonder. We shall speak of that later. But, for now, I have Miss Keay to entertain me. Oh, and Oskar?'

'What now?' he said, seething.

'A glass of wine would be most welcome. Something German if you can find it. I have spied two empty bottles in this room already, so I assume you need more. Take your time. Off you trot, as the English say.'

Maria expected Oskar to erupt as she'd seen him do before. But he simply grabbed his coat and hat and stormed out of the room, slamming the front door behind him. She was amazed at how, despite his clear anger, he obeyed his sister so quickly. She was certainly seeing a different side of him. And as for that darkroom . . . But she had to focus on Lina now, who was squeezing her hand. Maria looked at her and was perturbed to see the imperious smile had vanished from her face, replaced by worry.

'My dear, I am sorry to say in the brief time we have while he is gone – for, take my word for it, he will not be keen to leave you and I together for a moment longer than he has to – I have some uncomfortable truths to dispense today. Please tell me the nature of your relationship with my brother. You're not really his assistant, are you?'

There was something about the concern on her face that made Maria want to talk frankly with her. 'You're right, I inna Oskar's assistant. Truth is, I started as his model and now . . . he is my beau.'

It was the most delicate way she could think to put it.

'I suspected as much. Now, listen well, my dear, as we have little time. I advise you now, most strongly, to leave this room and never return. Never, do you understand?'

'Well . . . nay, I dunna understand. I dunna understand at all. Oskar and I are very happy together.'

The fear crept over Maria that she had been judged on sight by Lina as unworthy of such a wealthy man as Oskar and she was ready to battle for the right to see whatever man she chose.

'I am certain it seems that way now. It is the period of the honeymoon, where everything seems delicious and the future is laid out like a magic carpet and all is well. But all is not well, my dear. And it is no fault of yours. You see, the problem is Oskar. He has always been a problem and it is only getting worse.'

'What is? What's getting worse?' Maria asked, incredulous. So it wasn't her own class that was at issue. But what was this about Oskar?

Lina shifted forward and looked intently at Maria. 'We have so little time. I cannot break it to you gently, but he is no good. He is bad, through and through. I know you want details, and I will tell you what I can before he returns, but the truth is I have come to bring him home as he needs supervision.'

'Supervision, but why?'

'Let me speak, and if there is time, then you may ask questions after. Listen carefully now. Our family, the von Schoens, we come from a long line of poets and philosophers. Yes, we are wealthy, but we have tried to use our wealth to improve the common good. We read, we lecture, we write and paint. Growing up, Oskar was the odd one out as he had none of these talents and it infuriated him. We all did our best to accommodate him, find him something that we could nurture in him. But all he was interested in was hunting, shooting, killing things. And drinking. And taking laudanum with his rowdy friends. We thought it merely a phase of youth and it would pass. But he has been this way for years now, with no sign of abating. Moreover, he has been reading pamphlets from troublesome people that distribute their words of hate among the beer halls of Bonn, calling for rebellion in Germany against the government. His political ideas now are abhorrent to us. He believes in an extreme form of nationalism that wants to destroy democracy and install a strong leader who would have absolute power over all. He believes that the very fibre from which all humans are made is inferior in some, superior in others. And he believes this to such an extent that he wishes to see a government one day that would remove those types of people he sees as inferior from not only our country but from the face of the earth. It is a horrific philosophy, one with which the von Schoen family are in no way associated. It appals us – myself and our father. We are liberals. We believe in art and goodness, culture and responsibility for others. Oskar is, in every way, the opposite of everything we hold dear. And it is not simply a political disagreement. We fear there is madness in him. I came here to take him home and, once home, we will do all we can to persuade him to enter an asylum where he can receive treatment for his troubled mind and improve. If I do not succeed, I want to tell you, Maria, that I fear for you. I fear for your future, if you stay with Oskar. As much as I love him, for he is my brother, I would not wish to inflict his worst characteristics on my worst enemy and certainly not such a young girl like yourself, as I believe he will destroy you.'

Maria felt a chill run down her spine. Everything Lina said felt like listening to Oskar going on about science. She knew it meant something important, but her mind was not agile enough to keep up. How could all this be true of Oskar? Hadn't he been kind to her? Wasn't he a generous man? What did all this talk of nationalism mean? And madness? She wished she had Charlie's brain to understand it. Whatever it meant, it all sounded very, very bad.

'How . . . how could he *destroy* me? He loves me. I know he loves me.'

'I speak frankly, my dear. I see you are already in his thrall. I take it he's bedded you – more than once, I am guessing considering how comfortable you are in his lodgings here. He's been looking for a girl like you for a long, fruitless time. And now he's found you. He'll want a child from you. A perfect child to breed his new dynasty. And you will never escape him then. It may already be too late. But whatever you do, you must get away from him now and never see him again. If he knows where you work, where you live, it is best you leave the town, the county even. He will not give up trying to find you. I know for a fact he has a pistol. He stole it from our father, who kept it in the house for defence. He is dangerous, Maria. I fear this will all end in disaster for you.'

At that moment, the front door opened and in came Oskar with the wine. Lina's face changed in a split second, from earnest to smug.

'You took so long, my brother, I assumed you had gone to grow the grapes yourself. Here, pour me a glass.'

Oskar came into the studio and looked at Maria. The moment he saw her, it was as if he could read her face like a book.

'What have you been saying to her?' he said viciously to Lina. 'What poison have you been pouring in her ear?'

Lina answered in German and Oskar answered back. And thereafter, Maria was witness to a fully orchestrated, rage-filled argument in a foreign language. She knew not a word, but she absolutely understood the sentiment. After some minutes watching this terrifying performance, Oskar was pointing at the door, clearly yelling at Lina to leave, looking as if he'd throw her out himself physically at any moment. Lina kept her cool countenance throughout and, standing up, held her hand up and that alone seemed to temporarily subdue him.

Lina turned to Maria and said, 'My dear, I need say no more to you, except to heed my words. Do not allow yourself to become trapped by him, for the truth is, *meine liebe*, he loves you only for your blue eyes and your pale hair.'

'Get out!' Oskar screamed. '*Raus hier*! *RAUS*!'

Chapter 26

March – April 1893

There was a calendar pinned on the door in Maria's lodgings. She carefully went through it, counting the days since her last bleed. It was six weeks ago. She had missed a bleed this month. She wasn't going to panic. After all, in the days when her diet had been poor and she'd often gone hungry and been perpetually overworked she was used to missing bleeds. Even though she was eating better these days, at the managers' table, perhaps her body was still getting used to eating well and just needed to catch up. That was it, that explained it. She was not going to worry about being late. After all, Oskar had explained it. He was a scientist, who knew exactly when to indulge and when to abstain. He'd never have made a mistake. It just wasn't possible.

Maria still loved her job, but felt these days she was going through the motions. She found it difficult to concentrate. It had been a few weeks now since she'd seen or spoken to Oskar. She'd told him it was best to have a little break from each other. He'd been livid about it, but she'd stood firm. The moment his sister had left, he'd sat her down on the chaise

longue, just as Lina had, and told her a mirrored version of the
story. He'd said his sister was mad and they were trying to get
her committed to an asylum, that she drank laudanum and
dreamt up ridiculous fantasies about him and other people
they knew. Also, that she was horribly jealous of Oskar and
his talents in science, and sought to do all she could to ruin his
life. Their father was beside himself with worry and never
knew what to do about Lina. This was why Oskar always had
a difficult time when he went home. Lina was the family problem and he'd not told Maria about it as he was ashamed. He
didn't want her to think there was madness in his family.
Maria had said all the right things, that she believed him. But,
inside, she didn't know if she did. She'd asked him about the
darkroom, the mess in there and the ruined photos. He'd been
very defensive about that, saying he never claimed to be a professional. He was learning his craft and improving by the day.
Nobody expected Michelangelo to carve David on his first
day, did they? Maria had accepted that. Oskar had tried to
cuddle her and ease her back onto the chaise longue, but she'd
pushed him firmly off and stood up, saying she was going now
and needed time to think.

He'd replied, 'Do not go, my love. Stay. And marry me!'

'You're asking me to marry you?' she'd said, incredulous.

And he'd stood up, picked Maria up and kissed her passionately, professing his all-dying love for her.

'Will you say yes? Tell me yes!'

What could she say after a member of her intended's family
had just told her that her beloved was . . . was what? Mad?
Bad, all through? Could it be true? Oskar was moody, that
was true. But he was clearly a genius and Maria guessed that
geniuses were allowed to be moody. It was all part of being
extraordinary. They didn't react to things in the same way as
normal people, ordinary souls like shopgirls and schoolmasters.

She was proud to be with such an unusual man. And perhaps his sister was jealous. After all, she was a spinster. Maybe she envied her brother's talents as a scientist and his ability to travel unaccompanied throughout the world and learn about it.

But just as much could be argued the opposite way. And seeing Oskar regularly would only confuse things. So, Maria decided to be strong and not see him for a while. She'd said she'd come back to him when she'd had time to think. She wanted to mention the pistol to him, that Lina had said he had stolen from his father, but she was too worried about his response. So she kept it to herself.

He'd said, 'I will wait for you until time ends. I am not going anywhere. Come to me when you are ready to give me your answer. A week, a month, two months, a year. It will not matter. For I know that you love me and you will come to the right choice. And when you come to me, we will start our beautiful life together and it will be perfect, Maria. I will make it so.'

It was the right thing to do, to give herself time, to try to decide if she believed his sister or not. But now she'd ended her addiction to him so abruptly, she suffered daily from with-drawal. Maria missed him, his body, his kisses, his words of love. Their time together was an escape from the ravages of the everyday grind and her body reached out for his touch. And now she had missed a bleed. But she was still holding onto the fact that this had happened with her many times before and didn't prove anything. But as to when she'd be ready to go back to him, that she did not know. Many of the things Lina had said could be explained away, but one thing haunted Maria and that was what Lina had said about her col-ouring, about breeding, about the only reason Oskar loved her. That couldn't be true, could it? She'd always wanted to have raven-black hair and flashing dark eyes, like Polly. Why would her colouring be so important to an intelligent man like

Oskar? Maybe he just had a type, like Mr Harborne did. Surely Lina was talking nonsense.

* * *

April came to Shrewsbury, the spring flowers blooming in geometric patterns along the beds in The Quarry, not that she'd had time to wander through and see them. Maria's working hours were as ruthless as ever, especially now the spring sale was on. Saturday nights finished later again, with no extra pay. She came back to her bed each night and almost fell asleep standing before her head hit the pillow. Sundays she spent mostly in bed, though the other girls in her room insisted she must come to church with them. But she couldn't face it. She just wanted peace, quiet and rest. Often, she would lie there, drifting between wake and sleep, clutching the photograph of herself she'd taken from the darkroom floor. She looked like a spectre in it. And these days, spent entirely indoors, her colouring paler than ever, her days ebbing away, she felt like one too. It had been so long since she'd gone out for a Sunday gallivant with her previous girlfriends and she felt too awkward approaching them again now. Maria felt that opportunity had passed, and now she was either working, or alone in her room, or asleep. And this was when she missed Oskar even more.

Then came a Sunday when she couldn't wait any longer. The weather was warm and inviting. She didn't want to stay in bed alone. Her body felt alive with springtime, vibrant and ready for something new. She took this as a sign that she must see him, that new life was breaking through the earth all around her and she could not spend her days any longer in a kind of aching death. This dreadful feeling, that had dragged her down since she'd stopped seeing Oskar, proved to her that it was wrong, all wrong, and that she'd only feel right again if she saw him and gave him her answer. She dressed in her favourite new outfit, a sky-blue spring dress with yellow flowers at the hem, waist and collar, perfect for her colouring and the season of renewal. She walked swiftly to his studio, hurried up the steps and knocked loudly on the door. Maria couldn't wait to see him now and her whole body hummed with vivacity and expectation. But he did not come to the door. He must be out, in the spring sunshine, perhaps taking photographs of street scenes and landscapes as he once told her he did (though she'd not seen a photograph like that in the dark room). Yes, that was it. She'd sit down and wait. He wouldn't be long. He'd want to develop the plates in the studio.

She waited. And waited. Lunchtime came and went and her belly rumbled from hunger. She could wait no longer, as she felt weak from it and nauseous. She went to a bakery and bought a huge slab of fidget pie, bursting with potato, onion, apple and ham. She polished it off, straight from the bag, in a couple of minutes. She was so ravenous now the spring days were here. The slice of pie had given Maria the energy she needed to be sensible about this. She tried not to be too despondent about Oskar's absence. He had been so adamant that he would wait for her. And she was sure he wouldn't let her down. After all, he could not read her mind and predict the moment she'd come. She decided that next Sunday she'd come with a note and leave it there if he still wasn't home. There, that sorted that problem. She felt better then and spent the day in the spring sunshine. Everything around her was waking up.

At work after that, she felt enthused and renewed. She threw herself into her job every day that week and by Friday, when she was usually exhausted, she still felt bright as a button. Then, on Saturday morning just after start time, she stopped walking in the middle of the store and knew, with absolute certainty, that she was going to vomit all over the thick, red carpet. She hurried with as much decorum as she could to the privies for women staff, noticing that Gwen spotted her as she rushed past gloves. The relief, when she reached the lavatory and was able to hurl her breakfast up into it, was immense. When it had all come up, Maria sat back on the floor and had a moment of euphoria, a moment of clarity, the relief of the nausea gone. She had missed a second bleed and ignored it. She was fooling herself. She must be pregnant.

Maria went to the women's staffroom to splash her face with water and cool down. Gwen came in.

'Are you well?' said Gwen, with concern. She came over and put her hand gently on Maria's back. 'No, you inna well at all. Tell Miss L you need to be off work.'

'I inna sick.'

'Course you are. You look white as a sheet. Want me to tell Miss L instead?'

'Nay!' Maria snapped. 'Sorry, I didna mean to say it like that. But please dunna tell anybody.'

'Here, come on. Take a load off.' Gwen steered her to a chair to sit down. 'That's better. Now then, what ails you? What dunna you want Miss L to know?'

Maria looked up at Gwen. She'd missed her, and Polly, and all the girls from the dormitory from hell. Seeing her friend looking at her with such sympathy made her realise how much she'd lost by leaving them, how alone she'd been ever since. She burst out crying and wept and wept, wiping away tears and snot with the back of her hand. Gwen passed her a fresh hankie.

'Let it all out. What's up, eh? What's got you in a state like this?'

She could tell Gwen, couldn't she? Of course she could. All the shopgirls had a code of silence. They watched each other's backs. And Gwen might've been in this situation before herself, who knew? But also, it wasn't so bad as that, as Maria knew she loved Oskar now and wanted to accept his proposal of marriage. And maybe he'd be fine about the baby. Why wouldn't he? He loved her. And everything would be perfect, just as he said it would be. Wouldn't it?

'I'm in the family way,' Maria said, trying to sound hopeful, but it came out miserably.

'Thought as much,' said Gwen and folded her arms.

'Dunna lecture me, Gwen, please!' sobbed Maria.

'Too late for a lecture. What are you gonna do about it? Marry that German? If he's still in the country. Or get rid of it?'

Maria gasped. 'I couldna! I could never! How could you suggest such a thing?'

'Because I've done it myself. I was careful and nobody found out. There are ways.'

As Maria suspected, Gwen had had to deal with it too, but she was shocked to hear how lightly her friend seemed to take the illegal procedure that would kill the baby. As much of a mess as this was, she wondered at that moment what she would do if Oskar had left the country, left her forever, alone and expecting. Maybe she would get a backstreet woman to get rid of it. Maybe she would have to. It was either that or bring up a child alone, disgraced, in utter poverty, ending no doubt in the workhouse. She would do it to avoid that future. She would do it in a heartbeat.

'What are you gonna do then?' said Gwen again. 'It wonna be long afore it starts to show. There's only so many times you can let out a skirt before everybody knows.'

'I need to think,' said Maria.

'You do, and think hard. You've been a fool, Maria. At least when I did it, I did it for money, not for some notion of love. Let's see how much he loves you when he's presented with a child out of wedlock. Think on.'

Gwen left the room. How could she be so cruel? Then Maria felt maybe that's exactly what she needed at that moment. Gwen always knew what to do for the best. If only she'd listened more carefully to Gwen in the past. She knew the way Maria was going when she met Oskar. Gwen had warned her to take care. She never beat around the bush about these things. Gwen had made her see that she needed to grow up, and fast, to take responsibility for what had happened. Maria sat for a while, recovering, drank some water and stopped her tears. She dried her eyes, pinched her cheeks and tried to look less pale and wan, tried to open her eyes wide to make them look fresh. She would get on with today and do her best. And then she would send a note to Oskar, demanding to see him as soon as possible. And they would decide together what to do for the best. It was all going to be all right. She walked back towards her station in the dress materials department, determined to explain to Miss L that she was just a bit peaky today, that was all, but she was fine now. Everything was fine.

But as she approached Miss Lafitte's cutting table, she saw her mentor look up sharply at her, then put down her scissors and beckon to Maria.

'Come with me,' she said and abruptly turned and marched off to the back of the store. Maria would be reprimanded for being absent without permission, she knew that. She would probably have her pay docked. But she still had a bit of money left from her modelling days that could tide her over. She wasn't worried. She just felt annoyed at herself that this was her first misdemeanour under Miss Lafitte and she never wanted to let her mentor down. She followed her to the stairs up to the offices. But why were they going up there? Surely Miss Bytheway didn't need to know about such a minor infraction.

'Miss Lafitte . . .' she tried. She was going to say she'd been taken ill and could explain everything. But Miss Lafitte simply raised her pointed finger to her lips and issued a hard 'Sshh!' She mounted the stairs at quite a pace and Maria tried to keep up with her. She'd have to take her punishment for lateness, she supposed. But she'd been so good for so long, surely Miss B wouldn't condemn her too harshly. She stopped as Miss Lafitte knocked hurriedly on Miss B's office door. She went in and turned to Maria, saying, 'Wait here', before closing the door. Maria could hear their lowered voices inside but not what they were saying. All this fuss over a bit of lateness? Just typical, just what she needed on an already awful day. Then Miss Lafitte opened the door.

'Come in.'

Maria entered the room and felt an echo of the last time she was here with these two women, at her interview, that glorious day when she had got her job and rushed to Oskar's afterwards. She would have days like that again, when she saw him next, she told herself. Now to face the music with these two and get it over with, then get back to work.

Miss Bytheway did the talking.

'It has come to our attention that you are carrying an unborn child out of wedlock.'

What? How . . .? How could they know? She wasn't showing yet. And she'd only been sick once.

'Do you deny it?' asked Miss Lafitte.

There was a moment where Maria thought about lying, about protesting her innocence and saying how dare they! How could they think such a thing of her! But she knew it was hopeless because all it would do was buy her a few weeks, if that, and then the truth would show on her. But maybe it would be worth it, to give her a short while to sort everything with Oskar.

'I see from your hesitation that it is true,' said Miss Bytheway.

'Nay!' Maria cried. 'I mean, no! Miss Bytheway, no. I am sorry.'

'Are you sorry for using your common dialect or are you sorry for ruining your life?'

Maria looked at Miss B in shock. It suddenly hit her, full force. What she'd been running from, denying to herself and pretending would be fine, were the straight facts of the matter: that she was ruined. Unless Oskar married her immediately. And even then, she'd be stuck in a situation she'd never wanted to be in. She'd lose her job, lose her freedom, lose everything she'd worked for, all this time.

'I am sorry, for all of it,' she said wretchedly.

'Too late for regret now, Miss Keay,' said Miss Lafitte, shaking her head.

Miss Bytheway added, 'And to think, you were one of my little champions. My special girls. All set up for a long and successful career in retail. We've nurtured you and given you chances any other shopgirl would kill for. And what have you done in return? Wasted it all on a passing fancy, no doubt. No self-control, no morals. What is to become of you only God knows, but Harborne and Company will not feature in your future for one moment longer. You are dismissed, without notice, without reference, without pay. Leave the premises immediately and collect your things from your lodgings. Goodbye, Miss Keay.'

Maria left the office and closed the door behind her. Everything was over. Everything was ruined. What was there to do but leave as Miss B said? There was nothing to say, nothing to be done, only defeat. She walked down the stairs so slowly, watching each foot placed on each step, to lengthen every moment she could still be inside Harborne and Co's premises, because, within minutes, she'd be booted out of it for good. At the bottom of the stairs stood a figure in a black dress. Maria looked up at the face. It was Gwen. She was smiling, triumphantly.

Chapter 27

April – May 1893

The Studio
4 The Square
Shrewsbury
SALOP
20 April 1893

Dear Charlie,

I know we have been quiet for a long, long time, but I want to change this by writing to you to say I have a new address –
PLEASE SEE ABOVE. You might think it is to another Harborne lodging house due to promotion. That would be correct a little while ago as I did indeed succeed in securing a new post as assistant to the floor manager of dress materials, which I loved doing. However, other events have overtaken my career and so I am happy to tell you that I am engaged to be married to Oskar von Schoen. Therefore, I live now in a smart and comfortable new boarding house, as I have left my job in preparation for my marriage. We are very happy and

looking forward to our life together when we marry, and we think we might well move to Germany, which is something I could never have imagined in my life. It is exciting and good news, as I am sure you will agree. I hope that things are fine with you and Rosie and that you make each other as happy and excited as Oskar and me. For we are very good and happy and excited. I am sending all my best wishes to you and yours, as they say. If you want to write back to me, write to the address above at the top of this letter.

Yours faithfully,
Maria Keay

Maria hated writing letters. She felt that she never sounded like herself in them. She sounded like a school child. She was a better speaker than writer, much better. But it was her only way of reaching Charlie, as he hadn't been in touch with her since January and she hadn't left Oskar's house since she had moved in, on the day of her dismissal. There was no way she could travel to Ironbridge to see Charlie. Firstly, she couldn't bear to leave the house these days in case she bumped into one of her old workmates. The humiliation would be too great. The other reason was that she and Oskar were not yet married, so the fact that they were living together would be scandalous. Yet, the full truth was, even if she wanted to, Oskar had made it quite clear to her that she should not go outside as they needed to keep the baby safe and the best thing for that was to stay on the chaise longue and rest.

One day, he went to collect some new photographic equipment from another photographer in town, saying he'd be back later that afternoon. Maria took her chance. She hurried down the street to the post office, bought an envelope, addressed it to Charlie and paid to post it. Then hurried back home. It was silly, really, as everyone she knew best would be at work and would never see her during the day, except on Sundays. But even though she knew this, she dreaded even being on the same street as Harborne's. And maybe a delivery boy might see her and shout at her, laugh at her. She could only imagine what they were saying about her at work, what Gwen had spread around.

Gwen. The betrayal cut deep. She knew they'd had a troubled friendship, but Gwen herself had always made it clear that girls supported girls, above all else. So, for her to be the traitor was the hardest lesson to learn. People talked about loyalty, but, when it came down to it, it was every woman for herself. But then Maria recalled how they both had spoken about Miss Lafitte's previous assistant and why the job had become available in the first place. The girl had been cruelly used by Harborne and she had left her very good job to escape him. There was nothing they could do for her and so the job was up for grabs and she and Gwen went for it. Looking at it this way, Maria had been the one to make the foolish mistake of getting pregnant and thus she'd forfeited her job. Therefore, Gwen had stepped in and taken advantage. It was a cold thing to do to a friend, to tell on her, to spill her secret to management, especially while Maria was still unsure of what to do next. But the fact was, the moment Maria fell pregnant, she had sealed her own fate. Gwen had merely taken the spoils. Maria had had no contact with the shop since that day, but she imagined that it would be Gwen who took her place in the best job she'd ever had. *Good luck to her then,* she thought begrudgingly.

Not only had Maria lost her job, the support of her mentors and her friends, she had lost her freedom. Staying in the studio constantly was dreary. At least most of Oskar's books were in English. She read a lot, slept a lot and vomited a lot. Her cousin

Rhoda had told her once that pregnant women were only sick in the mornings, but for Maria it went on and off all day and night. It made her weary, so she welcomed the sleep. But she still felt like a prisoner, even more so than at the dormitory from hell at Harborne's. She never thought in her life she would ever miss that place, but she did, desperately. The camaraderie, the stories, the laughs, the friendship. Sunday evening out on the town. Just having friends, even one friend, had been heaven, she realised now. This was what prompted her to write to Charlie, to reach out to someone who understood her. She'd lied in the letter, she knew that, but it was better than silence. Maria needed to hear from a friend. And there was no better friend than Charlie in the world. Only now that she had none did she truly grasp this.

So this was her life now. Outside, Shrewsbury moved from April to May as Maria sat on the chaise longue. Oskar came and went. He had the freedom of men, in charge of his own destiny. She never knew exactly where he was going, but he always had a reason to leave for an hour or two or three. It was something to do with technical supplies or a chemistry chum or photographic mentor, or something. She wondered if any of it were true. He never came back with anything that might signal where he'd been. Perhaps he was even out whoring. She was a realist now, Maria. The last few weeks had broken her optimism, perhaps forever, she felt. Oskar had broken it, single-handedly.

She'd gone straight from Harborne's to the studio on the day of her dismissal. She'd knocked on the door, and again no answer, so she'd sunk down on the stairs and wept. And wept. And still he didn't come. Eventually, in her exhaustion, she had curled up on the top step, her bag as her pillow, and napped. He'd found her there around lunchtime. He'd woken her up and kissed and kissed her. She'd told him about the job and about the likelihood that she was pregnant. He'd swept her up and carried her inside, like precious cargo. He'd had a bag of groceries with him, including her favourite food she craved the most, fresh bacon. Oskar had fried it up for her and she ate it warm from the pan, salty and delicious. Then he'd wrapped her in a warm blanket and insisted she stayed on the chaise longue relaxing as he read to her from a book on chemistry, of which she understood virtually nothing. As the days went on, he fed her delicacies, such as seafood and fine cheeses, wine and little cream cakes. She certainly ate well with him. Nobody could say he treated her badly. He had his little rages and she tried to stay out of the way when he was in his black moods, cursing his family, or some academic he claimed rebuffed his paper on something or other, or the woman at the fish market laughing at his accent, or whatever new disgrace had irked him that day. Only seeing him once a week before she'd moved in with him had kept the frequency of his moods at a distance, but now she saw them in full force. Yet when he was in a good mood, Oskar treated her very well. He was at her beck and call whenever he deigned to stay home. He was sweet with her and tender when it suited him. On the worst days, she'd hide in the bathroom, shivering in bathwater long gone cold, just to prolong her isolation, away from that room, away from him. As the days passed, and her old life faded to a memory, Maria asked him several times what their plans were, what was going to happen.

He'd say, 'Do not worry your beautiful head about such things. All is in hand.'

And she'd accept it, because she was weary. But also, as time went on, her strength increased. Her sickness diminished, and with it came energy she'd not had in weeks. She felt stronger to take some control now, hence her subterfuge in writing to Charlie. Maria had to hope that if a reply came she'd be alone at home when it was received. She did far more around the apartment these days, as she could not stay on that damned chaise longue for a moment longer. Sometimes she eyed it with disdain, as if all her problems had begun on it, which, of course, in a way they had. He was out so often, Maria had the place to herself a lot, so she started to look around it, see what secrets he had stashed away. She found a hidden drawer in the wardrobe, where he kept a wad of cash. Mostly, she was looking for the pistol his sister had told her about. But it was nowhere to be found. Perhaps Lina was wrong about it. Perhaps a servant had stolen it from their father. It certainly was nowhere in this place. It gave her some hope that he had his rages, yes, but maybe he was not so bad and just needed to be manipulated and managed. The child she carried was what he cared about most, so she needed to get her way by using that fact. She began to ask him with more insistence about their future. One day in May, Maria said she simply must have a conversation with him. He sat down on a chair, looking a little annoyed. She decided to stand.

'What is to become of us, of me and our baby? I've asked you several times now and always you change the subject or . . . or pat me on the head, like a lapdog. And say I shouldna worry about such things. But I do worry. I am with child – I carry your precious babe – and I remain unmarried. You made it clear before that marriage was your heart's desire. But since then you have stayed silent on the subject. When are you going to marry me and make our child respectable? Where will we live? We canna stay here. My reputation is ruined here. We mun go. Will it be to Germany? Will I meet your father? What kind of home will our child have? Because living in this tiny studio without a bed is not the life I had in mind.'

He listened with little patience, making faces and rolling his eyes at every turn of phrase.

'Do you not trust me, Maria?'

How she wanted to say, 'Absolutely not.' But she knew it would set him off on one of his rages. 'Course I do.'

'Then trust me when I say all is in hand.'

'But what is in hand? What exactly? When will we marry?'

'If you must know, I have changed my views somewhat on marriage. I am sure we will marry in time. But have you ever considered, Maria, how it disadvantages women? If you consider it carefully, you must realise that women who marry become the property of men. And, as you know, I believe people should be free and not bound together by law. But if you want to be old-fashioned and behind the times, I will marry you in time, you silly little thing.'

'But we mun marry, Oskar. My disgrace is certain if we dunna marry. How could you leave me waiting for such a thing? We mun do it and do it now.'

His face changed. That signal always frightened her. She never knew what would happen next, whether it meant passion or fury. He was so hard to predict.

'Oh, and I see the little shopgirl of Ironbridge is in charge now, is she? This is the girl who believed the lies spouted by my evil witch of a sister over me, the man who loved the little shopgirl, who wanted to marry her and pluck her from obscurity to a life of leisure? But then she trotted off back to her work and her friends and abandoned the man who loved her most, just when he needed her? And then she finds herself in trouble, and she crawls back and he takes her in and treats her like a queen. And now she complains? She demands? Oh no, my shopgirl. You rely on me now and I decide what will happen with us and when. Your job is to protect our precious child you carry and one day you will serve your biological destiny and produce an heir for me, a perfect baby boy as I know it will be. It is my destiny, you see, to produce a son who will rise up with me and conquer all. You will be the vessel for that destiny. And as for marriage, it will happen when I decide it is best. As I have said, IN TIME. Hear it and be satisfied.'

After that, he grabbed his jacket and left, off to the freedom of outside. Maria found herself shut in and alone again, all her pleas talked over and ignored. She felt as if her very self was dissolving into a shadow of who she used to be. Her voice, her words were not listened to, as if all that came out of her mouth was unintelligible noise. The frustration was maddening! She screwed her eyes shut, gritted her teeth, clenched her fists and screamed in exasperation. Then she thought of her unborn child hearing such an unearthly sound and she patted her belly and said sorry, over and over. After that moment of release, she merely felt empty.

Maria walked over to the studio roof windows, looking out at the overcast skies of a May afternoon. She used to look through these windows and wish never to leave this room, never to go back to the slog of daily work. And now her wish had been granted. She was safe. She was not on the streets or in the workhouse. But there were some things worse than all of that, she now realised. At least at work, she'd had her own agency. She had moved up the career ladder, through sheer hard work and the talents she'd developed with a lively mind and an ability to assimilate everything she learnt and apply it. She'd served the customers best, so they always came back to her, and to impress and endear herself to her managers, who enjoyed mentoring this lively, ambitious young woman. Great things had been ahead. She had given up Charlie for it: Charlie Woodvine, the kindest man who ever lived, surely, apart from her own father. And now she had lost everything. She had gained a child, which grew inexorably each day inside her, but she had also chained herself to a madman. For surely, Lina had not lied. This man, who railed on about how the world was against him, how only he understood the intricacies of science and technology while his contemporaries ignored and belittled him, but one day, he was certain, he would achieve his destiny in ensuring Germany's greatness, by fathering a race of little Oskars, who looked like him and her, who would march forth into the future to rid the world of undesirables. Oh yes, Oskar was mad. Surely nobody else in the world talked of such things and believed them to be true, only other madmen. He would end in an asylum, she was convinced of that. But, for now, she was tied to his destiny, whatever that might be, as she had nowhere else in the world she could go and no one else in the world she could turn to.

* * *

Schoolmaster's Cottage
Ironbridge Day School
Church Hill
Ironbridge
29 May 1893

Dear Maria,

How good it was to hear from you! I can only apologise for not being the one to break the ice sooner. I am a coward, clearly, as you beat me to it. If you were here with me on one of our walks, I think we could talk about what happened the last time we met and all would be well. Thus, I'm very grateful to you that you have written to me and kept our friendship alive. Thank you, Maria.

Firstly, please let me extend my congratulations to you on your engagement. I know that your intended will be a good man by the simple fact that you love him, because only good can come for any man who receives your regard. I wish the two of you all the happiness in the world. I hope, now that you are free of the burden of retail work, you can finally rest a little, until the rigours of married life claim you. I know that you will make a wonderful wife and mother, running your household with precision and generosity, such is your way. Mr von Schoen is a lucky man indeed.

As for myself, I am glad to announce that I, too, am engaged, to Rosie. We are to be married in June and then Rosie will come to live with me in my schoolhouse. She tells me I must get rid of most of my books to make way for fashionable knick-knicks for the home! I suppose she is right, as I never read the same book twice! I am glad I can tell you this news of our marriage now, as I had held off after our meeting. I don't know why I held off, but I am glad to be rid of that burden now and know I can share my news with you as good friends should. I hope we can always share news with each other, good or bad. We have been friends for a long time, have we not, you and I?

So that is my big news. Other than that, my news is smaller but looms no less large in my life, as the school inspector paid his annual visit this last week. As you know, this is something that myself and Anny dread every year and, yet, this year it went surprisingly well. All of the children put themselves forward with grace under pressure and, in fact, it seemed that the pressure they were under turned them into little diamonds, as their performances in the question and answer tests the stern inspector subjected them to went ten times better than expected. We even have one girl – an undernourished little waif called Minnie – who has chosen to be a mute, since her father died in a coal mining accident hereabouts, but even she spoke up on the day of the tests and answered a question assigned to another child, which was: 'Who defeated King

Richard the Third of England?' Her friend struggled with his answer and looked about him at all four walls, the windows and the ceiling, as if the answer might be writ there, and this tiny tot who hasn't spoken a word in six months piped up with, 'Why, it's Henry Tudor, sir,' to the room's utter astonishment. I should add, however, that every Friday lunchtime of those six months, Anny has come to the school to take Minnie for a walk. What Anny said to the child on those walks, I'll never know. But it took six months for it to come to fruition, for at the moment she spoke aloud, she ran over to Anny and threw her arms around her. It was a touching scene to be sure, and not a dry eye in the house afterwards. Even our stern inspector seemed a touch moved when told the story. A grand day for all.

Other than that, I've been reading a book called Diary of a Nobody, which has entertained me immensely. I think that you would like it too. It is about a very ordinary man, his family and his suburban life, full of minor mishaps. What I like about it particularly is that it makes the case that stories of ordinary people are just as worthy of our attention as the rich and famous of this world. And despite the main character's rather pompous self-regard, I happen to agree with him. I think of all the children I teach every day, every year. All of them will go on to do nothing spectacular, I warrant, just as I myself have done nothing spectacular. And, yet, we are no less worthy of attention than a lord or lady, or a privileged buffoon who gets himself in the newspapers by dint of his wealth alone. The other thing I like about the book is how all of the conflicts within are decidedly of low stakes. Nothing earth-shattering is at stake there. And I appreciate that too, in a world where a little girl can lose her father in a mining accident and her mother to drink and laudanum, where her only sanctuary is a twenty-minute walk once a week spent with a *kind lady at her school. As history is the narrative only of the conqueror, so we nobodies should tip the balance in our favour for once and tell our own stories, to anyone who'll listen. This is my roundabout way of hoping that my letter holds some interest for you, even while harping on as it does about ordinary folk and their little dramas, despite your love of adventure stories and drastic escapes. That's a very wordy way of saying, I hope I'm not boring you to tears. Rosie has told me more than once that I talk far too much! Thus, I am trying to reform. But not, as you can tell, very successfully.*

And so, I must draw my very long letter to a close. My only excuse is that, as we have not written for so long, I had a store of words shored up to impart to you and your kind letter burst the ramparts and out came the flood. Forgive me, for too many of them.

Keep well and happy, Maria. Please do keep in touch and let me know your progress in the world. I will always, always want to know of it.

Very best of the best to you both,
Charlie Woodvine

Chapter 28

Oh, how Maria wept after reading Charlie's letter. She was lucky in that her hopes came true and the letter arrived early one evening when Oskar was out, though the odds of this were ever increasing, as Oskar seemed to spend more and more time away from the studio. He would come back either chatty and insufferable or hazy and wordless, clearly the worse for whatever he'd imbibed, though God only knew where he'd been to take it, perhaps an inn in a shady part of town or even an opium den, if there were such a thing locally. Thank heavens he was out when she received the letter so she could read it in luxury, alone, and afterwards allow herself to sob and sob for all she had lost.

Every word of Charlie's letter was perfection. Every thought was sweet and witty and fascinating. And to think, she used to sit at Oskar's feet and worship every word he uttered. And now every word he said offended her, with his horrid ideas about politics and the rights of the strong and which of the races of man were superior and other such nastiness. Or his flights of madness, when he proclaimed he would one day be the King of Europe and she would bear his dynasty. If only she had stayed in Ironbridge and married Charlie, she would be sitting at his kitchen table talking to him about who conquered King Richard the Third, and how the little waif Minnie was that day, and did she still talk, and oh, so many other things of import and consequence, not this sham of a life imprisoned in a poky little set of rooms with a rich lunatic who treated her like a brood mare. Of all possible futures, this had never occurred to her. Oskar von Schoen might be a somebody in Germany, with his wealthy, cultured family, but to her, he was a nobody. Charlie was the somebody – she knew now – she had been an idiot to leave. The simplicity of his life – that which she had run from in her adventure-seeking foolishness to exploitation on the shop floor in the big town – seemed like a kind of heaven to her now. The contrast with the chaos of her own life felt like a stab to the heart. What she wouldn't give to be carrying Charlie's child now, to be Rosie, to be moving in to his little schoolhouse in June. They were to be married in June! Only weeks away, maybe even days! How could it be true? And how could Rosie Green, of all people, about as peaceful as an ironworks, tell Charlie he talked too much? And say she'd get rid of his precious books? How dare she! Oh, the frustration of it all, the rage, the envy and regret. Maria cried so much, she dropped to her knees on the rug and shook her head, trying to rid herself of this tumult of emotion. But it was no good. Nothing would ever dislodge these feelings. The only thing she could hope for was to become numb one day, and feel nothing.

She sat on the floor, her hands on her belly, staring into space for a long time after reading the letter. The evening turned to night. Still she sat there, rereading the letter a dozen times and holding it close to her. Then she sat and stared again. Was she losing her mind? She stared at nothing for so long, she lost all sense of reference, time fading and meaning with it. She did not think when the door went and in came Oskar.

'Why are you sitting here in darkness, you silly goose?' he laughed and turned on the lamps, bathing the room in warm light.

He must've been at the wine tonight, as he was full of himself and bragging about a card game he'd won and beaten every other man in the room, those idiot Englishmen. She still stared into middle distance, not looking at him. She was tired of his hateful face. He did not even seem to notice as he spouted off more and more about his prowess at the card table. She did not even hear the words any more.

Not until he said to her, 'Is that a letter you are holding?'

In that moment, she awoke from her stupor and snatched the letter behind herself so he couldn't see it. How could she have been so careless?

He dropped down to one knee and looked at her, very calmly. 'Who is the letter from, Maria?'

'Nobody,' she said, quiet yet firm.

'Give me the letter.'

She didn't say a word. She only knew she would never give it to him. She had lost her voice, lost her will somehow. But she still had her determination in this one small matter. And that was Charlie's letter.

She did not move.

'Shall I be impelled to take it from you by force?'

'Do what you will,' she said. She was talking now like a soulless phantasm, a person whose heart had long ago been ripped out and there was nothing left but this one battle. 'But you will never get your damned hands on it.'

'It is from him, is it not? Charlie Woodvine. You should not be reading letters from another man when you are engaged to be married.'

Oskar was still calm, but it was an uneasy calm, the silence before the crack of thunder.

'Engaged to be married? Is that what we are?' she said and looked at him then, laughing bitterly.

'It *is* from him, I can tell. You are right. It is from *nobody*.'

'You're not fit to lick his boots.' Maria said it with such venom she'd never heard in herself before. How she hated Oskar at that moment. How she loathed every fibre of his being.

'Give it to me!' Oskar bellowed and lunged for her. She whipped round and held the letter to her belly, curling up tight like a hunted creature trying to survive. His hands were everywhere, moving hard and swift, like a beast from mythology with multiple arms. And he bested her, even as she groaned with effort, as she tried to stop him prying open her hand and ripping the letter from it. But she wouldn't give up, grasping for the letter, holding onto his waistcoat as he stood up, dragging her up from the floor.

'Oh, it is the little whore of a shopgirl we have here! How easily she reverts to type! What a sweet little bride she is, fat with child and weeping and screeching over her lost love. What a prize of a wife for the von Schoen heir!'

Oskar held the letter up above her reach and laughed at her. She punched him in the chest with all her might, but again all he did was laugh.

'I will never marry you!' she screamed, hopeless that she'd ever reach the letter he still held high above her head, taunting her with it.

'I do not need you for a wife,' he spat at her. 'Just the perfect Nordic boy inside you. As long as the child is safe, I care not if you die after. If need be, I'll rip it from your womb.'

'You are a monster!' she cried. 'I'd rather kill myself, and my child with me, than let it be in your hands. And I will do it. The moment your back is turned, I will do it. I will do it!'

She was screaming at him now, still reaching for the letter. He brought his fist down, filled with Charlie's words, and punched her hard in the face. She reeled backwards and he caught her, only to punch her again, and again. She heard her nose crunch and saw drops of blood fly. She staggered back, as he raised his fist once more, and she fell against the camera on its tripod, still set up there, though it hadn't taken a picture in weeks. It clattered to the floor, as she fell backwards, Oskar tripping over her feet as she kicked to free herself from him. His head was at her waist as he scrabbled on the floor to right himself. Maria glanced and saw the cracked wooden box of the camera beside her on the floor and she grasped at it, took a hold of it, lifted it high and brought it down on the back of his head with strength she had never known. So powerful it was that she screamed out louder than her cousin did in childbed. And then, at last, Oskar stopped dead.

Chapter 29

After so much sound and fury, the silence was unsettling. Maria felt paralysed for several seconds, staring at the back of Oskar's head as he lay across her unmoving. Then it started to ooze with blood. She panicked and pushed him off her to free her legs. He rolled over and ended on his back, his eyes closed, his body abandoned to oblivion. She stared at his chest. She couldn't see it rising and falling. She was frozen in fear. She'd killed him. She'd killed Oskar. She'd killed a man.

Then, she acted. She got to her feet, unsteady, leaning against the wall. She needed to flee, as soon as she could. What would she need? She went to her money stocking in her bag, with the little cash left she'd saved from modelling. It wouldn't be enough to get her far. She went to the hidden drawer inside his wardrobe and took his cash. She riffled in his waistcoat pocket and found his watch too. She might need that, to sell it. She looked at the time. It was just past nine at night. There would still be trains running, she didn't care where to, just a train to anywhere, away from here. She stuffed it all in her bag with a couple of outfits to wear, and she took a key to lock the door. She didn't want anyone to be able to get in easily. The longer it took someone to find him, the longer she'd have to get as far away from here as she could.

She looked down at the cream-coloured dress she was wearing and saw the bodice was spotted with drops of blood. His or hers? Perhaps a mixture of both. Then she remembered her injuries. She went to the mirror and saw her face was a mess. Big bruises would appear soon. She fetched a cloth and water and tried to clean herself up, wiping away the blood at least. She fixed her hair and found her bonnet that was the closest fit, to shield as much of her face from strangers as possible. She pulled off her dress and put on a plainer one, darker and less obvious. It was the dress she was wearing the day she met Lina. She couldn't think about that now. She couldn't think about how she'd killed that woman's brother. Maria buttoned up her bodice and threw a faded, old tartan shawl about her shoulders. She didn't want to look fancy, just ordinary. She didn't want to draw any attention to herself. She wanted to look like every other shopgirl on the streets. She wanted to look like a nobody.

Maria took one more look around the room, then hurried to the front door. She did not look at Oskar. She couldn't bear to. She went too quickly down the steps, almost tripping, then rushed along the alleyway and out into the street. The street lamp's glow hit her eyes as she looked up, making her wince. Her head was throbbing with pain. The punches he'd landed there were beginning to take effect. She had to keep focused. She had to put one foot in front of the other and get to the railway station. She had to look normal. She couldn't be doing with any questions, any concerned passers-by, not now. She kept her head down, eyes on her feet, walking forwards, slowly, making progress as her head felt like it would split open with the pain. She felt faint. Stopping, she closed her eyes. She had to stay calm, collect herself. She had to keep moving forwards.

'Maria?'

There was a voice, a voice she knew well.

'Maria! What . . . what's happened to you?'

She looked up and there was her erstwhile friend Gwen, dressed in the same smart outfit Maria herself had worn as Miss Lafitte's assistant.

'Gwen,' she muttered. She felt Gwen's hand on her arm. She had to keep upright. She couldn't faint here in the street.

'Lord help us, you look like a corpse,' said Gwen and put a firm arm around her. 'Where are you staying? Where's home?'

'Not home,' muttered Maria. Home was not a word she'd ever use about Oskar's hovel. And then the thought of Oskar being there, dead, assaulted her, and she cried out.

Gwen held on tight to her. 'Come on, Maria. Tell me where to go, where we can get you sat down at least.'

Maria thought of the steps up to Oskar's place. They could sit there a minute, she supposed. As long as they didn't go inside, never that.

'It's back there,' Maria gestured vaguely.

'Come on then,' said Gwen. 'Lean on me. Point out the way.'

She felt Gwen's arms tighten about her, giving her the strength to go on. Maria forced her feet to move, one step in front of the other, pointing the way out to Gwen.

'Is it here?' said Gwen. 'This alleyway? Those steps?'

'Here,' she whispered. But the steps . . . went up to the studio . . . where Oskar lay, dead. And again the memory assaulted her. 'Nay!' she cried. 'I canna go back!'

'What's in there?' said Gwen urgently. 'Is he there? That posh German? Did he do this to you?'

Maria was aware some had stopped to stare in the street. She had to be circumspect. She had to get away from the curious gazes of strangers.

'Let's go up,' she muttered. 'Sit on the steps.'

Gwen steered her into the alleyway and down to the steps. They were hidden from the main street, so Maria could sit at the end of the staircase, her feet on the ground, and hide for a moment out of sight and gather herself. She felt a little better now she'd taken the weight off. Her legs had felt like jelly, but now she could focus more. Gwen sat down next to her.

'Tell me what the hell he's done to you, Maria. What's happened here?'

Maria looked up at her friend's face, or, at least, a friend she had once. How nice it was back then, to have friends. Now she had none. 'I've missed you,' she said, simply, to Gwen.

Gwen's face was a picture of concern, then it softened. 'We've missed you too, me and Polly. And the others. But what's going on here, Maria? What can I do to help?'

At the thought of what lay at the top of those stairs, waiting for her life to implode on its discovery, Maria began to sob. 'I wish . . . I wish . . . I were dead.'

Gwen gave her a good hug again and said, 'Now then, enough of that. You're stronger than that, Maria Keay. Or the Maria Keay I once knew. Just think about what you did to Savage, that time. You didna take nonsense from any man. Now, what's happened to you? Your face inna pretty sight. Did he strike you?'

How she wanted to admit it all to Gwen, spill the whole sorry story. But she couldn't bear to, couldn't reveal the horrible truth, that she was a murderer. She just wept and let Gwen hold her. She felt as if she were at sea, on stormy waters, the world crashing around her. She reached out with her right arm and held on to the step for ballast. And then she felt the most curious sensation upon that outstretched hand.

She felt the warm, wet nose of a dog and its lick, saying hello in his uninhibited canine way. She opened her eyes and saw Biscuit first. Then looked up and there was his master, standing there, in the alleyway, looking mightily confused and worried. That face. The curly hair beneath a bowler hat. The soft moustache. The kindly eyes that always smiled at her, even when he was not smiling. She knew them so well. She'd prayed to see him so many times, but knew it was impossible.

'Maria,' he said, breathlessly. 'What . . . what has happened here?'

'You're not the German,' said Gwen.

'No, I'm . . . a friend of Maria's. From her home town. From Ironbridge.'

Biscuit bumped his nose against Maria's leg. He was whining at her, so excited to see her. Was she dreaming? Was she dead? Could it really be Charlie and Biscuit here, now?

'Charlie,' Maria whispered, still convinced she was imagining his appearance, despite Gwen having a conversation with him.

'Ah, you're the one in the letters,' said Gwen. 'Well, I dunna know what's happened here. She wonna tell me. I am sorely worried for her though. She needs medical assistance, I'd warrant.'

'She does indeed,' said Charlie. 'This is her address, I believe. I have it written on a letter. Shall we take her upstairs first?'

'Nay!' cried Maria, with such insistence it made Gwen and Charlie flinch in shock.

Maria's mind was racing, trying to work out what on earth she should do next. But her body felt as if it would come to pieces at any moment. She knew she needed help. And despite the welcome presence of her old friend Gwen, come to her aid at this moment of need, the only person she truly trusted in the whole world was Charlie Woodvine. And he was miraculously here. And she needed only him now.

'Gwen,' she said, pulling herself together. 'Thank'ee for

your kindness. I've Charlie here now and he'll sort me out. Honestly, I'll be fine with Charlie.'

'You sure?' said Gwen, glancing up at Charlie and back at Maria. 'I've never trusted any man in my life, myself.'

'This one's a good'un,' Maria said and smiled, trying to look normal. She felt she'd given away too much already, with her obvious fear of what was up there, in that studio. She had to take control of the situation and simplify it. The more people who knew what had happened, the more trouble it would cause all round. And that meant Gwen must go.

'All right, then,' said Gwen, standing up.

'Thank'ee again, for helping me,' said Maria, looking up at Gwen.

'It's nothing,' she replied, shrugging. She hesitated, then added, 'Listen, Maria. I'm sorry I told on you, at work. It was wrong of me to do that, just for a job.'

Maria said, 'It's all right. It's the same as we did to Miss L's last girl.'

'Not really. She'd already gone. But I wanted that job so bad. I needed it. I needed the pay rise. And I knew you couldna keep the job, not once you'd found yourself . . . well, you know. But I shouldna told on you. I'm sorry I did it and I'm sorry to see you like this, now. I shoulda helped you then and I didna. I feel partly responsible for how you are now, in this sorry state.'

'It inna your fault, Gwen, none of it,' said Maria, thinking of Oskar, the real culprit, with a shudder. 'Please dunna think that.'

'Well, I choose to disagree. You were right, about shopgirls looking out for each other. I said that once and I meant it. But it's hard, in a world where women are pitched against each other. It's not an excuse, but a reason, I suppose. But whatever the reason, I didna do right by you. I hope you can forgive me, just a little, for I wish you well in the world, Maria. I always did.'

'I understand,' said Maria, as Biscuit nudged up against her hand again, giving it a good lick.

'I can see you're in good hands,' said Gwen, smiling at the dog. She looked over at Charlie and said sternly, 'Look after her properly, mon. Or you'll have the shopgirls of Shrewsbury after you.'

'I will,' said Charlie emphatically.

Gwen nodded, looked at Maria, then glanced up at the top of the stairs. Then, finally, she said her goodbyes and left, walking away down the alleyway and into the streets beyond.

Immediately, Charlie rushed to Maria's side, crouching down before her and taking her hands in his own.

The relief of feeling Charlie's strong hands about hers, so reliable, so welcome. How safe she felt, with Biscuit beside her too. She could weep. But how was it possible? How could Charlie be here, now, in her hour of need? It still felt like a fantasy, born from her head injuries, surely. But Charlie was still here and he was talking to her. Biscuit was leaning heavily against her leg, the warm bulk of his body so solid and reassuring.

'Tell me what happened, Maria.'

'Are you truly here? Are you real?'

Charlie smiled and the sight of it made her sob with relief. Biscuit whined at her and she reached out and touched his silky ear, to ensure he was real too.

'Of course I'm here! Dunna cry. I am here.'

He sat down beside her and held her until she recovered herself.

'Maria, please tell me what has happened. I fear we must take you to seek medical attention.'

'Nay! Nay, Charlie. Just hold me.'

He did and they sat quietly a while longer. Just to sit there with the warmth of his body enveloping her felt like she'd died and gone to heaven. And she wanted that to be true, at that moment. For to be alive was nothing but pain, knowing what lay ahead if they went through that door above.

'Charlie, what are you doing here? How did you know I needed you?'

'I will tell all, but first you must let me take you to a doctor.'

'Nay, Charlie,' she said again, calm now, not hysterical, her decision a rational one. 'I canna see anyone. I mun get away from here.'

'Tell me first what occurred.'

'He beat me. You can see from my face that he beat me.'

'I shall kill him,' said Charlie. She'd never seen his face look that way before, as if all his goodness drained from it.

'Nay, nay, Charlie. No need. For I've killed him myself.'

Charlie's face was like stone. He hesitated, then nodded. He was thinking.

'Where? Up there?'

'Yes, up there.'

'Are you certain? Did you check his pulse?'

'I didna, nay. But he was dead.'

Charlie looked behind them at the top of the steps.

'Well, the door to your lodgings is open a crack so I'll go and have a look.'

'The door is open?' she said, perturbed, and looked up there. It was just a couple of inches. She hadn't noticed this before. She thought she had shut it. She thought she had locked it. But her mind was so befuddled by the shock and the pain that she couldn't be sure. She had no memory of doing it.

Maria stood up, unsteadily but successfully. Charlie followed her, his hand on the small of her back to help her, Biscuit shoving by them to reach the door first, his snout at the gap, sniffing wildly. Maria pushed the door open further, gingerly at first, as if something dangerous would rush out of the gaping doorway. She peered into the vestibule. All of the lights were still on.

'Let me go first,' said Charlie.

'It is a horrid sight,' she muttered, covering her mouth with her hand.

Charlie replied, 'Stay here.'

But Biscuit beat them both to it and trotted into the studio. Charlie followed him slowly. Maria stood in the doorway, sobbing, trying to stop her noise with her hand, but unable to control herself. She watched Charlie move into the room and disappear from view. She readied herself for his response. He would know she was a murderer and he would never look at her the same way again. She felt ruined for him. But also, she felt suddenly that she should never have involved him in this, not Charlie. He did not deserve to be caught up in a heinous crime. His innocent life that brought so much good to others must be preserved. Maria stepped forwards to tell him that, to make him go and leave her, so she had to face the music alone. It was the only way.

'Charlie?' she called. She would tell him to go.

'Stop that, boy!' she heard him say to Biscuit.

'What's happening?' Maria said and edged forward.

'There's nothing here,' he said, appearing in the doorway. 'There's a mess, but he inna here.'

She rushed through the vestibule, into the studio. The spot where she'd left Oskar was empty. The broken camera was there, a little pool of blood on the wooden floor, which had a smear of dog lick through it. But no Oskar. He truly had gone.

'I thought he was dead!' she gasped. 'I thought I'd killed him.'

'Well, unless he's arisen from the dead, I'd say you're off the hook,' said Charlie, taking off his hat and placing it on the side table, looking about at the disturbed furniture caused by their fracas.

She went to the spot where Oskar had lain, crouched down and touched it. Biscuit bumped up beside her, sniffing at the blood, throwing glances at his master, as he so wanted to lick it again, but he was a good boy and held off.

Was she losing her mind? Was Oskar really gone? She had never doubted her own senses so keenly in her life. She looked around and saw Oskar's jacket was not there. It was true. He'd left. She hadn't killed him. She wasn't a murderer.

'Oh, dear Lord!' Maria cried and sobbed, her head swimming, so she fell to all fours.

'Come, dunna fret so. All is well. Come, my love.'

Charlie took hold of her and soothed her. Biscuit barked and whined, trying to shove his nose in her face and lick her. It was so silly, it stopped her tears. They both laughed, her and Charlie, on the floor, Biscuit not understanding a thing, but doing his best to help. These two kind souls were the best of all possible beings on this earth. They must be cherished and protected at all costs.

'Charlie,' she said, suddenly. 'Why are you here? Now? Why are you not safe at home, with Rosie?'

'I canna love Rosie. Not when I love you down to my very bones.'

His expression was one of good-natured resignation. How she loved his positive outlook on life, at even the darkest time, whereas Oskar perpetually made the lightest moments dark.

'And I love you!' she said.

'I know you do.'

She turned her body to him and, on their knees, Oskar's blood spilt beside them, they embraced with a closeness and gratitude she had never known. How blind she had been to give this up for a pipe dream that had transformed into a living nightmare.

They kissed and laughed and held each other more in a tight and grateful cwtch.

'But how did you come to be here now?' she said, touching his cheek, watching his mouth, his eyes, as if he were a mirage, a miracle. He helped her stand up and held her at arm's length, scanning every inch of her hair, her face. He seemed to be in shock too that he was really here with her. Then he came back to himself.

'Well, it was curious. I just went for a walk, after work. I thought of you. I mean to say, I do not cease to think of you. But it consumed me today. I didna wanna stop walking, to go home, and face the fact of my life, the prospect of a loveless marriage. It seemed a good idea at the time, and Rosie was keen. But she didna love me either, it was a sham. You were right: she wanted me to spite you, I understood that in the end. I knew that tomorrow I would end it with her. She would be angry at first, but, underneath, she would know it was point-less, her and me. She definitely wanted no life in a schoolmaster's cottage, that was certain. So I had to wait until the morrow. And I paced the floor of my home. And I couldna stay there, confined, so I went out for a walk. I walked and walked and found my feet heading for the railway station and there waited a train at the platform that was travelling to Shrewsbury, as if it were waiting only for me. I boarded. I had no plan. I only knew that as the train moved off, I felt a lightness I hadna felt in months, not since I first saw you again in January, on your birthday. I thought it was hopeless. I hadna planned a word of what I would say to you. I only knew I had to come here. It was a dreadful plan, really. Shockingly bad.'

Maria laughed and wiped away her tears. 'I'm so, so happy

you did! But Charlie, I need to tell you what's happening here.'

'You dunna need to say a thing. I know you and that is all I need to know. I dunna know him, but any man who hits a woman deserves the worst that life can throw at him. Are you married yet?'

'Nay,' she said.

'Good, good,' he said, looking relieved.

But there was more to tell. It would take a lot of explaining. Then she remembered that Oskar was out there, at large. 'We mun go. He may come back at any moment.'

'You live here, together?'

Maria felt the weight of judgement upon her. Perhaps he could forgive her for living in sin. But . . . a child? There was nothing else for it. She'd have to tell him the truth. And now, so he could go in peace, avoid any contact with the sickness of Oskar and live his life without her, if that's what he chose. And why wouldn't he? Who could take on a broken, ruined woman like herself?

'We do. And there is more, Charlie, that you mun know . . . I am with child.'

She looked at him, ready for his face to fall with disappointment. She would understand, if he backed away. She would not blame him for a second.

Chapter 30

'I dunna care,' said Charlie. 'I love you and I love your child. I love whatever is a part of you.'

Biscuit sensed something important was happening and barked excitedly, pushing his muzzle into Maria's hand again.

'Biscuit agrees,' added Charlie. 'And I'd already guessed it. Your frame, your face, even beneath your bruises, I could see it. You have altered. You look quite different, you know. You are more yourself than ever, somehow. You've . . . come into focus.'

'Are you sure? I wouldna blame you, Charlie, for walking away. I wouldna blame you for a second.'

'I am sure. Do you believe me?'

'I do.'

'Then let's leave this place. Let's go home.'

'All right, then. Take me home, Charlie.' It was bliss to say this.

He picked up her bag. Then, she remembered, she'd taken Oskar's money and watch.

'I took some things from him, in that bag. I dunna wanna take them now.'

'Leave them behind. We dunna need a thing of his and we dunna need any accusations of thievery.'

Maria took out the money, keeping her own, and the watch, leaving them on the side table, from where Charlie retrieved his bowler hat. They moved to the door and Biscuit went ahead, as ever. But then he stopped and barked three times. They went ahead of Biscuit: Charlie first, carrying Maria's bag, and they both went down to the foot of the steps, the dog following them cautiously. He barked again and would not move.

'Time to go home, boy,' said Charlie.

But Biscuit curled his lip and started to growl, looking beyond her, down the dark alleyway.

Maria had never seen Biscuit like that, so riled and wolfish. She shivered, then, on a premonition, whipped round to see Oskar coming towards them.

He wore his jacket with one hand in his pocket, the other holding a white rag to his head. As he saw them all, standing on the steps, he stopped and threw the bloody rag to the floor.

'Here she is, the whore!' he shouted, laughing cruelly. 'And with her whoremonger!'

'That's enough of that rubbish,' shouted Charlie. 'Stand aside and let us go in peace.'

'I should call the police on her! Look at my head!' Oskar kicked the bloody rag. He was strangely vibrant, as if the whole thing were a great joke.

'Look at her face. I should give you the same. But we want no trouble. We're leaving.'

Oskar came closer and Biscuit's growl erupted into vicious barking. He had good instincts, that dog.

Charlie stood in front of Maria, his right arm held out across her. Biscuit ran down the steps and stood between them and Oskar, who laughed at the growling animal.

'It is a brave hound, but it is no match for this.'

He reached round to his back and retrieved something tucked into his trousers. He drew out a pistol.

'Steady on now,' said Charlie, moving completely in front of Maria in an instant.

Biscuit was unrecognisable, edging closer to Oskar, barking ferociously, his body taut and ready for anything, even a gun. There it was: the pistol she'd sought and never found. He must've carried it with him everywhere.

'It is a beauty, is it not? It was my father's, a *Reichsrevolver*. And I know how to use it. I know very well.'

Oskar always bragged about everything, but he usually lied. Perhaps he didn't know how to use it, she wondered. But it mattered little, as it was in his hand and he could shoot like a fool and still do a lot of damage.

'Let's just all calm down. There's no need for threats,' said Charlie.

'Oh, but that is where you are wrong. There is every need for threats!'

He waved the pistol around above his head and everyone flinched, even Biscuit.

'Do you play chess?' asked Charlie.

Oskar frowned. 'Of course. I am a gentleman. Unlike you.'

'What we have here, sir, is a stalemate. Nobody wins. I inna going anywhere without Maria and you wonna stop waving that weapon about till I do. So, you see, nobody wins.'

'But *you* see, Charlie Woodvine – yes, I know exactly who you are. The lower-class schoolteacher in a provincial town. How quaint! But, Woodvine, there will be a winner and only one of them. Because you and your dog and your bitch are trying to steal from me. She carries something that belongs to me. And I will have it. Unfortunately, it's too soon to take the babe from her by force and so she must stay. Until it is her time. And you must go. And that, as they say, is that.'

MOLLIE WALTON

Maria had listened to all of this, behind the broad shield of Charlie's back. But she could see that there would be no victory between these two men. Only a woman could win this battle.

She stepped out from behind Charlie and said, loudly and clearly, 'It inna yours.'

Charlie cried, 'Maria! Stay behind me!'

'What did you say?' Oskar said, squinting at her.

'I said, it inna yours. The babby. It's Charlie's.'

Oskar's mouth fell open and the gun drooped. 'You . . . I . . . It cannot be!'

'It can and it is. You know we met, Charlie and me, when you were away? Well, that wasn't the only time. We saw each other all through the month. I lay with him many times. And that's when I fell pregnant, not when you came back. It's his babby. I counted the weeks, I used science, just like you taught me. It's Charlie's child, all right. I only stayed with you as Charlie was to marry. But it's off now, so I'm going with him.'

'There is nothing for you here now,' said Charlie. 'Stand aside and let us pass.'

'You . . . you . . . you faithless whore!' Oskar screeched and lifted the gun.

'Stop!' shouted Charlie and, in one movement, he dropped her bag and threw himself at Oskar, but Biscuit was quicker and he went for the throat. In the moment they both fell upon Oskar, a gunshot rang out in the Shrewsbury night.

'Nay! Oh nay!' cried Maria and rushed to the heap of them, falling beside them to see where the gunshot had found its home, in her man or his dog. But it was Oskar who began to squeal and writhe in pain, reaching downwards. Biscuit leapt up and shook himself all through like a corkscrew, while Maria and Charlie looked down and saw Oskar's boot was welling with blood, oozing thickly in the lamplight. Charlie kicked away the gun that lay on the ground where Oskar had dropped it, while Biscuit nosed his way in and fell to licking Oskar's bloody boot with enthusiasm.

'Do you never feed this poor animal?' said Maria.

Charlie pulled Biscuit off, then looked up at her, still in shock, stared at Biscuit, stared at Oskar, then stared at Maria again. He let out a brief laugh, then expelled air from his mouth and wiped his forehead.

'Am I hit?'

'Nay, you inna hit,' said Maria. 'He hit himself, like the selfish fool he is.'

Oskar was groaning incoherently, his eyes closed, his hands reaching fruitlessly for his foot, as he was too weak to sit up.

'We mun stem the bleeding,' Charlie said, absently, staring down at the foot again. His schoolmaster ways came to him and he delved into Maria's bag, scrabbling around inside and pulling out a woollen stocking. He unlaced Oskar's boot and eased it off. Oskar moaned and sounded like he was cursing in his own language. Charlie looked at the wound, while Biscuit watched closely and licked his lips. Charlie shoved the dog's nose away, then wrapped the stocking, carefully, expertly, around Oskar's foot, tearing the end into two halves and tying it up tightly.

'That'll do it,' said Charlie and nodded.

Then there were voices nearby, coming from behind the alleyway wall.

'What's occurring yonder?' shouted someone.

'Sounds like a gun going off.'

'You dunna know what a gun sounds like, mon. I do, I fought in the Crimea, me, and heard no end of 'em. You were just a nipper then. You dunna know the sound of a gun.'

'All right, old lad. I needna fight in a war to know a pistol when I hear one. I inna half-soaked!'

They argued on and Maria said, 'Time to go.'

'Agreed,' nodded Charlie. 'He wonna bleed to death. He'll need it seeing to, but he'll survive, I warrant.'

Charlie took up her bag and Biscuit came to his side, mouth open, tongue lolling, ready to go. Maria looked down at Oskar, still groaning and moaning and muttering. She had not an ounce of sympathy for him.

'I'm leaving you, Oskar von Schoen.'

And with that, she turned and took Charlie's arm and they hurried down the alleyway, and out into the night. She could not run fast, her head aching again now the emergency had passed and her body remembered it had been beaten. And anyway, it would look odd if they ran down the street, and they needed to look the opposite of odd. They needed to look like nobodies. So they hurried along, trying to look normal, not speaking, Biscuit trotting along beside them happily. *If only I were as innocent of the world as a dog*, Maria thought. They had survived a scene fraught with danger, lived to tell the tale, except the tale would never be told. It would be their secret, forever. And what if Oskar came after them? Not now, but when he was mended. Came to Ironbridge and made trouble for them? Or sent police to find them, accusing her or Charlie of shooting him? They might be free now, but it would hang over them like a guillotine. She could only hope Oskar believed her about the child, for if he truly did, he'd have no business left with her and hopefully he would leave her alone. But a man like that, a man of addled mind, he might come to seek revenge, he might demand punishment, for his child he thought he had, for his foot, for his honour and his pride. She would not put that past him, not one bit. Would they always be watching their backs, expecting a knock on the door?

They reached the station. Charlie looked at the notices to find their train.

'Last train to Ironbridge long gone,' he said.

'What shall we do?'

'Get on another, any other. We can change beyond. We just need to get away.'

'Agreed,' she said and helped him look.

There was one train left to leave Shrewsbury that night and it was about to arrive. They hurried to the platform and it was puffing into the station. Luck was with them. They boarded and found an empty carriage for themselves. Charlie put the bag up on the rack. Biscuit slumped down on the floor, tired out with all the excitement. The train was going to Crewe. It sat in the station for several minutes, throughout which Maria and Charlie sat in silence, holding hands. Maria was by the window, scanning the platform for any signs of trouble. A policeman looking for a couple with a dog. A German gentleman waving a pistol. But nobody came. And the train pulled away, the window obscured by clouds of steam before dispersing, revealing the night's landscape beyond the train, deeply dark and secretive.

'We'll stay on for a bit, then get off, probably at Oswestry,' said Charlie. 'Prepare yourself for an uncomfortable night sleeping on a bench at the station. Then we'll get trains back to Ironbridge first thing in the morning. Back home.'

'All right, Charlie,' said Maria, nestling her exhausted head into his shoulder. She would go anywhere with him, do anything he required. She could have died today. But she didn't. Instead, she was free. And she loved and was loved. Rocked by the gentle rhythm of the train, within seconds she was fast asleep.

Chapter 31

June 1893

O n the walk into the woods in the misty morning, they heard the great Benthall waterwheel before they saw it, the river rushing through its huge structure at a speedy pace. It had been years and years since Maria had seen it last, when her father used to take her on walks in Benthall Edge Woods for Sunday picnics. She was glad it was still going. They passed it by and walked deeper into the woods. Morning fog hung about the trunks of the trees, ghostly in the early light. Birds flitted in and out of the mist, chirping the presence of the two walkers, with alarm calls for their canine companion trotting alongside its new mistress. Ever since dealing with Oskar, Biscuit had decided that his job was now to protect Maria and thus he hadn't left her side for a moment.

'Not long now,' said Charlie.

'Are you sure it'll be all right? I dunna wanna be a burden to any folk.'

'I am certain. It's family, after all. And you are family, my love.'

They came to a fork in the woods and Charlie led them on

the right path, nearer to the river. She could hear it plash and play in the quietude of the woods, not a soul in sight as they walked. Before long, they finally arrived at a clearing and there stood the house. It was large, detached, away from civilisation, a coach path snaking away to town behind it. The long structure was topped with two brick chimneys and clouds of wisteria hung over the upper-floor windows all along the façade. To the front and side lay an extensive vegetable and flower garden, canes carrying peas and beans beside fruit bushes and rows of cabbages, all in perfect, apple-pie order, like something from a fairy tale. In fact, the whole place held the atmosphere of folklore, nestled in the secretive woods. To think that Anny Malone had once been a girl of the working class like Maria and now she lived here.

It was so early in the morning, Maria worried Anny and Peter Malone would still be abed. She would hate to disturb them. They reached the front door and Biscuit yelped, then sat down before it, neat yet impatient. Charlie knocked firmly and a maid answered swiftly, looking the motley assembly before her up and down in unwelcome surprise. Maria realised they must all look a state and present a strange crew to be turning up so early on her mistress's doorstep. The maid particularly eyed up Maria's face, a look of pity in her eyes. Maria looked away, down at her feet. She was ashamed of her bruises.

'We're sorry to bother you at this time,' said Charlie, removing his hat. 'Is Mrs Malone at home, by any chance? I am her relation.'

'I know you, sir, if you'll forgive me being familiar,' said the maid, smiling shyly. 'You taught me and my brother at school some years back.'

'Ah . . . dunna tell me . . . Myrtle Webb! And your little brother . . . Roddy!'

'That's us!' cried the girl, then checked herself. 'I shall enquire within. Please wait in the hallway.'

They entered a narrow corridor and Myrtle gave Biscuit a tickle behind the ear, before she went off to find her mistress.

'Everyone in Ironbridge knows Charlie Woodvine,' said Maria, smiling. But smiling hurt her face and she winced in pain.

Charlie looked at her with great concern, putting down the bag and sliding his arm around her. He whispered in her ear, 'Not long now and you can rest, my love.'

But Maria's body had decided that it had held out quite long enough: from fighting with Oskar, to fleeing on foot, to a rough night spent on the hard wooden bench outside the railway station, to the walk up here. It couldn't wait one more moment and, before she knew what was happening, her knees had turned to jelly and she felt her legs give way.

When she opened her eyes next, she didn't know if it were Charlie or a manservant who'd carried her upstairs, but she vaguely recalled being weightless for a time, before finding the luxury of a bed with crisp sheets and plump pillows. She'd never been so glad to feel the softness of a bed in her life, after all that time on the unforgiving chaise longue and, before that, the questionable hospitality of Harborne and Co. There was something warm beside her leg and she looked down and saw Biscuit spread out beside her, sleeping deeply. He'd had a long, adventurous night too. The room was simple, with light blue walls and a large window that looked out on the woods. Maria felt safe. She went back to sleep.

Hours later, it must've been, as the sun was lowering in the sky for late afternoon, she awoke ravenously hungry, as she'd not eaten anything since an apple the night before that Charlie had given her, from his pocket. She simply must eat. Biscuit was gone, she knew not where. She climbed out of bed and saw that she'd had her outer layers of clothes removed and slept in her corset cover, corset and combination. It was a corset she'd been wearing loose so as not to confine the baby, so it wasn't too uncomfortable, but what a relief it was to drag it off now. There was a ewer and basin, and soap to wash with. She cleaned her whole body, then her face, carefully. Looking in the mirror, she saw she had a black eye and two bruises on her left cheek. Her ear felt sore as well. A hairbrush and comb had been laid out for her and she took her hair from its plait and brushed it out. The feeling of freedom with her hair down was delicious. She saw a plain white nightgown draped across a chair at a dressing table, as well as a gown with pink peonies on it to put on over the top. It was time to be brave and go out into the house and face the kind people who'd looked after her so well already.

Maria ventured out and the house was quiet, so she stole downstairs, barefoot, crossing a hallway with a floor made from tilework: black, white and terracotta decorated with a flower on each tile. It looked ancient, like the floor of an old church. The tiles were cold on her feet, but she stopped, as she didn't know where to go next. Many doorways led off the central hall and she hesitated until one of the doors opened and, thankfully, Anny Malone came through and saw her.

'Dear girl, you're awake! And up and about! Are you sure you're strong enough?'

'Thank'ee so much for . . . this,' she said, gesturing to her clothes. 'And for . . . everything.'

'It's my pleasure, my love. You must be hungry. Fancy summat to eat?'

'I'd kill for it,' Maria said, then grimaced at the thought of yesterday's drama, where she thought she *had* killed. Or maybe she still had . . . All night, in fitful sleep on Charlie's shoulder, her dreams had been haunted by thoughts of Oskar lying in the street, bleeding to death. Charlie had bandaged his foot well, but what if it hadn't been tight enough? Or Oskar, in his madness, had pulled the bandage off? Could a person lose enough blood from a wounded foot to die? What a ridiculous question to have to worry about, but it had tortured her dreams all night.

'Come with me and we'll get you comfy in the parlour and I'll let the kitchen know to bring you a plate.'

Anny showed her into a comfortable room with paintings of landscapes on the walls and photographs lined up on a sideboard in small frames. There were French windows at one end that looked out onto the vegetable beds. There was a warm, crackling fire in the grate. Maria sat down next to it, in a pale green armchair with a stiff back, which she needed or she would slump into sleep again. Only her hunger kept her awake.

'Oh, by the way, when we took your dress to clean, the maid found this in the pocket.'

Anny fetched something from the sideboard and handed it to Maria, then left the room.

It was the folded-up photograph of Maria she'd taken from the darkroom floor the day she'd hid in there from Lina. She recalled slipping it into her pocket. She'd forgotten about it and there it must have stayed, all this time. She unfolded it and stared at herself, sitting on the chaise longue, her hair down, facing the camera, staring at the photographer, at Oskar, with desire, hopelessly in love. Her eyes in monochrome looked like black holes in her white face. She shuddered. She couldn't bear to see this photographic evidence of her stupidity, to believe herself in love with such a monster. What she really saw was innocence and it made her heart ache to behold it. She ripped it in two. Then again, and again. She leant over and threw the pieces into the fire, sat back down and watched them curl up and burn. There, it was gone. That girl was gone now.

Anny came back in and sat opposite her on a deep green sofa, smiling.

'You dunna have to talk if you'd rather sit quietly, Maria. I have my newspapers to read. I like to keep up with current events.'

'I'm happy to talk, if I wouldna be disturbing you.'

'Not at all. How are you feeling?'

'Like death warmed up,' said Maria, not meaning to be so frank, but it just came out.

'I inna surprised, after everything you've been through. The most terrible trials, my dear girl.'

Just hearing someone saying it, and so kindly, brought it home to Maria just what she'd suffered recently in her life. A sudden sob escaped her, and she covered her mouth with her hand. Anny reached across and touched her knee.

'It's right and proper to weep, love. Let it all out, if you wish.'

She wanted to, but she felt embarrassed. She knew how lovely Anny was, but she felt ashamed of herself.

'I'll be all right.'

'I know you will. We all do. You're a strong'un. You've proven that to yourself and all of us.'

'Where's Charlie?' she asked, suddenly in need of the sight of him, for his face always gave her the reassurance she needed, that she really would be all right.

'He's at school, with Biscuit. We had to pull that dog away from your bed, he loves you so.'

'Charlie's teaching today? After the night we've had?'

'He insisted. I said I'd take the children on today, but he said nay, that I was doing enough for him. He'll be back, after his evening class.'

Maria recalled that Rosie went to that class, and she felt sick at the thought.

'It's the men's evening class,' said Anny, a knowing look on her face. 'And Rosie Green comes to my class on another night . . . if that's what you're thinking.'

'You read my mind,' said Maria ruefully. 'I dunna even know what to say about that. About anything.'

'You dunna have to say a word. It's your business. Charlie has shared some of it with me. What I know is that you're a very brave young woman who's been through a kind of hell. And that Charlie loves you more than his own self, more than his own life. He'd do anything for you. And he'll stand beside you through thick and thin, if you'll have him.'

'Of course I will. I'm the lucky one, to still have his love, after what I've done.'

There was a brief silence then. Anny was about to reply when the door opened and in came Myrtle with a tray for Maria.

'Thank'ee,' said Maria and looked at a plate of pork pie, apple slices, some kind of red chutney, cheese and a hunk of bread. No other meal had ever looked as good. She fell to eating, forgetting all manners, so hungry she was.

Anny reached over to an occasional table and took up her newspaper. Maria saw it was the *Shrewsbury Chronicle*. Perhaps, in the coming days, tomorrow even, there would be a story in it about a German gentleman found injured . . . or dead . . . and police were searching for a couple . . . and their dog who'd fled the scene. She stopped eating and felt a wave of nausea, putting her hand to her forehead and closing her eyes, chewing the food down, forcing herself to swallow so she did not bring it up.

'You might've eaten too fast,' said Anny gently.

Maria opened her eyes and looked up.

'Take it slowly. Your poor body has been through a lot.'

'I deserve it,' she said miserably.

337

'Now, now. None of that.'

'But it's true!' she cried and broke down. Through her tears, she admitted, 'I've dragged the kindest man who ever lived into my own unholy mess. And now you too. I mun go. I mun leave this place and Charlie. You canna be caught up in my disgrace. You deserve better, Charlie does too. Oh, my love. My life. What have I done?'

Maria sobbed and sobbed. Anny took the tray and placed it on a coffee table, then sat back on the sofa, waiting patiently while Maria wept. She did not say a thing, and Maria cried and cried until she could cry no more. Then, once it had subsided, Anny spoke.

'When I was a girl, I spent a spell in gaol. I thought my life was over. My father was killed. My mother died not long after. I had nothing. My Peter saved me with his love, his kindness. We had a son. He died. We had more children, and we gave a home to an orphan, Hettie Jones. She came into a fortune and married my son, Evan. It's her house you sit in now, or it was, before she gifted it to Peter and I. I worked for her charitable foundation for years until I retired a while ago. I have four children and three grandchildren. See, there they are, my beauties.'

She gestured to the sideboard and stood up, went over to it and showed some of the photographs in frames to Maria.

'Here's Evan and Hettie with their littlest ones, Johnnie and Dotty. And here's their eldest girl, Martha there. She's sixteen now and works with her parents at the foundation. It began by establishing some hostels in Ironbridge, but now it runs projects all over the Black Country, helping the poorest among us to get back on their feet. My daughter, Flora, works there too, twenty-eight now. She took over my job as chief clerk when I retired. She married a local man, James. He works at the fire station. And here's their bonny little boy. Five years old. They called him Owen.'

Anny sniffed and Maria saw she was overcome with emotion for a moment. But she went on.

'Here's my twins, Billy and Lily. They're twenty-four and both have ambitions beyond this place. He's training as a lawyer in London and she studied French at the University of Cambridge, and she's a librarian there now. Neither are married. Neither are even interested, as yet. They were always like that, independent and determined. They love their freedom, you see.'

At that moment, a figure passed by the French window and Maria looked up. It was a man with white hair, dressed in plain, comfortable clothes, gardener's gloves on. He went to the row of tall beans and was picking them, plucking off each pod and placing it in a shallow wooden dish.

'And that man there, who looks like the hired help, is my dear husband, Peter. The best man I ever knew. He's worked in the hardest jobs known to man. And now he lives in perpetual retirement, growing food for us and the foundation, drumbling about his garden, happier there than a pig in mud.'

Anny put the photographs carefully back in their places on the sideboard, then turned and looked seriously at Maria.

'I'm proud of my family. And I can only apologise for boring you silly with chunnering on about them all.'

'Nay,' said Maria, shaking her head. She loved hearing about them.

'But I have a reason. And that is to show you how rich a life is, any life. It inna defined by one thing, by one event, one mistake. I loved a cruel man once, and I suffered under another, who sent me to my imprisonment. I could've died in there. I could've taken my own life, when I struggled back home and found I had nothing left. I could've been dead long ago, and never given life to this raft of bonny young'uns who go out into the world now and do only good in it. But I didna. I put my misfortune and my disgrace behind me. But it was not *my* disgrace, in truth, Maria. For it is society that decides who is punished and who is rewarded, who is free and who is not. Sometimes our paths through life are blighted by storm and wrack, and we get stuck in the drowning mud, and fear we will never get out. But we do. We endure. And so will you. Life has thrown some punches at you these past months. You are bruised. But you are not beaten. You are strong. You survived. And so did your child. And your man, who loves you more than life itself, will be there by your side, along with that soppy hound Biscuit. And you'll be all right, my dear. You'll be fine. All this will pass, and you will walk into the rest of your life, beloved and safe. I just know it.'

Epilogue

56 Poppelsdorfer Allee
Bonn
GERMANY
2 April 1894

My dear Maria,

I hope this letter finds you well. In truth, I hope this letter finds you at all! I have sent it to your employer, assuming you are still there. However, I do not know what your current circumstances are. If you have left their employ, I hope some kind soul has forwarded this letter to your next known address. Enough of these logistics. The fact that you are reading this letter now proves that it has found its lucky way to you!

Let me explain why I have chosen to write to you. I was most moved by our meeting, Maria. I know how inauspicious it must have seemed to you, with Oskar responding the way he did to my visit. I heard nothing more from him after that.

My father and I decided that, short of carting him off in a white jacket, there was nothing we could do to contain him. Thus, imagine how surprised we were to see him return to us in June last year, with all of his possessions delivered soon after. He had a limp and would tell us nothing about how he got it. He did tell us that you had left him to have a child with another man. He said it meant nothing to him, but I could see how hard he took it. Since then, we tried to persuade him to seek medical help, but instead he surprised us again by getting engaged to his cousin, a very rich woman who has always taken a shine to him, much older. They married in the autumn and he lives in Berlin with her now, where he has taken up his studies in chemistry at the university there. He works with a friend of her family, a famous chemist called Fritz Haber, who Oskar is very impressed with and talked of nothing else the last time I visited him in Berlin. He is not as manic as he used to be, so perhaps his older wife has settled him a little. However, his political beliefs have continued to deteriorate into the most violent and abhorrent kind. I'm afraid my father has now banned him from returning home. Thus, I travel to see him intermittently, but even these visits are proving too much for me. I fear we have lost him to his madness. He is not the only one spouting such revolting views in my country, I am sorry to say, so he is encouraged in his dark ideas. I can only hope that this vehement nationalism he preaches is just a brief phase in our country, at worst. I can imagine nothing worse as the fate of my beloved Germany. We are a cultured country of great artists, composers, writers and poets. We are not the nation of my brother's insane vision.

I am supposing, at this point in the proceedings of this letter, that you are wondering why on earth I am writing to you and telling you all of this, when you have gone away into your own life and, no doubt, were very happy to leave it all

*behind, as far as the von Schoens are concerned. There is a
solid reason, so please bear with me. It is the child, you see. I
do not know how to explain this to you, other than to say it
is a premonition I had, or a kind of feminine intuition, as they
call it. But I have the idea lodged in my head that the child you
carried was Oskar's. If I were you, and it was his child, I
would have lied to escape his clutches, I am sure. I am not
calling you a liar, Maria. But I want you to know this: if my
suspicions are true and you did carry Oskar's child – and
perhaps you are in some kind of trouble now the child is born
and are in need of help and care – then I would like to extend
the hand of family to you. I want to assure you that I will do
anything I can to help you. I will never have children of my
own, of that I am certain. If I can help a niece or nephew of
mine to have a better life, then nothing would give me more
pleasure. Oskar's wife is in her fifties, you see, and her child-
bearing days are over. There will be no von Schoen heirs if
Oskar stays with her and, I must say, I think he should as it's
the best place for him. So, any child of our family is precious
to me. I believe your child is that child. You can write to me
here and I will send you money or anything else you require.
Or you can come to Bonn and visit us, stay with us, even live
with us if you so desire. My father is heartbroken over his son
and I know it would give him the greatest pleasure in his last
years to know the only von Schoen heir. We are here, waiting
for you, if you wish to come to us.*

Please consider it carefully.

All our very best regards to you, Maria.
Lina von Schoen

Maria folded the letter over and passed it to Charlie. As he
read it through, she looked at the envelope. It had been sent by

Lina to Harborne's, then that was crossed out and Maria's old address at her lodging house on Hodge Bower had been written instead, she supposed by some secretary there who'd forwarded it using the last known address. She could only imagine that Mrs Cribb, the landlady, had popped it through their door. When Maria had first picked it up off the doormat that morning, and turned it over to see Lina's name and the Bonn address on the back, she had felt sick at the sight of it. What if it were a threatening letter if Oskar had died of his gunshot wound, or if he'd survived but wanted revenge? What if the police were on their way from Shrewsbury at this very moment to arrest her ... or Charlie ... to say that Oskar claimed one of them had shot at and wounded him? Knowing his madness, and the chaos that surrounded his life, it could be anything. She and Charlie had scoured the Shrewsbury newspapers at Anny's house for weeks after, looking for reports of a German with his foot shot up. But there was nothing. They hadn't heard anything or seen anything in all that time. So when the letter arrived, it was like a terrifying spectre from their past arriving on the doorstep of their happy home in the schoolmaster's cottage. She had torn it open and read it in a panic. Charlie had found her there and asked her what it was, but she couldn't speak until she'd read it to the end.

'That whole family is half-soaked,' said Charlie, when he finished reading.

'Charlie ... I'm so sorry.'

'What for?'

'That ... I brought these people into your life. I thought I'd escaped from it forever. I thought I'd kept it from you.'

'Come here,' he said and took Maria in his arms. He held her close and kissed the top of her head. 'Dunna be glum. Nothing those mad folk can do can ever hurt us. We did nothing wrong. And they can prove nothing else. Dunna fret or spend a moment of your life thinking on them any more. Let's leave them to their madness. We're too busy being deliriously happy to let them rain on our parade, eh?'

'We are,' she said, and held on tight to him. Biscuit sidled up and pawed her leg, annoyed he was being left out of all this affection. Then baby Alfie called out from the other room, demanding attention in his own way.

'No rest for the wicked!' said Charlie, kissed her cheek and went to see Alfie. He stopped and turned to her, still holding the letter. 'In the bin?' he asked.

'Nay, let's burn it,' said Maria.

'Excellent plan. It'll be very satisfying to see it on its very own little funeral pyre.'

'Give it here,' she said, going past him to the fireplace and scrunching it up as small as she could and throwing it into the coals, still warm from the morning fire that had just gone out. Charlie lit a match and set it aflame. He didn't stay to watch, as baby Alfie was yelling now, and he hurried through to the bedroom to fetch him. Maria watched it burn, the paper disintegrating into blackness as the flames took it. 'Gone,' she said firmly to herself.

In came Charlie carrying baby Alfie, who was babbling on about something of great consequence in his infant mind.

'Listen to all that chunnering on!' Charlie cried and kissed his cheek. 'He'll be a schoolmaster before we know it.'

'Like his dad,' said Maria and smiled at them both.

'Right, I'm off. Those little terrors will be arriving soon. See you presently.'

Charlie passed his son over and left by the front door, followed by Biscuit, trotting behind. Maria cuddled Alfie, kissing his soft baby face, the most delicious smell she'd ever known: her baby's skin. He reached his arms round her neck and held on, his head on her shoulder. She looked back down at the ashes in the fire. The fear she'd felt on opening that letter still lingered about her. They'd come so far, she and Charlie. The day after she'd arrived at Anny's, Charlie had gone to the church in his lunchtime and arranged for the marriage banns to be published as soon as possible. They'd agreed that, on the train from Shrewsbury. He wanted to marry her straight away, if he could. She wanted that too.

She'd stayed with Anny until her wedding day. After Anny had so kindly put her at her ease, ensuring that any vestiges of shame and disgrace were banished, Maria spent a lovely few weeks at the old brickmaster's house. As Charlie had promised so long ago, Anny did know quite a bit about Maria's parents and together they compiled a family tree on paper, drawn up from all the folk Anny knew of in town who were related to the Keays and the Collies. Maria discovered that she had a couple of distant cousins she'd never heard of and so, along with cousin Rhoda and her daughter Matilda Rose, she knew that once she was married and the child had come, and she was able to rejoin Ironbridge society, she'd have new family to meet and get acquainted with, a marvellous thought. First, she had her own family to form, and that was with Charlie Woodvine.

The wedding had come less than a month later: a quiet, simple affair, with Anny and Peter as witnesses, a plain cream dress, no fuss or bother. It was perfect. On their wedding night, they'd both been ridiculously nervous. Biscuit had been shut out of the room and was scratching at the door. Charlie said he was worried about hurting the baby and Maria was worried about disappointing him, as she'd felt sullied by her past.

She'd said, 'We dunna have to do the traditional wedding night thing if we dunna want to.'

'You are right,' he said and went to his drawer and pulled

out a pack of cards. 'Let's play rummy instead. And let that damn dog in.'

So they'd sat on the bed, dressed only in their bedtime attire, joined by Biscuit. But they couldn't stop looking at each other, glancing over their cards and watching each other's movements, each other's bodies. Charlie had thrown the cards aside and kissed her passionately. It was glorious. And hilarious! They had laughed as they kissed. She'd never known love could be so much fun. Biscuit had barked his head off with excitement and Charlie had firmly put him outside and shut the door once more. After that, the fun continued, turning to something more serious, more profound, but also joyous. At last, for the first time in months, if not years, Maria had found herself deeply in love, happy and whole, utterly free from care.

She'd moved in with Charlie on her wedding night, at the schoolmaster's cottage. As her belly grew large, there were whisperings in town about how big she looked so soon after marriage, but, if anyone wondered about it, Maria and Charlie guessed they'd assume the two of them had jumped the gun before the wedding, rather than the actual provenance of the child she carried. There was more gossip about Charlie jilting Rosie than anything. Rosie found another beau within a couple of weeks, by all accounts, and the last they'd heard, she'd married him and they'd moved to Wem. It was a welcome release that they didn't have to bump into Rosie every time they walked through Ironbridge.

Baby Alfie – Alfred Woodvine, named for Maria's father – was born at home on the first day of December, weeks overdue and very uncomfortable he'd made her too at the end. The relief when he came out of her, healthy and hearty, was immense, as was his weight. Charlie nicknamed him King Alfred the Late.

Maria was awakened from her reverie by the sound of the front door opening.

'It's only me,' called a voice from the hallway.

'Morning, Anny.'

'Morning, you two. Look at this bonny boy!'

'Is it nappy day today?' asked Maria.

'It is indeed,' said Anny, coming towards her and reaching out for Alfie. 'We're going to teach those little'uns how to change a nappy, aren't we, eh? Bostin boy! That's what you are! A bostin, bonny boy!'

Alfie giggled and grabbed at Anny's nose. With no grand-parents of his own, baby Alfie had determinedly adopted Anny as his honorary grandmother.

'You take him. I'll be there presently.'

'Take the day off, if you want to, love. Have a rest.'

'Nay, I like coming in. I wanna take some pictures in class today. Show the world how we teach our little'uns everything they need. You could use it in the foundation's journal, if you like. Show it to sponsors.'

'Now, that idea is proper jam,' said Anny, then blew a big raspberry on Alfie's cheek and he screamed in delight. 'See you in there. Dunna hurry.'

Maria waved them off, then went to the sideboard and took up her camera. It was an Eastman Kodak Daylight. It was known as the 'detective camera' someone had told her once. It was easy to carry and perfect for her needs, capturing the fleeting lives of working folk, ordinary people – some might call them nobodies. Before she left, Maria stopped beside the mirror above the fireplace. She held up the camera, looked over it into the mirror and snapped herself, smiling.

Glossary of Shropshire dialect terms

Babby – baby
Beaut – girl
Beggar my tripes! – expression of surprise
Bostin – great/good
Cakey – simple-minded
Canna – can't
Chit – a forward young girl
Chunnering – chatting
Coulda – could have
Crink – an old wrinkly person
Cwtch – a cuddle or sitting up close to someone
Danker me! – I'll be damned!
Darksome – gloomy
Darter – daughter
Drodsome – dreadful, alarming
Drumbling – dawdling
'ee – you (a shortened version of thee, e.g. thank'ee)
Hadna – had not
Half-soaked – silly, stupid

Havna – have not

Inna – isn't

Judies – not limited to Shropshire, yet Victorian slang for prostitutes

Lark-heeled – an early riser

Lass – girl

Little'un – baby or child

Masher – not limited to Shropshire, yet Victorian slang for a rich gentleman who visits prostitutes

Mon – man, said to a friend

Mun – must

Nay – no

Needna – need not

No great shakes – not that good

Oss – horse

Oughta – ought to

'Ow bist? – How are you?

'Ow do – How do you do?

Proper jam – very good

Ratlin – the smallest of a litter of baby animals, the runt

Roadster – tramp

Scrudged – a bunch of people all pushed up against each other

Set you down – sit down

Shouldna – should not/should not have

Summat – something

Thank'ee – thank you

This'un – this one

Thumb lump – handheld food, usually meat and bread

To land the otter – doing something that's impossible or very difficult to achieve

Tommy rotter – liar

Wasna – wasn't

Wench – used for a young woman in a similar way to 'lass'
      and is in no way derogatory to females
Werriting – worrying distractedly
Winsome – pretty
Wonna – won't
Wouldna – wouldn't
Yer – your

Author's Note

Gosh, I loved writing this story. I've always had a thing for the whole shopgirl world. As it says of Maria in this novel, shopgirls inhabited a hinterland between the traditional working classes and the up-and-coming middle classes. It was fascinating to read and learn about their incredibly difficult lives. Just FYI, it might interest the reader to look more into the National Union of Shop Assistants, referred to by Charlie. An intrepid shopgirl, Margaret Bondfield became an undercover reporter of the appalling conditions in her efforts to improve the lives of shopgirls and later became a Labour Party MP. In the early twentieth century, shopgirls went on strike and conditions did improve. This was too late for Maria though!

Shrewsbury cakes – these delicious treats are still sold today and nowadays they're called Shrewsbury biscuits (yet I have it on good authority that they were known as Shrewsbury cakes back in the 1890s).

Payment by results – this unjust practice of pay for teachers was eventually abolished in 1897, just as Charlie hoped it would be.

Fritz Haber – the chemist mentioned as working with

Oskar – was a real-life German chemist, who went on to invent deadly gases used in WW1 and on whose work was built the origins of the WW2 poison gases used to such devastating effect in the Holocaust.

Now, if you like a Mollie Walton novel to read for an afternoon, I'm sure you're asking yourself, how are the Ironbridge and Raven Hall Sagas connected? So, for readers of all Walton novels (and those who might become so!), I'd like to explain the connection between the Ironbridge stories and the Raven Hall series. Namely, one of the main characters from each series are related by family. You can see this on the family tree diagram in this book, yet – if you really want to know . . . and I just know you do – this is the explanation of how Anny Woodvine/Malone from the Ironbridge Saga and Harry Woodvine of the Raven Hall Saga are related.

The Raven Hall Saga is about Rosina Calvert-Lazenby and her daughters in WW2, set in Yorkshire and beyond. Widowed Rosina meets young RAF sergeant Harry Woodvine in *A Mother's War*. Harry's father was Alfie Woodvine, who features briefly as a baby in *The Shopgirl of Ironbridge*, born in 1893. Harry's beloved grandfather – who he talks about to Rosina in *A Mother's War* – is Charlie Woodvine from *The Shopgirl of Ironbridge*. Charlie is related to Anny Malone – of The Ironbridge Saga – through her father John Woodvine (b. 1793), who features in *The Daughters of Ironbridge*. John Woodvine's father, James Woodvine, was born 1771 and John's uncle Matthew Woodvine was born 1770. Matthew had four sons, including Ebenezer, born 1790, who is John Woodvine's cousin. Ebenezer had a son born in 1810, Josiah, who had a son born in 1830, Reuben Woodvine. Reuben was Charlie's father. Thus, John Woodvine is Charlie Woodvine's great-grandfather Ebenezer Woodvine's cousin! Therefore (thanks for sticking with me!), Anny is Charlie's great-grandfather's cousin's daughter, i.e. his great-grandfather's cousin once removed. So, they are related, but distantly (and since you've read *Shopgirl*, you'll be aware by now that Harry Woodvine's father, Alfie, has quite a different lineage . . . which means Harry's relationship with Anny Woodvine is via family and love, rather than strictly by blood).

You can read every single Mollie Walton book as a stand-alone story, because each book also works as a separate tale, and you'll still get plenty of enjoyment from reading them that way. However, if you'd like to experience the full Walton world, you can also read an epic saga of all of the books in chronological order, if you wish, i.e. start with *The Daughters of Ironbridge* set in the 1830s and read all four Ironbridge books, then all three Raven Hall books, all the way through to the current latest in chronological terms, *A Sister's Hope*, set in the early 1940s. That'll give you just over a hundred years of story of one big family, connected by Anny Woodvine in the nineteenth century and Harry Woodvine in the twentieth. It does please me that all the Mollie Walton stories – whether set in Shropshire or Yorkshire or further afield – are connected by this one familial link that spans the Mollie Walton universe. Marvel movies, eat your heart out. That's enough to keep anyone going for a bit! Aren't you glad you asked?

Acknowledgements

Huge thanks go to:

Shroppiemon, AKA Stuart, for research help on all things Shropshire, at all times. And for reading the early draft. And for naming Charlie's dog Biscuit, who is hereby dedicated to Stanleydog, AKA Shroppiedog.

Alexis Donoghue, for kindly sending amazing pics of 1890s Ironbridge.

Shropshire Memories Facebook group members, for help on my research call-out post on 15 April 2024: Jan Haynes-Cockerill, Gillian Robinson, Rhiannon Urquhart, Vicky Jones, Margaret Ann Roberts, Nicola Edwards, Christopher Williams, Marcus Keane and Alan Brisbourne. And also for my post on Paradise & Hodgebower 18 June 2024: Graham Hickman, Michelle Brazier, Schofields Popman, Geoff Fletcher, Clare Dobson, Margaret Ann Roberts, Rita Rich and Stuart Geoffrey Davies.

Vicky Jones, for local history info on Ironbridge shops in the 1890s.

Tim Marchant, for excellent maps of Ironbridge and Coalbrookdale.

Nic Parker, for help with German language and culture.

My excellent editor Jenni Edgecombe for always giving me such clear and thoughtful editing, as well as the whole team at Headline for their dedication to all things Mollie.

My incredible agent Laura Macdougall, as well as Olivia Davies and Eleanor Horn at United Agents, for representing me in all things with candour and patience.

My wonderful family, friends and Facebook fam for always being there for me, especially when I'm a sickly child (which is often). Thanks too to the kind medical staff who've helped me.

Early readers – Lucy Adams, Stuart Geoffrey Davies, Lynn Downing and Pauline Lancaster. Thank you for your wonderful feedback, as ever.

Readers, reviewers and bloggers – writers would be totally at sea without you! Thank you for championing our scribblings.

Last but not least, as ever, my darlings Poppy, Clem and Tink. Thanks for all the laughs and light, especially when the world feels increasingly dark. Love you all.

DISCOVER THE RAVEN HALL SAGA

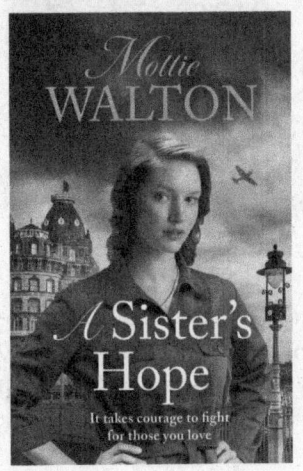

AVAILABLE NOW

About the Author

© Claire Newman-Williams

Mollie Walton is the saga pen-name for historical novelist Rebecca Mascull. She has always been fascinated by history and has worked in education, has a Masters in Writing and lives by the sea in the east of England. Under Mollie Walton, Rebecca is also the author of The Raven Hall Saga.